TWO KINDS OF STRANGER

STEVE CAVANAGH

TWO KINDS OF STRANGER

HEADLINE

Copyright © 2025 Steve Cavanagh

The right of Steve Cavanagh to be identified as the Author of
the Work has been asserted by him in accordance with the
Copyright, Designs and Patents Act 1988.

First published in 2025 by Headline Publishing Group Limited

1

Apart from any use permitted under UK copyright law, this publication may
only be reproduced, stored, or transmitted, in any form, or by any means,
with prior permission in writing of the publishers or, in the case of
reprographic production, in accordance with the terms of licences
issued by the Copyright Licensing Agency.

All characters in this publication are fictitious and any resemblance to real persons,
living or dead, is purely coincidental.

Cataloguing in Publication Data is available from the British Library.

Hardback ISBN 978 1 0354 0825 2
Trade Paperback ISBN 978 1 0354 0826 9

Typeset by EM&EN
Printed and bound in Great Britain by Clays Ltd, Elcograf S.p.A.

Headline's policy is to use papers that are natural, renewable and recyclable
products and made from wood grown in well-managed forests and other
controlled sources. The logging and manufacturing processes are expected
to conform to the environmental regulations of the country of origin.

MIX
Paper | Supporting
responsible forestry
FSC
www.fsc.org
FSC® C104740

Headline Publishing Group Limited
An Hachette UK Company
Carmelite House
50 Victoria Embankment
London EC4Y 0DZ

The authorised representative in the EEA is Hachette Ireland,
8 Castlecourt Centre, Dublin 15, D15 XTP3, Ireland (email: info@hbgi.ie)

www.headline.co.uk
www.hachette.co.uk

For my dad, Sam

PART ONE

@EllysLittleLife
Manhattan, New York

FOR VISION-IMPAIRED USERS, AUDIO DESCRIPTION OF LIVE VIDEO PROVIDED BY AI AUDIO ASSIST.

A young woman has the camera in selfie mode as she goes through a door into a modern apartment and walks into the kitchen area. She removes her overcoat and places some shopping bags on the kitchen counter.

ELLY: Hey there, friends, Elly here, thought I would do a live video and let you in on a little secret. It's our six-month anniversary tomorrow...

The young woman holds her left hand to the camera, displaying her wedding ring and an engagement ring with a large white diamond.

ELLY: ...And I wanted to surprise James tonight. Don't worry about him seeing this video, by the way. I noticed this morning that he's left his phone on the nightstand, so there's, like, no way this will ruin the surprise before he gets home from work. So, I've been shopping...

She puts a grocery bag on the counter and begins to unpack.

ELLY: I got some eggs, flour, cream, and, of course, this box of foolproof chocolate-brownie mix, because I'm terrible in the kitchen, as we all know. Like, I can't even make cookies. And brownies are a favorite of my gorgeous new husband, so, like, why not. Homemade brownies, from a box, but, like, maybe we could just keep the box thing to ourselves and pretend it's my own recipe.

She arranges the shopping on the counter and rolls up her sleeves.

ELLY: I know it's for my husband, but for me this still qualifies as my random act of kindness for the week, hashtag RAK. Let me know in the comments what your random act of kindness is going to be this week, or maybe you've already done it, so let me know. Spread the kindness, guys, and let everybody know...

thud

She turns round, distracted by the thumping noise.

ELLY: What was that, guys? Did you hear that? Whatever, ah, I... What else? Yeah, so the rest of my week is pretty exciting; On Thursday I'm having a girly night with my bestie Harriet. I feel like since we got back from honeymoon I've been so busy and I've seen Harriet at a few parties and we saw that play on Broadway last month and we had that lunch, but, like, we haven't just, like, gone out and hit a bar like we used to. So, you know, we're doing that on Thursday because she means so much to me. She was my maid of honor and I just need to make sure that we hold on to that special friendship...

thud *thud*

She turns and walks through the apartment.

ELLY: Did you guys hear that again? Like, I definitely heard something...

She opens a door. Inside is a bed. A man and a woman are in the bed. They are naked.

ELLY: Oh my God! OH MY GOD! How could you? How could you?

The phone falls to the floor.

♥ 45.6M 💬 132M 🔖 957,899

@kindsofkindness
😮 😢 Oh My God Elly! I'm so sorry.

@dailykindnessandkittens
Is that James and Harriet??!!!??!!

@betty2013
Oh sweetie! That son of a bitch! I'm so sorry! @Elly you so don't deserve this, you are the kindest sweetest person I know, I just can't believe they would go behind your back like this?

@startmeup56
How long do you think they've been cheating? Did this start before or after the wedding?

@commandgirl14
I never liked James. He's such a piece of shit and I never trusted Harriet. She's a model and you can't trust models. Elly I love you.

@Justice4peace60066
DAAMMMMM girl! You don't deserve none of that shit, after all your acts of kindness, and all dem people you helped. I know you all about the random acts of kindness, but that don't get you nowhere in this life girl.

@crystalcool47
I am shooketh! James!! Harriet!! My heart is 💔 for you Elly.

I
Elly

Elly Parker strode through the crowds in New York's Grand Central Station and thought about all that she had lost. The painted heavens on the ceiling above shone down on the crowds, but not on Elly.

She was twenty-seven years old.

Two weeks ago, she had everything.

Perfect husband. Perfect apartment. Perfect friends and the perfect job.

And everyone knew it.

She put journalist and social-media influencer on her tax return. She wrote lifestyle pieces for high-end magazines, but most of her income came via social media – YouTube, Instagram and TikTok. Her channels were filled with creative and highly produced videos of her amazing apartment, her *fits*, her make-up demonstrations – her *life*.

Because there was another reason Elly was so popular. Her series of videos on random acts of kindness. That is what set her apart. Her account wasn't just about her, it was about spreading a little love in the big city. Sometimes that was buying a meal for someone living on the street, or giving a bigger tip to a waiter, walking her elderly neighbor's dog, or even something as small as holding the door open for someone. These she captured and shared on her socials, in the hope that it inspired others to do the same.

It worked.

#RAK regularly trended across social media.

Not only did Elly have the life she had always wanted – she had the life that her five million followers wanted too. None of this had been given to Elly. She had worked hard to win every single one of those followers. They loved her because she never took anything for granted. She had her first ever video pinned to her profile. It showed a much younger Elly, taking thirty bucks to her nearest CVS and buying everything from the make-up counter that a young woman needs to create a great evening look. That video was a reminder, to her followers and to Elly, of how far she had come in six years, and that she was still that young woman who was excited and grateful for every break she got, every lipstick that she received in the mail, and every set of eyeballs on her channels. People loved Elly, because she was just like anyone else who had a dream – except Elly's dream had come true and she was going to share it with everyone – with grace, a smile, and heartfelt humility.

The problem with sharing your perfect life with millions of people is that millions of people are watching when it falls apart.

Two weeks ago, Elly's life exploded. And the world watched. She had taken down the video soon after it had happened, but by then it was too late. People had clipped it and were posting it all over TikTok, Instagram, YouTube – everywhere.

Elly's phone buzzed in her coat pocket. As she reached for it, she checked the time on the gold clock in the station. Almost noon. Her appointment with her agent, Giselle, wasn't until two o'clock. Elly wanted to ride the train uptown, find a Starbucks and relax for an hour; gather her thoughts, before her meeting. Giselle was fielding interview requests from the *New Yorker*, *Vogue*, *Rolling Stone*, CNN, MSNBC and Fox. Elly was a star in the making. She had opportunities in broadcast television, in publishing, and journalism. She was set to be one of the few social-media stars to jump into the mainstream legacy media. Not that Elly felt like being in the world, not even outside. Apart from the meeting with her agent every Tuesday and Thursday, Elly hadn't left the hotel. The same hotel she'd booked into the day she found James and Harriet together. She'd hastily stuffed a bag with essentials and retreated to the anonymity of the American hotel experience. She felt exposed. Too much attention for her to deal with right now. She hadn't posted anything online in two weeks.

Since that live video, everyone wanted her story. Everyone wanted Elly.

Except one person.

Her husband.

As she looked at the ornate celestial ceiling in Grand Central, she thought how different her life would now be if she had ignored the noise coming from her bedroom during her live video. Her friendship groups were all shared by James and Harriet, and she didn't want to speak to her friends because she knew whatever she said would get back to James and Harriet. Her agent, Giselle, was a shoulder to cry on, for now. But she knew sooner or later she was going to have to deal with her problems. If Giselle had her way, Elly would do that on *Morning Joe*.

Elly's boots found the stairs down into the bowels of the city to the subway. She broke left, headed downtown. Her hair tied up at the base of her neck bobbed with her movement. A navy beret helped disguise her general appearance. She didn't want attention.

She was moving forward. In every way.

She had no choice. She knew that now. The world had shared the pain of her betrayal, and Elly had tried to be strong.

But she wasn't. Not really.

She could not be in that apartment. It was the scene of their betrayal. She had checked into a hotel, to get away from everyone and everything. Hotels are not real life. They have dry-cleaning on demand, food twenty-four hours a day, and worst of all, a minibar. Except this was a really good hotel, and they had full bottles of wine in the fridge. Last night, after she had opened a second bottle of wine, Elly had sent James a text message.

A single word.

Hello.

No response.

She waited for a half hour. Had another glass of Chardonnay, then called him.

He didn't answer.

She called him again.

He didn't pick up.

Over the course of consuming the rest of the bottle, she had called him another six times.

It hadn't helped that James was now one of the most hated figures on social media. Elly's TikTok had seen to that. He'd deleted his Instagram along with the rest of his social media. It didn't stop the hate. Tens of thousands of people pouring abuse onto his name, contacting his friends, his family, his employers. In the two weeks since that live video outing James and Harriet, they had both suffered. Harriet got dropped by her modelling agency and James was fired for bringing his firm into disrepute.

Elly didn't ask for any of that to happen. She knew it could. And she didn't stop it. Couldn't stop it.

None of it helped Elly feel better. Revenge was not sweet. It tasted bitter. She still loved him. Now she had to bear the guilt of ruining two lives as well as managing the pain in her own.

Elly took off her brown leather glove, wiped at the tear on her cheek as she turned the corner for the downtown train and tapped her phone on the scanner as she went through the barrier.

A single set of stairs led down to the platform. It was midday.

Not too many commuters around, but New York is never quiet. There are always people.

A man stood at the top of the stairs. He had a cast on his left leg, from below the knee to the top of his foot, and held a crutch in each arm. Even though it was cold, he wore sweatpants with one leg cut away because of the cast, a sweater and a red jacket. He had a thin face, but he wasn't struggling to hold his weight on those crutches. Even from a distance, Elly could see he had powerful arms and shoulders. He reminded her of boys she knew on the swim team or gymnastics team in college.

But this was no college boy.

He was older. Ten, maybe fifteen years older than Elly. Yet he didn't look like most forty-somethings. Not to Elly. He looked . . . well, Elly thought he looked just great. He wore a blue baseball hat. He leaned down, still holding the crutch with his right hand, and tried to grab something.

There was a yellow hard-shell luggage case beside him, on rollers. He moved forward a little, gripping the handle and the crutch as he shuffled along, but now he had a new problem. He was trying to get down the stairs, but couldn't quite figure out how to carry the case and use the crutches to support his weight on the descent. A woman in a long black coat pushed past him, and he fell against the rail. She hollered an apology as she skipped down the steps. He simply smiled. Didn't show any anger or irritation, just a polite wave of acknowledgement.

After the last two weeks of carnage, Elly found herself stepping toward the man and saying, 'Do you need some help with your case?'

Perhaps because she wanted to help. Perhaps because she missed the warm feeling that came after she had completed one of her daily random acts of kindness. Perhaps because the guy looked quite pathetic and she felt sorry for him.

At first, he was surprised. His mouth opened and moved, but no words and no sound came out. At this point, she noticed a scar on his chin, just below his lower lip. Pale and wide. An old wound. Then he smiled and said gratefully, 'Thank you, I managed this far holding it with the crutch and dragging it alongside me, but that doesn't work with stairs. This is so kind.'

'No problem,' said Elly, reaching down. She pressed the button on the extendable handle at the top of the case, pushed it down, took the plastic handle, and picked it up. It wasn't too heavy, the type of case she liked to use for carry-on baggage when she flew.

A thought occurred to her that two weeks ago, before that viral video, Elly would have asked the man if it was okay for her to take a video for her socials. This would've been a good one for her daily random acts of kindness. But not now. Elly didn't know if she would ever post online again.

She waited a moment until the man got both crutches secure on his arms, lowered them to the first step and then hopped down. He'd bent the broken leg, using it to help his balance as the rubber feet on the crutches found the next step. The crutches clicked as they took his weight, and he said, 'People have been walking past me for the last five minutes. I didn't know how I was going to get down to the platform. People in this city are so busy they . . .'

SNAP!

The plastic handle broke off the case.

Not only did it stop the man speaking, but time itself seemed to stop for Elly. She froze. So did the man. They didn't try to grab the case – no point. Instinctively, Elly's hand reached for her mouth, and she drew in a fierce gasp.

They watched as it fell, almost in slow motion.

The case hit the steps and bounced into the air, somersaulting and then hitting them again, sending it tumbling down, down, down onto the platform with a dull *thunk*, and then the case burst open, charging cables, a laptop, underwear, socks – everything spilled out onto the platform.

'*Oh my God, oh my God,* I'm *soooo* sorry,' said Elly over and over again, like a breathless mantra, as she hustled down the steps.

'It's okay. It was an accident,' said the man, as he slowly and carefully made his way down.

Elly crouched down, instinctively, and began to gather the man's items, placing them back into the case. She felt sick and useless as she snatched his Calvin Klein underwear from the dirty platform, folded them and stuffed them into the open case. This was all so inappropriate that she felt her cheeks burning with the shame of it.

She was out of breath. Her neck flushed red. Her nervous system flooded with the adrenalin that comes with total, immolating embarrassment.

The man reached the platform and as he tried to bend down to help her retrieve his personal items he overbalanced and fell, twisting to save his broken leg and landing on his ass.

'Oh. My. God, are you alright? I'm so sorry! Jesus, what have I done?'

'It's okay. It's not your fault,' said the man.

They were both on the ground: Elly on her knees, the man on his ass. People walked past them, their knees, high heels, jeans and boots marching either side of them.

Elly and the man made eye contact and they both laughed, nervously. It broke the tension and Elly let out a relieved guffaw of laughter.

'Let me help you up,' she said, getting to her feet. The man got his good foot beneath him, took Elly's hand for balance, a crutch in the other, and soon was upright. She gave him his other crutch, and wiped sweat from her forehead. Everything was back in the case now. Not neatly, but it was there. Elly dropped to a crouch, closed over the lid of the case and then felt around the edge, looking for the zipper. She found it.

The zipper was already fully closed.

On closer examination, she discovered the fabric part of the case on one side had come away from the seam attaching it to the hard shell. The case would not stay closed.

She lifted it, one hand underneath, the other hand on top, and said, 'You don't have, like, a band or something to hold this together?'

The man shook his head, said, 'This has not been my week. I'll have to go repack, leave some stuff at my apartment and take my backpack. I've just got time to do that and make it to the airport for my flight home.'

She put the case on the floor, rubbed her head.

'I feel terrible, I'm so . . .'

'It's not your fault. Honestly, I appreciate you trying to help. I can't manage the stairs yet. I shattered my ankle at soccer practice and I'm still getting used to these damn things,' he said, holding up one crutch.

Elly felt sick looking at the busted suitcase.

'How are you going to get this case back to your apartment?'

He stared at it, said, 'Maybe if I jam it under my arm? That should keep it closed. Could you help me lift it under there?'

Elly sighed, checked her watch. She didn't have any appointments for hours. This was supposed to be preparation time.

'How far is your apartment?' she asked.

'Just a few blocks over.'

Elly picked up the case, held it closed in her arms, said, 'Come on, I'll help you.'

'No, I couldn't ask you to—'

'It's the least I can do. If I don't help you, then I'll just feel awful all day,' she said.

By the time the man had made his way back up the steps, he was out of breath.

'Thank you, I actually don't know how I would make it back without you. I'm Logan,' he said.

'Elly,' she said, and made sure to slow her pace, matching Logan's unsteady, halted movements with the crutches.

They made it out of the station onto 42nd Street and Logan moved to the crosswalk.

The case wasn't heavy, even with the contents inside, but it was awkward to hold and walk with the damn thing. She held it tucked underneath her left arm, her fingers just reaching the bottom side. She gripped it tightly and held it closed so it wouldn't open far enough for his underwear, or anything else, to fall out. As they crossed the street, her left arm began to tire and she switched, awkwardly, almost spilling the case again in the middle of the crosswalk.

'Jesus, there's no way you could've gotten this thing back to your apartment by yourself,' said Elly.

'I know. I was just too embarrassed to ask for help,' said Logan.

'You don't get to be embarrassed — you're injured. I'm fully functional, but it was me who managed to toss your case down the steps hard enough to break it.'

'It was the cheap handle,' said Logan. 'You've been nothing but kind. No one else stopped to help me.'

'Most people in this city are too busy to help a stranger,' said Elly. 'It's kinda sad. We should help out more.'

They reached the other side of the street and kept going south until they hit 40th. A man in a large, filthy coat sat on a cardboard bed on the corner. No way of telling how old he was. Homeless people age faster. The streets of New York are like time machines. One night on a sidewalk feels like a week. A week feels like a year, and it shows on the faces of the homeless, and in their eyes.

Elly slowed, shifted the case under a different arm so she could reach into her pants pocket. She brought out five dollars and handed it to the man. He looked sleepy. He took the money, quizzically at first, then stared up at Elly. He mouthed a *thank-you*.

Elly and Logan walked on.

'You're a good person, Elly,' said Logan.

'I try to do one thing every day to help somebody. I haven't done that in a while. I'm not really *that* good of a person,' said Elly, thinking about James and Harriet. They had both hurt her deeply. A wound that she would carry on her heart for a long time. Yet they didn't deserve to have their lives ruined for one mistake.

'You don't take compliments too easily,' he said, smiling.

'Like I said, I'm not so good. I just try to make up for my mistakes. Makes me feel better.'

'So I'm one of your charity cases? Like that guy on the corner?' he said again, smiling.

'Maybe,' said Elly, 'but he's in better shape than you. How did you say you broke your foot?'

'Ankle, playing soccer. Guy stepped on my foot when I was going for the ball.'

'Ouch.'

'You're telling me. I've got plates and screws and all kinds in there . . . Oh, wait, we're here,' he said, stopping outside an apartment complex.

It was an old building and from the bags of cement, plaster, buckets and tools piled up in the lobby, it looked as if it was about to get some much-needed maintenance and repairs. Logan hit the button for the elevator and waited.

It was cold outside, but surprisingly warm in the small lobby.

Elly noticed the elevator button hadn't illuminated when Logan hit it. She wondered if he had not pressed it correctly; he'd still had his arm slung through a crutch at the time. She pressed it, firmly. The button didn't illuminate. Logan leaned toward the elevator doors, rapidly pressed the call button, and listened for a few seconds. Elly couldn't hear any of the usual noises that elevators make. No mechanical whirr from the jib wheel lowering the counterbalance, no distant rattle of elevator doors closing on an upper floor. Logan leaned back and looked at the LCD display fixed on the top of the elevator doors.

'I cannot believe this,' he said. 'Yesterday, the garbage chute got blocked, today the elevator. I'm sorry, my building is a mess. My ankle is a mess, and my life is a mess.'

'It's okay. What floor are you on?'

'Third?' said Logan, the pitch of that one-word reply rising at the end, changing it into a question instead of a statement.

'Well, I've come this far,' said Elly. 'No point in leaving you with the case here. Stairs are not your friend. Come on, I'll race you,' she said.

'No fair,' said Logan, and they both laughed as he pointed Elly in the direction of the stairwell. This was, in so many ways, a pain in the ass for Elly. She hated stairs, but she thought Logan was funny and a little cute in his own way. More than anything else, she was glad of the distraction. This poor guy had busted his ankle, and then Elly had busted his case. For the first time in weeks, she wasn't thinking about the pain of having been betrayed by the two people in her life that she had loved and trusted the most – she wasn't thinking about the millions of people who had watched her walk in on her husband while he was in bed with her best friend, she wasn't thinking about the tsunami of abuse that followed James and Harriet and how, somehow, Elly bore responsibility for that too.

Logan's broken ankle, broken case and shit-out-of-luck life was making her feel better in every way.

It may have been the third floor, which was better than the eighth floor, but it still meant six flights of stairs, which were just as hot as the lobby. The old pipes snaked along the exposed-brick walls and followed the stairs upwards like thick iron and copper snakes. And, just like snakes, they hissed too. Whatever serious problems this building may have had, heating was not one of them. By the time they reached the third floor and the door to Logan's apartment, both of them were out of breath and covered in sweat.

'Thank God,' said Logan as he put his key in the door and pushed inside.

The apartment was like a lot of spaces in the city for young professionals – small but no doubt ridiculously expensive. A tiny kitchenette on the right. A living space with a tasteful leather couch pointed at a TV, some bookcases, and two doors beyond – one bathroom and one bedroom, she guessed.

Elly brought the case through to the living space, asked, 'Where do you want this?'

'Ahm, just dump it on the floor. I can slide it into the bedroom with my feet,' said Logan, breathing hard from the effort of hopping up the stairs.

He was being mindful that Elly was in a strange place with a strange man, and maybe asking her to step into his bedroom might make her feel uncomfortable. Even though her arms were aching, and she was out of breath and sweating from the stairs, she appreciated the thought.

Logan was alright. Considerate, even.

'It's okay, honestly. Where's the bedroom?' she asked, between breaths.

'On the right,' said Logan, who kept back, giving her space, allowing Elly to push open the door. The bedroom had a double bed, white sheets, a built-in closet and just about enough floor space to walk around the furniture. She dumped the case on the bed, came out of the bedroom and opened her coat, flapped it to help her cool off.

'I can't thank you enough,' said Logan. 'There's some water in the fridge if you'd like some. Help yourself to a carton. I'll just be a minute or two repacking. I just need to find my backpack . . .'

He moved into the bedroom and closed the door. Elly checked her watch. She still had a ton of time. No rush. Her lips were dry, and she really did need something cool to drink. She shook her arms, trying to get blood back into her biceps, then opened the refrigerator. While Logan may have seemed like a woke, hip, metrosexual type of New Yorker, he was still a guy, and this was definitely a guy's fridge.

Some elderly vegetables in a drawer, a jar of mustard, jar of peanut butter, some milk and half a dozen cartons of water. No plastic bottles; cartons of Icelandic spring water. Obviously, Logan was passionate about the environment too.

Elly exposed her neck to the cool air from the refrigerator, took a carton of water, opened it, and enjoyed a long drink. Still with the door open, the air cooling her skin, she drank most of the carton. Closing the fridge, she looked toward the bedroom. The door wasn't fully closed, just shut over. Elly took the opportunity to take a better look around the apartment.

It all appeared clean and nicely decorated. Neutral colors, two windows either side of the TV with a view of the street below, but not much light. A coffee table with some large art books carefully arranged on top. Copies of the *New Yorker* magazine in a rack on the bookcase. Most of the books were old – the classics, she guessed.

Elly loved books. She took a few minutes to study the racks, noting a couple of titles which were also among her personal favorites.

This Logan guy was really growing on her.

Two bulky garbage bags were piled up behind the door in the short hallway. The only things out of place, really. She remembered him mentioning the garbage chute was blocked, probably the construction workers' fault, throwing something down there that didn't belong. She imagined Logan would struggle to get those garbage bags downstairs on his crutches. Poor guy seemed to be having a bad time of it.

Logan was still in the bedroom.

Elly was in two minds. She could leave now, and head back to the station, but Logan was probably heading back that way too. And she wanted to make sure he had a backpack, and that he could manage. She decided to give it another few minutes, walk back that way with him. There was a charm to his helplessness.

And he was proving to be shelter from the nuclear heat of the explosion that had ripped through Elly's life these past weeks.

For a moment, her mind flashed on the night before, the calls to James that he didn't pick up. A drunken mistake. Even the thought of it sent waves of loathing through her stomach.

She tried to focus her mind on Logan, and his apartment, and how fate can sometimes lend a helping hand – making sure you meet the right people at just the right time in your life.

But thoughts of her pleasant morning with the man on his crutches didn't shift the uneasy feeling in her stomach. If anything, she began to feel worse by the second. Her stomach groaned and burbled, and a swell of pain washed her gut. She bent over, took a breath and it passed, but just for a moment. She straightened up and the pain came again. This time, her vision washed in a haze that made the titles on the book spines blur.

Vertigo now.

Her head felt far too heavy for her body, and she had to grab the shelves to maintain her balance.

Elly slipped the carton of water into the large pocket of her overcoat so she could use both hands to steady herself.

She needed some air. She thought of going to the window, but the room was suddenly terrifically hot. Sweat dripped onto the hardwood flooring as she turned and took a step toward the door. She took a second, gathered herself, did some breathing exercises she had learned in yoga class and her head felt a little clearer.

The door. The hallway. The stairs. Air.

In that order.

As soon as Elly let go of the shelves and made for the door, her vision swam, her head spun, and she stumbled. It was as if she was on the deck of a ship being tossed around by waves the size of skyscrapers. More faltering steps couldn't find her balance, and she fell forward, her hands outstretched to save her. Her left knee took a hit as she went down, and she collided with the garbage bags piled behind the door.

The red bark of agony from her knee somehow cleared her head and she was able to get onto her side and sit up. She blinked, winced and held her knee. There would be a hell of a bruise from that fall. But her vertigo had eased. As Elly slowly gathered her feet beneath her, and using the wall for balance she stood up, it was then she noticed the garbage bags had ripped when she landed on top of them.

They were quite firm and unyielding. As if a box was in the bag.

Elly wiped sweat from her eyes, and for a second thought how clumsy she was. Maybe she was just faint from the effort of carrying the case up all those stairs.

Then she saw something through the rip in one of the garbage bags.

Something that stopped her heart.

She leaned over, put her fingers inside the bag and tore it open. Then did the same to the bag beside it.

Elly froze. Shock rooting her boots to the floor like cement.

There, in the garbage bags . . .

Two.

Yellow.

Broken.

Suitcases.

The handle hanging limp at the top of each one.

The zippers closed.

The fabric between the zipper and the case, ripped.

Both cases were identical in every way to the case she had just carried up six flights of stairs.

Her gut squeezed.

Saliva filled her mouth and Elly moved.

Out the front door, not looking back.

Down the first flight of stairs, clinging to the rail with her left hand in case she lost her balance again and tumbled over the side.

Panting.

Heartbeat rattling like a snare.

Her feet matching that fast tempo, adrenalin taking her down those stairs.

As she half stumbled, half bounced down the steps, she realized, almost absent-mindedly, that her stomach and right leg felt wet. She grabbed the carton of water from her coat pocket. It was leaking, she probably hadn't sealed it again properly.

Another flight down. Quick turn on the landing, and down another set of steps. The door to the lobby visible now.

As Elly was almost at the bottom of the stairs, she was about to toss the water but saw, strangely, that it was indeed sealed with the cap.

But her hand was wet.

Elly reached the bottom of the staircase, thumped open the door to the lobby of the building and ran for the front door.

In the sunlight, and the cool air, she felt the pain in her knee and the churning nausea return.

Elly doubled over and vomited, violently. The suddenness of the reaction frightened her. She looked at the carton of water again, thinking about taking a drink to wash out her mouth, and then saw where the water was leaking.

A tiny hole in the top of the carton.

The kind that could be made with a pin.

Or the needle from a syringe.

Her vision whirled into a kaleidoscope of colors and random shapes as the carton fell from her hand and the ground came up to meet her. A terrible pain on the side of her head.

Elly used her arms to push herself off the ground and saw the pool of blood where her head had been.

She crawled forward, onto the street.

People passing by.

Knees and shoes and legs all around her, a blur, as she crawled toward the curb.

Voices. The sidewalk. And then the blue sky.

Elly saw a face before her eyes. She was lying on her back, and the homeless man she had given some money to was kneeling over her.

He looked concerned, and he was saying something, but Elly couldn't understand a word. More faces appeared, obscuring the sky above.

Strangers.

Their lips moving. But Elly couldn't hear anything.

Then black.

And a deeper, darker silence.

2

Eddie

I know two things about civil litigation.

You can win a case in the parking lot.

Civil litigation is anything but civilized.

Give me criminal law any day. With a prosecutor, you know exactly where you stand. They are going to try to bury you and your client. There's no subterfuge. It's two armies standing on opposite hills. They charge at each other and meet in the valley. There's a victor and a loser and a lot of blood left on the ground.

With civil law, your opponent can behave like your best friend, your worst enemy, or they simply hide in the long grass with a rifle aimed at your head. The only thing you can be sure of is that when your opposing counsel opens their mouth, what comes out is anything but the truth. The high-roller civil defense attorneys who represent Fortune 500 companies, insurance conglomerates and pharmaceutical giants, wear five-thousand-dollar hand-cut Italian suits like plate-steel armor. They've all been in the wars. They've seen things. They don't shake easily.

I've got a reputation as a trial lawyer, and before that as a con artist, but I'm still small-time compared to these guys. Oh, and by the way, they are nearly all guys. There's more testosterone in a

Wall Street civil litigation department than the locker room at the Ultimate Fighting Championship.

Yeah, civil law ain't civilized in the least.

Then there's the real battleground. If you can win a case without stepping into the courtroom, so much the better.

I liked parking lots for all major battles.

In every case ever tried, people make the decisions. Judges, or juries. You have to play the people and not the law or the facts.

All good lawyers know that you need a working knowledge of every judge's personality. Judges are like violins – if you don't know how to play them properly, they can make one hell of a racket. Great lawyers – they know a lot more. Like the best parking lot close to the courthouse. That's where the real knowledge pays off.

It was a cold, sunny Monday morning and I was on my way to Kings County civil court for a case discussion with the plaintiff's lawyers and the judge. My client was Morrie Sirico. He owns an Italian deli in Queens, passed on to him by his father, and his grandfather before him. The place opened in the fifties selling Italian cold cuts, cannolis, tiramisu, coffee and cakes. A sense of community grew around the deli. Old timers can be found there most mornings, blowing steam off their espressos and risking a dollar on the dominoes. Six months ago, the plaintiff, Neville Carmichael, is in the neighborhood and he happens to visit Morrie's. He buys some good cheese and is on his way out the door when he slips on some prosciutto, which somehow found its way onto the floor, and he lands on his back, injuring himself. The paramedics are called to Morrie's, and shortly after Neville goes to see a lawyer.

The lawyer sends a letter to Morrie claiming personal injuries for his client and seeking hundreds of thousands of dollars in damages.

A week later, Morrie lands in hot water with the insurance investigator. They're not happy with Morrie's paperwork, or his face, so they refuse to indemnify. Now Morrie was facing a lawsuit for half a million dollars in damages for personal injury and he doesn't have insurance cover.

Civil cases settle. The vast majority of them anyway. That's not to say the settlement is fair or that justice has been done, but money has been handed over to someone who was wronged or injured. In civil law, it's all about the money.

How do you get the most money for your client? Or, if you're a defense attorney, how do you pay the least amount?

You play the game.

Sometimes that's down to being a good attorney.

Sometimes that's down to cheating.

Sometimes it's hard to tell the difference.

Sometimes it comes down to where you play the game.

Like I said, I prefer parking lots.

Before I was a trial lawyer, I had a moderately successful run as a con artist hustling insurance companies, criminals and casinos. Grifting is not so different from filing lawsuits, persuading juries, or winning more clients. The big difference in the con game – the hours are better.

Still, the experience I had in my former profession sure helped when it came to the justice game. Like now.

The closest lot to the courthouse is just across Adams Street. This is where the defendants and their families park, corrections officers, bail bondsmen, probation officers, court staff, witnesses, those called to jury service and even the judges.

Just as it's important to know your judges, knowing where to park can save a lot of time and billable hours.

Only I didn't use the Adams Street lot. I parked further away, in the Pierrepoint mall, just across the street from Brooklyn Park. It's further away from the courthouse and it's more expensive. Seems a bad choice, but it was perfect for me.

There were two reasons to park in the Pierrepoint mall.

The first is the view.

The second is that prosecutors park here. They don't want to run into the family of a defendant they've just successfully convicted in a dark parking lot. So they avoid the lot closest to the courthouse in favor of a quieter place, further away.

I pulled into the Pierrepoint car lot via the underground ramp, but there were no spaces on the first three levels. I needed an elevated view anyway.

I parked on the fourth floor, killed the engine, and retrieved my case files from the trunk of the Mustang. The upper levels were open to the elements, no windows. Open sides to let in air, or let out the smells that accumulate in parking lots. I had made sure to park on the west side of the lot, with a view of Livingstone Street beneath me. I leaned over the concrete barrier and checked my watch.

Anytime now.

There was a federal building down the street, but most of the real estate in this part of Livingstone was occupied by small businesses.

Only three kinds.

Bail bonds.

Orthopedic medical practices.

Personal-injury lawyers. A *lot* of personal-injury lawyers.

And not all of them the best kind. Someone once joked that if an ambulance drove down Livingstone with its sirens on, before it got to the end of the street there would be fifty lawyers in suits chasing after it.

A brown SUV pulled up on the street outside the law offices of January Jeffers, Esq. Attorney at Law. Jan was one of those guys who would chase the paramedics. Not that there was anything wrong with that, and not that there would be any danger of him catching them. Jan Jeffers looked eighty years old when I passed the bar exam. Now, he looked like he was being held up with coffee, a thousand volts of electricity, and very thin strings.

A small man in an offensively bright orange button-down shirt and black pants got out of the SUV and made his way to the gap between the parked cars outside Jan's office. Before he could make the four feet between the SUV and the parked cars, his head turned sharply.

A food courier on a bicycle, wearing a green helmet, was almost on top of him. The guy in the orange shirt must've heard the screech of brakes from the bike. But the cyclist was going too fast, or the box on his back must've weighed too much because he wasn't slowing down fast enough. He put his feet on the blacktop and they skidded as the brakes on his bike whined. The man in the orange shirt jumped out of the way of the bike, leaping in between the parked cars, and the bike just missed him. He then quickly scrambled back up onto his feet to hurl abuse at the courier, who had managed to come to a stop just a few feet away.

They were too far away to hear what they were saying, but judging by the hand gestures and the hollering, I'd say there was a fair and frank exchange of views. The cyclist pedaled away and the man in the orange shirt was still cursing and waving his arms, and even taking a small run at the cyclist as he left the scene.

The guy in the orange shirt went into Jan's office. I took a few moments to turn and check the parking lot. No BMW M series in midnight blue. Not yet.

I turned back to the street in time to see Jan leading his client in his orange shirt back out the front door. They didn't go far. Next door was an orthopedic medical practice. I thought the words *medical* and *practice* were doing a lot of heavy lifting on that sign. It might have been more efficient for Jan to just install an internal door in his law office, so clients could walk straight into the orthopod's office without venturing onto the street. They were a team, Jan and the doc. Jan brought in the clients, the doc wrote up whatever kind of medical report Jan needed after a thorough examination of the client's wallet.

They were in there for maybe five minutes and hadn't come out yet.

I heard the sound of a BMW engine. Turned.

M series. Blue. But not the midnight blue Beamer I was looking for.

I swung around just in time to see Jan holding open the doctor's office door while his client in the orange shirt, now with crutches on each arm, managed to maneuver himself out onto the street. He walked stiffly now, throwing one crutch forward with his weight, then swinging his body, and then the other crutch. He was also wearing a back support, kind of like a girdle around his waist, except the thick part was on his lower back. I didn't know how effective it would be at supporting his back, but it at least helped hide some of his offensive orange shirt.

I looked up the street, saw the bicycle courier crouching behind a parked car. He got back on his bike and cycled away.

I heard another car come up onto my level.

This time BMW. M series. Midnight blue.

I turned away from Jan and his client and approached the young man getting out of the BMW. His name was Chris Doyle, a young up-and-coming assistant district attorney. Smart and fair. At least one of those qualities meant he wouldn't have a future in the district attorney's office. He wasn't long out of law school, and I figured he would last another six months before he'd go for a job in one of the old white-shoe law firms in Manhattan with his real-world criminal experience, his contacts in the DA's office, and his heart full of the pride and fulfilment that comes from public service. But you can't live on pride. Chris was working on a big payday that would come with a corporate job.

'Hey, man,' I said.

'Eddie, you waiting to beat me up?' he asked, with a smile.

'I don't beat anyone up any more, Chris. I've got people who do that for me.'

'Is Bloch on the other side of that pillar, then?'

'Nah, she likes you. Especially after that deal for little Jackie.'

Chris had taken pity on an old client of mine. Jackie was a great card player and an excellent hustler in his time. He got caught with cash that he couldn't account for when he was busted for assaulting an asshole who came after him with a ten-pound hammer. Jackie had cleaned the guy out at the card table and acted in self-defense. The police don't like Jackie, and they don't like illegal card games, so they arrested him. Chris did him and me a solid, and let Jackie plead out the charges for six months' probation and a confiscation order on the cash.

'You walking to court?' I asked.

'Why do I get the impression you want something from me?'

'I don't know what would give you that idea, but now that we're on our way to court together I figure I may as well pick your brains on money laundering . . .'

Chris had written a few articles for various law-review publications on the Banking Act and digital fraud. He knew what he was talking about. We found the elevator. Chris went in first and I followed.

He leaned over to hit the button for the lobby.

I asked him a question about digital fraud and RICO.

I didn't listen as he started to answer. I didn't want to know anything about digital fraud and RICO.

I just wanted to wait until he was distracted, focusing on the elevator panel, leaning over, turning away from me, so I could steal his car keys from his jacket pocket.

I learned from the best. My old man. Smart hands, he used to call it. To execute a clean pocket dip, you need to master two contradictory movements simultaneously. You need to be fast. And you need to be soft. Specifically, soft fingers. Moving your arm at speed tends to tense the muscles – the key is to keep a light wrist. A tense wrist means hard fingers, which means the mark will feel the lift.

I put his car keys in my pocket, and pretended to listen while he regaled me with the latest legal developments in an area of law that few understand. The elevator took us to the ground floor and we walked around the corner together, through Brooklyn Park to the courthouse. I told Chris he should go on ahead, I had to meet a client outside.

In truth, I just didn't want him to see me pulling his car keys out of my pocket and putting them in the plastic tray as I went through security screening.

He went into the building ahead of me. I waited ten minutes, then followed.

Civil court is on level three. Criminal, level four.

I took the elevator to the third floor and found my client pacing the hallway. Lawyers and their clients lined the benches and slouched against the painted concrete walls. Morrie was dressed in a white shirt, open at the collar, and black pants. His stomach hung, reassuringly, over his belt. Morrie liked cannoli.

'Eddie, where've you been?' he asked.

'I've been preparing. How are you feeling, Morrie?'

'I'm going out of my mind. I can't believe this. I swear to you I swept the floor the night before this happened. We hadn't cut any meat that morning, so I don't know how this man slips on a piece of prosciutto? It's not possible.'

'I know. I believe you,' I said.

'I don't have much money, Eddie. What with Gloria sick in the hospital . . .'

His wife, Gloria, was having treatment for ulcers. The doctors would never say it, but I knew the stress of this case was taking a toll on this elderly couple's health.

'How is she?'

'She's worried. The business has been in my family for generations . . . to think I could lose it . . . we could lose our home. It's too much for her,' he said.

'Look, Morrie, I'm going to do my best today. This is just a settlement discussion, but if everything plays out, we could finish this . . .'

'I told you, I don't have much money. The goddamn insurance company, I paid them every month for years and they leave me in the gutter,' said Morrie, and his right hand gripped his chest. His daughter, Julia, had told me Morrie was having chest pains since the lawsuit began. With the amount of damages Neville Carmichael was claiming, Morrie would have to sell his apartment and the store and he could still be in debt.

'You can't give them any excuse not to honor the policy, Morrie. I told you, paperwork . . .'

'Julia thought she did all the paperwork. That's what I told the insurance guy,' he said, throwing his arms up. His face, usually a pale red, was beginning to darken into a deep crimson. I could almost hear a hiss from his blood pressure rising.

'If you don't have paperwork logging the times and frequency of the floor cleaning, then that violates your insurance policy. It means you can't prove a reasonable system of maintenance and inspection. And you didn't write up an accident report, either. That's why the insurance company wouldn't indemnify you.'

'They expect me to write reports? Reports? What am I – the *Polizia*? If I knew how to write a report, I wouldn't be chopping meat for a living.'

'There might be a way out of this. I can't promise anything, but I believe you when you said the floor was clean. Let me see what I can do.'

I left him on a bench, panting. His head looked like somebody trying to blow up a red balloon. His hand, clutched to his chest, was trembling. I was worried for Morrie. The legal system in America can take lives, but putting a needle full of poison into someone isn't the only way to kill them. Morrie's wife, Gloria, was already in the hospital and if this case didn't go away fast Morrie could be in the bed next to her.

They were good people, let down by a rigged system. Like so many in the country.

And Morrie's insurance company wasn't the only one on the make.

As I moved through the crowd, trying to locate my opponent, he grabbed me by the arm and gently pulled me to the side.

Jan Jeffers moved quietly.

'Eddie, I see your client is here. Good, good. I know his insurance company has pulled the plug so I want to be fair . . .' said Jan.

He made a clicking sound in his throat as he spoke. It was some kind of tic, or nervous habit, but with the skeletal frame, the gray skin, gray hair, and big eyes, he looked like a dead stick insect in a suit.

'Jan . . .' I began, but he interrupted. He was one of those guys who was always on transmit. Like he communicated through a two-way radio, but Jan always had his 'talk' button held down. He wasn't interested in what anyone else had to say.

'Now, you're smart enough to realize liability is not going to be an issue for my client. He slipped on a piece of prosciutto on the floor of a deli – it's *res ipsa loquitor* . . .'

He pronounced the doctrine of law in what I guessed was his attempt at a Latin accent. It might have been correct, but I wouldn't know. I wasn't so hot on the law. That was Harry Ford's domain, my consultant, best friend and former judge.

Res ipsa loquitor is Latin for 'the thing speaks for itself'. It can apply in cases like this, where the plaintiff can't prove a specific act of negligence, like one of Morrie's employees dropping prosciutto on the floor and not cleaning it up, but it's clear that Morrie's people had control of the floor, and the prosciutto, and there must have been negligence for the meat to be there on the floor so his client could slip on it and fall on his ass.

'I don't think it's *res ipsa*—' Again, I was getting nowhere fast with Jan.

'Let me finish, Eddie. I'm going to do you a favor. My consultant orthopedic specialist says this is a compression fracture, tiny, but it's there, and with pain and suffering and loss of earnings you're looking at three hundred and fifty grand in damages, easy. Now I know your guy doesn't have that kind of money. I'll go easy. Settle today, I'll recommend two-fifty. That's the best deal you'll ever get in your life.'

'Morrie would need to sell the store and his home and he still wouldn't raise a quarter million dollars after debts and taxes,' I said.

'Shit happens, my client is horrifically injured and it's Morrie's fault. He's gotta pay up,' said Jan, pointing to his client on the bench.

The guy in the orange shirt I'd seen earlier. The crutches were leaning against his thigh. A pained expression in his face.

The plaintiff, Neville Carmichael.

'Here's what I'm gonna do, Jan. I'm going to make you an offer. This is a non-negotiable, one-time deal. You take it today, or it's off the table forever. You understand?'

'Don't low-ball me, Eddie. Just don't. What's the offer, 'cause I can't go below a quarter mil on this case or my client will sue me, and he'd be right.'

'Here's the offer. You like Latin? Morrie pays *nihil*. Nil. Morrie pays you zero dollars . . .'

Jan threw his hands up in disgust.

'Wait, I haven't finished. Morrie pays nothing. You, or your client, pay Morrie ten grand, for expenses, today. And you buy me breakfast. Final offer.'

'Eddie, have you had a stroke? Did you bump your freakin' head? What the hell is wrong with you?'

'Do you have any money on you?' I asked.

'Sure I do,' said Jan quizzically.

'Good, because here comes my breakfast.'

The food-delivery cyclist made his way through the crowd toward us. His name was Darius Johnson, but everyone calls him Pork Chop, on account of his father who worked at a butcher's shop in Bed Stuy and came home every night with a bag of pork chops. Since Darius is all grown up and recently left home, he's become vegan. But the nickname stuck.

He pulled the GoPro camera off his green bicycle helmet and handed it to me. I hit play, showed the camera to Jan.

'Your client is hard to miss in that orange shirt. See, he got out of his wife's SUV this morning, outside your offices, with no movement or mobility problems whatsoever. He even leapt out of the way of Darius's bike here then jumps to his feet straight after and shouts and screams at the bike rider. He goes into your office, a few minutes later he goes next door with you to the orthopedic clinic, again no problems with movement or mobility. Then there are two problems for you. One, neither you nor your client see Darius filming you from behind a parked car. Your second problem is that when Neville comes out of the medical practice he suddenly looks like he fell off the top of a four-story building. And Darius here got it all on video for me.'

'Shit,' said Jan. 'You set this up, Eddie?'

'You're damn right I did. Here's what's going to happen if you don't take my offer. This video is going to the judge in this case, and then the district attorney's office, and then you will be disbarred and prosecuted for fraud – your client too.'

'Bullshit,' said Jan. 'You're bluffing. No way would the DA look at this . . .'

I pulled out my phone, called the Kings County central office. This courthouse is renowned for having the most friendly, informed and helpful staff. And they loved me. I sent donuts at Easter and four food hampers at Christmas.

Anne McCartney answered the phone. She was seventy-one years old, single, wise, formidable and funny as hell.

'Eddie Flynn, when are you going to ask me out for dinner?' she said.

'I'm a divorcee workaholic, Anne – you deserve better. Do me a favor, please, would you page ADA Chris Doyle to the third floor . . .'

The announcement came over the public speakers almost immediately.

'Chris Doyle to level three, please, for Eddie Flynn.'

Jan folded his arms, but I could tell he was rattled. We had put our cards on the table. Now it was time to turn mine over.

I moved away from Pork Chop and Jan, and stood in front of the elevators. Couple of minutes later, the doors opened and Chris stepped out.

I met him, making sure to keep my back to Jan, and took Chris's car keys out of my pocket. He smiled, took them and I made sure to block Jan's view of this little exchange.

'Thank you. Where did you find these? I just realized they were missing a few minutes ago,' he said.

'It was Jan Jeffers who found them. See that guy behind me who looks like he hasn't eaten in six months?'

We both turned, looked at Jan.

Jan didn't look happy. Pork Chop was covering his mouth, trying not to let Jan see his silent laughter.

I pointed to Jan, and so did Chris, making sure it was the right guy I was referring to.

'I'll let you get back to putting innocent people in jail,' I said.

Chris patted me on the arm, waved goodbye to Jan and hopped back into the elevator.

I took my time making the short walk back across the hallway to where Jan was standing, his face dripping down to his knees.

'One time offer, Jan. You did get one thing right. It *is* a case of *res ipsa loquitor*. Morrie swept that floor the night before the accident.

He didn't cut any meat or sell any prosciutto before your client fell that morning. Your man fell on a cold cut because he put that piece of meat on the floor himself after he pretended to take a slip.'

'We withdraw the lawsuit and the video goes away?' he asked.

'And you pay ten large.'

'Today?'

I nodded.

'Deal,' he said, and turned away.

'Wait,' I said.

Reluctantly, Jan swung around, a look of total defeat on his face. I almost felt sorry for him.

'What?'

'You forgot something,' I said.

Pork Chop opened his delivery bag and handed me a sandwich wrapped in foil.

'Pay the man. You're buying me breakfast, remember?'

'That'll be five hundred dollars,' said Pork Chop.

'You gotta be freakin' kidding me,' said Jan. 'What the hell is in that sandwich, caviar and golden eggs?'

'Prosciutto,' said Pork Chop.

As Jan counted out five one-hundred-dollar bills like they were his last, I went over to see Morrie.

'It's done,' I said. 'The case is dropped. That guy over there is going to pay ten grand for your expenses. Some of that has to come out to cover some filing fees and my time, but you should have about eight grand left over. You are going on a health-and-safety course to learn how to complete the proper reports so you don't end up in this mess ever again. Whatever is left over, and it should be plenty, goes toward your wife's medical bills.'

'What the hell happened, Eddie?'

'Justice,' I said. 'It makes an appearance every now and then.'

My phone buzzed in my pocket.

It was my sixteen-year-old daughter, Amy. Usually, I get texts. Sometimes even words instead of thumbs up or thumbs down emojis, occasionally a little red heart. I like those.

I answered, 'Hey, sweetheart . . .'

'Dad, I need you to get over here right away . . .'

She sounded breathless, and there was something else behind her tone. Not excitement.

Fear.

'What's wrong?'

'It's Mom. She's in trouble . . .'

3
Elly

There was a dream.

The longest nightmare Elly had ever experienced.

First, there was darkness.

Then, Elly found herself standing at the top of a staircase in Grand Central. In the subway. She was watching a yellow suitcase as it tumbled down the long staircase, turning and whirling through the air, making deafening bangs as its corners hit the stairs and then launched upwards, and then back down, that sound hurting her ears every time, echoing in her chest, her entire body feeling the impact vibration, and the steps went on, and on, and on, down and down into nothingness . . .

Here and there, for mere moments, she saw different images.

A man with round, wire-rimmed glasses and curly brown hair. He had a kindly face and a white coat, like a doctor, and thick lips that parted as he stared down at her. His hand on her brow. His thumb gently tugging her eyelids, and then a blinding white light that burned her eyes and stayed there even after she closed them.

She saw him a few times.

Her stomach hurt.

Her throat hurt.

Her head was pounding.

And the dream . . .

The suitcase thumping off the sharp corners of the stairs, tumbling, and then thumping, and every hit was a pulse that sent a shockwave of pain through her skull.

Pounding pain.

And then her eyes opened, and she was looking at a dark ceiling. Painted white. It must've been nighttime.

But her body was surrounded by a white veil hanging down. Like the veil that lines a coffin . . .

Elly felt the panic rise. She wasn't supposed to be dead. She couldn't be.

She was twenty-seven years old. And she wasn't dead.

But the veil was so white and clear.

Slowly, her eyes adjusted, depth perception returning.

It wasn't a coffin veil. It was the curtain surrounding a bed.

Her hospital bed.

Elly's head hurt so bad. Her throat. She couldn't speak and her stomach was in pieces. Like she had swallowed a bellyful of acid.

She tried to feel her tummy, but she couldn't move her left arm. Her right hand moved, and she was able to hold it in front of her eyes. There was a sharp jab of pain on the back of her hand. She saw the butterfly needle taped there, and a drip line attached to it.

But her left arm would only move a little.

She had no memory. No idea how she got there.

The effort of moving her right arm was too much. Her eyes felt heavy, and she couldn't keep them open no matter how hard she tried.

The darkness. Welcome. Restful.

And then the dream . . . the suitcase, and the noise of it hitting the stairs . . .

'Elly . . .' said a voice.

She opened her eyes and realized instantly it was no longer night. Sun came in behind her. She could see it burning the doctor's white coat, making the sunbeam seem otherworldly, like a shaft of light from heaven catching an angel's wing.

It was him. The kind doctor with the wire-rimmed glasses and thick lips.

'Elly . . . do you know where you are?'

She tried to speak, but her throat and her mouth were so dry. Elly tried to move her left hand, to gesture to her mouth, but found once again that it would not obey her. She was too weak to sit up. Too frightened to look. There was a strange sensation in that arm. Her left forearm and wrist felt so cold. Like it was stuck in a freezer.

Had she been in an accident?

Had she lost her left arm?

She motioned with her right hand, feeling the pull of the needle again, dragging the drip line. Her fingers touched her cracked lips. They felt like grade-five sandpaper.

The doctor nodded. He dabbed something cold on her lips. Ice maybe, or cool water captured in a linen cloth. It felt good. So soothing. Like drinking from a cold mountain stream after days in a hot desert.

'Hos . . . hospit-al . . .' Elly said, her throat aching.

'That's right. You're in hospital. You're in Mount Sinai and you're going to be okay now. My name is Dr. Jones . . .'

'How . . . Wh-whe-whe-when?'

'It's okay. You've been here for four days. You're going to be just fine.'

Elly blinked. Licked her sore lips. And, like a sudden flood, her recent memories came rushing back, her consciousness filled.

James, her new husband. The love of her life. Seeing him in bed with her best friend, not six months since her wedding day.

The explosion of attention.

The hurt.

The betrayal.

Even though he disgusted her, Elly still loved her husband. That's why it hurt so much. She was not enough for him. He wanted the lifestyle she could offer, but he didn't want her. It wasn't like that when they were first dating. She met James through a dating app. They got talking and he seemed wonderfully, exceptionally, beautifully normal. He liked nice clothes, working out, books, movies, and he had wit. No baggage. No debt. He wasn't an asshole – something increasingly rare in online dating. He wasn't controlling. He was supportive. Clean. A junior trader on Wall Street with a career path, good teeth and a health plan.

They had been dating a month when Elly introduced James to her friends. At first, Harriet couldn't understand why Elly was so into him. Harriet wasn't into normal guys – she wanted someone special. It was James's normality that made him special, at least to Elly. She didn't know exactly when James and Harriet began seeing each other on the side, but she guessed it had happened not long after James proposed.

Harriet always wanted what she couldn't have.

She'd met Elly during a shoot for fashion week. Elly, being a social-media influencer, and Harriet a catwalk model, they had hit it off right away. They had gone out for cocktails after the shoot and neither of them could remember much about the evening except that they were clearly destined to be best friends. Harriet never felt human to Elly – she was some kind of goddess who didn't play by the rules of society, work, culture or anything else. And being around someone like that often felt like carrying a burning torch. It lit up the world around you, but you realized that sooner or later the torch was either going to burn out, or it would burn you.

And now the shame.

The drunken phone calls to James that he didn't answer.

All of it hit Elly again, afresh, in milliseconds, and with it came a tsunami of emotions.

And then the man on the subway stairs. Logan. The man with the scar on his chin.

The broken yellow suitcase. His apartment. The identical broken suitcases in his trash bags. The water. The tiny pinprick hole in the carton.

Vomiting. Passing out on the street.

Elly felt as if she might throw up again.

'There are men here from NYPD,' said Dr. Jones. 'They have to speak to you . . .'

Good, thought Elly. She'll tell them what happened. She must've been poisoned. That man with the suitcase and the broken ankle, he tried to poison her. God knows what would've happened if she hadn't made it out of that apartment.

She shifted her weight, tried to put her hands on the bed to sit up, but her left arm wouldn't move. Her head throbbed violently at the effort.

'My a-arm,' said Elly, still unable to move it.

'I've told them they should wait, but I can't stop them talking to you,' said Dr. Jones.

He stepped out of her view.

Another man appeared in front of her. He wore a plaid shirt and had ID badges hung around his neck from a yellow lanyard.

'Elly Parker . . .' he said.

Elly turned away from him. He had cold eyes and Elly's stomach clenched. She thought she was going to be sick. She turned to her left, gasped for air. She hated being sick, and didn't want to vomit on the cop.

It was then she saw her left arm. She realized why it wouldn't move and why it felt cold.

Her left wrist was handcuffed to the metal bed rails.

'I'm Detective Sacks, Mrs. Parker, you're under arrest for the murders of James Parker and Harriet Rothschild.'

PART TWO

ELL ellyparker ✓

Manhattan, New York

🎵 The Bangles – Manic Monday

AUDIO DESCRIPTION OF VIDEO PROVIDED BY META AI

A young woman dressed in flowing black pants and a white T-shirt smiles sweetly at the camera. She is sitting on a beige couch in a tastefully decorated apartment. She gets up, packs her backpack with a laptop and camera, and sprays perfume on her neck.

ELLY: Hi, guys, it's another gorgeous Monday morning in Manhattan. There's a lot to do today so I hope you enjoy coming with me for another NYC adventure...

She grabs a water bottle from a fridge.

ELLY: James is always telling me to hydrate more, so I can't forget this.

The young woman opens the door to her apartment, steps out and the door shuts behind her. She gets into the elevator. Doors close as she checks her phone. She goes out of the elevator. Camera sweeps up to the blue sky framed by tall buildings. The young woman opens a door and goes into a Starbucks.

ELLY: My day always starts with coffee. Can't resist an iced mocha from Starbies...

The young woman sits on a crowded subway train sipping an iced drink through a straw. The young woman walks through a gym. She is dressed in a blue sweat-pant suit.

ELLY: It's two weeks to the wedding so I've got to get my morning workout in. Must, must, must fit into that dress...

A montage of the young woman working out on various fitness machines, doing press-ups, squats, in time-lapse mode, so that the woman looks as if she is moving very quickly. The young woman dressed in black trousers and white T-shirt sits at a restaurant table.

A plate of scrambled eggs and toast with avocado. A fork dives into the eggs.

ELLY: After my workout it's a healthy breakfast and then it's time for work...

The young woman enters a building through a frosted glass door. The sign on the frosted glass door says WeWork.

The young woman sits at a desk, wearing AirPods in her ears. She types on a laptop. This footage is played at x10 speed, so it looks as though she is typing really fast.

The young woman exits through the same door with WeWork on the frosted glass. She sits on a subway train.

She enters a pet store. Walks through the food aisle.

ELLY: Guys, you know me. It's all about paying it forward. Like, I don't own a pet. Actually, my building doesn't allow it. If they did, I would love to have a cat. I used to have a cat called Mr. Smiggles when I was little, and it was so cute. My parents rescued him and he was with us for about five years before he passed. Good years, mostly. But just because I don't have a pet doesn't mean I can't use my daily RAK to help some furry friends.

The young woman exits the pet store. In her arms she is carrying a bag of dog feed, a bag of cat food and some pet toys.

She enters a building. There is a friendly woman in uniform behind the desk. The young woman puts the dog and cat food and toys on the counter and talks to the friendly woman.

ELLY: So, guys, this is Margie. She works for, like, the best animal shelter in the city, Lost Paws, and, for today's random act of kindness, we're donating some delicious food to the shelter and of course…

The young woman gives a rubber bone to a black Labrador cross in a cage. The dog sniffs the toy. The young woman gives a red-and-orange ball to a Border terrier, who takes it in its mouth. The young woman gives a ball with a string to a black-and-white cat.

ELLY: …TOYS! Because all good dogs and cats deserve some toys. I met the cutest doggies and cats today and I can't tell you how much they love their new toys. If you are looking for a pet, come down to Lost Paws or check out some of the great animal shelters in the city who find homes for these cuties.

The young woman sits on the subway, drinks from her water bottle.

The young woman slumps onto a beige couch, drops her backpack at her feet.

ELLY: I know I'm supposed to cook tonight, but, guys, I'm so tired I'll just order some sushi for dinner. It should be here by the time James gets home from work…

It's night. The apartment is lit with lamps. The young woman relaxes on the couch with a young man. They kiss. The young woman leans her head into the young man's chest. They lace their fingers together and stare into each other's eyes, lovingly.

ELLY: And that's my Monday. What was your random act of kindness today?

#NYC #randomactofkindness #RAK #gymgirl #writinglife #starbucks #nycsushi #petfriends

♥ 301K

▶ 424,023

4
Eddie

On the drive to Riverhead, I thought how strange life can be.

I loved my ex-wife.

Christine was one of the smartest people I know, which made it somehow even more incomprehensible that she had married me at some point. Maybe the fact she divorced me speaks more to her intelligence than hooking up with me in the first place. We met in law school. She was idealistic. I was realistic. That was the conman in me. She was a better lawyer. Fastidious and straight down the line. She stuck by me, through alcohol rehab and beyond, for longer than I could ever have expected.

It was never going to end well. Of course, we have Amy from that marriage, and I know she's the best thing in both of our lives.

My practice brought the wrong kind of attention to our family, and I found myself keeping my distance from my wife and child. In the final years of our relationship, we were separating and getting back together and then falling apart again. I think Christine did the right thing when she pulled the plug. I had romantic ideas of finding a no-risk job and enjoying the quiet family life.

But I am not a quiet man, and sooner or later someone would come to me for help, and I would not be able to turn my back. That's part of what makes me a bad father and a bad husband. I help those in terrible need and sometimes that brings trouble. No matter how much I wanted Christine, I knew she and Amy would have a happier, safer and more contented life without me in it so much.

When Christine met Kevin, at first I was jealous. I hated him. But I came to realize that Christine's and Amy's happiness meant more to me than my own. I knew he would make her happier than I ever could.

And being apart from me would keep them safe. It broke my heart to let Christine go, but I did it because I loved her.

Amy wouldn't say what was going on over the phone. Just that Christine was in trouble. Her mom would never call me and ask for help. Too proud and probably too smart. And, more than likely, she didn't need my help. Christine was a strong woman, stronger than her new husband, Kevin, and my solutions to some kinds of problems are a little too unorthodox for my ex-wife's liking.

I pulled up outside Amy's school, killed the engine and sent her a text message.

> Do you need me to come in and sign you out?

Her reply was quick.

> I already faked Kevin's signature.

The doors to the school opened and Amy walked out with her book bag slung over her shoulder. It had been two weeks since I'd last seen her. She looked like she'd grown. Her hair seemed longer and it had definitely lost its summer shades.

Shrugging the bag from her shoulder, she got into the passenger seat, kissed me on the cheek and buckled her seatbelt.

'Thanks for coming, Dad,' she said.

'What the hell is going on with your mother? I've been worried sick driving over here.'

It was right then that I noticed Amy was looking over her shoulder, checking the side mirrors.

'Did you just ditch school? You worried the principal is going to come chasing after you?'

'Nah, it's fine. I signed out. I promise. Look, Mom is worried about some asshole coming after Kevin . . .'

It wasn't like Amy to use bad language in front of me. I guessed she was at the age where it was kind of acceptable. As long as the language didn't get too salty.

'What asshole?'

'I overheard Mom and Kevin arguing about it a while back. One of Kevin's cases. Some guy lost a lot of money because of a problem with inheritance law, or something. I don't know what. All I know is this guy is bad news and your name was mentioned.'

'My name?' I asked as I pulled out onto the street, headed for Christine and Kevin's home.

'Mom and Kevin were arguing. She was mad at him. She said she wanted a quiet life. That she divorced you because of all the trouble you got into . . .'

Amy suddenly realized what she had said, and the uncompromising way it had come out. She always told the unvarnished truth and often it was only after a word had been spoken that she realized the weight of it. In this way, like so many others, she was just like her mom. I was afraid that forging Kevin's signature was a little too much like *me*.

'Sorry, Dad. She was pretty upset about the whole thing. She cried.'

'She cried?'

Amy nodded.

Christine hardly ever cried. She wasn't the type. Kept all her emotions bottled up inside, the Irish way.

'Must be serious,' I said. 'So has he threatened your mom, or Kevin?'

'I don't know. I think so. Kevin seemed afraid of this guy.'

'Kevin's afraid of his own shadow,' I said, without meaning it. It was a cheap shot, and I regretted it almost as soon as I'd said it.

'He's different from you, Dad. If that's what you mean.'

'So why didn't you call me before? More to the point, why didn't your mom call me?'

'I asked her to call you yesterday. She said it would only make things worse.'

She knew me too well.

'So has he done anything, this guy?'

'We don't know for sure. He hasn't broken the law, anyway. Kevin says he thinks the guy followed him home last night. This morning Mom found a letter on the porch, addressed to Kevin.'

My hands tightened on the steering wheel, making the leather squeak.

'What did the letter say?'

'I don't know, but it mentioned our family. I heard them arguing about it.'

My jaw clamped down.

'Your mom should've called me. She contact the police?'

'I think so. They're both trying to act normally so they don't freak me out. I saw this guy across the street once, from my bedroom window. He's creepy. They tell me not to worry, but I know they're really worried. Mom is working from home. Won't go out. Insists Kevin drives me to school and back. I just don't want to see her like this. She's acting really strange. She even got a new home-security system.'

'Thanks for calling me – I mean it. I *hate* to see your mom upset.'

'I know,' she said, with some sadness in her tone. 'That's why you gave her the divorce, right? So *she* could be happy.' There was a little bite in that sentence that she probably meant.

'I tried, Amy. But I couldn't give her what she wanted, what she deserved. What you both deserved . . .'

'I wanted you to be my dad. That's all I ever wanted from you,' she said, and my chest tightened to absorb the impact from that one. 'I need you to make her feel better. You can do *that* for me.'

Nobody can hurt you like the people you love.

I didn't argue. She was right. I was wrong.

We drove on in silence, regret filling the space between us like a bad smell.

I pulled into the pea-gravel driveway of Amy's home. A white house sitting on a wide green lawn in a quiet suburban area where most American families can only dream of living. A big house, with large windows and a porch. Two-car garage.

As I stopped the car and got out, I heard footsteps approaching, with purpose, on the gravel. The footsteps belonged to a pair of black leather boots, with light blue jeans pulled over them, a white knitted sweater and dark hair tied back.

'What's going on?' asked Christine, her arms folded. Then she saw Amy and her expression changed – like her question had already been answered. 'Oh, I see. Anything you want to tell me, Amy?'

'I called Dad. He can help . . .'

Throwing up her arms in frustration, Christine did a one-eighty on the gravel and marched right back to the house, shaking her head the whole way.

Amy ran after her, shouldering her bag. I followed, around the corner of the house to the front porch. I saw Amy follow her mother inside, and there, standing on the porch, was Kevin. He wore tan chinos and a blue button-down Oxford shirt. His hands were by his sides. His right hand held a silver revolver.

Kevin forced a smile as he saw me approach.

'Eddie,' he said, nodding in greeting.

'Hi, Kevin, maybe we should talk.'

He gestured for us to go inside. As I stepped over the threshold, I glanced over my shoulder, saw Kevin scanning the neighborhood, the gun tight in his fist. As he turned his attention to the house, he saw that I'd noticed him checking the street. He tried to force another smile, but gave up halfway.

The hallway had black and white tile and a grand staircase, with an alcove underneath it. In it was a coat rack and a bench with shoes stored underneath. Kevin was in his thick woolen slippers. I heard Amy's voice in the kitchen and followed the sound of her protests and her mother's bootheels on the tile. Then Christine's voice. She was speaking through clenched teeth – always a bad sign. On the Christine scale of pissed-off, clenched teeth ranked way above shouting. I had a lot of practice in gauging my ex-wife's levels of rage.

Both Amy and Christine bit their tongues when I entered the kitchen.

'Somebody want to tell me what's going on? Amy called me and said you were in trouble. Something to do with a guy stalking you because of an inheritance case.'

'Amy, you should've told us you were going to call your father,' said Kevin, but in a placatory tone. He was making a point, in an attempt to close the matter and move on.

'I need permission to call my dad, now?' said Amy.

Christine gave her a look, side-eye. A warning – *don't you dare*. That shut up Amy. She was just as smart as her mother.

'There's nothing you can do, Eddie,' said Kevin. 'I've already obtained a restraining order.'

I'd had no idea this thing, whatever it was, had gotten that far.

'Who is this guy? Who exactly is threatening you?' I asked.

Kevin approached the kitchen counter and upon it, lying open, was a lockbox, with a digital number keypad, for the gun in his hand. He put the piece inside.

'His name is Arthur Cross. About two years ago, he began a

relationship with one of my clients, Betty Le Saux. She was in her seventies, widowed, had a lot of cash and stocks and a big property portfolio. Cross is in his mid-thirties, ran pyramid schemes and sold shady bitcoin to the elderly, who all lost money – if it stank, he was into it. Did some time too.'

'You know a lot about this guy,' I said.

'When Betty's nieces and nephews met Arthur, they were suspicious, and rightly so. I handled Betty's will and estate planning. They came to me to make sure she hadn't changed her will, but when I told them a marriage can invalidate previous wills they told me about Cross. I was concerned for Betty, so I got a PI to look into this guy. That's how I know so much. Three months ago, Betty died. Fell over the rail on the second floor of her mansion and broke her neck. Police carried out an investigation – accidental death. Betty's family were convinced Cross had arranged the accident. She was no spring chicken, but Betty was solid on her feet.'

'Don't tell me a new will appeared . . .' I said.

Kevin smiled, said, 'Exactly. It was handed to me by Arthur the same day the police ruled Betty's death as accidental. The will he gave me left everything to him. It was signed and witnessed by two people the family had never heard of. One of them was called Bruno Mont – he did time with Cross. Also, the private investigator couldn't confirm it, but he was convinced Bruno Mont killed people for money. And that Cross, who had a perfect alibi for the night of Betty's accident, had paid Bruno Mont to kill Betty. The family instructed me to contest the will and we got it thrown out in court, and her prior will upheld, which left Cross with nothing.'

'You shouldn't have gotten involved,' said Christine.

'I had no choice. I had to do what was right for my client,' said Kevin.

'Where have I heard that before?' said Christine, managing to land a blow on me and Kevin at the same time.

'After the case, Cross started following me around the courts.

Standing outside the office. Even our home. Then there was a letter yesterday – anonymous, of course, telling us to be careful. That our family was in danger. I got an emergency restraining order yesterday afternoon.'

'You think the letter came from Cross?'

'Had to be. The order says he is not to come within one hundred feet of my office, or our home. I saw him out there last night. He stood on the sidewalk across the street, exactly one hundred feet away . . .'

'Then he showed up at my school this morning,' said Amy.

'*What?*' said Christine and I, simultaneously.

'I didn't want to worry you,' said Kevin. 'I'm on it already. I've petitioned the court to amend the restraining order to include Amy's school too.'

'What did he do at the school?' I asked.

'He just *stared* . . .' said Amy, and shivered at the memory.

I felt my fingers tightening into fists.

'I was with her this morning. He wouldn't try anything with me there. We're making sure Amy is protected,' said Kevin.

Reaching for the lid of the lockbox for the pistol, I saw Kevin's fingers tremble as he closed it, picked up the box and put it up high on a kitchen shelf. He turned and smiled. Kevin was trying to keep a calm façade. He was scared, but there was no way he'd admit that. Not to me. And especially not in front of Christine.

'Amy, why didn't you tell me this in the car?' I asked.

'I didn't want you freaking out when you were driving,' said Amy.

'Was he stalking you during the case?' I asked Kevin.

'Yes, just outside the office, mostly. That's when I got the pistol. I have a pal in City Hall who helped me get a permit.'

'How long has this been going on?'

'About six months. Low level at first. But things have gotten worse,' said Kevin.

'Can I see the letter?' I asked.

'The original is with the police,' said Kevin as he took out his phone, brought up a screenshot and gave it to me.

YOU MADE A MISTAKE COMING AFTER ME. YOU SHOULD HAVE THOUGHT ABOUT YOUR FAMILY . . .

'How much was Betty Le Saux's estate worth?'

'Just shy of twenty million. She gave everything to her daughters, split down the middle. But she had already given Cross some cash for his businesses. He did alright out of his little con.'

'But you got the fake will thrown out, so what does he want? Money?'

'He just wants to make our life a living hell,' said Kevin.

'Maybe I should talk to this guy?' I said.

'No! Look, everything is under control,' said Christine. 'We don't need you making things worse. We've got a restraining order, and Kevin has a gun.'

'What happens if he busts through the front door when Kevin's not at home?' I asked.

'Then I'll put a bullet through his head. Kevin took me to the shooting range. I know how to use that thing,' she said, pointing to the gun in the lockbox.

'I get it,' I said. 'But Amy is scared. Hell, you're all scared and I don't blame you. This guy sounds dangerous. Maybe Amy should come stay with me for a while.'

'No,' said Christine. 'I want her here where I can keep an eye on her.'

'I haven't spent a lot of time at Dad's recently. I miss our nights together eating pizza and watching Detective Palumbo.'

'Columbo,' I said.

'Right, it would be good for us to—'

As much as I loved hearing this, before Amy could finish her sentence, Christine had brought me down to earth.

'What you really want is to spend more time in the city. I don't want you running around Manhattan on your own,' she said to Amy, and then, as an afterthought, 'No offense, Eddie. But she's sixteen and she's not responsible yet.'

'But, Mom—'

'I don't need to fight with you too,' said Christine.

Backing away, her hands raised in surrender, Amy left the kitchen and pounded upstairs.

'Teenagers . . .' said Kevin.

I wanted to say a lot more. That I could keep Amy safe better than anyone, but I held my tongue. There was an atmosphere in the house now. I wasn't welcome. It was emasculating for Kevin, having his wife's ex-husband come in as the protector, and as for Christine – there was too much history there. Too many old wounds and broken promises between us. And there was no doubt that my presence brought danger to those around me. It was just a fact.

Silence filled the kitchen. Hard as concrete. Freezing everyone on the spot.

'I should go,' I said. 'But, look, if this guy comes around again, I would appreciate a call. Maybe there's something I can do. If you want, I can get Bloch to come and check up on you. I know Amy likes her.'

My investigator, Bloch, pronounced *Block*, had met Amy a few times when she visited me on weekends. I was always working on something and that meant Bloch was too. It's funny how some people just take to Bloch. She doesn't say very much, but when she does, people listen. Not good with people, but brilliant with logic, science and deductive reasoning. Somehow, she got on well with Amy. Maybe young people have an honesty that Bloch appreciated. She didn't have to decipher intentions and emotions through subtext.

'Thank you, that would be fine. But there's really no need. We're okay,' said Kevin, before Christine could object. I felt for Kevin. He was a good man, way out of his depth. No point in me making him or anyone else feel worse about that. The fact that he'd gotten himself a gun showed me just how afraid Kevin was feeling.

'I can see you got this covered, Kevin. I feel better knowing you're looking after Christine and Amy. I'll take off – sorry to intrude,' I said.

Kevin and I shook hands at the front door. Here was a regular, straight-up guy who loved Christine and had grown to love Amy like she was his own daughter. It had taken me a while, but I was glad. Christine was happy. Amy was happy. They were well looked after and cared for in every way that I couldn't quite manage. And, more than anything, they were safe.

Until now.

I had almost reached the Mustang when I heard Christine's boots on the gravel again.

'Eddie, I'm sorry,' she said.

I stopped at the car, turned around.

'It's okay. I know it's a stressful time. Kevin is doing his best. You're lucky, you know? He's a good guy.'

She stepped closer, put her hands on my shoulders. I felt that warmth from her touch the way I did when we'd first met.

'Thank you for saying that. I know this hasn't been easy for you. Thanks for coming over. Amy shouldn't have called. I guess she got scared. She admires you, you know? She follows your cases, you know that?'

I didn't.

'Look, if this gets any worse, then maybe she should come and stay with you. Thanks for the offer. But don't go doing anything about this man Cross. Just leave it alone. Okay? I'm sorry for how I was in there. We split up because I couldn't live that life. I couldn't spend my days looking over my shoulder, worried about you pissing off some crook who would come after us. I thought I'd left that life behind. I thought I was doing the right thing . . .'

I got the impression she wanted to say more, that part of her still loved me, that maybe she had made a mistake getting divorced. Or maybe that was all in my head.

She leaned in, kissed me on the cheek, then turned and left.

With my cheek and my heart burning, I reversed out of the driveway and headed back to the city.

I called Bloch on my cell phone.

'I need you to look into someone for me. Guy named Arthur Cross.'

'Who is he?'

'He lost a lot of money in an inheritance dispute. Looks like he shacked up with a little old lady who mysteriously fell to her death leaving him everything in her will. Turns out the will was no good and the family took the money. He's stalking the lawyer who acted against him.'

'Who's the lawyer?'

'It's Kevin Pollock.'

'Christine's Kevin?'

'The same. This guy Cross even made an appearance at Amy's school this morning.'

There was silence on the other end of the line. I guessed Bloch was getting her anger under control.

'Any explicit threats?'

'A veiled threat in a letter left at the house. Kevin has got himself a revolver for personal protection. This guy Cross has a record. Did some time with a guy named Bruno Mont. There's a suspicion Cross paid Mont to kill the old lady while Cross had an alibi. He's a real piece of work, this guy.'

'I'll look into Cross.'

'I wonder if you paid him a visit, if it might help cool things off. Stalkers work well when their targets are isolated. It would be good to let this guy know there are people looking after the family. Take Gabriel Lake with you. Just *make sure* Lake doesn't shoot him.'

'I'll try. Kate's looking for you, by the way.'

'I'll call her later. Thanks, Bloch.'

She hung up. I called Gabriel Lake. Ex-FBI Behavioral Analyst. Works with me and Bloch from time to time. When he's not working cases for me, he catches serial killers.

He answered the call, and I filled him in on Arthur Cross. Told him Bloch would want him to ride along for a visit with Mr. Cross.

'It's just a hello,' I said. 'I want him to understand that Kevin has powerful friends, and he should back off. You're an extra body. And you're there to *make sure* Bloch doesn't break any of his bones.'

There was a pause on the other end of the line. I heard rustling. Lake was one of those guys who was always fidgeting – especially when he was thinking. And he just happened to be someone who was almost constantly living inside his own head. So he made a lot of noise. Like a motorcycle idling.

'I'll try to keep Bloch from damaging him. Just out of interest, when you spoke to Bloch, did you tell *her* to make sure *I* didn't shoot the guy.'

'I might have said something along those lines.'

Lake was just as smart as Bloch, but, where her mind didn't fully comprehend the remits of human action and emotion, Lake was all about psychology.

'I figured,' he said. 'I'll keep Bloch on a leash. And I won't shoot him. Happy?'

'Ecstatic. Seriously, thank you. I owe you and Bloch.'

'It's fine. Kate is looking for you.'

I flicked a finger across the phone screen. I had two missed calls from Kate. Two from our office secretary, Denise.

'I'll call her. Any idea what it's about?'

'Nope, I'll let you know how it goes with Cross.'

He hung up. I tried Kate's cell phone, but it went straight to voicemail. That either meant she was in court, or she was somewhere with no reception. I called the office instead and Denise picked up.

'Kate's gone to the 27th Precinct with Harry. We've got a new case.'

'What is it?'

'We're defending a celebrity accused of double homicide. *The New York Times* is calling it the TikTok murders . . .'

5
Kate

Denise had taken the call and transferred it straight through to Kate Brooks.

The offices of Flynn and Brooks, attorneys at law, had been quiet that morning. Harry Ford was reviewing files while he listened to a Rolling Stones album that played softly throughout the office. His dog, Clarence, lay peacefully at his feet. The phones had been mostly silent, and Kate had sat in her office working cases and dictating letters and motions for Denise to type.

The call came in from the desk sergeant at the 27th Precinct. Of course, he'd called looking for Eddie. He made a point of getting to know the booking sergeants in most police precincts in the city. If a good case came in, Eddie wanted to know about it first. Kate didn't exactly agree with this type of practice, but she had learned that sometimes it was better to look the other way as Eddie slipped fifty-dollar bills into the hands of those officers, loaded the trunks of patrol cars with cases of whiskey and kept Mets and Knicks tickets flowing to the friendly cops.

This was modern legal practice. Except, it felt just like the old legal practice.

Kate told the sergeant that Eddie was out, but she would see the prisoner. When she asked about the case, she wasn't expecting to hear that their firm had been requested.

'She told me she wanted Eddie Flynn. So I'm calling Eddie Flynn,' he said.

'I'll call Eddie, but in the meantime I'll be right over. What's the client's name?'

'Elly Parker. She's some kind of famous YouTuber.'

Kate knew the name. She'd seen the viral videos of Elly Parker catching her husband and best friend in bed together. Tens of millions of people all over the world had watched it too.

'You mean the famous TikToker,' said Kate.

'Whatever, she's gonna be charged with double homicide. Soon she'll be the famous murderer.'

'Who are the alleged victims?'

'Her husband and some chick he was banging on the side . . .'

She closed her eyes, tried to swallow her anger, said, 'Chick? Is that official NYPD terminology for female murder victims?'

'Maybe I should just give this one to another lawyer.'

'Didn't you just say she requested our firm?'

'Do I still get my fifty bucks?'

Kate sighed, said, 'I'll talk with Eddie. I'll be right over to consult with Ms. Parker. Make sure she's looked after until I get there.'

'I'll give her the best cell we got,' he said, and hung up.

On the way out of her office, Kate grabbed her backpack, which held her pens, laptop and charger, business cards, legal pads, retainer agreements, nicotine gum and bottles of water for the clients. Her police precinct bag. Everything she needed for a jail visit.

Harry closed a file on his desk, nudged his reading glasses onto his forehead, pinched and then rubbed the bridge of his nose.

'You want to come with me to the 27th Precinct? I think this could be a big case. Celebrity TikToker accused of a double murder.'

'What's a Tikky Tokker?'

'Someone who posts videos on TikTok?'

'Is that a dating website?'

'Nope, it's where people share videos about all kinds of things – pets, their lives, book reviews, cruise-ship travel – you name it.'

Clarence looked up at Kate, then looked at Harry before rolling onto his side and closing his eyes. Harry stood up from his desk, shuffled around it. He had been seriously injured a few months ago and wasn't yet back to full health. A little unsteady on his feet from time to time, and he tired easily, but his mind was still sharper than a cutthroat razor.

Harry put on his jacket. Clarence barked.

At first, Harry ignored him. Clarence barked again, more insistent this time.

Harry turned, picked up his walking cane, said to Clarence, 'Alright, goddamn it. I've got the cane. You happy?'

Clarence settled back to sleep. Harry had been known to leave the cane in restaurants, or at home, mostly on purpose, but Clarence wouldn't let him go anywhere without it.

Clarence was a good dog.

'You drive,' said Harry, taking his cell phone from his jacket pocket. 'I want to look at TikkyTok.'

'TikTok, like a clock,' said Kate.

'I prefer TikkyTok,' said Harry.

An hour later, they both sat across a steel table in an interview room in the precinct, waiting for their new client. Kate had her legal pad on the table, retainer agreement, a blue and red pen at the ready. She had a system for taking notes. She had a system for most things.

Harry took his cell phone from his jacket and opened the TikTok app.

'You're supposed to put your cell phone in the locker before you come in here,' said Kate.

'Yeah, that young officer asked to take mine. I told him I didn't want to.'

'What did he say to that?'

Harry gave Kate a warm look, dipped his chin, said, 'He didn't say anything. I used to be a senior judge in this city. That still carries some respect, even from the NYPD.'

He turned his attention back to the phone, quickly found Elly Parker's account and scrolled through the first few videos until he found one he hadn't seen yet.

The door opposite opened and a police officer led in a young woman in handcuffs and gray jail sweatshirt and pants – the outfit given to detainees who either have their clothes taken for examination or don't have anything warm to wear when they are arrested.

She was shorter than Kate. Her head down. Hair stuck to her cheek with sweat or tears. Tears, probably, thought Kate, judging by the inflammation around both eyes. Her skin was the same color as porcelain, making her eyes and her lips stand out. It wasn't lipstick making them red – they looked sore and cracked.

Kate noticed Harry doing a double-take, looking first at the profile photo of Elly Parker on her TikTok and then again at the young woman shuffling toward them.

She looked as if she had been hollowed out. Whatever life had animated the Elly who lived in the virtual world had left her in this one. She looked as if she was recovering from a terrible illness.

Elly took a seat at the table opposite Kate and Harry. The cop left and closed the door behind him.

'Elly, my name is Kate Brooks, from Flynn and Brooks, attorneys. This is Harry Ford. He's a consultant with the firm. We work with Eddie Flynn. Whatever you tell us is confidential. We're here to help you.'

'I didn't kill James and Harriet,' said Elly, leaning across the table, her eyes wide and desperate, her voice hoarse and raspy. 'I've been in hospital. Someone tried to kill me four days ago. The police don't believe me.'

There was a look on her face, a furtive speed to her eye movements and a tremor in her ruined voice – utter fear and desperation.

'Someone tried to kill you?'

'I told all of this to the police. They don't believe me. His name is Logan, but that might not be his real name. I can tell you where he lives. He tricked me into coming to his apartment. I drank some water. It must've been laced with something bad. I almost died. You can find him. He has a scar on his chin, just below his lip. He had a broken leg. Crutches. He's the man on the subway. The man with the yellow suitcase.'

6

Logan

Drip . . .
Drip . . .
Drip . . .

The watercooler in the reception area needed a new seal. The steady drip from the faucet into the tray made Logan clench his teeth, and the scars on his back began to feel hot and itchy.

He closed his eyes, breathed in and exhaled. Tried to black out the monotonous

Drip . . .
Drip . . .
Drip . . .

'They're ready for you now,' said the blond assistant with the ten-thousand-dollar smile.

At first, Logan didn't move.

He sat on the post-modern couch, back as straight as the mast on a ship, chin up, right leg crossed over the left, palms on his thighs, heart rate at fifty-one beats per minute.

When a suitable delay had passed, Logan gradually angled his gaze to the blond assistant. Then nodded and smiled. He uncrossed his legs, stood, but he took his sweet time about it.

His gestures and movements were slow and precise. Unhurried.

Powerful.

Logan had sat on a thousand extravagantly priced and uncomfortable couches in a thousand designer reception rooms, and had a thousand blond assistants tell him that *they* were ready for him. He'd been in those receptions when other guys got called ahead of him.

They're ready for you now.

He'd watched those guys bolt off the couches as if they'd just heard a starting pistol. Invariably, they were nervous, eager to please the people they met. Their sweat stank of desperation. And people with true power could smell it on them.

No matter where Logan found himself, no matter what situation, he always understood the power dynamic and that meant he could take control. Through his body language, through his speech, or lack of it, through his eye contact, his demeanor, his gestures, his dress – Logan was in charge.

Today he wore a tight cashmere rollneck sweater with a navy suit over the top. Black shoes, polished. The suit was bespoke – cut in Hong Kong. The black designer glasses held clear lenses. He had 20:20 vision, but he also knew that in these kinds of meetings those glasses gave him an extra twenty IQ points.

No briefcase. No pen.

His phone buzzed in his jacket three times on the way to the conference room.

It took nerve not to take the device in his hand and at least check it.

He knew it would distract him from the job in hand.

The phone notification was for later.

When he could have time to enjoy it.

The blond assistant let him into a wide conference room – with panoramic views of Manhattan and the park. An oval-shaped conference table was lined with five guys in business suits on one side, and a single chair on the other side for Logan.

The assistant closed the door behind her as she left. Logan stood behind the chair. His hands lightly clasped in front of him.

'Logan, you know everyone here, I think,' said Josh, Vice President of Marketing. 'But I don't believe you've met our CEO.'

The man who took up the seat at the center of the table was older than the other four, losing his hair at the temples. Tanned, bulky, leaning back in his chair. Pale suit. Blue shirt open at the collar. The only one with no tie.

'Mr. Hartfield, of course,' said Logan, leading with an open hand.

Hartfield didn't get up. He stretched out a soft, meaty paw across the table and Logan took it gently, didn't squeeze. But Hartfield crushed Logan's hand, or at least tried to. That was a powerplay that never worked. Nothing betrayed weakness like an overly firm handshake.

'You're the man I'm paying twenty-five thousand dollars to, just so that you can tell me what I already know,' said Hartfield.

'Let's hope not,' said Logan.

'Okay,' said Hartfield, 'let's get this show on the road. You've got a presentation to show us?'

Logan casually flicked his eyes to the wall and the large screen there.

'No Powerpoint presentations today, Mr. Hartfield. Do you mind if I sit?'

Slightly puzzled, Hartfield nodded, leaned over the desk and studied Logan as he pulled out the chair with one hand, undid his blazer with the other and then sat down. Slow, deliberate movement. It gave him a certain kind of class.

'We've had six marketing companies carry out extensive market research studies. They've all come in here, one after the other, and given us detailed presentations. You understand this is a pitch to lead our next major campaign? Are you seriously telling me you don't have anything to show us?' said Hartfield.

'I thought we could talk, like grown-ups. Now, those marketing experts all came in here and said how much they love your restaurants. They showed you some colorful graphs and bar charts based on the consumer research you asked them to conduct, essentially justifying how they spent the twenty-five grand. They all concluded your sales are down because of the economy, – so you should bring out new burgers, some vegan options, and lower your prices.'

Hartfield's left eye twitched. He said, 'They all came up with the same strategy because they all got the same answers from the consumer research. Thanks to those companies, and their extensive Q & A's with over ten thousand consumers, we have a strategy. You're telling me that data is worthless?'

'The advertising legend, David Ogilvy, once said that the problem with asking questions of members of the public is that people don't think how they feel, they don't say what they think and don't do what they say,' said Logan. 'I didn't speak to a single consumer. Didn't spend hours on creating digital bar charts and smiley faces on a graph. Your fee paid for my time. I spent that time visiting five of your fast-food outlets. And, by the way, lowering prices is not a strategy – it's a tactic. There's a difference.'

'So I paid twenty-five thousand for you to eat at my restaurants? Is that it? I only ask out of politeness, because I think I'm going to want it back.'

Logan smiled, looked to the man sitting to the right of Hartfield. His name was Todd Summers, President of Marketing.

'Todd here isn't going to like what I have to say, because it involves some investment. Marketing men hate having to spend. I'm afraid some outlay is required, over and above your usual ad spend.'

'I have to spend money to sell my burgers cheaper?' asked Hartfield.

'Who said anything about cutting your prices?' said Logan. 'If you adopt my strategy, your prices should go up.'

Hartfield leaned forward, said, 'Up?'

'Why do people eat in fast-food restaurants?' asked Logan.

'Because they want quality food, fast,' said Hartfield.

'No, they want something that is reliably *okay*, and they want it quickly. But there are other fast-food outlets that dominate that end of the market – McDonald's, Burger King, KFC, Chick-fil-A, Popeyes and half a dozen others. You have a large company with a lot of restaurants, but you're *not* McDonald's. Their ad spend over a single day exceeds your total marketing budget for the last two years. They are one of the dominant global brands. You simply can't compete. But you have an advantage. Your food is better. I think that is your strength, and in order for people to appreciate that, your prices have to go *up*.'

'You're telling us that people will appreciate the same Hartfield Cheeseburger Deluxe if it costs more?' asked Todd, a derisory tone cutting his voice.

'Yes,' said Logan, 'and if you don't understand that you shouldn't be in marketing. It's human behavior. People believe a more expensive bottle of wine tastes better than a cheap bottle. Price determines their view and enjoyment of wine before and during the drinking. And it will *actually* taste better on the palate. In wine terms, McDonald's is a cheap liquor-store Chardonnay, and you're champagne in a screw-top bottle. In other words, you need a new bottle with a cork. You must reposition your brand.'

'But this is a family burger restaurant . . .' said Hartfield.

'Of course it is, but in the future it will be a *higher-end* family burger restaurant. Put your prices up twenty-eight percent, refurb your older stores – more ambient, luxurious lighting. Make it *feel* like a restaurant instead of an airport lounge and write off the cost for tax purposes. Invest in additional cleaning staff. Four of the restaurants I visited had dirty floors and tables. Your cleaning staff are just as important as your cooks and servers. Half of the experience in a restaurant is the place itself, the other half is the food. Both are equally important. Doesn't matter how good your food is if you have to eat it while sitting next to a pile of garbage on the table beside you. The fact is it just won't taste as good.'

Hartfield blinked rapidly, as if his brain was suddenly bombarded with brand-new information.

'When the prices go up, don't try to hide it. Embrace it. The new ad campaign I will design for you is in two parts. For the initial relaunch it's *Hartfields, You Pay for Quality*. Hardly original, but it works. When the Belgian beer company Stella Artois launched in the United Kingdom they couldn't match the prices of regular beers. Their ad campaign had the slogan *reassuringly expensive*. They sold a lot of beer. You're going to sell *a lot* of hamburgers.'

The room was ominously silent. The other department heads were all focused on Hartfield. They were waiting for his reaction. None of them really mattered in this room, and Logan had focused on Hartfield. As he had laid out his plan, he'd kept a close eye on Hartfield's expression. At first, he hadn't bought it. Then, slowly, the idea had taken hold.

'It's risky,' he said.

'It carries some risk, as does all repositioning of brands. The alternative is to cut staff and install digital ordering screens in all of your outlets. They make money because people order more food when they use touch screens. The forty-year-old father of two, on his lunchbreak, doesn't want to have a conversation with an eighteen-year-old cashier to explain why he wants a Hartfield meal and an extra burger on its own – not *two* meals for *two* people. The soccer mom doesn't want to see the look on the face of that same cashier as she orders two Harty Sundaes to go and one non-fat latte. The screens take away most of that guilt at the point of ordering. So your sales will go up, and in a year you'll have paid for the refit of the screens, but guess what? You're still not McDonald's. That's your strength. And that's what you will tell people. That's the second part of my marketing campaign – you're going to ditch the line about paying for quality. Your main campaign will be – *Hartfields*, and a picture of the most delicious burger you've ever seen. Below it, the slogan – *We're **not** McDonald's*.'

The department heads held their breath. They didn't know whether Hartfield was going to throw Logan out or kiss him.

Hartfield didn't keep them waiting much longer. He pushed his chair back from the table.

Stood.

Laughed and applauded.

One by one, as predictably as the sunrise, the department heads stood alongside him, beaming smiles at Logan.

'Logan, you're a goddamn genius, you know that?' said Hartfield. 'Where did you learn marketing? Harvard? Yale?'

Logan stood, shook Hartfield's hand, said, 'I've never studied marketing. I'm a behavioral psychologist. I know what people think. I know what they do. I know what they feel. More importantly, I know how to make people buy whatever I want them to buy . . .'

'We've been playing this the wrong way all these years. We do have a good product, and we should be making more money from it. Thank you.'

'My pleasure,' said Logan, and as he released Hartfield's grip he felt his phone vibrate again, three times. Three notifications.

His very teeth ached to look at that phone. But he resisted.

'I'll be honest, Logan, I've been looking for a creative guy like you to spearhead a new direction for this company. We'd love to have you join Hartfields as Vice President of—'

'I'm afraid I must refuse. I like to stay in private consultancy, Mr. Hartfield. Don't worry, you'll be paying me a lot of money for these campaigns, but I like to be flexible and work with different companies. It suits my lifestyle better.'

'Oh, sure, God, tell me about it. Nothing like being your own boss. Say, what do you do in your spare time? Racquetball? Golf?

I would love to take you out on the course for an afternoon. We could hit nine and then hit the bar.'

'I'm afraid I don't play sports.'

'But you look like an athlete. What is it? Running?'

'Yes, in part, but I run alone. And I train alone.'

'Come on, Logan. I'm trying to seduce you into my company here. Let's do something together, get it in the diary. What do you like to do to relax?'

A slow, long smile spread over Logan's face as he said, 'I kill people.'

All the air left the room. Silence and shock. The room was frozen, like a cold breeze on an Alaskan lake.

Logan let his grin widen further, his eyes playful.

Hartfield pointed at him, the laugh came deep from his great belly, then he said, 'You sonofabitch, you're fucking with me. Damn, you almost got me on that one . . .'

Logan made pistols with his fingers, mock shooting him, laughing along with Hartfield as the rest of the room joined in with nervous laughter.

After ten minutes, and more congratulatory talk and plans, they agreed on half a million dollars for Logan to prepare a detailed strategy and tactical marketing plan.

Contracts would be sent in a few weeks. Logan left the room.

He walked along the corridor to the sound of Hartfield, still roaring with enthusiasm in the conference room, his obnoxious voice growing fainter with every step. Logan walked into the elevator, and could feel the phone in his jacket, heavy and delicious, loaded with notifications that would spike his adrenalin, giving him a dopamine hit and releasing juicy pleasure endorphins. The anticipation was intoxicating.

Delayed gratification is sweet. Logan knew this more than most.

It wasn't until he was on the street and headed for the subway that he took his phone from his jacket pocket. Logan could easily afford a town car and a driver. And, for a time, he had enjoyed those pleasures – but he missed the subways. It was on the trains that Logan had time to study people. Their faces, their reactions to different social and environmental situations. Ride the subways in New York for a week and you will learn more about human beings and psychology than spending a week in close study of the great textbooks.

Once you understood the mechanisms and triggers for human behavior, the subway becomes an entire psychology course. Logan liked to be among people, so that he could watch them unobserved. People of all walks of life used the subway, rich and poor, because it was still the fastest way around the city.

But, for now, his phone had his full attention. He had set an alert for news articles with specific search terms. Now, the results were coming in fast.

> TikTok Star Elly Parker charged with double homicide in Manhattan.
>
> The TikTok Murders: Influencer Charged in Revenge Slaying.
>
> Social Media Kills. Elly Parker, TikTok Star, and Her Descent into Murder.

Logan smiled to himself, descended into the subway from the street. He swiped his MTA card at the turnstile, walked down the stairs and stood on the platform.

Elly was not supposed to survive the visit to the apartment. It reminded him that he could control the environment, the decision-making and a person's reactions to psychological, social and environmental stimuli, but he could not predict an individual's biological reaction.

Vomiting shortly after she had ingested the treated water had saved Elly Parker's life.

It wasn't supposed to be a revenge killing – it was supposed to be a murder suicide. That's why he hadn't balked at giving her his name. Elly kills her husband and her best friend, the people closest to her who had so utterly betrayed her, and then Elly takes her own life.

Still, the first part of Logan's narrative had worked perfectly – the double homicide.

Elly would be telling her story, or as much of it as she could remember, to her lawyer. She would tell them about a man named Logan she met on the subway steps. About his yellow suitcase and his broken leg and his crutches. And his vulnerability. And her guilt at having lashed out at James and Harriet by nuking their lives online. And then she would tell them how she dropped the gentle, vulnerable stranger's case. How it had burst open. How she had felt utterly compelled to help this man.

Then the apartment, and the broken elevator, and the stairs and the sweat and the cold water from the fridge and how good it had tasted, at first. Logan's only distinguishing mark was the small scar on his chin. In every other way, he had a plain, angular face. A sketch artist would draw something that resembled a quarter of the population. But Logan knew he had no real need to worry about being recognized by Elly, the police would not believe her and there were no witnesses nor any physical evidence to corroborate her story.

She could not tell them what she did not know.

That the man would be impossible to trace.

That the man had spent time strategizing, testing suitcases and how they would break when he removed a screw from the handle and cut through most of the fiber weave below the zip with a razor blade so that a heavy blow would rip the remaining threads holding it together, how he had rehearsed his lines, studied her routine, when she went out, what time and where she was going, to make sure she would be the one to offer him help at that precise moment at the top of the stairs leading to the platform.

Like much of the world, Logan had never heard of Elly Parker before he'd watched the video of her accidentally discovering her husband in bed with her best friend. She had looked so shocked, so utterly betrayed. The pain was writ large on her face. The reality of that discovery is what fueled the viral reaction to the video. Logan then watched some more of Elly's content, and discovered her daily acts of kindness.

That made him feel sick.

It seemed performative to Logan. Not only was Elly deriving the endorphin pleasures of goodwill from her acts, but she was doubling those little rushes of satisfaction by filming these so-called kind acts and lapping up the praise from her followers.

Logan realized then that he had found his next masterpiece. He'd drunk in the hate from Elly's followers directed at her husband and the friend who had broken her heart. If anything should happen to those two, Elly would be the prime suspect.

And if she was genuinely a kind person, then this was an aspect of her personality he could exploit.

Her act of kindness for Logan would be her last.

A train pulled in, Logan waited with a few other passengers on the platform while people got off and then he stepped inside.

He was looking for a female butterfly.

She was not in this carriage.

He checked his watch. She would likely be on this train or the next.

He stepped out of the train car, ran to the next and hopped on just as the doors closed.

There she was – his butterfly girl.

Following her through the subways and the city as he had done for the last months, he had been reminded of a particular summer when he was seven years old. That year, his parents went traveling alone, leaving him in their mansion in the Hamptons with his nanny. He spent those two months alone, in their garden. It was hot that summer and for some reason their garden was filled with the most beautiful colorful butterflies. And his father wasn't there to punish him or beat him. Instead, he chased butterflies.

This woman reminded him of that happy summer. She was his butterfly.

Logan took a seat and for a moment, reflected on his business meeting as he tried to ignore the young woman sitting opposite him. He took out his phone and let his mind wander.

Logan had told the truth to Mr. Hartfield.

He liked to kill people.

For Logan, killing was a lot more fun than golf. And probably easier.

Even though he had turned his admission in the boardroom into a dark joke, the thrill of merely speaking those words was enormous. Logan liked to talk. To *really* talk. There was, he knew, a deep psychological need for conversation.

Mostly, Logan talked to the dead.

They were excellent listeners.

His intellect had given him insight, and he knew that talking to the dead was merely an outlet, or a symptom of a deeper problem.

Logan was, and perhaps always had been, lonely.

He looked up from his phone at the commuters in the subway car around him. Directly opposite, sat the young woman he had been following for some time now. He had been alone for so long that even following this young woman, this butterfly, felt like a relationship.

The only question in his mind was how this relationship might end. Normally, they ended in a pool of dark blood.

7
Eddie

An office meeting in my firm isn't exactly what most lawyers would call professional.

For a start, Harry hates these meetings. He's always sipping out of that hip flask, and he's not drinking mineral water. Clarence, unusually, doesn't sit at Harry's feet. Instead, he snuggles up in the corner of the office so he can keep an eye on everyone. Denise, the office secretary, gives him a marrow bone to chew on. She thinks Clarence sees us as arguing and, of course, he doesn't like it. The bone and an occasional pet from everyone help keep him calm.

It was the afternoon, and Kate had called Bloch in. Denise had made coffee for everyone, but I preferred making my own. It was a weird thing to me, having someone who works for you prepare your drinks. I never got comfortable with it. Denise didn't mind. Plus, her coffee was terrible.

Our office sat above a tattoo parlor in Tribeca. It wasn't spacious, and didn't look much like a law office, which was the way I liked it. Our conference room felt cramped with all of us sitting inside, so we stood around the two desks in the large space that encompassed the reception area, Denise's workstation, Bloch's desk and Clarence's bed. And the Xerox machine, which needed such skill and finesse to operate that I stayed away from it like it was radioactive.

'She's innocent,' said Kate. 'And she's terrified. Someone tried to kill her and she doesn't know why. Someone, possibly the same person, murdered her husband and her best friend. She has been all over social media recently. She discovered her husband, James Parker, and her friend Harriet Rothschild were having an affair while she was live on TikTok. The DA has more than enough motive to bury her, but I want this case. And she wants us.'

The district attorney, Robert Castro, had history with my firm. We had recently wiped the floor with him in a murder trial he had handled personally. Despite this, he had gotten re-elected as DA shortly afterwards. Castro wore a white suit and ran as an anti-corruption candidate, but the suit was just for show. He was in the pocket of every crook on Wall Street and the fundraisers he got from his corporate friends had been enough to blow out his opponent in the election. In the US, whoever spends the most money in an election usually wins.

Castro had some bad press lately after an inmate named Ruby Johnson escaped from a maximum-security women's prison. Castro wanted a high-profile scalp to take away the bad press from the prison break and I guessed Elly Parker was going to be his target.

'Kate's right. She didn't do this,' said Harry. 'She looked really ill. Like she had been knocking on death's door.'

I noticed Denise, Bloch and Kate gave Harry a particular look. They didn't want to say it, didn't want to recall it, but it wasn't so very long ago that Harry had stood in front of that same black door. He'd been shot, almost died in the hospital and then fell into a coma. That was a hard time for all of us. We loved the old man, and for a while it looked like he was never going to wake up. The polished cane in his hand was the legacy of that injury. He hated the thing, and kept leaving it behind. Harry Ford is one of the strongest men I ever met. He would work his way off that cane if it killed him.

'Okay,' I said, 'what do we know and what did she tell the police?'

'Same story she told us. The man with the yellow suitcase who said his name was Logan. The lead detective is Bill Sacks. He didn't give much away about the circumstances of the case. James Parker and Harriet Rothschild were found dead in Elly's apartment. Five days ago,' said Kate.

'What's the cause of death?' I asked.

'We don't know,' said Kate. 'Detective Sacks's questions to Elly weren't specific enough. He didn't give anything away. He basically focused on the fact that Elly was the only person alive with motive to kill them.'

I thought for a moment. Bill Sacks was a long-serving homicide cop. Smarter than most.

'There are two explanations,' I said. 'Either he hasn't found a murder weapon he can tie to Elly, or he doesn't yet know the cause of death.'

'Maybe both,' said Harry.

'So what *do* we know? Elly has motive for the murders. A ton of it. It's all on social media. We need to download hard copies of those videos before any of them disappear. We don't know the cause or even the time of death for the victims so we can't chase down an alibi. What can we do to verify her story about this guy she met on the subway with the suitcase?' I asked.

'I'll take it,' said Bloch. 'I have a contact in the transit police. I'll see if we can find some security footage from Grand Central. I'll look into the apartment she visited, find the lease.'

I nodded, said, 'Now our big problem. When is the arraignment?'

Kate said, 'Tomorrow morning. I think the DA will get a grand jury indictment fast, but you're right: bail could be a major problem. Elly's parents are out of the picture. Her mom, Susan Yorke, died a few years ago from a car accident, and her father, Stewart Yorke, not long after – heart attack. She has savings, but not a lot. If bail is set over a million dollars, then she can't make the bond.'

'Then what happens?' asked Denise.

'Then she goes to Rosie's until her trial,' I said.

The Rose M. Singer Center on Riker's Island was named after a former Board of Corrections member who advocated for incarceration reform. The center was opened in the late eighties and was meant to be more rehabilitative than punitive with work programs, art therapy, gardens and access to secure open-air areas. Rose M. Singer's granddaughter once said it's a disgrace that this facility bears her relative's name. Rosie's, as it is known, is one of the most violent, overcrowded and dangerous places on the planet. And it's not just the inmates that make it unsafe – the threat of physical and sexual assault from corrections officers is very real. Just ask the City of New York, who had paid, and will pay, many millions of dollars in compensation to the inmates who were victims of rape and sexual assault in Rosie's. The plan, and hope, was for Rosie's and Riker's to close, and end the decades of suffering on what was rightly called Devil's Island.

'She won't survive in there,' said Bloch.

It sounded even more like a factual statement coming from Bloch, who was clinical with both her language and her thought.

'She may not have a choice,' I said. 'We know a few inmates who can look after her.'

'But we don't know anyone in maximum security,' said Harry.

Shit. He was right.

'Let's hope it doesn't come to that. Kate, how much can Elly raise for a bond?'

'Like I said, she has savings, but not serious bail money. I already discussed with Elly setting up a GoFundMe, or asking her followers for donations. That's a double-edged sword. She thought about it and doesn't want to take the risk. Right now, that's the right call. She may change her mind after a night in Rosie's. Asking the public for bail money might get her out, but it's going to throw gasoline on the media frenzy happening around this case.'

I nodded, said, 'Let's hope we don't get a crazy judge who'll set bail above a million. As a back-up, I'll talk with the usual bail bondsmen – see if there's something we can work out.'

'Are you going to appeal to their better nature?' asked Harry. 'Don't bother. Bondsmen are as tough as they come. They've heard every sob story on the planet.'

'I'll bear that in mind. If the angels of their better nature can't be reached, maybe I can find one who is on the side of the devil.'

8

Logan

While he pretended to look at his phone, Logan admired his butterfly.

She had long blond hair in tight curls and wore a floral-print dress and a bright green cardigan. She'd worn that cardigan last week. It suited her. Large, coke-bottle glasses. A line of freckles crossed her nose, from cheek to cheek. A backpack with a fake sunflower pinned to it sat in her lap, and in her hands a romance novel with a thick, transparent plastic sleeve on the cover, obviously borrowed from the library. She must've finished the book he'd seen her reading last week, the one with the crown on the cover. This one had a woman wrapped in a shawl watching the sunset on the prairie. He couldn't read the title or the name of the author because of her thin fingers wrapped round the book. A pink butterfly tattoo wrapped its wing round her right wrist.

He tried to think whether he had noticed this detail before. He thought he must have, and had not given it any further thought. It was, after all, an innocuous detail, but perhaps that tattoo was what had reminded him of that butterfly summer, and had prompted him to give her that nickname.

Her legs were crossed, and Logan could see a hole had worn almost the entire way through the sole of her Converse sneaker.

Logan thought she was very beautiful, in a strange and perhaps sad way.

He'd first seen her a couple of months ago.

He still remembered that day. He'd taken her picture, performed an image search. Even an enhanced search using AI.

She wasn't online, far as he could tell. No photos anyway. He wondered why, considering she was so stunningly beautiful. Perhaps she had ventured onto social media, and her looks brought the wrong kind of attention. Logan had noted which train she had ridden, and when, and had looked for her the next day. Sometimes he got on the right train, sometimes not. Sometimes, like today, he would catch the right train but not the right car. He would see her getting off at 42nd Street. Headed back to her apartment, or to her part-time job waiting tables in a steak house.

Sometimes extraordinary people caught Logan's attention.

Not long afterwards, they ended up dead.

Logan was buzzing from the meeting he'd just aced with Hartfield's. And today was the first time he had sat opposite her. He had never gotten this close.

Her face was so full of life it made him wonder what she would look like dead. He had done the same thing that magic summer, when he was seven and his parents had gone on vacation. Logan had managed to trap one of those beautiful butterflies from his garden. He'd taken it in his hand, and slowly crushed it.

He noticed her eyes would occasionally flick away from the pages of her book, down and to her left, toward the bag of groceries on the floor of the train. The bag sat in between the feet of a middle-aged woman in jeans and a thick brown waterproof coat. A ring of dirt and grime surrounded the cuffs on the woman's coat. She was huddled into it for warmth, and she was dozing.

Then Logan realized what had distracted the young woman from her book, and why she kept looking down at the bag of groceries.

With the motion of the subway car, a packet of noodles had wiggled its way to the top of the grocery bag and with every sway of the train, it got closer to falling on the floor.

A squeal of brakes sounded in the carriage as the young woman leaned down, grabbed the noodles before they fell and then tucked them deep into the grocery bag.

The older woman with the bag at her feet didn't open her eyes.

Before his butterfly went back to her book, she looked straight at Logan. Perhaps she had felt his eyes upon her.

She smiled, but it was not merely a polite acknowledgement. Logan knew that he had a handsome face, and he liked to dress well.

'That was kind of you,' said Logan.

'I'm sorry, what . . . Oh,' she said, glancing down at the groceries next to her. 'I wouldn't want to lose my noodles on the train . . . so . . . no big deal. It's just noodles.'

Her accent wasn't New York. There was a hint of the south in her voice. And the smile she gave him, which carried a hint of embarrassment and self-consciousness, sent a quiver of excitement fluttering in his stomach.

'You didn't tell that lady that her shopping was spilling, you just acted. You helped her, and she'll never know. No one would know. That's a *real* act of kindness,' said Logan.

She smiled back, let out a nervous giggle and swept some of her curls behind her ear.

'Well, *you* saw me, but I didn't know anyone was looking.'

'Exactly my point. My name's Logan,' he said.

'Grace,' said the young woman, still smiling. A good name for a butterfly.

The older woman beside her opened one eye as the train slowed for the next station, then closed it again.

The act of kindness came with selflessness. Different to what he thought of Elly. Logan had never known kindness. It was alien.

Something else to be studied, understood. He found himself wanting to get to know this woman. She seemed so rare to Logan, like fine gold dust running through the torrent of a dirty river.

'It's rare to meet genuinely kind people in this city. Maybe I could repay your kindness and buy you a cup of coffee?' said Logan.

Grace closed her book, stood and said, 'I can't right now. My shift starts in ten minutes,' she said, beaming a perfect smile.

Logan nodded and smiled back, said, 'That's okay. Maybe another time?'

'Have we met before?' asked Grace.

This time it was Logan trying to quell the self-consciousness that threatened to burn his cheeks. He said, 'I get this train sometimes. Maybe you've seen me before?'

'Maybe . . .' she pondered, then said, 'Sorry, this is my stop.'

'Sure. Maybe I'll see you again. Next time I'll bring noodles.'

She laughed.

'Or I could get your number, and we could meet for a drink. Or coffee?' he asked.

The train slowed. Logan looked once again at Grace's face. Her skin was pale and perfect, even her cute brown freckles. He wondered again, just for a second, what her face would look like dead.

Still smiling, Grace took her phone from her backpack, held it out toward Logan's as she got up to exit the train.

Air Drop Request – Accept Grace's contact information?

He looked up, Grace had her phone pointed at his.

'I'm free tomorrow?' she said, but her intonation was that of a question.

The train stopped and the doors opened.

Logan hit the accept prompt.

'See you tomorrow, Good Samaritan,' said Logan.

Grace smiled again and got off the train.

The doors closed and the train pulled away from the platform.

With Elly surviving the attack, he had some things to take care of. Someone once said that a killer makes fifty mistakes with each murder they commit, and if you can predict half of them you are a genius.

Logan didn't make mistakes. Elly had been given the correct dose. And it had taken Logan longer than he had anticipated to break the cast off his leg in the bedroom. If he had gotten to her sooner, he would have made sure that she never left that apartment.

He had contingency plans for multiple scenarios. Some of those plans would need to go into operation.

First, he needed to make sure the NYPD were convinced Elly was the killer.

Second, no loose ends.

The homeless man who had given assistance to Elly while she lay on the street. He had seen Logan with Elly while she carried the suitcase. She had given him five dollars. And he had looked around while Elly was lying on the street. He had seen Logan watching the scene unfold.

One person accused of murder telling an extraordinary story of how she was almost killed – police will not believe that. But an independent witness corroborating some of Elly's story? That was different. Logan had already cleaned out and left that apartment, rented under a false identity, and with no security cameras in the building to record his movements. Even if the police checked out that place, they would find nothing. Logan had studied the NYPD. He knew them, just as good poker players know their opponents. Now, he needed to learn about the new players in Elly Parker's life.

He continued scanning the news articles on his phone.

. . . the Post *understands that Kate Brooks, of Flynn and Brooks, is acting for Elly Parker. Eddie Flynn and Brooks are a formidable legal team with a string of high-profile victories in criminal trials. We have reached out to Mr. Flynn and Ms. Brooks for comment. If Elly Parker's*

fans are hoping for a miracle to save their idol, Flynn and Brooks are their best chance yet . . .

Logan flicked his thumb to the left, bringing him back to his search page. With both thumbs he typed into the search bar . . .

Eddie Flynn Kate Brooks

Hit search.

And began to read.

9
Eddie

There are a lot of things in this country that can kill you.

Guns. Drugs. Disease. Car accidents.

Add to that list being arrested and charged with a crime. The so-called justice system can rip you apart just as fast as an assault rifle or a bag of heroin.

The first thing it takes is your dignity. Sitting in a cage with thirty other people whose lives have had a catastrophic turn is not good for the soul. Those who think they've hit rock bottom don't know that there's a whole other subterranean level. Your dignity is continuously peeled away.

Sitting in an interview cell awaiting her bail hearing, with Kate beside me, Elly still had a lot of layers of dignity intact. She had washed her face. Tied up her hair. My hope was that she could cling on to that fight. The worst thing that can happen is to give in to the process.

'This is Eddie. He and I will be representing you in this case. How are you feeling?' asked Kate.

'I still can't eat. My throat and my stomach are just . . . not good. Thank you for helping me. I'd heard about you two on TikTok. I followed some of your cases. I really need your help . . .'

I'd sat across from every kind of person in this situation. It's easy to spot the people who half expected to find themselves in handcuffs wearing jailhouse sweats. They stand out. There's a resignation to their demeanor, not acceptance exactly, but not far off. The people who unexpectedly find themselves in the meat-grinder that is our legal system have the same expression. Shock. Horror. Total fear. They don't know what's going to happen to them and they have no idea how they got there.

'Did you find out any more about James and Harriet? I still don't know what happened to them . . . *Jesus* . . . their parents . . . You have to tell them I didn't hurt them. I'm not a violent person . . . Something fucking terrible has happened and I . . . I . . . *loved* them . . . They hurt me so bad, but I *loved* them . . .'

She collapsed into terrible, racking sobs, holding her sides in case they burst apart. She was young, and obviously she had talents, intelligence, but more than that she had been through an inferno in the last few weeks. The infidelity, her life blowing up for the world to see and now her husband and friend dead. And she had only just survived an attempt on her life.

And yet here was Elly Parker . . . She wasn't feeling sorry for herself, or firing a hundred questions at us about what happens next and how she can get out of here – she was mourning the loss of her husband and her friend. And thinking of the howling pain that James's and Harriet's parents would be feeling.

I liked Elly Parker.

'We haven't heard anything more from the police,' said Kate. 'We're trying to get more. And we're looking into ways to verify your evidence about the guy with the suitcase – Logan. Right now, we don't know if that's a real name, and if it is we don't know if it's his first name or a last name, which means there are thousands of potential Logans in the New York area alone. We need a lot more if we're going to find this man.'

Elly's face was soaked in tears, and yet she nodded at Kate, trying to listen through the pain.

'Elly, the only way through this is to take one step at a time,' I said. 'The first step is we have to get you bail. You've given all your financial information to Kate. You earn around one hundred and fifty thousand a year, some years more, some less. You have sixty grand in savings, and you can cash out some securities to add to that total. With bail, the judge usually sets a bond. It's basically a financial promise to return to court for trial. If you don't show, that money you made your promise with is gone. Now, we think altogether we can come up with what, a hundred grand?'

Elly nodded.

'Okay, now that should be enough. You only have to pay a percentage of the bail bond the court sets. As long as we don't get a crazy judge who sets bail at an extortionate amount then you are getting out of here, today.'

She covered her mouth as she cried. She was listening, understanding, but this was a young woman barely clinging on with both hands.

'Elly, I need you to sign this. It's a release for your hospital records. We need to try and find out what happened to you in that apartment.'

She got herself together a little, signed the form and pushed the pen and the paper back across the desk.

'We'll see you a little later this morning, in court. Don't talk to any of the other detainees in your holding cell,' I said, but this part, I thought she wasn't taking seriously.

'Elly, I know you're going through hell, but you need to listen to Eddie,' said Kate. 'You can't trust any other person around you except us right now. The DA, or the cops, will likely ask one of the detainees to talk to you, and get some kind of confession. Don't. Talk. To. Anyone.'

She heard that. Wiped her eyes. Nodded.

'Thank you. I'm so sorry. I'm so sorry. I won't talk to anyone . . .'

Trembling, she rose and the door opened behind her. The corrections officer towered over her. She was in her mid-twenties, but she looked much younger. Those jailhouse sweats were way too big, and she was small and frightened of this place. In that moment, the look of fear on her face reminded me of my daughter, Amy. I had caught the same look in Amy's face when I picked her up from school. I suddenly felt very protective of Elly Parker. Amy had her family around her, and Bloch, Lake, Harry and me. Elly's parents were gone. Her husband murdered along with her best friend. She was alone in this nightmare.

But she wasn't alone any more.

The CO led Elly out through the security door, and Kate and I made our way back to the court.

'Kate, we're going to save this kid,' I said.

'I just hope we get her out on bail,' said Kate.

I nodded, but didn't say anything. Kate was experienced enough and brilliant enough, and she had been through the wars of major trials, but she hadn't yet had her heart ripped out by this system. I hoped she never did, but in this line of work it happens. Even the jaded lifers in criminal defense work, with hide as thick as a longshoreman's hands, occasionally get their tickers punched by a client. Elly was about Kate's age. I guessed she saw herself in Elly, or part of herself. That's the thing about our legal system – doesn't matter who you are, it can come for anyone, and when it does, the destruction is just the same.

In the hallway outside the arraignment court, people lined the benches set along the gray walls.

'Any word from Bloch yet?' I asked.

Kate shook her head.

We made our way to the court dockets pinned up on the wall and checked for Elly's name. She was on Judge Busken's list. Not the worst judge we could've drawn. The thing about a judge setting bail is that there are no hard and fast rules – there's convention and rough guidelines, but bail can vary between ten dollars and three billion dollars – sometimes even higher. It's supposed to be related to the defendant's earnings, and the seriousness of the crime they are charged with, and the amount is set to ensure that they don't skip bail. If they do, it will hurt them.

Busken, with a double homicide – murder one for the husband and Elly's best friend? I could see Busken going as high as three million. Maybe higher. We needed a plan B. A bail bondsman. For a price, and security on the bond, bondsmen can help people get bail. But there are limits on what they can offer. Most bondsmen run a mile from murder trials – the price is just too damn risky – usually there is no security sufficient to cover the bond and, if the accused split, the bondsman can go out of business.

'You okay to handle the hearing if it comes up? I want to see if I can find us a bail bondsman,' I said.

'Sure. Who are you going to speak to? A good bondsman, I hope?'

'Oh no,' I said, 'I want the worst one possible.'

Kate looked at me strangely.

'Is this an Eddie Flynn thing that I don't understand and it's best if I don't know anything about it?'

'Could be.'

'Great.'

If you want to know what's going on in a courthouse, you have two options. You can get to know the security personnel or, if there's a coffee shop in the courthouse, get to know the staff who work there. There's a tiny coffee shop in the back of 100 Center Street that sells sandwiches, donuts and, if you're the right kind of customer – gossip.

'Can I get a hot cup and a glazed, please, Renata?'

Renata had worked the shop for ten years. Pouring cups of Joe and making sandwiches, occasionally cleaning the illuminated sign above the sandwich counter, which was so old that when the plastic and magnetic letters fell off the sign, and broke, they could not be replaced. A sharpie had been used to make up the letter O in COFFEE.

They don't take cards. Just cash. And you make sure it's a silent tip that goes into the tip jar – any rattling of dimes that go in that jar is likely to provoke a mean gaze from Renata.

'Eddie Flynn, you working with all the bad people today?'

'I got no choice – there's always a prosecutor involved.'

'You're a very bad man,' she said, laughing.

'I have my moments,' I said, slipping a twenty into the tip jar, and making sure Renata saw me do it. 'Say, I'm looking for a bad man right now.'

'You're in the right place.'

'I don't mean a defendant. I need a bondsman. Someone with a bad rep. I know a few, but I want somebody who is hot right now. You hear any stories lately?'

She put a napkin on top of the glass deli counter, and two donuts on top.

'I just wanted a single donut.'

'You're too skinny. You need to eat,' she said. 'I know a man. I heard some folks complaining about him. Richard something . . .'

'Richard Reynolds?' I asked.

'That's him. He's charging people a lot of money. Charges they don't expect.'

I'd heard of Reynolds – a few stories some years ago, along with half a dozen other bondsmen. In the justice system, there was always a way to skim off the top, rip somebody off or worse. Most bondsmen did a good job, yet the profession had a bad rep. Not as bad as defense attorneys, of course.

Still, Richard Reynolds's reputation was bad enough to earn him a nickname. The obvious one.

'Thanks, Renata,' I said, taking the coffee and the donuts.

I walked round the corner from the shop, took a mouthful of the coffee and gave the donuts to two young kids, obviously brothers, sitting on the floor with their backs against the wall. They looked like they were waiting to see if a parent got bail. Hard to know if they were praying they got out or praying they stayed in. The kids were maybe sixteen and thirteen, if that, and they looked as if they hadn't had a good meal or a new pair of shoes in a long time.

They didn't say anything as I gave them the donuts.

They didn't need to.

They just ate them. That was thanks enough.

I hung around the hallways while Kate was in court, keeping an eye on the lists and gauging the mood of Judge Busken.

I was looking for cops.

It didn't take me too long to spot detective Bill Sacks. He was wearing his uniform. Not a cop uniform, at least not in the conventional sense. Sacks wore a plaid shirt tucked, under strain from his small belly, into his navy chinos. He was a little overweight, nothing wrong with that, but he was one of those guys who wore a shirt and pants one size too small. Because of his gut and his profession, his belt had to do a lot of heavy lifting: an empty holster for his Glock on his right hip (police are required to check their firearms at the security gate), a keychain with three pounds of keys and keyrings dangling off his left side, perhaps to help balance the weight of the Glock on the right. Half a dozen lanyards, including his NYPD badge, hung round his neck. Two Velcro pockets on the back of the belt held extra magazines for the Glock and his cuffs, and a large pocket beside it held his notebook and pen.

Sacks had reached the level of experience and seniority where he wasn't required to chase down suspects on foot. Just as well. It had taken him ten years as a patrolman to work up to detective, and that time had taken a toll on his feet.

Whenever he could get away with it, like today, Sacks wore a pair of black Crocs over thick black woolen socks.

A moustache and pair of Oakley sunglasses finished the ensemble.

He was the kind of guy who read the instruction manual for every device in the house, cover to cover. Twice.

He was talking to Bernice Mazur, another one of the workhouse civil servants in the justice system – except Bernice worked as an assistant DA. She had come up under former District Attorney Miriam Sullivan, my old sparring partner. Bernice was forty-one years old with five kids under eighteen and a divorce two years behind her. She wore dark green suits, white shirts and thick glasses, which either hung off the end of her nose or dangled on a gold chain round her neck. She always had a thick armful of files, which she carried with ease, and a large purse hung off her elbow, which must've weighed twenty pounds. The purse was stuffed with a laptop, glasses cases, half a dozen legal pads and fifty ballpoint pens – and only half of them still had ink.

Because Miriam had been a mentor for Bernice, or perhaps because Bernice already possessed the character that Miriam expected of her ADAs, I always found Bernice to be ruthlessly fair, highly skilled and good natured.

Bill Sacks was talking Bernice through a file of papers. He was briefing her on the Elly Parker arraignment.

I left them to it and went into court, found Kate sitting on a bench while other cases proceeded.

'Bernice is handling Elly Parker's case,' I whispered.

'That's the first piece of luck Elly's had. I like Bernice,' said Kate.

'Me too. I just hope Judge Busken behaves himself. He's normally fine, but sometimes he gets ideas. No good ever comes from a judge with ideas.'

'He's been pretty reasonable this morning. No one has pissed him off so far. I think things might turn out okay today, touch wood,' she said, and tipped her fingers to the bench beneath us.

It wasn't long before Bernice entered the courtroom, Bill Sacks behind her.

Bernice called the Elly Parker case. Kate and I made our way to the defense table. Soon as the name of the case was called, I saw something flash over Busken's chops. He recognized the case. He must've heard about it on the news – who hadn't? Still, it made me nervous, and I suddenly had a bad feeling.

Kate and Bernice went through the formalities. Elly was led into court, in handcuffs and tear-stained prison sweats, wide-eyed and trembling. I told her to take a breath, and that this hearing would be over in a few minutes.

'Your Honor, the prosecution opposes bail. This is a double homicide. The defendant is a high-profile individual, but the People recognize the defendant has a clean record. If the court is of a mind to grant bail, we would ask for bond to be set at one million dollars . . .'

Bernice had read our financial statements. She was being fair. And I silently thanked her.

'One million?' asked Judge Busken. 'Isn't this the TikTok murder case that is all over the news?'

Oh shit.

Busken was having an idea.

'Correct, Your Honor. I've spoken to the probation and bail officer regarding the defendant's circumstances and financials. One million dollars should be sufficient to secure the defendant's attendance. The sum is in keeping with the seriousness of the charges. It is however a matter within the discretion of the court,' said Bernice.

Before Kate or I could say anything, Busken was straight out of the traps. Like all judges, he wasn't a fan of publicity for bad decisions. If this was a case that came under media scrutiny, the last thing Busken wanted was some legal analyst on CNN criticizing him for setting bail too low. The general public figured that anyone who was remotely famous was also a multi-millionaire, and of course this couldn't be farther from reality. Busken wasn't thinking about the defendant, or securing her attendance at trial – he was thinking about column inches and the media saying he was soft on celebrities.

'The court has to be assured that the defendant will return for trial, and it is cognizant of the defendant's celebrity and financial means. I will set bail at a bond of one million dollars . . .'

I heard Kate, beside me, breathe a sigh of relief, her shoulders easing out of a knot as she exhaled. We could just about secure a bond that amount.

I was still holding my breath. Busken hadn't finished.

'. . . and a further cash deposit of one million dollars. Next case.'

Kate objected, I objected, Busken gave us a dirty look and the clerk was already calling the next case. Elly just about had enough to pay the percentage court bond of one million. She didn't have a million in cash on top of that.

Elly Parker was shaking as the correction officers on either side of her half dragged her out of court. Panic had taken her limbs; she wasn't resisting the officers.

She could barely stand. She said, 'What's happening? What's happening? What's happening to me?'

I turned to Kate, said, 'Go tell her I'll have her out in forty-eight hours.'

'I'm not going to lie to her. Where the hell are you going to get a million dollars cash?' she asked.

I pressed my lips together tightly.

Kate got the picture.

She shook her head, said, 'I don't want to know.'

10

Eddie

As Kate ran off to grab a quick word with Elly, I stopped Bernice in the hallway.

'Hi, Eddie, I'm sorry. I tried. You should appeal. Busken is way out of line,' she said.

'An appeal will take too long. I appreciate you being straight up. How's the kids?'

'The five-year-old is just getting over chickenpox so my whole house is smeared in calamine lotion, the eight-year-old has joined the school band and is torturing a violin every night for three hours, the twins aren't speaking to each other and my eldest just broke up with her boyfriend. It's Armageddon. How's yours?'

'Amy's fine,' I said without thinking. She wasn't fine. I was worried sick about her and her mother, and Bloch was going to pay a visit to the creep who was stalking the house. 'Look, what can you tell me about this case? I know the DA is mad at me, but Elly is barely holding on . . .'

'Castro absolutely hates your guts, but this is about your client. You're on the wrong side of this one, Eddie. That's all I can say . . .'

'Give me something. This is like the secret police prosecuting this case. What's the COD? Do you have a murder weapon? Forensics? Come on, Bernice.'

Something caught her eye, and she glanced to her left.

Bill Sacks slowly folded his thick arms across his chest. Even though his eyes were covered with his Oakleys, we could both tell he was watching Bernice carefully. Cops don't one hundred per cent trust prosecutors, and decent prosecutors should never, ever, fully trust cops.

'I can't say anything at the moment,' said Bernice, still with her gaze on Sacks.

'Either that means you don't have a cause of death, you don't have forensics, you don't have a murder weapon, you don't have a timeline, you're working to kill the defendant's alibi or you don't have a case at all. You've got motive and jack shit.'

'I can give you an early trial date. That's it.'

I half expected Bernice to give me some hint of the case against Elly, but not this. It was way too early for a trial date.

'You haven't even convened a grand jury. You want to set a date?'

'Grand jury is just a formality. We're fast-tracking this one. February twenty-first. Two-week trial. I already spoke to Judge Quaid. You want it?'

Quaid was a ball-busting Superior Court Justice who dreamed of dunking defense attorneys into vats of acid for fun. He would be my last pick for a judge for this case, but that trial date sounded like a lifeline for Elly.

'That's three months away? This has to be the fastest trial in history. What the hell is going on?' I asked.

'You want it?'

'I don't want Quaid, but I'll take the date. Why so fast?'

'I can't say any more,' she said. 'I'll book the trial date. Grand Jury before the week is out. I take it your client won't testify before the Grand Jury.'

'Of course not.'

'Good. Let's get this show on the road. I hope you get her out, Eddie. I wouldn't put a rabid dog in Rosie's.'

Bernice left me in a cloud of lavender perfume, her bag rattling with pens as she made her way down the hallway, where Sacks fell into step alongside her, shuffling along in his Crocs.

I called Harry.

'Busken got scared of bad press. Set a million-dollar bond and a million in cash. I'll take care of it, but I wanted to ask you something. Bernice is prosecuting and she just offered me a February trial date.'

'February next year? Three months away?'

'Yep.'

Silence. Harry was just as perplexed as I was. It wasn't unusual for defendants to wait two years for a trial date.

'She hasn't even sat a Grand Jury yet,' said Harry.

'That's happening this week, so I'm told.'

'Did she tell you anything at all about the case against Elly?'

'Nothing,' I said.

Harry fell silent again.

'I've never heard of this. Something is up. Bernice gave you that trial date because she had to. There's some need or advantage to the DA's office in getting this case to trial fast. Right now, I can't think of anything specific. Unless . . .'

'Unless what?'

'It's a long shot, but it could be a witness problem. That's the only thing I can think of. Your evidence dictates your trial. If you've got a witness who is key to your case, then you schedule your trial around their availability.'

'Can't they set a date that suits them and just subpoena their witnesses?'

'They'll subpoena them anyway, but if you've got a professional witness you have to incorporate their timetable because they might be under subpoena in a dozen cases.'

'What kind of professional witness? Maybe forensics?'

'Yes, maybe. Let me ask around. What are you going to do about Elly's bail. Is Kate filing an appeal?'

'That'll take too long. I'm just going to get her out.'

'Are we breaking people out of Riker's Island now? I've got a steel file and Denise could bake a cake and send it to Elly.'

'If Denise is baking, we won't need the steel file. Elly could use Denise's meatloaf to breach a steel door.'

'I don't like to cast aspersions on her culinary expertise.'

'Leave Elly's bail to me. I just need you to get me a couple of things first. I'll pick them up at the office later.'

'What do you need?'

'Our filing fee receipts from the court office for last year. I don't need all of them, maybe three months' worth, copied.'

'I can't work the damn Xerox . . .'

'Ask Denise to do it. That's not all. I need a roll of duct tape, a pillowcase and a .45 caliber ACP cartridge.'

'A cartridge . . .'

'From the magazine of the Colt 1911 that's in the holster under your left arm.'

'I'm not sure the New York Bar Association would approve of your methods of legal practice.'

'What they don't know won't bother them.'

II
Elly

She couldn't remember when she'd last eaten.

The peanut-butter-and-jelly sandwich she'd been offered that afternoon in the holding area had a strange smell. She'd tried a little of it, but her stomach threatened to throw up the first bite and she put it back on the paper plate and left it in the corner of the holding room. No sooner had she put it down than two women in the cell began fighting over it. The smaller one whacked the other in the mouth with a closed fist and this seemed to be enough to claim the prize. The large woman with the dreadlocks who got punched, spat blood on the floor and walked back to her bench. The other ten women in the holding area watched her walk the whole way, like she was prey. She had exposed weakness, and now wore it like a badge of shame.

Elly made a mental note never to put herself in that situation. This wasn't high school. There would be no teachers to break up a fight. This was survival, all over again, but for real this time. She had kept her eyes on her rubber gym shoes and sipped the juice box. It was sweet and full of sugar, but she didn't care.

Kate had told her they would get her out in forty-eight hours.

Elly desperately wanted to believe that.

She couldn't remember the journey from the courthouse to Riker's Island. Elly had sat in the prisoner van and wept in her transport cell. Like a closet, not much bigger than a coffin set upright, but with a chair and metal hoops for the chains on her wrists and ankles.

She remembered the vague smell of the river. Then getting off the transport, her gym shoes hitting wet concrete as she stepped onto the island; the rattling of the chains as they shuffled into another holding room.

The smell of disinfectant.

Stripping naked. Trembling with cold and fear. Spreading her legs while a female corrections officer laughed, barked instructions and shone a flashlight at her genitals and anus.

A cold shower. Fresh, thin orange clothes. A cloth bag with more of the same clothes, a towel, a toothbrush and toothpaste.

There was a line of fresh detainees ahead of her, but Elly only stared at her new gray slip-and-slides over gray socks. She picked up a thin rubber mattress, which was also surprisingly heavy despite its appearance, and dragged it, along with her bag, along endless gray corridors, with steel bars painted blue every hundred yards. She passed the overflowing dorm rooms – fifty beds, fifty women, to every dorm – to the clanking of the steel doors, and the buzzing of the electronic locks, and the hollers of the women.

Elly's arms were aching by the time they got to Max. That's what the male CO called it. Maximum security house 421 looked like a cave built with cinderblocks, painted white. Lights hung from the high ceiling. Several steel tables stood in the center, with stools around – all bolted to the ground or cemented directly into the floor. She could see fifteen steel cell doors – five on the bottom, ten one floor up accessed by a steel staircase and walkway. At first the house looked deserted. All the doors were closed. The correction officer led Elly up the steel staircase and along the walkway and told her to wait outside cell M8. He called for an unlock on M8. The buzzer, more high-pitched than the others, signaled the CO to yank open the cell door.

She wished it had never opened.

It was a single cell, obviously designed for one prisoner, but inside were three women. Steel plates secured to the wall with chains acted as bunk beds. Bunks on either side of the narrow cell, a toilet in the corner. Just enough space to walk in between them. The lower bunk on the right was empty, and Elly stepped in, put her mattress over the steel and her bag on top. She took her rough blue blanket from the bag. She didn't look at the other women in the cell. She just crawled onto the bed, still clutching the cloth bag with her meager possessions inside, and turned to face the wall.

The CO said, 'Play nice with the new fish.'

Elly heard his boots on the floor as he turned, and the steel door slammed shut.

She was in darkness.

She cried as quietly as she could.

The other three women didn't speak.

They tutted, and one of them sucked their teeth, no doubt irritated by the further erosion of what little space they had left by a fourth body in a cell that would be cramped for two.

In the dark, she heard the singing, and the crying and the screaming and the banging, and all the sounds of two thousand women in torment.

Right then, at that moment, she just wanted her father more than anyone else on this earth. He was the one who always made things right. Over these past torturous weeks, she had thought of him often and her pain caused by James and Harriet's betrayal mixed with her grief for his loss. Her mother was practical, but never an optimist. Her father, Stewart, balanced things out in that marriage. He always told Elly that everything would work out just fine.

She needed her dad to tell her that right now. To give her one of his big hugs, to smell that old aftershave on his shirt and the faint odor of motor oil that somehow never left his hands. When Elly was at her lowest, Stewart had always been there for her. The last time, before he died, when Elly was struggling badly for money, he had taken her in his arms and told her he would pay her rent, but the relief didn't come from the handout, it came from the love and warmth of her father. They weren't religious. Never went to church, but Stewart had been raised Catholic and that never really left him.

He sometimes told Elly to say a prayer if she was really worried. That this would help, no matter what.

Elly, shaking in her bunk, said a silent prayer.

She prayed for Eddie Flynn, and Kate, and Harry, and for them to get her the hell out of here.

PART THREE

ELL **ellyparker** ✓

Manhattan, New York

🎵 Taylor Swift – 'Shake It Off'

AUDIO DESCRIPTION OF VIDEO PROVIDED BY META AI

A bedroom. Painted gray. Morning sunlight through the blinds. A young couple in bed. The young woman throws back the covers, stretches her arms to the ceiling. She leans over and kisses the still-sleeping young man beside her. She gets up.

ELLY: Hey, people, Elly here. It's a Saturday and, even though it's been almost two weeks, I still can't believe I'm married...

The young woman walks through a kitchen. She holds up her left hand. She is wearing a diamond ring and a gold wedding band. She fills a barista coffee machine with coffee beans and water. She drinks a large glass of iced water.

ELLY: I need coffee first thing, but these last two weeks I've been starting my day with water. James swears by this cool app, so I can track my hydration.

Close-up of her iPad. On the screen is a graphic of an empty glass. A thumb presses an icon on screen. An animation plays of a small amount of water trickling into the bottom of the glass. An animation of a thumbs up appears on screen. And then a message – KEEP GOING – ONLY 0.45 GALLONS TO GO...

The young woman exits an elevator, then crosses a lobby and exits a building. She goes into a Starbucks.

ELLY: Water is great and all, but, like, I still need coffee. Luckily, we have a Starbies right next to our building.

She exits the Starbucks with a coffee. She walks through the crowded streets of Manhattan, smiling. She enters a CVS.

ELLY: I've been meaning to stock up on essentials. It has been such a crazy, busy, amazing time lately that I've run out of my go-to everyday products.

The young woman grabs a basket and starts filling it up with beauty and grooming products as she moves through the store. She picks up two tubes of toothpaste, two packs of dental floss, two rolls of antiperspirant deodorant, two bottles of hair spray, two bottles of hair mousse, two tubs of moisturizer, two tubes of foundation, two bottles of eyedrops, two tubes of face wash. More products fill the basket too quickly to see, faster and faster.

A bedroom. The young woman pours the contents of a CVS bag onto the bed. She picks up the first item. Then the next as she describes them.

ELLY: Everybody needs a good toothpaste. Turns out they're, like, pretty much all the same, so I just buy one with a flip top, so I don't lose the cap. Next, eye drops. If you're living in a city like New York, yes, you will have an amazing time, but air quality is just not great and my eyes tend to dry out. These eye drops, just once or twice a day, total game changer. No point in having gorgeous eye make-up if your actual eyes make it look like you're in a zombie movie. Moving on, facial wash. I need to use this every day. It's really like a facial scrub, but it's not too harsh. You know what I mean. You can feel like you've been washing your face with sandpaper sometimes. And the rest of the stuff in here, well, you don't need me to go through it all again. You know my choice bargains. Anyway, I didn't just buy one bag...

The young woman holds up a second CVS bag.

The young woman walks through city streets. The Empire State Building is visible behind her. She enters a brick building and speaks to a woman in an office.

ELLY VOICE-OVER: This is a women's shelter in SoHo. Some women escape abusive, violent relationships with just the clothes they're standing in. So, when I stock up on essentials, I always buy two of everything. One for me, one for someone who might really need and appreciate it. This is my random act of kindness for today. If you want to be a part of the daily RAKs, but you can't think of what to do, my advice is to just buy two of something that you buy regularly. Could be you get an extra sandwich at lunch for a homeless person, or even something as small as an extra tube of toothpaste. I know somebody will really appreciate it.

It is later in the day, and the young woman sits in a Starbucks at a table beside a good-looking young man in a suit, JAMES, and another young woman with blond hair and a black coat, HARRIET, who sits opposite.

ELLY: I'm so glad I have you both in my life.

JAMES: Aww, I love you, princess.

HARRIET: You two are so sweet.

Elly closes her eyes. James glances at Harriet, then lightly kisses Elly. Elly smiles. The three of them laugh together.

ELLY VOICE-OVER: I'm so lucky to have a husband and a good friend that I can always rely on. What was your last RAK? Let me know in the comments...

#cvs #cvsessentials #Starbies #RAK

♥ 347K

▶ 757,899

12

Logan

The Manhattan skyline, in winter, set behind a huge moon, is one of the most beautiful sights in the world.

Logan stood in one of the best spots to take in this view.

It wasn't from the top of the Rockefeller Center.

It wasn't from the viewing platform of the Empire State Building.

Logan stood, in total darkness, surrounded by three million dead.

On a hill, among the tombstones of Calvary Cemetery in Maspeth, Queens, his breath misted as he took in the island of Manhattan. The electric glow from the city towers stretched and rippled upon the surface of the East River, like starlight trapped deep beneath tinted glass. Gravestones, mausoleums and commemorative statues surrounded Logan and occasionally caught fragments of light here and there, and appeared to him, for a moment, as a miniature reflection of the city – as if the tombstones were tiny buildings, and Logan a dark giant among them.

New York's necropolis had first opened in 1848, a Catholic burial ground with its inaugural internment, reportedly, a woman named Esther Ennis, Irish and poor, who is said to have died of a broken heart.

The cholera, influenza and tuberculosis epidemics quickly filled what would become the first section of the cemetery. Half of those who were buried here during those periods were poor Irish children. It is one of the largest cemeteries in the world, with burials still taking place in different sections. It is the resting place of entertainers, military heroes, mobsters and ordinary citizens of New York.

Before he got back to his work, Logan quietened his breath, listened hard and silently turned three hundred and sixty degrees, taking in this corner of the cemetery, watchful for anything that might look like the traces of a flashlight. Due to some recent vandalism, and the usual problem of kids drinking six-packs and getting high, the security patrol had stepped up its game. Three weeks ago, the security guard would sit in his little booth at the cemetery gate and watch YouTube until sun-up. Relatives had complained about the levels of vandalism and the mess the kids left behind, which prompted the guards into regular patrols. Logan had taken some time to get to know the security patrol schedule and routes. Few people came to this part of the cemetery at any time, and Logan had yet to see the patrolman anywhere near this section after eleven at night. During his scouting walks, he'd come across numerous empty beer cans a quarter mile to the east, gathered around a collection of large, flat stone tombs and ornate statutes in a wealthy family plot. An ideal spot for underage drinking. That's the hot spot the guards focused on. Far away from Logan and his business in the cemetery.

He was a cautious man. He gathered data, planned, tested. He knew he could work undisturbed, but he took no chances.

The area was silent and dark, and Logan was all alone with the dead.

He lifted the black iron-head military folding spade from the ground with both hands and arced it overhead, leaned forward, folding at the waist until the shaft touched his ankles.

Breathed.

Stretched up and backward, contracting his spine.

Breathed.

Logan had already been in the cemetery for an hour, first hauling all his equipment and gear over the iron fence, then preparing for the dig. Three tarps had been laid out beside the grave, and he had used a pick and an edging tool to measure out his excavation – forty inches, by fifty-five inches. This was a gamble. He wasn't digging out the entire length of the burial plot because the metal casket below was a half-couch – the lid was split into two parts to allow only the top half of the body to be visible for the memorial service. He'd seen some pictures from mourners on social media, and recognized the half-couch lid.

He switched on the LED head flashlight stretched over his black beanie, and thrust the spade downwards, biting into the cold earth. He stood on the edge of the spade until it sank into the soil, then levered down, lifting a chunk of topsoil free, and then dumped it on the first tarp.

This grave sat below the branches of a tall tree, it's trunk perhaps ten feet away. Still, the branches overhead were a welcome shelter for the dead below.

One thirty in the morning.

He had calculated it would take him three hours for the dig.

Logan worked the spade and occasionally took up the pick, making sure to keep the edges and wall of the grave intact. He found that he couldn't work with the headlight lit, he was having to stop and swat moths fluttering for the light above his face. So he worked in the dark. The first hour passed quickly, and he had a mound on the nearest tarp of about four hundred pounds of topsoil.

He drank from his water bottle, stretched his shoulders. Sweat drenched his back, like a sheet of ice with the nighttime temperatures, making his scars itch.

Some wounds don't heal.

The darker soil would be next, separated into another layer on the second tarp. This soil gave just as easily as the first layer, with roots spread throughout. Another hour, and the cushioned protective gloves were still not enough to prevent his callused palms from bleeding.

Logan liked the calluses that sat on the ridge of his palm, below each finger. He had earned them, with thousands of hours lifting iron dumb bells, barbells and kettlebells. This and the calisthenic exercises he practiced daily had built a powerful body. Supple, flexible and incredibly strong. He had a gymnast's physique and an endurance athlete's conditioning.

Every morning, he took an ice bath. Three minutes of immersion. He was so used to it now that he didn't even feel the shock from the cold. Then ninety minutes of training. It paid off.

The second layer of soil covered the second tarp.

More water. He needed to stay hydrated.

The final layer was the toughest, mostly clay. By the time the third tarp was filled it was almost three a.m. and Logan's shoulders and back were aching gloriously, the muscles filled with blood.

Not all graves are six feet deep. This one, about four feet. The ordinance and regulations for the depth of graves varies from state to state. At three feet deep, most carrion and wild animals cannot smell a cadaver, and will leave it undisturbed.

As he got closer to the casket lid, he switched to a large plastic shovel scoop. The kind used for snow. He didn't want to damage the coffin lid. It was imperative that his work go unnoticed.

Using his gloves to clear away the final thin layer of dirt from the chrome-colored casket, he reached to the left side, his fingers searching for the latch. Most steel caskets are latched. If it didn't have one, he would need to use a coffin key. If he couldn't find a keyhole on that side, he would need to abandon the dig, and return another night to dig up the entire coffin.

His fingers probed, tight against the side of the casket lid and the wall of earth.

And there it was, a latch.

He climbed out of the grave, retrieved his leather bag, which he had hung on the tombstone, and opened it. Inside was a bum bag that Logan attached to his waist. He took off his gloves, opened the bag.

Dealing with a decomposing body is not like it is in the movies. He'd watched scenes where coroners smear Vicks Vapor Rub on their top lip, to mask the odors. Logan had tried this once before. It didn't work. In fact, he was reasonably sure it had made the smell worse. The Vicks had opened his sinuses – so he could smell the decomp gases better.

He tore the seal on a medical mask. He still had a box of these at home, the leftovers from the Covid pandemic. Removing the plastic packaging, he slung the mask over his wrist then retrieved a small bottle from his bag. He then unscrewed a cap on the vial of peppermint oil and tipped half a dozen drops onto the mask before sealing the bottle, placing it back in his bag and putting on the mask.

He dropped back down. Instead of putting on his soiled work gloves, he put on latex gloves with thick, ridged sections on the palm and the fingers for extra grip. He went back into his bum bag, retrieved the syringe and slid it into his wristband. The cap still covered the eight-inch-long hypodermic needle.

His fingers found the latch again. He took a deep breath and unlocked the upper half of the casket.

The smell hit him immediately, despite the peppermint oil soaking the mask on his face. The oil helped dull it, a little, but there was no combatting the stench of decay. It got into the very fibers of clothing and could remain there for days even after a laundry cycle.

Logan would be dumping everything he was wearing, anyway.

He needed to see clearly for this part of the job, and he flicked on his headlight.

The beam fell on the face of the corpse.

Hollow cheeks, sunken eyeballs – the lids stitched shut as well as the lips. Teeth were visible through the decayed, paper-thin skin.

Logan worked quickly, first unbuttoning the jacket, then lifting up the shirt. The ribs were visible through the skin. This helped Logan. No point in injecting anything into a vein. There was no blood flow. For all he knew, there was no blood at all, just embalming fluid.

The air was thick with the smell of the dead. He didn't know if it was the odor or the light from his flashlight, maybe both, but moths gathered and swooped around him, the beam catching their wings – some were pale and some bright colors.

Logan ignored them and concentrated.

He inserted the needle at an angle between the ninth and tenth vertebrochondral ribs. The liver is the largest internal organ in the body; he knew with the correct angle, and using those ribs as a guide, he couldn't miss the liver.

A small injection. About a third of an ounce. Two teaspoons.

That was enough.

There was no blood as the needle withdrew. He capped it, put it back in his bum bag, and rearranged the clothing on the body. Closed the lid, killed the beam on the headlight and climbed out.

Filling in a grave is much easier than digging one up. He'd stitched a rod into one end of each section of plastic sheeting. This meant he could lift it, and tip most of the earth straight back into the hole. He set about doing just that, making sure the separate piles of clay and soil were returned in the order that they were removed. It was due to rain heavily that morning, which would help with settlement.

He used a tool to help level the topsoil layer, then from his bag he removed a roll of lawn. Same dimensions as the section he had dug up. He rolled it out, bedded it in. Checked the surroundings to make sure there were no security personnel, then lit up his headlight for a final inspection. To the casual observer, nothing would seem out of place. Only if someone took time to examine the ground would they notice a little difference in the shade of grass and the composition of the soil.

Logan stretched his back, lifting his arms and stretching out his hands toward the tree canopy overhead. It was a peaceful resting spot for the dead.

He gathered his tools, packed up, shut off the headlight and made his way toward the railings. His feet crunched through leaves and twigs. He couldn't help the noise, but he guessed unless there was someone very close by, no one would hear him. Speed was better than silence at this point. His eyes adjusted to the dark once again. A dull throb of pain in his shoulders and back accompanied every step. Even though he was in peak condition, tonight's work had been heavy and hard. He'd had to be fast.

He thought an ice bath, followed by a sauna, would aid recovery.

Maybe afterwards he might call Grace, the beautiful butterfly girl from the train.

These thoughts were floating in his mind as he walked through the small city of tombstones. They were chased away, suddenly, by a blinding light in his face.

'You there! What are you doing here at this time of night?'

Logan stopped, held up his left hand to shield his eyes, and disguise his face. In his right he had a pick, a hoe and his spade. The flashlight was like the sun; he couldn't see anything but the vague outline of a silhouette behind it. He angled his stance, trying to hide the tools in his right hand behind his body.

The flashlight angled down to his waist, and just for a second Logan could make out the figure of a security guard. A man in his fifties, in a dark uniform. One hand on his belt, but not on a gun – on a radio.

He would have preferred a gun. The radio was more dangerous.

'You heard me – what the hell you doin'?' said the guard.

'Sorry, I'm just looking for somewhere to sleep,' said Logan.

The guard said nothing. He was perhaps ten feet away. Logan began closing the gap. One step at a time.

'It's okay, sir. If I can't camp here, I'll just leave. No need to call the cops or anything. I'm really sorry.'

Another step toward the guard.

'Stay right there, mister,' said the guard, plucking the radio from his belt.

Logan heard it come out of the Velcro sleeve.

Saw his arm come up with the radio in his hand.

As well as weight training, and endurance, Logan took care to spend five hours a week training muscle twitch fibers in his upper body and legs, so that he had the capacity for incredible speed from a standing start. These were advanced speed drills, the same training that Olympic fencers, boxers and sprinters do every day. It's one thing to be able to run a marathon, or bench three hundred pounds, but this was different. This taught the body how to get from zero to thirty miles per hour in the blink of an eye.

Logan kept hold of the shovel with his thumb, opened his fingers and the other tools fell from his grip. As he did so, he sprang forward in an explosive movement, his right arm arching up.

The shovel came whipping forward.

The guard began to swear, leaning backward, raising his hands instinctively to protect himself. But Logan had elevation and momentum, and there was no stopping him.

As Logan landed, he swept the shovel down, feeling the ripple of impact through the shaft as the iron edge bit into the guard's face like a blade. The sound made by the shovel cleaving flesh, sinew and bone sent a wash of goosepimples over Logan's skin.

The force of the blow brought the guard to the earth instantly, as if he'd been flattened by a ton weight.

This was now messy. This was not how things were supposed to play out.

The guard's head had been caved in by the blow, but his limbs still twitched.

Logan lowered himself down into a crouch beside the body.

'What *are* we going to do with you, my friend,' he whispered.

Instantly, Logan made calculations. What would the police think?

More importantly, what did Logan *want* the police to think?

He hid his gear behind a large tomb, sprinted to the family plot a quarter mile away from him and, still wearing his gloves, picked up a few of the discarded crushed beer cans. He returned to the body of the guard, tossed the cans around him, some of them spilling beer on his chest. The NYPD would assume an altercation with drunken teens had gotten out of hand. They would trace the boys from their fingerprints and DNA on the beer cans.

The remaining problem was that the fatal wound was inconsistent with the story Logan wanted to tell.

He stood beside the dead guard, raised his right leg off the ground, and stamped down on the man's skull.

Again. And again. And again. Until his boot found solid ground.

The earth was hard from the cold temperature, but still he thought there might be some tracks.

The heavy rain would help cover them. There was nothing more he could do, but trust the NYPD to do what they always did – to use the data available to come to the easiest logical conclusion.

Standard procedure.

That's what had brought him to the cemetery that night. That's why he had dug up a corpse.

NYPD standard investigative procedure.

The best insurance policy in the world.

13
Bloch

As a private investigator Bloch should only have had access to a limited number of databases that provide information, including criminal convictions, on individuals within the state.

Bloch had a habit of rubbing certain cops up the wrong way. It was possible that they were intimidated by a female former officer who was stronger and smarter than them. Or, Bloch thought, it was more likely that they were just a-holes. But they were fewer in number than when Bloch was on the force.

The more intelligent police officers quickly recognized Bloch's forensic thought processes and respected her. The rest, with the exception of the a-holes, knew her by reputation and valued their limbs being attached in all the right places. This brought a different but equally useful level of respect.

The result was that Bloch, with a few calls and encrypted text messages to former colleagues, could get a lot more information on an individual than the average PI. Not just a complete criminal record, but police reports, tax returns, social-worker reviews, every little document generated in a life that could hold some clue or insight. All this she had printed out and it now lay in a folder on Gabriel Lake's lap.

He sat in the passenger seat of Bloch's Jeep as they drove to the last known address for Arthur Cross, the man who had been harassing Eddie's ex-wife, her new husband Kevin and Flynn's daughter.

Lake flicked through the last pages of the dossier, closed it.

He sat quietly for a moment as Bloch weaved through the light evening traffic on Long Island. Bloch wasn't great at reading people, but detected a change in Lake. It wasn't that he had restless limbs – it was more a case of having a restless body. He was always tapping, or fidgeting, or clicking his tongue, or cracking his knuckles – something – always in perpetual motion, a physical manifestation of his mind, which was continuously dialed up to eleven.

But, having closed the folder on Cross, his right leg stopped hammering his heel into the footwell. His hands rested lightly on top of the file, his head still and his gaze fixed on the road ahead.

'What's wrong?' asked Bloch.

'Huh? Nothing, I'm fine . . . I . . . I'm fine,' he said.

Bloch said nothing.

They drove for another half a mile.

'What's wrong?' asked Bloch again, uncomfortable now with Lake's calm demeanor. She had never seen him like this. It was almost like he'd been unplugged.

'Nothing.'

'What did you see in that file?' she asked.

'Same as you.'

'Come on, what's on your mind?'

'This isn't going to work,' said Lake. 'If this guy Cross has a problem with somebody, there's no way we're going to persuade him to let it go. There are a lot of red flags in this file, particularly in his juve history. The illegal images of children on his laptop, the animal cruelty . . .'

The steering wheel squeaked as Bloch strangled the leather at the memory of reading that in the file herself. She couldn't abide any kind of mistreatment of children or animals. Cross had three juve convictions for torturing neighborhood pets. There was a detailed history of what had happened in each case, but Bloch couldn't bring herself to read any of it. When he was arrested, they checked his computer and found something worse than animal cruelty.

Lake continued, 'He was bad before he did his first year in an adult prison. Seems like he learned a lot from his time inside, mainly how to play the system. He has a long list of known accomplices, but most of them are dead or back in prison. Apart from one – Bruno Mont. I saw his rap sheet. He met Cross in juve?'

'Timeline fits. And I made some calls. Mont was fifteen years old, locked up for assault. He'd knocked out four of his mother's teeth. After that he graduated to armed robbery and spent another eight years inside. It's not in the file, but he killed a man during that stretch,' said Bloch.

'How come it's not in here?'

'He was initially charged, but the DA bought a self-defense argument. Mont refused to join a neo-Nazi gang; one of their crew tried to take him out. A CO caught a shiv in the leg during the attack. Mont was stabbed eight times, but still managed to kill his attacker. He's a steroid junkie and the rage took over. The attacker bled out after Mont tore his jaw off of his face.'

'Holy shit, how big is this guy?'

'Six-five, three hundred pounds and change. Cross is cruel and dangerous, but he's smart. I think he likes to get Mont to do his wet work. Like killing his elderly wife.'

'Any sign of Mont being involved in the beef with Kevin?' asked Lake.

'None so far, but we need to be careful when we pull up at Cross's place. Make sure he doesn't have any visitors before we knock on his door.'

Lake opened his mouth to speak, hesitated, then decided to spit out.

'Cross is a sociopath and an obsessive compulsive. I don't think he's gonna back off no matter what we do here.'

'We know he's smart,' said Bloch. 'The smart play is to drop this and move on.'

Lake nodded, said, 'I don't think it's a question of intelligence. There's a narcissistic element to his personality. In his eyes, Kevin robbed him of a lot of money and he wants payback. He won't stop.'

'Let's see how it goes. Be positive,' said Bloch.

'You've been reading those self-help books again.'

'Being positive doesn't hurt.'

'Okay, then, I'm *positive* we're not going to achieve anything tonight.'

Bloch drove the rest of the way in silence, unnerved by Lake's stillness.

She pulled up outside a one-story stucco house in a neighborhood that had once been perfectly pleasant, but which time and weather and neglect had rendered poor. Garbage littered every sidewalk. None of the neighbors cut their lawns, and the white picket fencing that surrounded them had fallen down or rotted away, or been replaced altogether by aluminum poles and chicken wire.

There were no lights visible from the front windows of Cross's house. A single car in the driveway. No signs of visitors.

'Doesn't look like he's home,' said Lake.

'Let's see. And if he is at home, remember *don't* shoot him.'

Lake drew his Glock from his shoulder holster, put the gun in the glovebox, said, 'Eddie told me to tell *you* not to hurt him. No broken bones. No pieces missing. He is to be left as we found him.'

Bloch tutted. Flynn knew her all too well. She got out of the Jeep, closed the door. Lake hadn't moved. He seemed to be thinking. He leaned over, opened the glovebox and retrieved the Glock. He put it back in its holster and got out of the car.

Bloch raised an eyebrow.

'It's just for emergencies,' he said.

Together they made their way along the flagstone path to the front porch of the house. Weeds grew a foot tall in between the cracks in the paving. The front door was heavy hardwood, no glass. Iron latticework, painted black, covered the door in a grid pattern, to make it appear old, like something you'd see on a medieval castle. It looked cheap on a house like this. But it would help strengthen the door in case anyone tried to put their foot through it.

No cameras outside. Bloch checked every corner on the porch.

She pressed the doorbell.

Lake stood beside her, and a little behind. Letting her take the lead.

They waited for thirty seconds, Bloch counting time silently. She reached for the doorbell again, but hesitated when she heard movement on the other side of the door, the rattle of a security chain being slipped into its housing.

Bloch lowered her arm, waited. The door opened six inches.

The brass security chain snapped taut, preventing the door from opening any farther, and in the gap she saw the face of Arthur Cross.

Twenty years had passed since his last mugshot. Thin lines crossed his wide forehead, and above it was short dark hair. His skin was pale and dry. Hollow cheeks. Lips that appeared slightly feminine, but with no color, as if the blood had been drained from them.

These details she scanned quickly, but it was his eyes that held her attention.

Large eyes. Round and almost too big. And even though it was nighttime Bloch knew those eyes would look the same beneath a clear blue sky.

They were black.

Of course, they were not actually black. Not really. Dark brown, but so dark as to make the irises indistinguishable from the pupils. Those huge eyes dominated his aspect, as if he was a creature that lived in the dark and his senses had evolved to accommodate his surroundings: his eyes grown larger to suck up even the smallest slivers of light.

Long fine eyelashes only served to make his appearance feral, as if something wild and dangerous lay behind this façade of a human face.

He wore no expression. No curiosity. No alarm.

His face seemed dead.

But his black eyes burned into the night.

Bloch's lips parted, but she said nothing. Cross didn't show the slightest hint of intimidation, nor curiosity. Bloch had no words. Her body and mind were engaged in more primal functions. She realized that she had clenched her fists, gooseflesh covered the back of her neck. Every nerve-ending was screaming at her to beware. To be ready.

'Mr. Cross, we have a matter we would like to discuss. Can we come in?' asked Lake.

For a moment, Cross didn't reply. At first it appeared as though he didn't hear Lake. But then he slowly shook his head, said, 'Who are you?'

His voice sounded childlike. A sing-song pattern, high and strange for a man in his mid-thirties. The sound of it made Bloch clench her jaw.

'We're friends of the lawyer you're harassing,' said Lake.

'Who are you?' asked Cross again in that unnerving voice.

Lake said, 'It doesn't matter who we are. You're going to leave the lawyer and his family alone.'

'Who *are* you?'

'We're going to be watching them closely. You need to back off,' said Lake.

Cross blinked his eyes, lazily, and Bloch realized it was the first time she had seen him blink. Those black eyes stared out constantly. Alive and full of wickedness.

His lips curled a little at the edges, not a smile, but more of a sketch of a smile drawn from distant memory.

'You're not police. What are your *names*?' asked Cross.

'You don't know us. We know you. Back off from the lawyer,' said Lake.

'I don't know what you're talking about,' said Cross innocently, but that strange smile on his lips betrayed the statement.

They all stood in heavy silence for a moment. None of them moved. Lake had been right. Cross didn't scare easily.

That smile on his face broadened, as if an evil thought played out in his mind.

'Oh, wait. I know who you're talking about now. Kevin, yeesssss. Oh, I have no interest in him. Or his bitch wife, but . . .'

Bloch dropped her right foot behind her. A fighting stance. Her muscles tight. She could feel her heartbeat quicken.

'. . . the *daughter*, Amy. Yeah, I *like* her. I think she likes me too . . .'

Cross's gaze switched from Lake, to Bloch.

'. . . I think Amy and I could have a lot of *fun* together . . .'

One moment, Bloch stood very still. The next moment, the sole of her right boot hit the front door parallel with the security chain, her weight and momentum busting the chain housing free from the frame, wood splintering. The door swinging open knocked Cross off his feet, flat on his back.

Black eyes wide open.

Bloch was still moving, dropping to her knees, instinct and training taking over.

She trapped his left wrist with both hands, kicked her feet out to land on her butt, with legs over Cross's torso. Her heels dug in, dragging her tight against him. Her left leg went across his body, keeping him on the floor, her right leg covered his face, pinning him down. She gripped his wrist tightly, and leaned back. His arm was trapped across Bloch's body, his elbow at her waist and she held his wrist centered in her chest.

She arched her spine, the back of her shoulders hit the floor.

'Bloch!' cried Lake.

She engaged her core muscles.

Cinched the hold.

'Don't do it!' cried Lake.

She drove her hips toward the ceiling.

Hard to tell which bone fractured first as Cross's arm bowed, sickeningly, in the wrong direction.

Most certainly the lateral and medial epicondyle, then the radial head. Like a twig being snapped in the middle.

Bloch heard the bones cracking, cartilage snapping like a whip, and pushed harder, twisting her body away from Cross, making sure to tear his shoulder out too.

Cross let out a high-pitched scream, like a deer caught in a steel trap.

And then another voice. Lake was screaming at her.

'Bloch!'

She let go of Cross's ruined limb. Let the small of her back hit the floor, then curled her legs up and over her head in a smooth backward roll. Her boots found the floor, and she pushed herself upright.

Stared down at Cross.

He was panting, but had managed to sit up. He cradled his arm, got onto one knee and stood as Lake put an arm round Bloch's waist and hauled her out of the house. She let him, of course, but all the while she stared at Cross.

They walked backward over the flagstone path, both keeping Cross in their eyeline. He was panting, his expression twisted in pain, but there were no screams now. Just the sound of his breath.

Just as Bloch and Lake reached the car, Cross spoke.

'*Bloch*,' he said, slowly. Letting every sound linger on his lips, the *K* on the end of her name clicking his tongue.

'B-L-O-C-K . . .'

Lake told her to get in the car. Bloch turned away from Cross, got into the driver's seat and fired up the Jeep. They pulled away in silence. Lake's fingers drummed on his knees.

Neither of them said a word until they were crossing the Queensboro Bridge over the East River and Roosevelt Island lay beneath them.

Lake drew breath, said, 'That didn't go—'

'I don't want to hear it,' said Bloch.

'I told you it wouldn't work. That guy is a pure sociopath.'

'I could tell. But you're wrong. It *did* work.'

Lake angled in his seat to face Bloch. 'How exactly do you figure that?'

'He wasn't going to listen to us. He wasn't going to back off. Now, he's got no choice – he's only got one arm for six, maybe seven months. He's a lot less dangerous if he only has one hand.'

She could tell Lake wasn't sold on the methods, but there was no denying Bloch's logic.

The head-up display on the Jeep's console lit up with an incoming phone call. Caller ID said *EDDIE*.

Bloch looked at the screen. Then returned her gaze to the front.

Lake hit the answer icon on the screen.

'How did it go?' said Eddie.

Lake and Bloch's eyes met for a second, in silence.

She looked back at the road.

Lake said, 'There's good news and bad news.'

'What's the good news?' asked Eddie.

'I didn't shoot him . . .'

14

Eddie

Bail bondsmen keep odd hours.

Part of the game. Mornings are for court. Getting paperwork signed for bail – application forms, indemnity agreements, promissory notes and confessions of judgement, all the pieces of paper to cover their business. Afternoons are most often appointment times. Their customers check in by phone or call into the office to confirm they are still where they are supposed to be, they are keeping to their curfew if any, they will make the next court date, and they haven't jumped bail.

Evenings vary – but most bondsmen are on the clock, charging by the hour, hunting down wayward defendants who haven't turned up for a court appearance that day and had a warrant issued for their arrest. The bondsmen find them and bring them in or sometimes manage to persuade them to surrender to the court with an excuse, and a higher bail bond, which means more money for the bondsman plus the fees for finding their asses in the first place.

Richard Reynolds got out of his Mercedes and opened his shop at seven in the morning, hauling up the graffiti-covered rolling shutters and letting himself in to the office.

I waited in my Mustang, watching him through his shop window. He switched on the office lights, took off his coat, went in back. Probably to make some coffee. I waited for six minutes, the average time it takes for a cheap machine to brew a pot, picked a gym bag off the passenger seat beside me, locked up the Mustang and crossed the street to Richard's place. As I did, I passed Richard's Mercedes. It was registered to him, personally. One of three cars. The second was a brown ten-year-old Ford, which he used for chasing down his wayward customers, and the third was a Bentley Continental.

Richard, like a lot of guys who suddenly find themselves making a lot of dough illegally, was terrible at hiding money.

The sign above the window said *Richard Reynolds, Bail Bonds* in white lettering on a red board. Below it was his phone number and below that – *BONDS 4 U.*

He hadn't locked the front door, and I pushed it open. Heard the *ting* of an electronic bell to tell Richard a customer had come in.

Richard Reynolds was in his early fifties with a full head of silver-blond hair, a jaw that looked like the engine block from a Chevy Chevelle and a moustache that might have been the same color as his hair at some point, but which was now much darker either with age, coffee or an inability to match it with the dye he used on what remained of his hair. He was a big man. He'd been into bodybuilding semi-professionally for years. Even though his tan suit had been made for him, it didn't quite fit. It was still too tight around the shoulders, which either spoke to the lack of talent on the part of the tailor who cut the suit, or Richard had been through a bulking phase since he'd bought it.

'We're not open,' he said, coming out of the back office, a cup of coffee in his hand. There was one desk in front of him, with two chairs, a phone and a laptop on it. The rest of the shop was a waiting area with cheap plastic office chairs that looked like they'd been accumulated over many years from several different fire-damage sales.

'My name is Eddie Flynn,' I said.

He paused.

'I know you. We've never met, but I've seen you in court.'

Richard was now interested. He smiled, offered me a chair. I could almost see the dollar signs rolling around his eyes like they were in a slot machine.

I slipped the gym bag off my shoulder and let it hit the floor as I sat down.

'How's that coffee?' I asked.

'Oh, I'm sorry. Would you like one? Fair warning, it's an old machine and it's not great.'

'Sold,' I said.

He smiled, put his coffee down and disappeared in back to fetch me a cup. He returned with hot coffee for me in his best branded mug – *Reynolds Bonds*, white lettering on red.

'Do you have a client who needs a bond?' he asked. 'I do a lot of white-collar crime. No problem.'

'Have you heard of the TikTok murders? It's all over the news,' I said.

'Sure, sure, I heard about it. Elly Parker, right? I heard Busken set bail at a one-mil bond and a million in cash. I can help with the bond, that's no problem, but the premium will cost her . . .'

He opened a desk drawer on his left, brought out a folder, opened it and began to shuffle through blank forms.

'Payment isn't going to be a problem,' I said, taking out my bill fold from my pants pocket. 'I'll pay her premium in full, right now.'

Richard watched me peel off a single bill from the fold, put it on the table and slide it toward him.

He stared at the bill. Looked at me.

'One dollar?' he asked.

I nodded.

He laughed, said, 'Eddie, you know my premium fees are set by law as a percentage of the bond. Ten per cent of the first three grand of the bond, eight percent from three to ten grand, and then I charge six percent of any amount over ten thousand. For your client, you're talking about sixty thousand dollars.'

'Don't ever try to lecture a lawyer about the law. Those are the *maximum* fees. There's no minimum. Is that what you tell your customers, that your fees are set down in law and you *have* to charge them that rate? Things aren't looking good for you.'

'My charges are fair. I got no complaints . . .' He didn't quite finish his sentence. He'd fired back without taking in every word I'd said. Now it was beginning to sink in.

'What do you mean, things aren't looking good for me?'

'You're about to have thirty plaintiffs in a class action lawsuit set your ass on fire. Right now, I'm not going to ask you to work for me for free. A buck seems about fair considering what you've been up to these past few years. You see, I know you, *Richard*. I know what your clients call you – *Tricky Dicky*. I know about the overcharging for copies of court records. I know about busting your own clients' bail so they get hauled back to court and the bond increased. I know about the overcharging for hours, for incidentals. I know all of it . . .'

I reached into my gym bag and took out the thick file of court receipts from my office, dumped them on the table.

Tricky Dicky said nothing, he could plainly see from the first page of the bundle that it was a receipt from the court office. He reached for it, and I slammed my hand on top.

'I know the Department of Financial Services will shut you down, and the DA will prosecute, and they'll seek a fine in the millions plus jail time, but that's the least of your problems . . .'

I took out the pillowcase, laid it flat on the desk, then the duct tape and the .45 ACP cartridge.

'I asked one of your former clients what they would expect in compensation. He gave me this crap. Said the bullet had your name on it. I was talking about him coming in on a class action suit against you, but he said it would take a lot of money to spare your life. He says he's going to put this pillowcase over your head, duct tape it in place then load this round into his gun and fire it through your skull.'

Sweat broke on his forehead. The perspiration caught the ceiling lights, made his head shine like a glitterball.

'What client?'

'You think I'm going to break confidentiality so you can take out a hit on this guy? No, thanks.'

He stared at the file of papers, then the pillowcase, duct tape and his eyes settled on the cartridge and stayed there for a while. His hand shook as he tried to bring the coffee mug to his mouth.

'There's a way out of this for you, *Dick*, and I'll even throw you a bone if you co-operate,' I said.

'What do you want?'

'I want my client, Elly Parker, out of Rosie's today, if possible. I know a bond of this size takes some time to arrange with the insurance company so tomorrow morning is acceptable. You'll write the bond, pay the cash surety and when her case is over you'll close up shop and move to Canada.'

'I can't do that. I have a business. I have responsibilities. I have—'

'You've got a house of cards and there's a hurricane on the way. Here's how we settle this. You get the bond. You put up the million in cash. And you sell your Bentley.'

'Wait, *what*?'

'Hear me out. The reason you got caught isn't because you're stupid. It's because you got greedy and you're shit at hiding money. I need your files. Everyone you overcharged in the last year, to the dollar amount. You're going to sell your Bentley and divide the proceeds up among the worst affected. Here's your bone, Dick – when the Parker case is over, and that million dollars is returned to you, guess what?'

'What?'

Right then I knew I was on a winner. Dicky had a million in cash, somewhere, that I hadn't been able to find during my research. He probably had more, but a mil was all Elly needed.

'Because you're a bondsman and you deal in cash with the courthouse all the time, and you already have a bill of good health from the Department of Financial Services, no financial checks are going to be done on that million dollars you deposit . . .'

His eyebrows lifted. I guessed he had finally seen the bone that was coming his way.

He said, 'So when the million comes back to me in cash, after the case, it's clean.'

'No finer money-laundering service than the New York Criminal Court Funds Office,' I said. 'You do this for me, the class action goes away with the proceeds from the Bentley sale. I hold off on the DFS report and I throw some extra cash to the guy who wants to kill you. When your million comes back, you disappear. I hear Canada is a nice place to live . . .'

'What if I don't want to go to Canada? I've got a good thing going here.'

There was no class action lawsuit. No threats to kill him. It was likely the vast majority of Dicky's clientele didn't even know they'd been scammed, and the rest couldn't do anything about it other than complain. There was no justice for these people other than to close Dicky's operation, try to throw them some money by way of a refund and make sure he never scammed another poor defendant.

'It's up to you. But you can't spend that clean mil in cash when you're in a wooden box.'

He took a moment to stroke his big chin.

'Maybe Canada doesn't sound so bad,' said Dicky.

15
Elly

There are no clocks in jail. No one has a watch, other than the correction officers.

Time is marked in routine.

Six in the morning, the lights buzzed into life inside Elly's crowded cell. From total darkness to shocking, blinding illumination. An inferno of light that burned through her eyelids into her brain. A reminder that in this place there were no choices. There was light, or there was darkness. Not even that was within her control.

She hadn't slept. But she had managed to make it through the night without disturbing her other cellmates, smothering her sobs in her pillow. Even though Rosie's wasn't exactly quiet in the dark hours, Elly had still worried about making any noise. She needn't have. The sounds of crying, screaming, steel banging on steel, songs, howls, harsh voices wielding hard words – it all floated in the dark, all night long. And somehow every sound spoke of the pain behind the one who made it.

Elly stayed very still. She waited while the woman in the bunk above her shifted and a foot appeared in the air above her, angling down until her toes found the edge of Elly's bed. The woman who descended from the bunk was dressed just the same as the other detainees. Same uniform. Same look in her eyes – anger and frustration, just simmering under the surface, held in check by the knowledge that nothing she can do will change her situation. The woman stepped down onto the floor, staring at Elly. She had pale skin and short dark hair that was wet, but not from washing. Sweat covered her face and neck and had stained the chest and armpits of her jail clothes.

'What are you looking at?' said the woman.

Elly turned away to face the wall.

'I said . . .'

'Stop it, Nance,' said another voice. 'Leave her be.'

Elly shifted, tilted her head back. The woman who had defended her leapt off the top bunk opposite. She was tall, with long lightbrown hair. She tugged and curled that hair into a bun then tied it up. While she did this, her hard gaze was fixed on the short darkhaired prisoner Elly now knew as Nance.

Nance held the gaze of the tall woman, then rubbed the back of her wrist across her mouth and turned to face the door. The woman on the lower bunk opposite was small and blond and wiry, with faded blue tattoos on her neck and a rash covering her mouth. She fell into line behind Nance.

A buzzer sounded and Elly heard the clanks and groans of the cell door opening. It was much louder than the night before, and soon she heard voices outside the cell. All the cell doors were being opened. Nance glanced over her shoulder at Elly, smiled, but it was not a friendly look. There was malice in that expression. Then she slid out of the cell, the small blonde following.

'Watch yourself in here,' said the tall woman.

Elly sat up, swung her legs off the bunk and said, 'Thank you. I didn't mean to annoy your friend.'

'She's not my friend. She got here day before yesterday. She a fish, just like you. But she been here before. You don't look like you done no time.'

'No, I haven't been in any place like this before. It's all some kind of terrible mistake—'

'Hush, don't tell nobody why you're here. It ain't none of their business. And don't ask nobody else, neither. Nance is sick. You see the sweat on her?'

Elly nodded, asked, 'What's wrong? Is it the flu? Covid?'

The tall woman angled her gaze, giving Elly the side-eye, said, 'You really don't know shit, do you? She's a junkie. There's plenty of shit in here, but not the kind of shit she needs. Weed takes the edge off. Crack too. But she's gonna be hard to deal with for a couple weeks or so until her body adjusts. Junkies be like that coming off their regular fix. Don't look her in the eyes. In fact, don't you look nobody in the eyes. Not in this place.'

'Thank you. I'm Elly,' she said, holding out a hand.

'Suze,' said the woman, ignoring Elly's outstretched hand. 'Stay by me for a couple of days, so you can get used to the way things work around here. You're in my cell. You follow my rules. Okay?'

'Of course, thank you so much. That's so kind. I'm really scared in here.'

'It's not kindness. Not for its own sake. You should be scared. Rich white girl like you? You'll get your ass killed in here in a heartbeat. And they do it in your cell. *My* cell. I don't need to be washing your blood off my walls, you hear?'

Elly swallowed, feeling suddenly very cold.

'Good enough,' said Suze. 'Let's get breakfast. I want your bread roll.'

'Sure, no problem.'

Elly followed Suze out of the cell and down the metal stairway. The women who occupied the rest of the house were milling around the recreation area, or seated around the tables. Everything was nailed down. Chairs, tables, TV behind a thick piece of plastic high up on the wall opposite the cells. The news was on.

Elly's picture flashed up on the screen, along with images and video from her Instagram and TikTok.

The chyron running along the bottom of the screen read – *The TikTok Killer.*

Elly felt something pulling her eyes away from the TV.

Half of the women in the room were staring at her.

'*Oh shit, lookee here, the TikTok killer, in da house . . .*' said a voice, but Elly couldn't discern who had said it. She kept her head down, followed Suze to a table and sat beside her.

'Keep your head down,' said Suze. 'Shit, I didn't know you a *famous* bitch. They'll all want a piece of you. Stay out here, where the COs can see you with the cameras. Don't go back to the cell until lights out. Be ready. One of these bitches is gonna come for you.'

16

Bloch

Bloch stared at the ceiling in Grand Central Station and tutted.

The celestial ceiling in the main concourse is a representation of the ancient heavens, with the zodiac constellations rendered in gold on a turquoise background. Electric light bulbs illuminate the stars that form the original Greek signs of the zodiac – the crab depicting Cancer, the winged horse of Perseus, Orion as the figure of the hunter and so on. It is one of the most beautiful and breathtaking public artworks in the world.

Bloch shook her head, dug her nails into her palms, then looked away from the ceiling and tilted her head to the right, cracking her neck.

She looked around the concourse and spotted Lake approaching. He had his cell phone in his hand and he was flicking his thumb across the screen. He stopped in front of Bloch.

'Did you get some pictures?' she asked.

Lake nodded, said, 'There's an MTA security camera at the turnstile and two on the platform. None on the stairwell.'

Bloch nodded. They were checking out Elly's story of the man with the yellow suitcase, identifying the cameras that would have picked him up. While New York's public transport system was one of the easiest and cheapest ways to navigate the city, Bloch never used it. She drove. She liked driving, but there was another reason.

The tunnels and platforms of the subway made her feel uncomfortable. Bloch couldn't handle any kind of confined space, particularly underground. Lake had to be the one to enter the subway and scope out the camera locations.

Lake paused, stared at Bloch. She clenched her fists, relaxed and then clenched again. Cracked her neck.

'What's bothering you? You don't have to go into the subway. I'm pretty sure I got everything we need,' said Lake.

'It's not that – it's the ceiling,' said Bloch.

Tilting his head back, Lake smiled as he took in the artwork.

'What's with the ceiling? It's gorgeous. Is it too high? Don't tell me you're claustrophobic and agoraphobic too.'

'I'm not claustrophobic. I just don't like being underground. And I like the height. It's the painting, it's backward,' said Bloch.

'It's what?'

Bloch pointed to the ceiling said, 'The constellations are facing the wrong way. It's like someone drew the stars from a mirror. Or they had the drawing at their feet and then copied it the wrong way onto the ceiling. It makes me . . . uneasy. It's like a stone in my shoe. It's not right.'

Lake nodded, said nothing. Only Bloch would notice small imperfections. It was what made her a talented investigator, but this ability also drove her crazy from time to time.

He followed Bloch out of the station, and they walked the route described by Elly, back to the building where she had been poisoned. There were two more cameras, in Pershing Square and at a crosswalk on 40th, that could have picked up images of Elly and the man with the suitcase. They also looked for cameras in stores pointed at the entrances and which might pick up passers-by on the sidewalk.

They tried the stores, but they struck out. Camera footage was erased after forty-eight hours.

When they reached the building, Bloch made a note of the address. Elly didn't know the exact address or apartment number, but she had given Kate a good description of the building and this was the only one that matched. Bloch took some pictures, sent them to Kate so she could confirm this was the correct address when she next saw Elly.

They walked on, and Bloch made a call as they moved. Her contact in NYPD. She gave all the relevant information – approximate times of Elly entering the subway and camera locations. If there was anything remotely matching the description of the man, then her contact would find the footage and send it to Bloch. If it corresponded with Elly's story, Kate could then subpoena the relevant security footage so that it could be used in court as evidence.

First, they wanted to see all the video. Make sure it backed up their client's story. No point in obtaining evidence officially that only damaged their case.

Bloch hung up the call, said, 'It's going to take a day to get the footage. Anything else we can do?'

'The homeless man who helped Elly,' and he pointed to the corner of 40th Street. One of the buildings on the corner had an alcove. There was a large shopping bag filled with rags and a bundle of cardboard boxes tied up with string tucked into the corner of the building recess.

'Nobody's home,' said Lake.

'Age range mid-thirties to early fifties. Caucasian. Unshaven. Red coat. Blue beanie hat. He was in the alcove on the corner of the street. That's all that Elly could remember about him. Not much to go on,' said Bloch.

They scanned the area, looking for other homeless people. They both knew that this was a community. Those who live on the streets get to know each other. And most help each other too, when they can.

'I don't see anyone. Let's walk the blocks. We're bound to find somebody.'

They circled the block, didn't see anyone who might have been part of that community. Until they walked back toward Grand Central and saw two men on the corner of 41st Street. Bloch always felt a pang of guilt when she saw people living on the streets. It was not their fault. Poverty, addiction, mental-health problems and sometimes even just bad luck could put almost anyone here. The hardest thing was to climb back onto their feet and get out of that spiral.

Lake and Bloch approached the two men. One was tall, with sharp eyes and a long gray beard. The other was short and wore odd boots – one brown and one black. They both wore beanie hats and thick coats. A shopping cart filled with bags of empty plastic bottles and cardboard sat between them. They were sorting through the bags and talking.

'Excuse me, guys, we're looking for the man who lives on the corner of 40th Street, in the alcove. Any idea where we could find him? He's not in trouble or anything. We just want to talk to him,' said Lake.

Both men halted their conversation and eyed Lake warily.

'You a cop?' asked the tall man.

'Used to be. Private investigator. My name is Gabriel Lake, this is Bloch. We just want to talk to the guy. He saw a client of ours, a lady who had been attacked. He helped save her.'

'You mean the girl who was puking in the street?' asked the short man.

Bloch stepped forward, said, 'Her name's Elly Parker. We need to talk to your friend. Do you know his name and where we could find him?'

Both men looked at each other for a moment. Something passed between them, their eyes searching each other's faces for the appropriate response.

'He helped her. Made sure she didn't choke while they were waiting for the paramedics. Is she alright? The lady, I mean?' asked the tall man.

'She recovered, but she's in a different kind of trouble. We're hoping your friend could help,' said Lake.

The tall man stepped back, shook his head, said, 'I'm glad she's okay, but we ain't seen the guy you're looking for. Don't know him. Sorry.'

The short man took the big guy's lead. He too backed away, dragging the cart, shook his head, said, 'Sorry, can't help you.'

'Wait, I thought you knew him? The guy who lives in the alcove on 40th?'

'We ain't seen him,' said the big man.

'Do you know where else he might hang out?' asked Bloch.

'Sorry, lady,' said the short one. 'Like he said, we ain't seen Joe in days.'

'Joe? What's his last name?' asked Bloch.

The short man swore under his breath, and turned away from the accusing look shot at him by his friend.

'It's none of our business. Like we told the other guy, we don't know shit,' said the tall man.

'What other guy?' asked Lake.

'The cop who came by the other day. If *Joe* is in trouble –' and as he said 'Joe' he gave his short friend another withering look – 'we don't want no part of it.'

'A cop? Was he in uniform?' asked Bloch.

'Nah, detective.'

'What was this cop's name?' asked Bloch.

'Didn't give no name. Just asked if we'd seen Joe or if we know where else he hangs out.'

'Did he leave a card so you could call him if you see Joe?' asked Bloch.

'Didn't leave no card, neither. Just asked about the guy in the blue hat who stays on the corner on 40th Street.'

'Did you tell this cop the guy he's looking for is called Joe?' asked Lake.

'Nah, we didn't slip up that time,' said the tall man.

'Shit man, I didn't mean to,' said the short man.

'Okay, what's Joe's second name?' asked Lake.

'Don't know. We don't know shit. Now leave us be,' said the tall man.

Bloch took two fifties from her wallet, gave one to the short man, and the other to the tall man, along with a card with her name and cell phone number.

'If you see Joe, or you see this cop come by again, call me. There'll be another fifty for each of you. What are your names?'

They looked at the bills in their hands, then each other. The short man was waiting for his pal to take the lead.

'I'm Pat, this is Sean,' said the tall man. 'You sure Joe's not in trouble?'

'None at all. The cop who asked about Joe, do you know what precinct he was from?' asked Lake.

'Didn't say,' said Pat. 'I thought it was kinda strange at the time. He didn't show no badge. Just said he was a cop and he was looking for Joe.'

'The guy gave off a weird vibe,' added Sean.

'Weird in what way?' asked Lake.

'He was wearing all black. Combat pants, shell hoodie. Sunglasses and a black baseball cap. Had a big-ass Rolex on his wrist too. Never saw a cop like that before,' said Sean.

'Was he tall? Short?'

'Average height. White guy. Built like a sprinter, or an athlete or something. Strong and lean. Had a little scar on his chin.'

'I don't like the sound of this cop. If he comes around again, you let us know,' said Bloch. 'We really need to find Joe. He might be in danger. Any ideas?'

Pat shook his head, but Sean looked at his friend then said, 'His name is Joseph Novak. Try the VA. Joe was gonna try and get into a program again. If we see him, we'll let you know.'

No rebuke from Pat this time.

Lake and Bloch thanked the men and headed back to Bloch's car.

'The Veterans Administration office is on West Houston Street,' said Bloch, pronouncing it *Howston*, like all New Yorkers.

'What kind of cop goes looking for a witness and doesn't give a card or a contact number, or his name?' said Lake.

'The kind of person who isn't a cop. Could be Elly's man with the suitcase is trying to take care of loose ends.'

'Or it could be nothing to do with this case. Might be a coincidence.'

'You don't believe in coincidences,' said Bloch.

'I believe in logic. Why draw attention to yourself by hunting down a homeless man who may or may not be able to identify you? Think about it. Soon as we get the MTA footage from the subway, we're going to know exactly what this guy looks like anyway.'

Bloch's phone rang.

She picked up. Listened. After thirty seconds, she ended the call.

'My contact is gonna check the traffic and NYPD Argus cameras. There's no subway footage for the day Elly was poisoned,' said Bloch.

'What?'

'It's gone. Could be a technical glitch. The footage is live-streamed to the MTA security office and the NYPD monitoring center, but sometimes it's not saved. Remember the subway shooter in Brooklyn? The Wi-Fi was down in the subway and the cameras didn't upload the recording to the cloud. PD had to identify the shooter from cell-phone footage of the attack,' said Bloch.

'Or it could be somebody wiped it. Somebody who doesn't want to be identified. Could be the same guy looking for Joe,' said Lake. 'How the hell do you wipe camera footage from the MTA?'

'Let's find out. If it is the man with the suitcase, then he's thorough. If we can find Joe first, then we might be able to find our mystery man.'

'How do you figure?'

'Because he's smart. He'll find Joe Novak eventually. And we'll be waiting.'

17

Logan

Karl Kaplinsky was a sad little man.

Karl sat in the driver's seat of a van parked in a disused lot beneath the Williamsburg Bridge. His neck arched; the back of his skull nestled on the head rest. Mouth open. Eyes open and fixed. In as quiet a spot as one could hope for this close to Manhattan, Logan, in the passenger seat of the van, unfolded a sun-shade and spread it across the inside of the windshield for some additional privacy.

The van didn't belong to Karl. The logo SECURE ONE in red lettering was displayed across the sides of the vehicle. Karl had worked as a technical specialist for Secure One for almost ten years. The van was filled with high-speed cable, wiring, power cables, dongles, servers, hard drives and various technical pieces of equipment that Karl used daily.

It wasn't Karl's job that made him sad. It was his life outside of his job. That's the way he had described his life on Reddit when Logan and Karl had first interacted. Karl identified as an incel. A man who was involuntarily celibate. Logan was looking for Karl, of course, as well as finding and interacting online with a number of Secure One employees of a certain kind. Karl was the most interesting to Logan, because he was sad and lonely, and lacked the intellectual rigor to divine that he was sad and lonely through certain life choices. Karl was, despite his decent career in IT, a failure. A loser.

Logan liked losers.

Inherent in each of them are the seeds of their own condition. All of these markers of failure were evident in Karl's social media. His personality flaws writ large in his posts on X, Reddit and Truth Social.

The real truth was that Karl's isolation and depression had pushed him ever further to the extremes of society and politics. In these chat forums and digital communities, there existed valid reasons for Karl's unhappiness – woke culture, liberalism, political correctness, immigration, the deep state and equal opportunities. Here, in the far reaches of extremist groups, Karl had people to blame other than himself.

Logan had learned that the Karl Kaplinskys of this world were among the most susceptible to manipulation and control. Essentially, they were already deluding themselves. Logan's interactions with Karl fed that delusion, and so it was easy to quickly gain his trust and exploit it.

In the passenger seat of the Secure One panel van, Logan scrolled through the list of dates and times displayed on Karl's laptop screen. He found the last entry for the date he'd met Elly in the subway – marked 6p/12a – and deleted the file from cloud storage. He had already deleted the previous three recordings for that day. The security system uploaded recordings to the cloud every six hours.

The Manhattan Transport Authority subcontracted its digital file storage maintenance to Secure One for an eye-watering amount of money. It turns out that storing data in cyberspace for thirty days is about as expensive as storing it in a suite at the Regency Hotel. In contrast, the steps Karl had taken to disguise his online personas were less than adequate.

Logan turned to Karl in the driver's seat, said, 'You've been most co-operative, but I'm afraid I still have to show your online activities to your employer . . .'

Karl said nothing.

'I know I said I would keep it secret if you co-operated, but, unfortunately, Karl, I have no choice.'

Reaching inside his jacket pocket, Logan produced what looked like a small sampler bottle of perfume, no bigger than his little finger, with an aerosol top. Inside was a clear liquid. Logan sprayed the laptop keys and the trackpad, liberally, then used a cloth to wipe it down. Some of the liquid had run beneath the keys, causing the screen to freeze and then go blank. He put the bottle back in his pocket and put on a pair of black latex gloves. He shut the laptop, wiped it down again and placed it on the floor of the van.

'The email you have scheduled to send tonight won't be read by your boss, Mr. Telford, until tomorrow morning. He'll choke on his granola when he opens that one. But don't worry, Karl. It's good to get everything out in the open: your views on immigrants, women, African Americans . . . It's a good thing that the world will finally see the *real* you. There's no reason to be afraid any more . . .'

Logan's nostrils twitched.

Karl had soiled his pants shortly after he had given Logan his log-in details to access the MTA security-footage archive.

He leaned forward and angled his view so he could take a good look at Karl.

Both his eyes were bulging and black with eight-ball hemorrhages from the bullet that had ripped through his skull. Both his front teeth were chipped. They might have been damaged when Logan put the gun in Karl's mouth, or maybe when he pulled the trigger – the kickback or perhaps the slide had broken Karl's teeth. Logan picked up the Ruger pistol from Karl's lap, unscrewed the silencer and placed that in his jacket pocket. Then he sprayed the gun, wiped it clean, dried it. He lifted Karl's dead hand, put the gun in it, to make sure Karl's palm prints were on the grip, then let go. The Ruger tumbled to the floor of the van.

'You've been most helpful, Karl. And you are at peace now. I hope you enjoy that gift. You see, I don't care that you are dead. I liked killing you. It feels . . . *empowering*,' said Logan.

He enjoyed talking.

Logan knew the importance of talking openly about one's feelings and emotions. Studies had shown that even patients who attend bad psychotherapists often get better purely because they have voiced their fears, their desires, their guilt and unhappiness. The mere act of speaking about problems makes people feel better. Not that Logan needed to feel better about his activities – the act of killing exhilarated him. He felt nothing for his victims. He'd realized, early on in his studies of psychology and human behavior, that he was a clinical sociopath – uninhibited by moral conscience. With that knowledge came self-awareness. Neither psychopathy nor sociopathy were classified as mental disorders in and of themselves.

Logan knew he wasn't sick. He merely had psychological traits enjoyed by a small percentage of the population.

Was he born that way? Or was it his upbringing? Logan tried not to think too much on this. The past could not be changed. He could only move forward.

His phone buzzed in his pocket. He took it out, smiled.

Grace, the girl he had met on the subway, had replied to his message.

> A drink sounds good. See you there at 8?

He texted a reply confirming the date. As he hit send, he felt something strange.

It wasn't excitement, not exactly. Not like the delicious thrill that had shuddered through him when he put a bullet into Karl's skull. This was different.

Strange.

For the first time in a very long time, Logan felt nervous.

He made sure no one had entered the lot. Then he opened the door, got out and shut it quietly. As he stepped away from the van, a boy wearing a puffer jacket and sweatpants pulled up on his bicycle at the mouth of the lot.

Logan couldn't see his face. His cap was pulled down too far.

Logan tensed. The boy was twenty feet away.

The boy sat on his bike and stared, then said, 'You can't park in here.'

Logan stopped, just a few feet past the van. The lot had brick walks on either side. On one of them someone had spray-painted, in white, *No Parking*.

'Are you the owner?' asked Logan.

'My dad owns this lot. You can't park here. See the sign,' he said, and pointed at the wall.

Logan reached into his jacket and took out his wallet.

'Sorry, didn't see it. My friend here, he's on the job, but he's had a rough day and put down a few beers with lunch. He just needs twenty minutes to sleep it off. How about twenty bucks, for the use of the space?' said Logan, retrieving a twenty and holding it up for the kid.

The boy stared at the bill clamped between Logan's fingers. The boy kicked off the ground and rode his bike into the lot. As he got closer, Logan was able to see his face.

No more than fifteen years old, if that. His puffer coat was old and ripped in a few places, with graying tufts of insulation peeking through the tears. His sweatpants were of a similar age and covered in lint balls. The kid pulled up on his bike, just within reach, and stretched out a hand to take the twenty. He had dirty fingernails.

'Why aren't you in school?' asked Logan.

'My old man doesn't care.'

Logan had felt the same way, at that age.

He nodded. He stretched out his right hand, let the twenty fall and grabbed the boy's wrist.

Logan leaned back, quickly, yanked the kid clean off the bike and pulled him toward the van. Pivoting as the kid came stumbling forward, Logan put his left hand on the back of the kid's head and drove his face into the front grille of the van.

The *thump* of the kid's head hitting the grille was accompanied by an equally loud *crack* as the boy landed on his chest in front of the van.

His dead eyes stared back up at Logan, his neck horribly twisted.

Logan sat on his ass, and with his feet pushed the boy's body underneath the van. It was more difficult than he first thought. The van didn't have great ground clearance. As he kicked the boy's legs underneath, he thought about what he might wear when he met Grace tonight. The Armani charcoal suit, certainly, perhaps with the black Versace shirt and the polished, calfskin Salvatore Ferragamo Oxfords. For his timepiece, either the Patek Philippe Golden Ellipse or the vintage Cartier Tank. He didn't want to look too formal, so perhaps the Cartier would be preferable.

Once most of the body was underneath the van, he got to his feet and lifted the boy's bike, smashed the handlebars into the hood, to make a dent and ensure mutual transfer of paint for the forensic investigators.

He stood, took out his phone and exited the lot. From his VPN, he accessed a secure internet connection and logged into Karl Kaplinsky's email. He made one addition to the draft email to Karl's boss. Karl's depression and isolation were bad enough, but the last straw had been when he'd run over a kid in a parking lot. Karl knew he was going to jail, apologized to the boss for the damage to the van and had decided to check out permanently.

Logan hit send on the email. No point in waiting any more.

The only problem with killing is making a mistake. One little error, one oversight, or one piece of bad luck could lead to a lot more work in covering his tracks.

A quiet street. No one around. Only the thrum of traffic on the bridge above.

He walked back to his car, parked a block away. Before he got in, he took the cloth and the gloves from his jacket and knelt at the curb, as if he was checking his front tire. Logan casually tossed everything into the storm drain, and had just got into his rental car when his phone began to ring.

Caller display read *Tokyo Management*. A brand and marketing company that had Logan on an extravagant non-exclusive monthly retainer as a fixer. He hit answer.

'Logan, Brett here, we need you to come in. Full crisis on the perfume launch. It's not selling.'

The company specialized in product placement with celebrities who wanted to sell tequila, vodka, wine, perfume, clothing or even phone cases – it was all part of brand extensions and maximalization.

'I can't right now. What's the problem?' asked Logan.

'I've got a mightily pissed-off A-lister and a shitload of terrible perfume that won't move on the website. Sales are ninety per cent down on launch week.'

'Any badpress issues I should know about?'

'None. It's just a bad product. What do we do? We can't lose this client.'

'Having a bad product doesn't matter,' said Logan. 'It's demand and saturation that we have to control. We don't have the balance right on the universality and scarcity scale.'

'What does that mean?'

'People buy new products for two reasons – either because everyone is buying it, or because hardly anyone can buy it. Both have value. It's the way we humans are programmed. You want something because few people can have it, which increases its value, or because everyone has it and you don't want to miss out. Put a notice on the website saying that due to demand you can't fulfill orders for twenty-four hours. Issue a press release to confirm it. Hike the price by a hundred dollars and reissue the product for sale tomorrow and watch those sales numbers go through the roof. Got to go now, Brett. Good luck.'

He ended the call, and hit the ignition button on the car. The radio came on.

'*Our phone-in today is all about the TikTok murders. What are the latest theories doing the rounds on social media? When will Elly Parker break her silence? And then later we're going to be talking to Chef Tommy about the ultimate omelette . . .*'

The Toyota's navigation system sprang into life and Logan entered his next destination.

A business in Tribeca.

It sat above a tattoo parlor.

The offices of Flynn and Brooks, Attorneys at Law.

18

Eddie

'Eddie, call on line three. It's that guy again from *The New York Times*,' said Denise, hollering at me from her desk at reception.

I was in my office, working on my third coffee of the afternoon, feet on my desk, pen tumbling through my fingers as I thought about Elly's case.

'You know you can call me on my office phone and tell me that. You don't need to bellow it out across the whole office.'

'I called your phone three times,' said Denise. 'You didn't pick up. You're miles away.'

She was right. When I get lost in thought, I go somewhere deep. The building could crumble around me and I probably wouldn't notice.

'Sorry, Denise. I'll pick up next time.'

'What do I tell the guy from the *Times*?'

'Tell him we're not ready to make a statement yet, and I got today's Wordle on my second try.'

Swinging my feet off the desk, I got up and took my coffee to Harry's office. He was behind the desk, a stack of files on one side, which he was ignoring, a cup of coffee in one hand, his phone in the other. Clarence lay in his bed in the corner, dosing. The Rolling Stones were playing from Harry's work laptop. Kate had set him up on Spotify. Harry liked listening to music as he worked, but didn't want to haul his records and record player into the office.

'Working hard?' I asked.

'Hardly working. I'm watching Elly's TikkyToks.'

'I don't think that's the right term.'

'I'm old. What's up?'

'I'm going slightly crazy thinking about this case. I don't like prosecutors keeping me in the dark. We can't build a defense if we don't know what case we have to fight.'

Harry put down his phone, took a sip from his coffee, said, 'You have no patience. Just wait for the indictment.'

'If we're going to trial at lightning speed then every day we spend sitting on our asses while Castro's office builds a case against Elly is against my religion.'

'She should be out on bail tomorrow, if your bondsman comes through. There will be plenty to do then. Just try to relax. Wait for Bloch and Lake to come back.'

'I can't sit here. I've got to do something.'

'What can you do?'

I thought for a moment. Looked at Clarence. He wasn't bothered by any of this. His master was at peace in his chair, he'd been fed and walked, and all was right with the world. I needed to think. Which meant I needed to move. There was one thing I could do that might help us get a jump start on Elly's defense.

'I've got to know more about the murders, but it might get us into trouble,' I said.

'What kind of trouble?'

'The serious kind. Want to come?'

Harry thought for a moment, asked, 'Whose car are we going to take?'

Harry drove.

I needed to make some calls on the way.

He still maneuvered his green convertible sports car way too fast. It was very old and very British. Harry loved this car. Nobody else did. It had a suspension system that I guessed was made out of old boots and tree branches, the steering made a horrible noise if you turned left hard and the brakes were either fully on or fully off, which made stop lights damn dangerous. We drove with the top down, despite the cold. Having the top up was an arcane puzzle that Harry had never quite mastered. Even with it up, it leaked and sent concentrated icy drafts of air across your face.

'Why don't you get this car fixed?' I asked, holding my cell phone to my ear.

'I can't. This thing was hand-built in England. If it broke down in the factory, surrounded by the guys who built it, they still wouldn't be able to put it back together.'

'Then buy a new car. This one is dangerous.'

'I like this car. It has character.'

'You mean you like it because it doesn't work properly?'

We were coming up on a red light. Harry touched the brakes, throwing us forward as the wheels locked up. The seatbelt bit into my shoulder.

'Yeah, that's kind of the point,' said Harry. 'Think about our office. You think any one of those people function properly? You never left the con game, not even when you're on your feet in court; Kate is an obsessive workaholic; Bloch is the best investigator I've ever seen, but she's like an AI robot most of the time; and Lake is a bumbling mass of anxiety who likes to shoot people every now and again. If it wasn't for Denise, the whole place would collapse. None of you can function properly. We're all flawed, Eddie. That's what makes us human. That's why I love this car.'

We drove on in silence.

I called the prosecutor's office. Bernice was out and her secretary said she was on her cell and gave me her number.

It took almost thirty seconds, but Bernice answered the call.

'You know, you shouldn't keep your cell phone in that handbag,' I said.

'My life is in this bag, Eddie. What do you want? I already told you I can't divulge anything about this case. Grand Jury empaneled tomorrow. You should have discovery in a week or two.'

'I need something else. My client is going to make bail in the morning. I need to get some clothes and essential items from her apartment. I'm on my way there now.'

'Her apartment is sealed. She can't stay there. You want in there you need to file a motion.'

'A lady from my office wants to go over there and pick up some of Elly's clothes and personal items. I don't need to file a motion for my client to access her underwear drawer.'

'It's a crime scene, Eddie.'

'You've gotten all the forensics you need from that apartment. Or are you telling me there's evidence in that apartment you're not showing to the Grand Jury? Maybe I should ask Kate to file a motion to dismiss on grounds of withholding evidence.'

Bernice sighed, said, 'I'll ask the detective to meet you there. Give me an hour. And don't screw me on this.'

She hung up.

We were almost at Elly's apartment building.

I called Bloch. She was in her car, with Lake, on speaker.

'I need you and Lake at Elly's apartment. Police will be here within an hour to supervise. They're letting us inside to grab some stuff for our client. You're going to pack up some clothes and personal items for Elly.'

A pause.

'You want to tell me what we're really doing?' asked Bloch.

'The apartment is still sealed. We need access and time to examine the crime scene *alone*. You and Lake can grab our own forensics. I just need to get rid of the detective who's supervising the visit.'

'How are you going to do that?'

Harry pulled up across the street from Elly's apartment building. She lived on the fifth floor. I glanced up, checked out the four windows of her apartment. Construction workers were on the sidewalk and the street outside the building, with about thirty feet coned off, taking up one of the eastbound lanes.

I said, 'When you're on your way here, stop by Times Square and pick up some flyers for whatever's hot on Broadway right now. Maybe a dozen should do.'

Bloch didn't ask questions. She just agreed and hung up.

'You gonna bribe the cop with tickets for a show?' asked Harry.

'Not exactly,' I said.

Con artists, like lawyers, have to be able to adapt and improvise on their feet.

Quick thinking. Fast hands. Ideally, you should have both. That's what my father used to say. And if your head ain't as quick as your hands you can still get out of a tight spot, just with a little less elegance.

Harry leaned on his cane outside Elly's apartment building, Bloch beside him. I was across the street in the driver's seat of Harry's car, Lake beside me in the passenger seat. I'd put on Harry's overcoat and turned up the collar. I added his Yankees baseball hat and my sunglasses. Lake put on a beanie and folded up the collar of his overcoat. It was just a precaution. I didn't think for a second our mark would ask someone to check the city cameras. He would likely want to forget the whole episode. Still, it paid to be careful.

Lake had an old canvas shopping bag between his legs filled with an assortment of latex gloves, bottles of chemicals, evidence baggies and forensic kits. He fished out a pair of gloves and started putting them on.

'How much time do you think we'll have?' he asked.

'Best guess, eight minutes. Maybe longer.'

The elastic at the base of the glove snapped over his right wrist and he began wriggling his left hand into the next one.

'That's not a lot of time.'

'It'll have to be enough. Right now, the cops and the DA are holding all the cards and the trial will be right in front of us before we know it. The longer they hold out on us the less time we have. We need to get ahead of this.'

The second glove snapped over the skin on the back of his hand.

'I get the feeling we're already too late,' he said.

'The subway footage?'

He nodded, said, 'Someone knew we were going looking for that footage. Either the police or the guy with the suitcase.'

'Can you find out who it was?' I asked.

He looked at me, asked, 'Does it really matter? The footage is gone either way.'

'It matters. If we can prove the cops deleted the footage, then we have grounds for a dismissal. Shaky grounds, but it gives us a shot at killing the case against Elly. If it was the man with the suitcase, then maybe we get a step closer to finding him.'

A Silver Ford Taurus pulled up outside Elly's building, in a no-parking zone, about twenty feet from the construction barriers. Before Detective Bill Sacks got out of the Ford, he reached into the passenger footwell and came back up with a laminated, letter-sized card, which he laid on the dash. The suspension rocked as he got out of the car and stepped to the curb, shortly joining Harry and Bloch on the sidewalk. I could see a clear, plastic evidence bag in Sack's hands containing Elly's keys and the fob to access the front door.

A glance from Harry over Sacks's shoulder. The slightest nod. Sacks hadn't seen me.

We were on.

Sacks held out his empty hand to Harry for a handshake.

Harry looked at him and smiled warmly. But he didn't take it. Before he retired from the bench, Harry would have had no trouble in shaking Sacks's hand. It was probably Harry's former profession that provoked the greeting from Sacks: a mark of respect for the judiciary. He certainly didn't extend his hand to Bloch. But now Harry was a consultant in a criminal-defense firm. And you never knew who might notice you shaking hands with a cop. We had hundreds of clients, and those clients had relatives and friends, and any such sighting could look like some kind of shady deal.

Criminal clientele are the most suspicious people in the world.

I could see Sacks nodding, then waving that same hand, no doubt waving away a kind explanation from Harry on why he couldn't shake hands.

Sacks was an old professional. He knew exactly how the game was played and would take no offense.

Harry and Bloch turned, and the three of them made their way to the front of Elly's building.

I checked my watch, dialed 311 and gave a description of the Silver Ford Taurus and its exact location, then hung up.

I climbed out of the driver's seat. Lake came round the car with his bag of tricks in hand. We crossed the street and I checked Sacks's windshield.

The laminated card was blue, with the NYPD logo in one corner, the license plate of the car below it. The card said this vehicle was a property of NYPD and detectives were on call. With this card, Sacks could park anywhere in the city, any time of day or night, and he would never get a ticket, even if he was parked in front of a fire hydrant on double red lines.

In New York, everywhere is a tow zone.

I took the bundle of flyers for theatre shows out of my jacket pocket.

Lake went to the front of the vehicle, took a knee and bent the number plate up from the bottom, bent it down again and worked it back and forth a few times. The aluminum plate didn't take much effort to bend it out of shape.

This is the fastest way to take off a license plate. No tools required. Bending it back and forth enlarges the fixing holes on either side of the plate. Lake leaned back, pulled the plate right off over the screw heads.

Ten seconds.

Done.

I finished covering the windshield with the flyers, and Lake started on the back plate.

Ten seconds later, with the license plates in a storm drain, we made our way to the Starbucks next door to Elly's building. Lake ordered green tea. I ordered coffee. I took my bill fold from my pants pocket to pay the cashier.

'That's eleven seventy-five. Sorry, we only take cards,' she said.

I checked my back pocket, remembered I'd left my wallet in my other suit.

'Do you have any cards on you?' I asked.

'I'm lucky I remembered to wear socks,' said Lake.

'Please, allow me,' said the guy behind me in the line. He wore sunglasses and a bucket hat. He touched the card payment machine with his phone and it beeped.

'That's very kind of you,' I said, pulled a twenty from my fold and held it out to him.

He waved it away.

'Please, I insist.'

'It's fine. Anyway, I don't have change,' he said.

'Don't worry about it. Please, for your kindness.'

He smiled, nodded and took the cash.

New York had a bad reputation for many years. It still does, in certain parts of the city and the subways. What most people don't understand is that what makes this the greatest city in the world isn't the architecture and the history, it's the people.

The server put our drinks on the counter. We found a table.

'What the hell is green tea, anyway?' I asked.

'Now that I come to think of it, I have no idea,' said Lake.

'Is it, like, tea leaves and something else? Like mint? You should know this.'

'No clue, actually. It's not mint. That would be mint tea. Never thought about it before. It's green. It must be healthy.'

'It smells terrible.'

'Then it's definitely good for you.'

Lake talked more about his morning with Bloch. The VA hadn't been much help in finding Joseph Novak, the homeless man who had helped Elly when she got out onto the street and had vomited and passed out. A volunteer at the VE Center said they would pass on a message to Joe Novak, but they wouldn't give out any further information.

After a few minutes, an NYPD patrol car came in answer to my 311 call. It pulled up behind the Silver Taurus. A patrolman got out, checked the vehicle and got on his radio. If he had read the license plates and radioed for a check, it would have come back that this was an NYPD pool car.

No license plates, parked in a no-stopping zone and, considering the amount of flyers on the windshield, it had probably been there for some time.

Three minutes later, the tow truck arrived.

I took out my phone, sent a text to Harry. He would be standing near Elly's window, checking the street and keeping Sacks talking while Bloch took her time in Elly's apartment packing her a bag. Then when Harry saw the police towing Sacks's car, he would take a moment to point that out to the detective. That left us with a window of time where we could get in and search.

That was the plan.

We got up, left the coffee shop and stood with our backs to Elly's building, ten feet from the doors.

Detective Sacks came charging out of the building, his hand in the air, waving to the tow driver who was shackling straps to the wheels of the Taurus. I moved, caught the door before it shut and together we slipped inside, called the elevator and rode it to Elly's floor.

Harry was waiting outside the elevator.

'What took you so long?' said Harry.

'Sorry, how did it go?'

'Sacks is a baseball fan. I know nothing about baseball. It was hell. Bloch had to pretend she was looking for a purse that proved impossible to find. We'd better be fast. I got the impression he's already suspicious.'

Bloch came out of the bedroom, dropped a gym bag off her shoulder and put on latex gloves.

'I didn't see any bloodstains. The apartment looks normal apart from the bedroom. The bed is stripped to the mattress, but I didn't see any blood or signs of violence,' said Bloch.

'Let's go dark and take a look,' said Lake.

Harry and I closed the curtains in the kitchen, the living room, then went to every room, closing the blinds to ensure the place was as dark as possible.

Lake tossed Bloch what at first looked like a plastic bar about two feet long. She pressed the bottom of the bar and one side of it lit up with bright purple light. She moved into the corner of the room and began to sweep the floor. Lake had a similar dark light, and he started in the kitchen area, sweeping the light over the kitchen work surfaces and the floor.

It didn't take them long to clear the room. Even less time to sweep the bathroom.

Harry watched in silence. While the apartment was dark, I could still see well enough. There was nothing remarkable about the place. By Manhattan standards, it was a really nice apartment and would've cost a bundle every month. But there didn't appear to be any sign that this was a place where two people had been murdered not one week ago.

'Some spotting in the sink drain. Not enough. James probably cut himself shaving at one point. Let's go over the bedroom,' said Lake.

As they moved into the bedroom, I closed the door behind them. Harry and I then opened the blinds and curtains in the kitchen, living room and the bathroom. I checked the street, saw Sacks still arguing with the tow-truck driver and the patrolman. He outranked the patrolman, who would've ordered the tow-truck driver to unhook the vehicle. But the tow-truck driver was having none of it, by the looks of things. The Taurus was still halfway up the trailer ramp. It wasn't moving further up the ramp, but nor was it coming back down.

Tow-truck drivers, as a rule, don't give a shit.

'We'd better hurry,' I said.

I left the window, entered the bedroom behind Harry.

Lake had his light focused on the mattress. There was some spotting, but not a huge amount. UV lights, in the correct range, show up all kinds of stains that are not visible to the naked eye. Blood, bacteria and other bodily fluids are visible because they do not reflect the light back from the surface. He sprayed some of the spots, took a Q-tip to the stains and then placed it in a plastic tube.

Beside the double bed, Bloch was on her knees on the floor.

She swept the light over a large stain, the size of a dinner plate, only visible on the hardwood floor under the UV light. It was strange to see something materialize under the violet and purple light, and then disappear just as light left it. This staining did not appear as dark as the area that Lake was examining on the mattress.

Bloch took a sample, same method Lake had used: collecting the material on a Q-tip and then placing it in a sealed plastic tube. She'd send everything to Raymond, a forensic DNA expert in a local lab who did all of her work and brought back results quickly and efficiently.

'We're done,' said Bloch.

Harry swept open the curtains. I ran back to the living room, and checked the window, which gave the best view of the street below.

The Taurus was off the ramp. The NYPD patrol car and the tow truck were gone.

'Sacks is on his way. We need to move now,' I said.

Lake took Bloch's evidence tubes and the light, putting it all in his bag as Lake and I left the apartment, ran down the hall, past the elevator and through the door leading to the stairwell. Soon as we got down a floor, we slowed, and took our time on the stairs.

'Looks like that place has been cleaned up well. What do you think?' I asked.

'I've never seen a murder scene quite like it.'

'Could the cops have destroyed the scene on purpose? All the bedding was taken.'

'It will be in evidence. We don't know how the victims were killed, but at least we know how they weren't killed. They weren't shot or stabbed, nor did they die from any kind of blunt-force trauma. There's just not enough blood around.'

'What about the area Bloch found on the floor?'

'That wasn't blood, at least that's my best guess. Blood looks like a black hole under dark light. This was much lighter staining. Best guess, it's a concentrated area of bodily fluid and bacteria.'

I nodded, said, 'Then we do know how they died.'

Lake stopped on the landing, turned to face me.

'How?'

'The stain on the floor is probably vomit residue. My guess is James and Harriet were poisoned, same as Elly.'

My phone buzzed in my jacket.

Caller display read *CHRISTINE*. I hit answer.

'Hi, are you okay?' I asked.

'I'm just *peachy*. I take it you completely ignored everything I said to you the other day and you went to Cross's place and fucked him up?'

'Ah, I didn't touch the guy. Bloch and Lake went to see him and things got out of hand. I'm sorry, but maybe it will teach the guy a lesson.'

'It taught him a lesson alright. I just got out of the precinct. He's alleging I paid someone to beat him up. I got arrested and questioned by police. He's getting a restraining order against us. Don't do us any more favors.'

19

Logan

Logan watched as Eddie Flynn pulled a roll of cash from his pocket, peeled off a twenty-dollar bill and held it out to the Starbucks cashier.

She said they only take cards.

Flynn was embarrassed. He patted his pockets and turned to his companion, who said he didn't have a card with him.

'Please, allow me,' said Logan.

Logan pulled down the bucket hat on his head, leaned over and tapped his phone on the card-payment machine.

Eleven dollars and seventy-five cents to buy Eddie Flynn and his companion a coffee and a green tea. But Logan knew he would be buying a lot more for his money.

'That's very kind of you,' said Flynn, offering Logan the twenty-dollar bill.

Flynn was the same height as Logan. Perhaps a little slimmer, not as much muscle development, but he was fit and Logan knew he could be fast. You could see it. He had that way of moving, every footstep sure, body in perfect balance, shoulders back. The lawyer exuded confidence like an aura that glowed off his skin. He wasn't cocky. This wasn't false swagger. This was the real thing.

Logan waved away the twenty bucks.

A polite first refusal was customary. It was made in the knowledge that Logan's act of generosity was genuine. He didn't wish to diminish this selfless act, because he didn't wish Flynn to guess at an alternative move.

'Please, I insist,' said Flynn.

Various studies have been done on this very human, everyday scenario. Most of these behavioral studies had been commissioned by major charities – what makes people donate money? Why do people commit an act of generosity and in what circumstances? This precise scenario, buying a stranger a cup of coffee when they didn't have the correct method of payment, had been one such study.

Logan knew from the statistics that only twenty per cent of the sample study would be insistent, at this stage, on reimbursing the person who paid for their coffee.

Logan decided to push the interaction further.

'It's fine. Anyway, I don't have change,' said Logan.

'Don't worry about it. Please, for your kindness,' said Flynn, with a handsome smile.

A third and final offer.

Only eight per cent of the sample in the behavioral study offered to reimburse the person buying them coffee a third time. When he followed Flynn and Lake into the coffee shop, Logan had simply wanted to eyeball Flynn. Man to man. You can observe someone forever. You can know their routines, listen to their conversations, watch their every move until you understand exactly how they think and interact with the world, but Logan believed that you never truly know what is in someone's mind and heart until you look them in the eye.

Perhaps this was his psychology training. Perhaps it was some deeper knowledge.

But he needed that look from Flynn. To hold those eyes in his vision for a moment, stare into them and glean their secrets. He took as much from that as the experiment in paying for the coffee.

Logan nodded, took the twenty with a smile.

The entire interaction with Flynn had taken less than ten seconds. In that time, Logan had learned much.

Flynn was in the top eighth percentile of the population when it came to selflessness and generosity. This percentile group were also known for high intelligence, morality and empathy.

This fitted with Flynn's job – he was a lawyer. His entire career was dedicated to helping his clients. Given his talents as a lawyer, Flynn had to be a student of human behavior too. He would know Logan's initial refusal to take the money meant his initial act of paying for their drinks was a sincere act of kindness, made selflessly without expectations. And that, now, taking the money from Flynn was the polite thing to do. Reciprocal acts of kindness – so that both men could take the dopamine hit from goodwill.

Flynn and Lake took their drinks to a table. Logan ordered an espresso, paid with his phone again and then took a seat behind Flynn and Lake, a few tables away. The tables in between them were dirty, with used cups, plates and napkins on them. No one would sit there and block his view while there were clean tables free behind him and at the window. He could watch them, unobserved as they kept an eye on the cop's Ford Taurus.

Only problem was the coffee spill on one of the tables.

And the drip . . . *drip* . . . *drip* . . . onto the floor.

Logan gritted his teeth, tried to ignore it.

Sound can evoke powerful memories. For some, it's a song – usually from childhood. For Logan, that particular sound brought back memories that he would rather stayed buried.

His mind flashed on an image.

Red.

So much red.

He shook his head, tossed a napkin onto that table to stem the dripping and listened hard.

The coffee shop was busy, like everywhere in the city, so listening in was more difficult. They kept their voices low and their eyes on the street. Logan was good at listening – part of his job. The man sitting with Flynn was about five-ten, wearing a creased white shirt, open at the collar, and a black suit, which could have used a press and dry-clean. His hair was curly and kind of wild, and he had a large shopping bag at his feet.

Logan caught some of their conversation. Enough to discern their relationship. The man was a private investigator. They had been looking for security footage to corroborate Elly's story. They had found none so far. Logan knew their search would find nothing. He had been careful. It was clear from their conversation they were also looking for someone. A witness. The homeless man. They had spoken to two men and gotten a name.

Joseph Novak.

They had tried the VA. They would keep looking.

The homeless man was still eluding Logan's efforts to find him. He was the only living witness who could corroborate Elly's story. It was essential that this man disappear, permanently.

Now Logan had a name to go with the face. Joseph Novak had helped a woman in the street, a stranger who was in trouble. Who was sick.

He would pay for that act of kindness with his life.

An NYPD patrol car pulled up outside the Starbucks and it drew the attention of Flynn and his companion.

Just before they had come into the coffee shop, Logan had watched Flynn cover the windshield of a Ford Taurus with flyers, and Lake had removed and discarded the vehicle plates.

Shortly after, a tow truck arrived.

Flynn was a serious player.

Smart. A risky move to pull, but one where the risk could be assessed and minimized.

Logan leaned back in his seat, took a sip of espresso and smiled. In all these years, he had never felt in any real danger. With this project, Elly had survived. And she had asked a stranger for help – Eddie Flynn.

This man, Flynn, was a clear threat. He would have to be neutralized.

And now, having bought him a cup of coffee, Logan knew Flynn's weakness.

And exactly how to exploit it.

He opened the browser on his phone, accessed the public-records website and typed in Flynn's name, paying the search fee on the credit card he'd saved to his phone. First, he searched birth records. There were not many Flynns in the database, and only one equating to Flynn's approximate age. He paid the fee for the birth record, made a mental note of Flynn's date of birth and then paid for another search. He had needed Flynn's date of birth for a criminal records check.

No results.

He typed in Flynn's name and date of birth into a general public records database, and paid another ninety-five dollars for a search.

Flynn had been married. Christine White. Birth records flagged his name again as the father of Amy Flynn. The last entry was for a divorce. Christine White and Eddie Flynn had gone their separate ways just two years ago.

Logan searched under the name Christine White.

She had remarried a year ago. There was an additional entry, with today's date.

Restraining order. Christine White is not to be within one hundred yards of Arthur Cross. There was an arrest record for yesterday.

Logan leaned forward. He searched the internet for Arthur Cross.

And he read all that he could on this new, intriguing individual.

Mr. Cross had potential.

Logan left the Starbucks, dipped his head, using his hat to obscure his face as he passed the cop arguing with the tow-truck driver. Logan crossed the street and turned a corner, heading back to the lot where he had parked his rental car.

Cross would have to wait. Tonight, Logan had a date.

20

Elly

Elly picked through the items on her breakfast tray. Powdered eggs that tasted grainy. A yogurt from a brand she had never heard of before. She didn't go near the fruit in a sealed plastic cup.

Suze took her roll.

She wasn't hungry, and knew that if she did eat something there was every chance she would vomit it up within minutes. Her stomach was going crazy. As she sat at a table with Suze, she noticed blood on the table. Fresh blood. It came from the cuticles around her thumb. Elly had picked the flesh away from her nail.

Same thing had happened in high school.

Elly was smart, kind of geeky, not funny, and she didn't think of herself as good-looking or cool. She guessed that none of her fellow high-school students did either. She had few friends. Kept to herself. Did her homework over lunch, alone, picking through a different meal from a plastic tray in her school cafeteria, with the same kind of anxiety ripping through her system, and the nail on her index finger unconsciously ripping through the skin on the left side of her thumbnail.

She remembered one particularly bad lunch in that old cafeteria. She had saved up for a new pair of boots. Black biker books, ankle length. With a silver buckle. She'd seen a picture of Katy Perry wearing the same boots on Facebook and desperately wanted to emulate one of her teen idols.

Only problem was Elly never wore anything with a heel. Vans and cheap Nikes had been staple footwear growing up. She remembered that morning, and the looks from the blond witches who hung around the staircase at the entrance, the jocks who gathered at the lockers in the hallway and the geeks too – everyone noticed her boots. And Elly never forgot that attention, because it was the first time she had ever felt even a modicum of self-confidence.

The confidence lasted until lunchtime, when she stumbled on the way to her table in the cafeteria, spilling half her lunch tray on the floor in front of the whole school. Everyone laughed.

Things were different back then. In the hell of high school, Elly could always come home to her parents. She was an only child, so she got a lot of love and attention from her parents automatically, but they were the kind of people who loved being parents. Family was a big thing in her home. Her mother, Susan, always described herself as a homemaker, even though she had her own pottery business, which she ran from the garage. Elly remembered long evenings in the garage during the summer, her mom at the potter's wheel, clay in her hands and her foot depressing the pedal to spin the wheel in time to the music her father had playing in the house. Her dad, Stewart, owned a car-repair shop. They would sit on old car seats that Dad had brought home from a wreck and watch her mom, listening to Dad's records from the eighties, sipping coffee and talking. She remembered that her parents worked with their hands and their hearts. A lot of love went into everything they did, be it making a fruit bowl or fixing a clutch – the oil and dirt engrained in her father's hands and the clay residue that coated her mom's fingernails – it was all evidence of the love they put into their work, and their family. Elly could never master pottery, and she was no good with a wrench either. Instead, when Elly was nervous, she picked at her cuticles until they bled.

She didn't have clay dust, or oil on her hands – only dried blood. Perhaps her parents sensed her anxiety. Elly could tell her mom and dad anything. Even falling over in the canteen because of her stupid expensive boots. They had laughed when she told them the story, and their laughter took away her embarrassment and shame at the memory.

Falling over was part of life, her father had said.

You always get back up again.

She missed her parents a lot.

Now, more than ever.

Elly sat alone, again, at a table, in a max-security facility, and picked at the skin surrounding her nails until she felt the blood on her fingers.

Rosie's wasn't high school. It was much worse. She guessed she was still in shock about the murder of her husband and best friend, because, while she had cried for them, she was also crying for herself. She had no time to process what had happened to her. She couldn't mourn her husband or her friend. Her emotions were already messed up, because these were the two people who had meant the most to her in the world, and they had betrayed her – and now they were dead. Somehow, it made the betrayal permanent.

It could now never be resolved. There was no reconciliation, no closure, no way of dealing with those emotions. Their deaths were a wound to Elly. One she knew would never heal.

Even now, sitting with Suze, watching her, Elly's fear and anxiety was constant. Yet some part of her brain told her to pay attention to Suze. That this was important.

This was survival.

She noticed the way Suze hunched over her breakfast tray, never once looking at what she was eating – her eyes forward, scanning the room, scanning the faces of the other detainees, assessing threats, watching hushed conversations, calculating, eating and waiting for the first move.

'You bleedin',' said Suze.

'What?' asked Elly.

'Your thumb. You bleedin'.'

'Sorry, I do that when I'm nervous.'

'I got some Band-Aids in the cell. You better keep that shit clean in here. All kinds of infections going around.'

Elly nodded, was about to speak.

'Don't thank me yet. You could be doin' a whole lot more bleedin' before tomorrow,' she said, and gave a slight nod by way of indication.

Following Suze's gaze, Elly saw the woman, Nance, and the small blond girl huddled in the corner with five other women. At first, Elly didn't notice anything sinister about the group. Then she saw that as they spoke, they covered their mouths, and their eyes collectively zeroed in Elly's direction. Nance took something from one of the other women. It was thin and black, but it had a shine to it.

'She got herself a shiv,' said Suze.

Fear is a strange thing.

It's hard to tell if it's physical, emotional or psychological. Maybe all three.

But when it bites it bites hard.

There is nothing else like it on this earth.

Elly felt every limb freeze. Her muscles. Her lungs.

Her heart.

Every nerve ending, every tiny hair follicle on her skin, tightened in alert. Her mouth was suddenly dry, her throat tight. With her eyes frozen on the thin black blade that Nance slid into her sock, Elly's mind shut down.

'I told them to lay off,' said Suze. 'They're not listening. They gonna cut you. Then they gonna ask you for money.'

Elly's mouth opened, but no words came. Tears filled her eyes and she started to shake.

'Wo-won't the guards see?' said Elly.

'Sure. They gonna take a cut of whatever you give to Nance. There ain't no way out of this for you. You gotta pay 'cause you sure as shit can't fight.'

'I don't have any money in here. I'm not sure I have anything left once I pay for my bail.'

'They don't care. You get cut and you pay. Or . . .'

'Can you help me?' asked Elly.

'I can try. Stay here.'

Suze got up and strolled over to Nance and the group of women in the corner. Elly tried to listen, to hear any snatches of their hushed conversation, but all she could hear was her own heartbeat thumping in her ears.

The group of women crowded around Suze. Elly heard them whispering.

To any casual observer it was nothing more than a conversation. Until it wasn't.

Until the scrawny blonde from Elly's cell stepped forward.

Something shiny flashed in her hand.

And she stabbed Suze in the belly.

The alarms sounded like thunder. Steel doors banged open. Boots thudded on the floor. Cries and screams rent the air and Elly looked on as Suze fell to the floor, and the blonde continued to stab at her left side.

They landed in a pile and were enveloped by corrections officers, one of them grabbing the blonde round the waist and hoisting her clean into the air before pivoting and slamming her down onto the concrete floor, face first.

Calls for a medic.

The blonde was cuffed, unconscious, and dragged out by two COs, her face a bloody ruin. One of the COs picked up the shiv, while more worked on Suze.

Elly got up, moved toward them, trying to help, but she was told to back away.

The chaos was over as a medical team came in, and the house fell quiet.

Suze was carried out in the arms of a medic, her blood dark and shiny on the floor.

And, in the corner, her back against the wall, Nance glared at her, wearing a wicked smile.

There would be no one to protect her in the cell tonight against Nance.

With all that she had been through, Elly knew if she didn't do something she may not live another day. She stared at the bank of three phones on the wall. Soon as the COs left, she had to make a call.

Her life depended on it.

21

Logan

Logan sat at a bar in the St. Regis, wearing his Armani suit, Versace shirt, Ferragamo Oxfords and the Cartier wristwatch.

He had made a mental note to take off the watch if things turned dark later. He didn't want to get blood on the timepiece.

He swirled the hand-cut cube of ice in his whiskey glass. He drank Nikka Yoichi, twenty-year-old single malt. Depending on the bar, you could pay between two hundred and three hundred and fifty dollars for a single pour. The bottle was six grand, retail, if you could find one. He only drank one glass, though. Not because he couldn't afford it, but because he didn't want the alcohol to dull his senses.

'Hello, stranger,' said a voice.

He got up off his barstool and smiled at his date.

Grace wore a little black dress, silver heels and a delicate silver chain round her neck. The pendant was a heart-shaped locket. Scratched. A little beaten up, but clearly treasured. The dress was off the rack, and the color had faded slightly on the shoulders, as if it had been worn on many hot summer days. Still, it fitted well. Her hair was up. She smelled sweet, like strawberries and lime.

'You look wonderful,' he said.

'So do you,' she said with a smile, a little out of breath, and not from the exertion of walking through the lobby. Logan noticed a vein pulsing in her long throat.

She was nervous.

He pulled out a barstool, and held it steady while Grace stepped up and shifted onto the seat. It was then that Logan noticed the seam at the back of her dress, just to the right of the zipper. The stitching was thicker for about two inches on this side of the seam, and some of the thread was a dark navy color instead of black. This suggested the dress was not only cheap, but old, and had been repaired more than once.

She ordered a mojito and they talked a little about life in the city. As well as studying English Literature at NYU, Grace worked in a Starbucks in the Bronx five days a week and waited tables in a restaurant on the weekends.

'When do you have time to study?'

'I'm always reading. On the subway, on my break – books for college and for me. Mostly I like dark romance.'

'What's dark romance?'

'It's like a romance novel, but it's fantasy and the characters kinda hate each other at first, or sometimes the girl has sworn an oath to kill the guy, or the guy is a vampire or a monster or something, but they fall in love despite their differences . . . that kind of thing. It's cool. What do you read?'

'Mostly academic studies and non-fiction, for work.'

'What do you do?'

'I work in behavioral psychology and behavioral economics. I advise companies how to sell their products.'

'And you do that through psychology?'

'Yeah, once you understand why people buy something, then you can sell them anything.'

'How does it work?'

'Well, take you for example. You performed an act of kindness on the subway—'

'Not the noodles again,' said Grace, laughing.

'Come on, you asked. You did that because you had the personal, environmental and situational capacity to do so.'

Clasping her hand to her forehead, Grace laughed again and shook her head.

'I don't get it,' she said.

'Okay, so there was a study done by John Darley and Daniel Batson. They took seminary students studying for the priesthood and asked them questions about why they wanted to be priests – was it about helping people or was it to do with their faith? Now, the questions had nothing to do with the study. The students were told after they had completed the questionnaire to go to another building on campus and give a presentation. Some were told they were already late for the presentation, and some were told they could take their time to get to the other building. This is the real part of the study: on their way across the campus, every student saw a guy lying in a doorway, coughing and groaning. Only ten percent of the students who were in a hurry stopped to help the guy. Sixty-three per cent of the students who were informed they could take their time getting to the next building stopped to help.'

With her elbow on the bar and her large blue eyes fixed on Logan, Grace smiled and listened, transfixed.

'Here's the kicker,' said Logan. 'Half of the students were on their way to give a talk about what they'd learned in seminary school and how that could be applied in later life, the other half were giving a talk on the parable of the Good Samaritan.'

'The Good Samaritan?'

'Yes, the story of the Samaritan who stops on the road to Jericho to help a wounded traveler, after a Jewish priest and a Levite had passed the wounded man on the road without helping.'

'Okay, so the priests who were on their way to give a talk on the Good Samaritan, they all helped the guy lying in the doorway?'

'No, it made no difference, even if that Bible story was right in the forefront of their minds. The only thing that made a difference was whether they had time to stop and help the man.'

'Wow. So, most of the priests didn't stop to help the stranger because they were worried they'd be late to give a talk on the Good Samaritan. That's crazy.'

'It's how most people's minds work. Kindness is relative to our capacity, which includes whether we have the time and the inclination to help others. So, getting back to the noodles—'

'Not the noodles *again*?' she said. A flush of embarrassment painted her cheeks a darker shade of ruby.

'Yes, the noodles. You had three choices on the subway. You could have ignored the situation and let the woman's groceries fall on the floor. You could have woken her up and told her about the bag spilling, but you did something else – you just helped her, not expecting any reward nor anyone else to see this small act of kindness. What academics forget about that study with the trainee priests is that ten per cent of them who were in a rush to get somewhere still stopped to help. I think you're one of the ten per cent, Grace. And I like that.'

Logan hesitated, staring at Grace, a strange warmth flowing through him, suddenly embarrassed – worried that he had perhaps said too much.

'I think you're weird, Logan,' she said with a smile, and added, 'And *I* like that.'

That warm sensation became hot blood flushing his cheeks.

'You're very special,' said Logan.

'I'm not special,' said Grace. 'Where I grew up, you helped your neighbors.'

'Where are you from originally?'

'Just outside of Maysville, Georgia. My family worked the watermelon farms. Nobody in that area ever had very much, but what we had we shared with those who had nothing. It was just the way I was brought up. I remember one time old farmer Greggs went missing. He was the meanest old son-of-a-bitch in the whole county. But his wife was a gentle soul. Greggs treated everyone like they were dirt on his boots, but when he went missing everybody went out looking for him. We searched those fields all summer long. It was hot too, but we never gave up, because there was a woman in that farmhouse going crazy with worry. That's where I come from. That's how I was raised. You help people, and you don't expect anything in return.'

'Did they ever find the melon farmer?'

She laughed, said, 'That's the worst part. His wife got a letter from him a couple of months after he went missing saying he was living in Atlanta. He'd met a stripper named Candy and he wanted a divorce.'

'So you all went through that for nothing?'

'It wasn't for nothing. His wife saw us out there every day. Looking for him. She felt the community's arms fold around her. That's what really mattered.'

This woman he had seen who had so intrigued him was now sitting enjoying his company. She had an easy manner, but it was more than that. When Logan was growing up, his family lived upstate, and there was a lake surrounded by woods not far from their house. When his dark thoughts seemed overwhelming, he would ride his bike through the trail in the woods until he found the lake, and he would sit on an old tree stump and watch the autumn breezes rippling the water's surface. It was quiet and peaceful, and it soothed his troubled mind. After an hour at the lake, Logan's thoughts of murder were dulled. His desires cooled.

He had not been back to that lake in many years. He had missed it.

Being with Grace, he felt the same soothing sensation as when he had sat on that old stump by the lake. He didn't want to kill her. Not yet at least. For now, he wanted more of this feeling. She was a cool balm on his wounded soul.

But more than anything else, for the first time in his life, Logan didn't feel alone.

'Do you want to go somewhere and get some food?' he asked.

'Sure,' said Grace with a smile, 'as long as it isn't noodles.'

22

Kate

Kate held her cell phone to her ear, and listened to the dead silence as Elly ended her call.

It was late. Everyone else had left the office. She was alone, panicked and had no idea what the hell to do. Elly would be calling her back in ten minutes. Kate had told her she needed a little time to think.

She got up from her desk, took a breath, put her hands on top of her head.

They don't teach this shit in law school. You learn case law. Statute. The basics. How to prepare for a trial. How to write a legal brief. How to stand up and speak in court.

There's no class on what to do when your client is about to get stabbed in jail.

She called Eddie, relayed Elly's conversation.

'They stabbed her cell mate Suze so Elly would have no protection tonight. The COs told her Suze is stable in the hospital wing, but she won't be back in that cell for a long time. There's a woman in her cell called Nance who has a shiv. She thinks Elly has money. Elly thinks she's going to get cut up in her cell tonight. She's in real danger, Eddie. We don't know anyone in her house who can protect her.'

'Goddamn it, all this because of Busken. There's no way we can get anyone friendly transferred to her house. Not this fast,' said Eddie.

'What if she tells the COs about Nance's shiv and the threats? Or I could try and get hold of the governor and tell him?' asked Kate.

'That's the worst possible thing that could happen. If we do that, or, even worse, *she* tells the CO, then Elly becomes a snitch. That makes her a target for *every* inmate in that jail. They won't just hurt her or threaten her, they'll kill her.'

'Then what the hell are we gonna do?'

'There's only one thing she can do. You're not going to like it. She's not going to like it, but there's no alternative . . .'

Kate listened, began to make notes on her legal pad, then stopped.

She didn't want to write this down, not anywhere.

'Eddie, I can't do that. I can't tell her this. I'm a lawyer.'

'You're *her* lawyer, but the law won't keep her safe in Rosie's. I know there's risk in this for both of you. But it's way less risky than Elly spending a night in a pitch-black cell with someone who is going to cut her up or worse. There's no other way.'

Since Kate began working with Eddie, she noticed pretty quickly that her partner didn't have much respect for the law. Eddie stepped over the line when he needed to, but always to help someone else. She had looked the other way so many times when her professional duty as an attorney was to abide by the law. In many ways, Eddie had never really left his con-artist life behind. He'd never left those streets where he had plied his trade.

But she took no part in his schemes. That wasn't the way she was brought up. Sure, she was different now to when she first started. Sometimes, she had to push right up to that dividing line of what's legal and what's not, but she never crossed it.

This situation was crystal clear. There was only one way to help Elly make it through the night in Rosie's. And if she did what Eddie suggested then Kate would be jumping over that line for the first time. Whether she got caught or whether anyone could prove what she had done were other questions, and in many ways the answers to those questions didn't matter.

Because Kate would always know what she had done.

'There's really no other way, is there?' she asked.

'Not that I can see. I know this is difficult for you, but—'

'Difficult? It's illegal.'

'Of course it is, and you don't have to do it. I can call Elly and—'

'I know she's our client, but she reached out to me. I can't throw this all onto your shoulders. I have to stand on my own two feet sometimes.'

'You stand a lot taller than I do, Kate Brooks. You're smarter and tougher than me, and you're a better person too. It's okay to let me take one for the team. I don't mind. It's not like I haven't done this shit before.'

'And what happens if I have to do something like this some day, and you're not here? It's my responsibility. I just wish there was another way.'

'If you don't do this, Elly is going to get hurt. They don't want to kill her, but they could put her in the infirmary and accidents happen. We can't rely on the crazies in Rosie's not to go too far. She could die in there tonight.'

'So either I compromise everything in my professional duty or Elly gets beaten and stabbed? That's what you're telling me?'

'Welcome to the New York criminal bar practice. If you can't do it, I understand. But somebody has to tell Elly what to do. For what it's worth, there's a way to tell her this without you losing your law license or the DA prosecuting you . . .'

'I know how to do it and not get caught. Whether Castro or the NYPD can prove I broke the law, doesn't matter. *I* will know what I've done.'

'Then let me—'

'Eddie, it has to be my decision.'

She heard him sighing on the end of the line.

'I know you'll do the right thing, Kate.'

'Yeah? And what's the right thing here, exactly?'

She hung up the call and then tore the page out of her legal pad, ripped it up and put it in the trash.

Elly would be calling back in less than sixty seconds. Kate stared at her cell phone on the desk and chewed her lip. Eddie once told her that sometimes a case takes away a little piece of you. The question is whether you let that happen. The best lawyers, the ones who care most about their clients, they pay that price.

She picked up a pen and tapped it on the desk, staring at the phone.

She didn't want to give up this piece of her. It belonged not just in her mind, but in her soul. Her father had been a cop. Twenty years in the NYPD. If she had asked him what to do, he would say there's nothing she could do. That what will happen in that cell, in the dark, wasn't her problem. She was just a lawyer. She could only do so much. Her responsibilities were to represent her client, in court, and that's it.

The screen on her phone lit up. The pulsing vibration from the incoming call sent the device dancing across her desk.

Kate's mouth was dry as she picked it up, answered the call.

And made her decision.

All of the detainee's phone calls are monitored. It didn't matter if she told her lawyer she was under threat; she hadn't made a complaint to the COs so they could do nothing. But it also made things difficult for Kate, because she couldn't tell Elly exactly what she had to do. Not outright.

Kate was subtle in relaying the information from Eddie.

Hypotheticals.

In the unlikely event that this might happen, this is what the CO response will be.

They talked for a few minutes.

Elly hung up.

Kate leaned back in her chair and stared at the ceiling. She had crossed a line tonight. She told herself this was a one-off. Never to be repeated.

Part of her knew that once she had opened this door, she would have to keep walking through it. That there was no going back.

She closed her eyes and thought about Elly.

23
Elly

'Hey, bitch, you done on that fuckin' call yet?' said the woman standing behind Elly.

It was difficult to tell the woman's age. She had been standing behind Elly in the line for the payphones for only a minute, but patience clearly wasn't one of her virtues. Elly had turned round only once, when the woman first came up and stood behind her. She had her arms folded across her chest, a comb stuck in matted hair, lips pursed tightly together. Tattoos, some animals, some indistinguishable words and letters, crisscrossed her chest and throat and crept up onto her cheeks and pock-marked face. Perhaps some of the tattoos were there in an effort to hide some scarring, but they were so poorly done it was hard to tell. It looked as if she had fallen into a printing press.

The woman had hungry, fierce eyes and scars on her knuckles and hands.

Elly listened to Kate, and the woman behind her tapped her foot.

'Bitch, you better hurry the fuck up or I'm gonna beat your ass.'

As Elly listened, she understood the subtext of what Kate was saying. She couldn't spell it out, but the advice and the path ahead were clear.

'Kate, I-I understand. I'm scared. I'm so fucking scared,' whispered Elly.

'You have every right to be scared. But I know how strong you are,' said Kate.

Elly's heart hammered in her chest. Her fingers trembled as she raised them to wipe the tears from her face. Her legs were shaking, and she held the phone to her ear with one hand, and the other hugged her belly.

The woman behind her sighed and cursed and tapped her foot impatiently.

'I don't know if I can do this,' said Elly.

'You have to survive in there,' said Kate. 'Don't forget who you are. You've been through hell, but you're still here. We're going to fight for you when you get out. We'll be standing right with you, but now you've got to do whatever it takes.'

'Thank you,' said Elly.

Elly hung up the phone.

Fear shuddered through her entire body.

She had felt like this before.

At college, in class one day, when a cop walked into the lecture hall. He interrupted the lecturer, Mr. Connors, and he had looked at the class until his eyes settled on Elly. And he pointed at her and then gestured for her to come down.

She had followed the cop and Mr. Connors into the hallway, at first afraid in case the police had made some kind of mistake and thought maybe Elly had done something wrong. Elly had her parents' conscientious nature – she never did anything wrong – not even a parking ticket.

The cop told her that her mother, Susan, had died in a car wreck. That she should go see her father, Stewart, who was at the hospital. Mr. Connors asked if she had a friend who could drive her. She didn't. Mr. Connors drove, and Elly spent the entire journey in total fear. The shock was taking care of any sense of loss at her mother's death – that crushing grief would come later. She remembered her father sitting on a metal chair in the waiting room of the hospital, consumed by loss and sorrow.

Her fear disappeared when she saw him. She felt his pain.

After the funeral, she had stayed home for a while, and they comforted each other. At that point in her life, Elly was almost out of money anyway – college was a struggle; she had to work jobs most nights and her credit cards were still maxed. But she didn't care, she had to be with her father for a while. Until he sent her back to college, back to her life, because that would be what her mother wanted.

Her father died a year later. A massive coronary at home, while he slept. But Elly knew otherwise. It wasn't heart disease that killed her father. His heart broke when he buried his wife. Even after he was gone, he still looked after Elly. She inherited their house, and sold it to pay her debts and find a place in the city.

Elly had to stand on her own two feet. She couldn't rely on anyone else. She had learned that through her husband's betrayal with her so-called best friend.

Elly couldn't let loss kill her like it had her father.

She had to stand.

She had to listen to Kate.

She had to fight.

'Move your bitch-ass—' said the woman behind her.

Elly swung round and punched the woman, hard, in the face.

Her momentum sent her off balance. She had never hit anyone before. A shooting pain bit into her wrist, she fell on top of the woman and they both ended up on the ground.

Cries and howls and whoops went up from the other women in the house. The woman began to claw at Elly's back and grabbed her hair just as the doors banged open and the COs rushed in.

One moment Elly was on top of this woman and, the next, two men, either side of her, had picked her up by the arms and legs and were hauling her out of there.

Elly was panting, the adrenalin coursing through her veins robbing her of breath.

'Solitary twelve,' she heard one of them say as they slammed the house door closed behind her.

It was the only way.

Outside the house, in the corridor, the COs placed Elly on the ground. One of them flipped her over, face down on the cold painted concrete floor. Their hands were hard and strong on her wrists as she was shackled, and she knew there would be bruising, but she also knew that she was out of that cell for tonight.

Kate's words echoed in her mind.

Elly, the communal areas of your detainment house are constantly monitored by security cameras. If one inmate launches a violent attack on another, then that inmate is removed from the house and placed into solitary confinement . . . It is unlikely that the victim of the assault will co-operate with authorities, because they don't want to be seen as a snitch.

Elly would spend the next twenty-four hours, at least, in solitary. A small bare cell with a bed and a toilet, and nothing and no one else.

For some, it was torture.

For Elly, committing that assault had probably saved her life.

24

Logan

Logan sat in his rental car outside the clinic, waiting for the man to come out.

He took out his phone and opened the photo album.

It was a picture of a refrigerator door, with bills and final demands pinned to it with magnets. The photo had been taken last night, in Grace's apartment. Rent, tuition fees and electric – Grace was behind on everything. She had come back into the kitchen after using the bathroom and they had enjoyed a coffee together.

It had felt awkward. Logan liked Grace. Last night, sitting beside her on her old couch, he knew what could happen next. It was a question of who would make the next move. Logan had felt sweat on his forehead. His heart rate was up. His stomach churned, and not just from the bad coffee.

She was beautiful, sweet and somehow remarkably innocent. Something in her eyes captivated him.

Logan had felt confused on that couch. Not about the situation. This was an internal conflict.

Sitting there, listening to Grace talk about her love of books, he couldn't help but wonder what she would look like in bed, asleep, with the morning sun's first rays falling across her face. And yet another part of him wondered whether her eyes would still have the same glow after he had strangled the life from her body.

Sitting on that couch last night, he had blinked and cleared his throat, as if this might help clear his mind.

It didn't work.

Images flashed before him.

The two of them in bed. Grace's soft hair on his shoulder, her breath on his cheek and her fingers stroking his bare chest. He could almost feel the softness and the warmth of her.

And then the image was replaced by one of shock on her face as Logan grabbed her throat and squeezed.

He shook his head, as if he had been trying to dislodge that last image from his brain.

'It's funny, you know?' said Grace. 'Where I grew up, I could walk for a mile and not see a single other person on the road. Here, I'm just surrounded by millions of people, but the difference is at home I never felt like I was alone. I never had that feeling until I came here.'

His heart was beating way too fast, the pulse loud in his ears along with a single thought – God, we are so alike. She understands me. I understand her. We feel the same way. The connection with Grace made him feel like he was a puzzle piece that never quite fitted together with the rest, and it wasn't until he'd met her that he realized she didn't fit in either, but together everything made sense – together they fitted.

It was a joyous moment for Logan. But also terrifying.

'I'm sorry. I have to leave,' he said.

He watched the surprise register on her face.

'Oh, you have to be somewhere now?'

'It's not that,' said Logan, getting up and moving to the kitchen. He poured his coffee into the sink and rinsed his mug, then placed it on the drainer.

'It's just, if I stay here, I don't know what might happen between us,' he said.

Grace said, 'Wait, you don't have to go. We can just talk if—'

'No, I'm sorry. I don't . . . I don't really date. Things are moving fast. I'm going to be busy for a few days with work. Maybe I can call you at the weekend?'

She got up from the couch and followed him to the hallway.

'Look, I'm sorry if I said something to offend you or—'

'No, Grace,' Logan said firmly. A trickle of sweat ran down his left temple, onto his cheek. He was breathing hard now, fighting the urge to take her head in his hands. For what reason he didn't yet know. Either to gently draw her into a passionate kiss, or violently twist her head, snapping her vertebrae.

'You are just . . . perfect, Grace. And I *will* call you. The truth is I like you. I like you so much that I don't want to do anything tonight that might mess this up.'

Her confusion and slight irritation seemed to disappear with those last words, as if she understood. She smiled.

Logan didn't want to kill Grace. He knew that. The images of her death were simply his subconscious warning him. He could not remember having had such a special evening before. Even though he had just met this woman, he had watched her from afar for a long time. His feelings for her were somehow supercharged. It was more than a crush, or any base desire.

If he were not a sociopath, he might simply surmise that he was experiencing the first flush of love.

And it frightened him.

The memory of his hasty exit from her apartment brought heat to his neck, and he found himself clenching his jaw. Logan stared at his phone, at the picture of bills and final demands on her fridge and decided then to help Grace with her problems.

Logan loved solving all kinds of problems.

When he was a child, he never really understood toys. He once caught his mother looking at him strangely. He was in kindergarten, surrounded by other boys and girls who were involved in roleplaying games – making up their own stories as they ran around with plastic unicorns, soldiers, fluffy animals or wearing cowboy hats or long scarves, which doubled as the veils of a princess on her wedding day.

Logan had sat in the middle of the floor, bewildered by the goings-on around him, unable to see the attraction of inventing stories or living in a fantasy world. He couldn't understand why anyone would want to do that when the real world was so fascinating. While the other children played, Logan sat with his puzzle books.

He could read and complete simple math problems from the age of three. The problems came from a book that had a shiny red apple on the cover, one which Logan thought was particularly juvenile. One day, when he was much older, he found his father's sudoku book. It was only half completed, and he finished the rest of the book in a single afternoon.

When his father came home from work that night, he grabbed the book from the coffee table and showed it to him. Logan expected his father to be pleased. He wanted him to be proud. Something that Logan had not yet experienced.

Logan had completed twelve puzzles to finish the book.

That night, his father lashed him with his belt twelve times. One for every puzzle. That was his father's way. No emotion. No love. Nothing but pain. His father wanted Logan to know that he shouldn't take things that didn't belong to him. The twelve bloody welts on his back were a reminder for a month or two.

So Logan did his own puzzles. Crossword puzzles were a new challenge, but he found, as he grew older and read more, and his vocabulary expanded at an exponential rate, he could decipher the clues more easily.

Logan was perhaps fourteen years old when he realized that there was a greater mystery out there in the world. Something that had baffled the world's greatest minds for centuries. The problem was understanding the human mind. Why do people do the things that they do?

Why did his father beat him so much?

And why didn't his mother care?

His father was a banker, and his mother held parties in the house that he wasn't allowed to attend. He understood their so-called social roles, but he couldn't figure out why they didn't love him.

What determines human behavior? It wasn't an equation that could easily be written down, nor was it a cryptic, or linguistic question. Numbers, letters and words – these things were tools that he could easily use. People were what ultimately confounded him. And at that age, and ever since, his lack of understanding of people, their emotions and behaviors, had led him into isolation.

He could stand in the middle of the schoolyard, surrounded by hundreds of his fellow students and classmates, and feel totally and completely alone, like an alien that had just landed on earth. His comprehension of science, mathematics and language far exceeded most of the school faculty, yet he could not understand why girls sometimes giggled as he passed them in the hallway, why the boys were obsessed with sports, nor why music played such a huge part in all of it.

Logan didn't get it.

There had to be a process, a method, an approach, some tactic or way of understanding other people.

In high school, he bought his first book on psychology. It was an old, out-of-date textbook he'd found in the Strand Bookstore. That night, he'd read it cover to cover. All two hundred and thirty-eight pages. When he'd finished, it was almost dawn. He'd made a mental note of some of the names that had kept cropping up in the text – Freud, Adler, Wundt, Jung, Pavlov, Skinner, Thorndike and Piaget. It was a night he would never forget. He felt as though he had found a key to what he had been looking for all his life. A way to understand the people around him.

Most of the book dealt with something called mental disorders, or diseases of the mind. But there were other sections that simply talked about behavior and why people do the simplest things, why they make the same mistakes. This subject was a map he could follow. The names of those psychologists were markers along his route to knowledge and understanding, not just of other human beings and wider society, but also a mirror through which he could look deeper into himself.

For Logan had read something in that book, a chapter about a category of people known as sociopaths. According to the book, and backed up later by further reading, these people did not have a mental illness, although some had symptoms of mental disorders including narcissism and a lack of empathy. Logan knew that night that he was reading about himself.

And he was reading about his father.

He wasn't scared. He didn't really feel fear, which could also have been part of his symptoms. If anything, he felt calm. He was not alone in this world. There were others like him. There had always been others like him. That was also the brilliant part of the book. He learned that certain aspects of human behavior had not changed in thousands of years, perhaps hundreds of thousands. And whatever the book said about sociopaths didn't really change his view of himself. He could already see the advantages open to him.

He could do things that others could not.

There was no doubt what Logan would study in college, and beyond. He would dedicate his life to this field so that he could first know himself, and then know everyone else.

So that he could understand people.

And control them.

He wondered how long it would take to understand the man he was waiting for.

That man had just walked out of the clinic across the street from where Logan had parked. He had his arm in a sling and an elaborate padded plastic brace covered the same limb. He looked pale to Logan. Like he didn't enjoy the sun. He wore a white T-shirt and gray pants. White sneakers. His feet tended to flap on the sidewalk, his stride wide. His legs didn't move straight ahead – they tended to be thrown to the side with every step. It was a strange gait. Arthur Cross walked like an exotic bird, more at home in the air than on the ground. His eyes were very large and dark, his eyebrows drawn together in a tight scowl, which may have been due to the pain.

The injury to his arm appeared extensive and was no doubt painful.

Logan glanced at his phone, closed the photo album and returned to the search results on Arthur Cross.

Had Logan and Arthur met when they were younger, perhaps Logan's early upbringing would not have been so solitary. There was something about this man, something familiar.

With his history of criminal fraud, cruelty to animals, sexual deviancy and violent behavior, Logan supposed Arthur had undiagnosed narcissistic personality disorder with psychopathic or sociopathic tendencies. The first restraining order had been obtained by Kevin Pollock, which also covered his wife Christine White and her daughter, Amy Flynn. The restraining order appeared to stem from intimidating behavior exhibited by Cross. An earlier search of court records had revealed the origin of the dispute. The last will of Arthur's late wife, Elizabeth Le Saux, whom Logan had no doubt that Arthur had married and then murdered so that he could benefit from her estate. Except his late wife's lawyer, Kevin, had gotten in the way. And Arthur was putting as much psychological pressure on Kevin and his family as possible, perhaps in the misguided view that it may change things for him, or perhaps because of a more primal instinct – revenge.

The restraining order Cross had obtained alleged that Christine White had arranged for hooded men to visit Cross and assault him.

Cross had dark potential, but he lacked the clarity of mind

that Logan enjoyed. This is what made Logan non-existent to the authorities. While Logan knew how to control others, he began to wonder about his own self-discipline. He had almost lost control last night in Grace's apartment. No one is perfect. Not even Logan. Certainly not Arthur Cross.

Yet Arthur could prove most useful.

He watched Arthur get into the back of an Uber. Logan turned on the engine of his new rental car and followed Arthur home. At first, he kept his distance, always allowing at least one car between him and Cross's Uber. As he drove across the city, he wondered how he should handle the approach.

Cross was not the first psychopath that Logan had encountered. Dealing with large corporations at the highest levels, one invariably encountered the more ruthless and selfish of human beings, individuals whose psychological states gave them every advantage in climbing over their colleagues to reach the top. In Logan's experience, these people, while not always very clever, possessed an animal or primal instinct. They could very easily discern when someone was telling them a lie. It was almost as if untruths had a smell that only they could detect. He would need to tell the truth. A direct approach would be best.

As Cross's Uber entered a suburban area, there was no longer a buffer car for Logan to hide behind. He decided not to hide and tailed the Uber through the streets until it stopped outside a low 1960s suburban home with an unkempt lawn and rusty chicken-wire fencing surrounding the property.

Cross got out of the Uber.

Logan killed the engine and got out of his car.

He had been right not to try to hide. Cross was waiting outside his home, staring at him as he closed the car door.

The Uber driver took off.

Logan didn't move. He stared at Cross.

Cross didn't move either. He stared back.

For a moment, neither of them moved. Neither of them spoke.

It wasn't a stand-off. This was something else. An appraisal, of sorts.

He could feel Cross's eyes lazily roaming over his body and finally settling on his face. Cross's face appeared dead. Blank. No emotion. No fear. If Cross had looked this way at someone without Logan's own psychological fortitude, they would feel deeply uncomfortable. Cross's gaze was not one which most could withstand for very long. Perhaps Cross knew this on some level, because when Logan didn't move or flinch, or break his gaze, a small twitch fell across Cross's right eye.

It was momentary. But the first sign of irritation or, perhaps, unease.

Logan approached, stood at the bottom of the path leading to Cross's front door.

'Mr. Cross, I would very much like to talk to you,' said Logan. 'We appear to have some mutual acquaintances. I have a problem with a lawyer. I think you have a similar problem. Perhaps I can help you.'

'What makes you think I need your help?' said Cross warily.

'I think we can help each other. I think we are not so different, you and I. You are smart enough to see that for yourself.'

Something else about the human psyche that has not changed in millennia – a predator can easily spot another predator.

Cross held Logan's eyes in his iron gaze for a few moments.

Then Arthur Cross smiled.

It was a smile as cold as a silver coffin plate.

25
Logan

The small house was well kept and clean.

Still, there was a smell that permeated throughout the dwelling. Something that Logan could not at first recognize. It was chemical in nature, but not something familiar. And not something used for domestic cleaning. Logan sat on Cross's couch, a glass of water in front of him on a hardwood coffee table. He had taken a small sip, out of courtesy, but nothing more. He did not trust Cross at all. The feeling was mutual, as he had seen Cross slip a pistol into his waistband in the kitchen.

They were still feeling one another out, carefully.

'So you've read all about *me*, Logan,' said Cross, 'but I know nothing about you.'

'As I already explained, Flynn and I have a personal matter. Not something I can discuss, not something in the public domain. I want him to suffer. Isn't that enough?'

'Not nearly enough,' said Cross, leaning back in his chair and smiling, as if Logan should know this.

'We don't know each other. I grant you that. Neither of us are individuals given to placing trust in others. I've always been an outsider, Arthur. My guess is that you are too. We are not like other people. We can accomplish things that others cannot. We are unbound by the societal norms that tie other men down. We don't need to exchange vows. This isn't a marriage. It's an alliance. Nothing more.'

'And yet I don't trust you. How do I know you are not working for Flynn? How do I know this isn't a trap?'

Logan had spent an hour talking to Cross, letting him know how he had discovered him and why he had sought him out. Everything he'd said was the truth, precisely as it had happened. The only information he'd kept to himself was why he was interested in Flynn. As he had laid out his story, he knew Cross wasn't just watching him. He was being studied, his every move minutely weighed and judged by a fellow predator – one who was looking for warning signs. Lies were red flags and to be avoided, but Logan could not risk telling this man the truth. Cross wasn't to be trusted. His whole life and everything in it had been obtained by exploiting others.

'What if I told you I am not working for Flynn?' said Logan. 'You're a man who can easily spot a lie. Tell me, am I lying?'

'You haven't said it yet.'

'Clever. Alright, Arthur, I am not working for Flynn, nor any of his team. I am here because I want to see Flynn suffer.'

As he spoke, Cross stared at him intently. He felt as if every word, every gesture, wasn't just seen or heard by Cross – it was being absorbed. Weighed. Tasted.

Cross said nothing.

Then he sat upright in his chair, placed his good hand on his knee and spoke with a different intonation. It was more direct. No longer soft, his words came faster and harder than before.

'Say I do believe you. What exactly do you want from me? I'm hardly in a position to back you up if you decide to corner Flynn in a dark alleyway. Besides, I have a friend who is going to help me.'

'Bruno Mont?' asked Logan.

'You *have* done your homework. Bruno is going to seek justice for me, in his own particularly brutal fashion.'

'What might that entail?'

'Something violent, if I know Bruno. He has a talent for it.'

'And you don't?'

Arthur's thin lips pressed together then spread into a smile. It was an unnerving sight.

'I don't have Bruno's taste for it. He will choose his moment and hurt the ones who hurt me.'

'But that's not enough, is it, Arthur? You've been looking for revenge since the day Kevin got that will overturned in court.'

'Kevin took everything from me. I want to take everything from him. Slowly, methodically. This . . .' he said, holding up his ruined arm. 'The ones who hurt me will feel the same pain, but it's nothing compared to what I want to do to Kevin and his family.'

'It's not so easy, though. You have your friend, Bruno, but my guess is if you had a plan to hurt Kevin and his family you would have done it sooner. If you could do this on your own, then you wouldn't have invited me inside. Brute force can only get you so far. Flynn has a weakness – his family. I want to hurt him in the worst way possible. That means targeting his ex-wife and child.'

Cross's dark eyes flared, and for a moment Logan thought he could see a scarlet spark dancing in those black pools. A trick of the light, somehow. Logan noted that the reaction came at the mention of Flynn's daughter. This wasn't just about revenge for Cross. Logan had stumbled upon something important to Arthur.

Logan sensed that Cross wanted the girl.

He did not want to know why. He could guess, but such thoughts were pointless.

As much as Logan understood Flynn's weakness, he had also just discovered a weakness in Arthur Cross.

'What if I brought you Amy Flynn? You could take her some place where she could never be found. If Flynn's daughter went missing, the pain and the fear would tear him and his ex-wife to pieces. Kevin too.'

Cross's gray tongue wet his lips and he allowed his eyelids to close and open again.

'You could do that?'

'My only issue is getting inside the house. That's why I need you, Arthur. You are a resourceful individual and every bit as watchful. You've been watching the den of our lion for a long time. I need to know where the cub sleeps and if there is anything in that particular den that might cause problems for a hyena creeping in at night.'

'They have a gun.'

'Where do they keep the gun?'

'Downstairs, on a high shelf in the kitchen. It's in a lockbox with a keypad.'

'How do you know this?'

'I saw the wife grab it when that delivery driver appeared. I have been watching for a long time now.'

'What kind of home security do they have?'

'There's a full security system.'

'Do you know the brand?'

Cross smiled coldly, said, 'Nici. It's on a decal sticker in the corner of the front window and the alarm box below the eaves of the house.'

Security companies are in the business of selling home-security systems. They tell consumers that showing potential robbers that this home is protected can be a powerful deterrent. This is at least partly true. The companies brand their alarm housing, which is bolted high up on the front of the house, and they always include decal stickers with their products for display in their customer's windows. Logan had advised several security companies and even introduced branded decals to some of them.

This home is protected by Simply Safe.
This home is protected by Ajax Home Security.
This home is protected by Ring Alarm.

In the marketing trade, it's free advertising. Someone sees a nice house and the type of alarm system they use. Maybe they can't afford a house like this, but they can afford the same quality of home security. This works. It sells products.

In reality, from a security perspective, it's a terrible idea, because it tells every potential intruder exactly what *type* of system is being used. No system is perfect, but knowing the mechanics of an operation of a particular security system is a huge advantage. May as well leave an instruction manual on the porch on how to disable or bypass the security system. It was always an argument in the boardroom of home-security companies: the security professionals wanted their products to have a generic decal – *This home is protected by a security system* – which has the same deterrent effect for potential burglars, but it doesn't help sell *your* products.

Logan's branded decals won in the boardroom. To hell with security.

'So you're just going to break into their house and steal the girl from her bed?' asked Cross.

'Yes,' said Logan.

'And what happens if the girl screams and wakes up her parents?'

'Well, then I'll just have to kill them all, won't I?'

PART FOUR

26

Eddie

It was a busy morning.

Tricky Dicky had come through, as good as his word, and the release papers were en route to Rosie's for processing. Kate and Bloch were on their way to meet Elly coming off the prisoner transport from Rikers.

Lake was out pounding the sidewalks, looking for our missing homeless veteran, Joe Novak, the only living witness who had seen Elly and the man with a scar on his chin and his leg in a cast, the man who called himself Logan.

Denise was typing up legal briefs for Kate. Harry and Clarence were in his office, and as usual Harry was glued to his phone watching TikTok.

Bloch had told me we would get some analysis results this morning. First, DNA results – we needed to know whose body fluids those were we'd found on the floor. I guessed it was vomit, from the pattern and the odor, but we needed to be sure. Then a more detailed analysis: whatever unusual chemical or compounds that were in the staining on the floor of Elly's apartment would be picked up by the lab tech. With any luck, the poison used would be exotic – something we could use to help track down the man with the yellow suitcase and the cast on his leg.

Until then, there wasn't much I could do but worry.

'Eddie,' cried Denise, 'email hitting your inbox right now. It's Elly's medical records from the hospital.'

'Just print them for me,' I said.

The printer beside Denise's desk hummed into life and began spitting out warm pages. I heard Harry coming out of his office, and the little bell on Clarence's collar jangled. The dog followed Harry into every corner of the office.

I grabbed some pages from the printer, read them and, when I'd done so, held them out for Harry while I grabbed more records hot off the printer. He stood beside me. The only sound was the crinkle of paper in our hands and the buzz and mechanical whirr from the printer.

As if on cue, the printer stopped. I took the last page.

Read it.

Gave it to Harry.

'Where's the rest of it?' I asked.

'That's it,' said Denise.

'There's nothing in Elly's toxicology report,' I said.

'I wasn't expecting anything,' said Harry. 'Unless they test for a specific type of toxin, most won't show up on a standard blood screening. Still, we've got something to start with here.'

'What? What have we got?' I asked.

'We have her symptomology. She had nausea, vomiting, drowsiness and dizziness. When the paramedics picked her up, she was fully unconscious. Her blood pressure was really low. She came round in the hospital enough to vomit, but couldn't answer any questions or give a history to the treating medical team. Even though she was vomiting, her heart rate never got above fifty-two beats a minute. They had to shock her heart and give her a clot-buster injection, IV fluids and ACE inhibitors. Strange that they gave her ACE inhibitors.'

'What are they?'

'They open up the blood vessels, allowing the heart to work a little less hard, but her heart wasn't working overtime at all. I don't understand. You should speak to the doctor who treated her. Something's not right here.'

The name of the treating doctor was Ted Jones. I asked Denise to try to get him on the phone. It was already close to noon.

Denise called out, 'Doc Jones on line three.'

I took the call in Harry's office and put it on speaker.

'Doctor, thank you so much for taking the call. I'm here with my colleague Harry Ford. We were just looking over our client's medical records and we had some questions.'

'Any questions about your client's treatment should be addressed to the hospital's legal department. I can't discuss this . . .'

'No, you misunderstand. This isn't a lawsuit. The release our client signed for her medical records states that we are not seeking these documents in contemplation of litigation,' I said.

'Wait a second – let me check that.'

He put us on hold.

Came back after thirty seconds.

'I see the release here on her file. How can I help you?'

'Our client believes that someone spiked her water with some kind of poison. Something that would cause the symptoms she was treated for. I don't know if you are aware, but her husband and her best friend were murdered some time just before Elly was admitted to hospital. We're not sure when they were murdered, but we believe they may have been poisoned too. We were wondering if you might have an opinion on Elly's condition and if it's possible she was poisoned?' I asked.

'Oh, she definitely had some kind of toxin in her body. A healthy female of that age does not present with those symptoms without something being introduced to her system to cause it. You know, I've been in the ER six years now. When I first started, I thought I'd be dealing with stab wounds, gunshot wounds, broken bones from falls and all the usual illness and disease. I never thought I'd be treating ten, sometimes fifteen young women a week who are brought in because some asshole spiked their drink.'

'Do you know what the drug might have been?' asked Harry.

'We screened for the usual date-rape drugs, but didn't hit a match. Thing is, these assholes are using ever more exotic cocktails to drug these young women. Unless we screen for a specific drug, we're not going to know, and you can only take so much blood for screening. In this case, like many others, we find that it's better just to treat the symptoms and if the patient shows signs of recovery then that's about all we can do.'

'I noticed Mrs. Parker was given ACE inhibitors, but her heart rate was fairly low. Would you mind explaining that?' asked Harry.

'Her blood oxygen level was eight-five. We had to increase her SATS. The ACE inhibitors worked. They opened up her veins and her SATS returned to normal very quickly.'

'Doctor, do you have any idea what kind of drug she might have been given to induce those symptoms?' asked Harry.

'Hard to tell. Like I said, it could have been a cocktail of drugs, maybe a vasoconstrictor of some type, which would account for the narrowing of the blood vessels – maybe epinephrine, and, again, that could have been cut with Fentanyl, PCP or something else. Whatever it was, unless she got treatment for those symptoms she would've died.'

We both thanked the doctor and I hung up the call.

Harry took out his phone, and started working on a search.

'Holy shit,' said Harry.

He gave me his phone.

He had been googling *Vasoconstrictors*.

He showed me one of Elly's social media videos.

She had been to CVS for all the essentials a young woman needs. L'Oreal shampoo, Colgate toothpaste, nail clippers, make-up, eye drops . . .

'What am I watching?' I asked.

I heard footsteps on the stairs leading up to our office.

Harry took his phone back and paused the video.

Kate and Bloch came in, Elly followed behind wearing the clothes Bloch had picked up from her apartment. She looked as if she had lost ten pounds and hadn't slept in days. Kate introduced her to Denise and the three of them went to the kitchen.

Bloch came into Harry's office holding her phone.

'My lab guy came back. That stain on the bedroom floor is vomit. There was enough saliva to do a DNA comparison – he believes it's a strong match for Harriet Rothschild. And there's something else. The vomit residue contained high levels of . . .'

'Tetrahydrozoline,' said Harry and Bloch, simultaneously.

'How did you know?' said Bloch.

'It's a vasoconstrictor,' said Harry. 'We got Elly's medical records and talked to the doctor. He thinks at least one of the drugs she was given was a vasoconstrictor. Look at Elly's Instagram . . .'

Harry wound the video back on his phone, and hit play.

Elly's voice resonated from the speakers on Harry's phone. Bloch and I stood beside him to watch the video.

'Everybody needs a good toothpaste. Turns out they're pretty much all the same so I just buy one with a flip top so I don't lose the cap. Next, eye drops. If you're living in a city like New York, yes you will have an amazing time, but air quality is just not great and my eyes tend to dry out. These eye drops, just once or twice a day, total game changer. No point in having gorgeous eye make-up if your actual eyes make it look like you're in a zombie movie. Moving on, facial wash . . .'

'I don't get it. What am I looking at here?' I asked.

Harry sighed, said, 'You're looking at evidence that will convict Elly of double homicide.'

27

Logan

Logan entered the Wholefoods store, and took the escalator up one level to the Amazon lockers. He keyed in the PIN to the locker and retrieved his items, opened the packages and dropped the boxes in the recycling bin.

He placed the items in his backpack and returned to the street, stowing the bag in the trunk of his rental car before driving uptown.

The situation with Elly Parker had to be managed.

No loose ends.

Joe Novak, the homeless person who had helped Elly, was priority one. He had spent every available minute searching for the man along street corners, in homeless and migrant encampments all over the city, and so far there was no sign of him. Bloch and Lake, the investigators who worked for Flynn, were also looking for this man.

Logan was not a trained investigator. He was smart, but finding people who didn't have an address was not something he had experienced. It had felt hopeless, these past few days. A day after Elly had been admitted to hospital, Logan had begun scouring that area of Manhattan, and when he didn't spot the man he began to talk to other people who lived on the street, asking if they had seen him.

It would have been more useful to simply bang his head against a wall.

There are many mistakes and errors that can occur in planning a murder. Logan had covered most eventualities. Two elements had gone wrong in these murders.

Elly had survived.

And before she had gotten to the apartment she made contact, in Logan's presence, with another human being: the homeless man whom she had given money. He had seen Logan with Elly. After Elly managed to get out of his apartment before Logan could cut the cast off his leg, the homeless man had come to her aid. Logan had made it down the stairs, and onto the street. And he had seen the man leaning over Elly. Asking other passers-by to call a paramedic. Before Logan had turned and fled back upstairs to clear and clean the apartment, he had watched from the entrance to the building.

To this day, he didn't know why, but Joe Novak had glanced up and seen Logan.

Not the genial, clumsy young man with the broken ankle and crutches.

The real Logan.

It was the last time Logan had seen Joe Novak. He had to leave the scene, clear the apartment. He would find the homeless man later.

But, so far, Logan had not laid eyes on him.

No one else in the city would remember Elly and Logan's walk from Grand Central to his apartment. But this man, Novak, he would remember.

He had gone to extraordinary lengths to make the situation appear as a murder suicide to the police. Elly surviving wasn't a problem because no one would believe her. But an independent witness corroborating Elly's story about a man with a suitcase poisoning her, well, that changed things considerably.

He had to kill this man, Novak. Killing Elly would only raise suspicion.

Novak had to die, and because he lived in a different world his death could be explained by other means. The police weren't looking for him, so his death could be because of a drug deal gone bad, a debt or a random encounter on the dark, dangerous streets of this city.

He drove around the city until it grew too dark to see the faces of those huddled on the sidewalks or doorways. Another day trawling the streets with nothing to show for it.

He wondered if Novak hadn't gone into hiding. Perhaps something had happened to him.

His phone buzzed and he pulled over.

A text from Grace.

She enjoyed last night. Wanted to do it again.

She didn't know yet, thought Logan. Grace hadn't realized what he'd done.

She would find out, soon enough.

He drove to one of his apartments, the loft in Midtown. Parked the car and took the elevator to the top. Once inside, he told his home hub to play Beethoven. While the music filled the sparse, industrial space, Logan went into the bedroom, laid out his clothes for the evening and the items he'd bought from Amazon.

A Wi-Fi blocker.

A radio jammer.

A large, soft make-up brush for applying foundation.

A small bottle of titanium dioxide powder.

A flashlight.

A powerful, tube-shaped magnet about six inches long.

A roll of trash bags.

A bottle of water.

Wet wipes.

And his lock picks.

Nothing here was illegal. It was all freely available to purchase from the world's largest store. Apart from one item, of course.

A nine-millimeter Beretta. Just in case things went badly wrong. Some years ago, Logan had arranged, through the dark web, to meet a man beneath a bridge in Brooklyn at three in the morning. The man arrived in an old Cadillac, popped the lid of his trunk and showed Logan an array of handguns and small assault weapons. They were ex-military hardware that had fallen off a cargo plane and miraculously lost their serial numbers when they landed. Logan had chosen the Beretta, one extra magazine and a box of ammo. He had yet to use the weapon, but he kept it well maintained and knew how to use it.

He exercised: pull-ups and push-ups, crunches and squats.

It had cost a quarter million dollars to install in his bathroom, but the plunge pool was Logan's happy place. He kept the temperature low — ice-bath low — and stayed in three minutes, until his hands began to shake. Then he got out and into a hot shower. He scrubbed every inch of his body with a hard brush and soap to remove as much dead skin as possible. When he was done, he stood in front of the mirror.

He didn't look like a man, he thought.

His skin was red from the heat of the shower and the body scrub. He could have been a demon, born from flame.

He put on skintight Lycra leggings, and the same style long-sleeve shirt. This would cut down on the DNA from sweat that went into the black combat pants and black sweater. He would dispose of all his clothing afterwards, of course, but it paid to be careful.

He put on black socks and molded, flat-soled moccasins, the kind of footwear that leaves only a blank, foot-shaped print in soft earth. No tread. Before he put on his balaclava, he rolled it up so it looked like a beanie, then placed it on his head. Slowly, he packed his backpack, careful to make sure he had everything he needed.

It was time.

*

Logan parked a mile away from the home of Kevin Pollock and Christine White.

Past midnight.

While he waited, he roleplayed what he was about to do, and all the possible things that might go wrong.

Coming up on three thirty in the morning, the perfect time, he drove closer to the house and parked one street over, behind the property. This was a main route into town, and the only thing on this street was a gas station two hundred yards away and a strip mall in the other direction, which was dark and long closed for the night. A tall, thick hedge separated this street from the rear of Christine's property, and, if his estimations from Google Earth were correct, he was parked precisely behind her backyard.

Logan plugged the Wi-Fi blocker into the twelve-volt port in the car using an adaptor. The radio jammer had a USB, which he plugged into the socket beside the twelve-volt. He turned the key to bring the battery to life, but didn't ignite the engine, then hit the Wi-Fi icon on his phone and searched for nearby networks.

A couple of available networks showed up. One caught his interest.

The White House.

He smiled at that one, then touched the display to join. The phone display read *internet available* then asked him for a network key.

He switched on the radio jammer and the Wi-Fi blocker, waited for the lights on the displays to turn green and then checked the White House Wi-Fi network. The information below the network had changed.

No internet available.

He plugged wired earphones into his phone, and checked the app that accessed the FM tuner built into the device.

No signal.

Logan got out of the car, pulled the balaclava over his face and approached the tall hedges. Hunkering down, he spread the lower branches apart, closed his eyes and forced his way through.

On the other side, he found himself at the rear of the White property, in their backyard. The pristine lawn glistened in the moonlight, damp with dew. He hopped the fence separating the enclosed yard and approached the side of the house.

A double-glazed side window, closed and locked, had a decal with the name of the home-security system affixed to the glass.

Logan checked his phone.

No Wi-Fi, no radio signal.

Everyone likes to feel safe in their home. No one wants to have their walls and floors ripped up by security engineers laying cable and wiring to connect all of the motion sensors.

Wi-Fi and radio-signal security systems don't need any of that intrusive work. They take a little more technical equipment than a pair of wire cutters, but they can be bypassed just as easily.

Logan put away his phone, pulled on his gloves and took the magnet out of the backpack. He placed it over the window, in the exact position that corresponded with the lock mechanism, felt the pull of the magnet grabbing the lock, and then slid the magnet to his right and listened for the click of the mechanism unlocking.

He threw open the window, and climbed inside silently. No alarms. No sound.

The house was dark and silent.

He found himself in a hallway separating the rear lounge area from the kitchen. He made his way to the kitchen, softly, silently, and clicked on his flashlight. The lockbox containing Kevin's pistol was high on a shelf that sat above a small kitchen dining table. He reached for the lockbox. It had a nine-digit keypad.

He laid out some gear on the dining table. First, he peeled off a trash bag and opened it on the table. He put the lockbox inside, popped open the lid on the titanium dioxide powder and dipped the make-up brush inside. Carefully, gently, he brushed the keypad.

Titanium dioxide is found in a lot of products. Toothpaste, sunscreen and other cosmetics. In this powdered form, it was primarily used as dusting powder.

For fingerprints.

Shining his flashlight on the keypad, prints appeared on four of the numbered keys – 1, 5, 6, 7. These were the four keys Kevin used to make up his combination. By isolating those keys, he had just gone from a possible ten thousand different combinations, to sixty-five. He didn't have time to punch in sixty-five different combinations of those numbers. He didn't need to. Kevin would use a memorable combination. Something he and his wife would easily remember. Either Kevin's date of birth, or Christine's?

Logan thought back to the documents he had read, and in particular the supporting affidavit accompanying the motion to the court for the restraining order against Arthur Cross. This affidavit had given Kevin's age. He was born in seventy-six.

Logan keyed in 1, 5, 7, 6.

Nothing.

He tried 5, 1, 7, 6.

The small green light on the keypad blinked. Kevin was born in seventy-six, the only thing he didn't know was whether it was January or May.

Logan opened the lid, drew out the revolver. Checked the load.

He closed the lockbox, used the wet wipes to get rid of the dust, and then placed the lockbox back on the shelf, and the trash bag and wipes he returned to his backpack.

Not a sound in the house.

Logan walked upstairs, the revolver in his hand.

The first bedroom belonged to Amy. Her door was not fully shut. He glanced down the hallway. The master bedroom at the end of the hall was closed. Next to it was a dressing room. No more than a box room, it could perhaps have been used as a fourth bedroom, but it contained a make-up table and mirror, and his and hers closets.

He returned to Amy's room and stood silently in the doorway.

Amy Flynn lay in bed. A soft, warm light glowed from a lamp on her nightstand. She lay on her side, facing the light.

Sound asleep.

Logan's finger curled round the trigger of the revolver.

He felt the heat flood his cheeks, blood pumping through his adrenalized system, the excitement building, sweat soaking through his mask.

He slipped the bottle of water from the side pocket of his backpack.

An hour later, Logan pulled up outside the home of Arthur Cross.

He got out of the car, walked round to the trunk and paused to scan the street once again. He listened, hearing the sound of a car in the far distance. A light rain was falling. No lights were on in any of the windows of the neighborhood.

Arthur opened his front door, and beckoned Logan inside.

Logan placed his hand on the trunk of the car and smiled at Cross.

A white panel van sat in his driveway. Something Cross had discussed. He would use it to transport Amy Flynn to a quiet location.

Logan stepped away from the car and walked up the flagstone path to Arthur's house.

'Well?' said Arthur, standing on his porch. He was different from the last time Logan had seen him. At first, he couldn't quite work out what was different. His eyes were still black as a moonless night and his skin paper white.

But it was the still, almost deathly calm that was absent from Cross.

Sweat beaded his forehead. His leg shook. He was fidgeting.

Anxious with excitement.

'Where is she? Is she in the trunk? Is she alive?' he asked, all in one breath.

Logan stopped a few feet from Cross, smiled and said, 'She's alive.'

'Did you have to kill the parents?' asked Cross.

'No, they're still sleeping soundly in their beds, for all I know, so—'

'Did anyone see you?'

Logan took a half-empty bottle of water from his jacket pocket. It was cold outside, but he was still a little dehydrated from his efforts. Adrenalin always made Logan sweat. He took a long drink, finishing the bottle.

'No one saw me, but you didn't let me finish. The parents are still asleep in their beds. So is Amy.'

'What? Did something go wrong?'

'I'm afraid, Arthur, everything went exactly as I'd planned.'

Logan calmly took Kevin's revolver from his jacket pocket.

And shot Arthur Cross in the face.

28

Eddie

We gave Elly the day to get back into the world.

Kate put her up in a hotel downtown. Somewhere expensive and quiet. She needed time to adjust to the hurricane of pain, loss, confusion and terror that had hit her for the past few days. We had questions that had to be asked, but now was not the time. People have remarkable strength, but everyone has their limits. We said we would talk after she'd had a good night's sleep, a shower and some decent food.

Yesterday, even as I'd told her to get some sleep, I realized how foolish that had sounded. Elly didn't say anything; she'd just nodded. I got the impression she hadn't slept properly in weeks – not since she'd found her husband and her best friend in bed together: the betrayal that had started this nightmare.

This morning, we are all in the office early apart from Bloch, who had gone to pick up Elly from the hotel and bring her in.

Bernice had gotten her grand jury indictment and we finally had some discovery.

Not much. But at least we had a cause of death and, thanks to Harry, we also knew why the DA's office was pushing for an early trial.

'How do you think she's going to take this?' I asked.

'I think she's going to be okay,' said Kate. 'Right now, she's hurt and she's confused. This explains a lot. And it means we know what we have to deal with. Then we can make a plan and let her know that we're fighting for her. That will make a difference.'

'Any word on the security footage for the route from Grand Central to the apartment where Elly was poisoned?' I asked.

Lake said, 'I talked to Bloch. She said there's nothing. She got all the files from the stores. This man knew to walk a few feet from the entrances to the stores so the security cameras wouldn't pick him up. The footage from the NYPD cameras were linked to the same cloud as the MTA. She tracked down the company who is supposed to store the footage. They're called Secure One. She's trying to get more out of them, but the company are stonewalling her.'

'Probably afraid of being sued,' said Harry.

'I'm not sure,' said Lake. 'I'll tell her to keep pushing.'

'We could subpoena the CEO,' I said.

'That's going to backfire,' said Kate. She had more experience in the politics and corporate mindset of company executives. Roasting Fortune 500 CEOs over a pit was her specialty. 'If we issue a subpoena, they'll just lawyer up and the shutters come down hard. Then there's no way of getting information out of them without a hearing. We need to dig into Secure One a little more, find out what's making them nervous about talking to us. If we find that, then we've got leverage to force a meeting.'

While we were talking, Lake stood, head down, looking at the scuffed toes of his shoes.

'Any more leads on Joe Novak?' I asked.

'He's disappeared. Either the stranger with the suitcase got to him, or he's left the city, or he's hiding somewhere. I can't draw a bead on him,' he said.

'Have you tried talking to the HOME-STAT people?'

'I got nothing from them either. They're super tight with security.'

There used to be a basic human right for New Yorkers to have shelter. In recent times, those rights have been loosened to an obligation to only provide between thirty and sixty days of shelter a year. This was due to an influx of migrants, people fleeing warzones to take up residence in the Land of the Free. In order to help with the overall homeless problem, the city employs survey-takers who walk Manhattan every day, taking a census of who is on the street without shelter and where they are located that day.

The problem is that a lot of people without homes don't want to take up shelter for various reasons – addiction, mental illness and many other factors all play a part.

'Try them again. Get to someone on the street conducting the surveys. They don't make a lot of money. Find the right HOME-STAT survey taker and make the right play,' I said, and peeled off five hundred bucks and gave it to Lake.

The office door opened and Bloch came in with Elly Parker, who still didn't look as if she had enjoyed much sleep at all. She was young and didn't have a single wrinkle on her face, but there were bags under her eyes, which were red and swollen. Her hair looked clean, and she wore fresh clothes and a little make-up. It was easy to see the burden of recent life-changing events crushing down on her shoulders. She even walked as if she was bent over, head down, eyes scanning the room fearfully. Still, there was a world of difference between the way she looked now and the time when I'd first met her in the interview room below the courthouse.

And yet, thinking of the way she looked in her social-media videos, she was half the woman she used to be. She'd lost weight and all her confidence.

The world had fallen on Elly Parker hard.

Bloch led her to the conference room. Kate exchanged a look with me.

We had no choice but to tell Elly what we had learned. We didn't know how she would react. There was no way to know until it hit her. I didn't want to lay this on her. Not now. She had been through trauma after trauma, and this just might tip her over the edge. But, at the same time, I had to save her. *We* had to save her. That meant we had to do our jobs, even the parts that are most difficult for our clients.

We piled into the conference room, and sat around the table, Elly at the head of it. Denise brought her some herbal tea, and she made a point of thanking Denise, reaching for her arm and placing her hand gently upon it. When the world is hell, any act of kindness, no matter how small, helps put out some of those fires.

'Elly, we've had some discovery from the prosecution and some results back from our own labs. There's . . .' began Kate, and paused.

Elly held her mug with both hands, her red, tortured eyes fixed on Kate. Elly was smart, she knew we were gathered here to tell her hard truths, the battle for her life that she now faced. None of us were smiling. I'm sure it felt to her as if we were there to help her plan her funeral.

'This isn't going to be easy to hear, and it's not easy to say . . .' said Kate.

Elly's gaze didn't waver from Kate.

'It's okay, Kate. I can . . . I . . . I . . . can take it. I need to hear this,' said Elly, her voice breaking, but behind the fear choking her there was something else. I suspected Elly Parker had a great deal of courage.

We were about to find out.

'I'm just going to say it,' said Kate. 'James and Harriet were poisoned.'

At the word 'poison', you could almost see it hit Elly physically. Her shoulders bowed, her chest caved and her chin dropped, like she'd taken a punch to the solar plexus.

'We got the reports from the medical examiner and we analyzed some staining on your bedroom floor. Harriet vomited and it wasn't cleaned up. We tested it and found a substance called tetrahydrozoline. It was also found in toxicology tests carried out postmortem. This poison is something called a vasoconstrictor. It causes blood vessels to constrict, stopping blood flow and causing other problems. Both Harriet and James died of cardiac arrest . . .'

Elly didn't move. Didn't react. She held on to the mug as if her life depended on it and she never broke eye contact with Kate. The only change was the small drip of tears falling into her herbal tea.

'Elly, we believe you were given the same substance.'

A small tremor began in her shoulders. Elly was shaking.

'I've never heard of this tetra-whatever-you-call-it, before.'

Kate leaned back in her chair, and looked to Harry. He nodded, taking out his cell phone. Harry had a way of speaking that most people found soothing. Something in his deep, baritone voice carried empathy and understanding and compassion.

'We know you didn't poison your best friend or your husband. We damn sure know you didn't poison yourself, but we have a problem, Elly,' said Harry, flipping round his phone. 'The prosecutor is going to show this to the jury. It's one of your videos where you go to the drug store to buy beauty products. See this . . .' He flicked his finger across the screen, searching for a particular point in time in the video.

'You bought a bottle of Visine eye drops. The main ingredient in these drops is tetrahydrozoline. It's a vasoconstrictor – gets rid of those little red blood vessels in the eyeballs. But if you have more than a few drops of this, and you take it orally, it can be very serious. It can stop the blood flow around the heart. It can cause a heart attack. This video is a problem. Essentially, the prosecutor can show the jury you going out and *buying* the poison, because you recorded yourself doing it and posted it on social media.'

Elly lifted her hands to her face. The mug tilted over, spilling tea on the conference table. Elly's eyes were wide with shock. A small pool of tea spread across the table. Denise brought over a napkin and wiped it clean. She put a hand on Elly's back and told her it was going to be okay, before she went back to her desk and manned the phones.

'I didn't . . . I didn't . . .' said Elly.

'We know,' I said. 'Now we have a story to tell the jury in your defense. Someone has been watching you, Elly. Our guess is someone saw your viral video – the one where you discovered James in bed with Harriet. They followed the story in the news. Your heartbreak. Your pain. They used that against you. This stranger knew that if anything happened to James or Harriet, then there's no one on the planet with more motive to do them harm than you. This stranger went through your entire life on social media and they saw this video of you going to the drug store. This individual is very sick and very smart. They knew Visine in high doses was poisonous. Now they know if James and Harriet get tetrahydrozoline poisoning, you are the number-one suspect, and the DA can prove you had access to it. The last part of the plan was to target you. To give you the poison as well and make it look like you poisoned your husband and his mistress in a desperate act of revenge and then took your own life. We think that was his play. Maybe, after you died in that apartment, he would have had access to your cell phone and social media. He could've written a suicide note, posted it on your socials. He kills three people, and the police already have a story ready-made for how it all happened. The police wouldn't look for anyone else if it's a murder-suicide pact.'

'Oh my God, this man was so . . . so convincing. I felt sorry for him at first. And he was so charming. Jesus Christ, what am I going to do?'

'You have to trust us,' said Kate. 'We have a plan. We're going to find this man. We're going to find Joe Novak, the man who helped you. We can put a living witness on the stand . . .'

'What about his apartment?'

Bloch said, 'We checked with the building supervisor. This

apartment was let out on Airbnb. The person paid with a credit card in a false name. They paid for a month and used fake credentials. There are no security cams in the building. We've tried to get hold of some of the neighbors. We spoke to the four apartment owners on the third floor and none of them saw this man. I'm trying to get in touch with the owner to see if he can let us take a look inside. Our guess is this man cleaned up well before he left, but we'll check it all the same.'

'Elly, this is a difficult question,' I said, 'and I don't want to upset you, but I have to ask. Anything we can do to try and trace this man is important. It's vital for your defense that we find him. To do that we have to work on what we know, and then think backwards. We know that James and Harriet were poisoned with large amounts of Visine drops. From the medical examiner's report there are no signs of any kind of violence having occurred. Neither James, nor Harriet, have any bruising of any kind. So they were not held and forced to drink this stuff. Now I know this is an awful thing to have to imagine, but we need to know. How do you suppose he might have gotten the poison into their system?'

Elly wiped the tears from her face, folded her arms and thought about it.

'I don't know. I mean, my husband and my best friend had a whole secret life together that I knew nothing about. I just don't know.'

'The poison acts fast, according to what we've read about it,' said Harry, and Elly nodded along.

'Yeah, it took maybe a couple of minutes before I felt the full effect,' said Elly.

'And considering both James and Harriet were found in the apartment, we're guessing that's where they ingested the poison. When did you leave the apartment?' he asked.

'The same day I found them in bed. I hastily packed a bag, and I left, and I haven't been back since. I stayed at a hotel.'

'There were no signs of a break-in at the apartment,' I said. 'I take it you still have your key. You didn't lose it?'

'No, I have it.'

I looked at Harry and then Kate. We were no closer to finding out how the victims were poisoned.

'Elly,' I began, 'we think the DA knows how they were poisoned. Tetrahydrozoline has to be ingested, so it had to be in something they ate or drank. They're going to say there was no sign of a break-in. That you had the only other key to the apartment. And that you hated James and Harriet for betraying you, so you snuck into the apartment while they were out and dosed some food or drink with tetrahydrozoline. We don't yet know the vehicle for ingestion, but we'll find out once we get further discovery. That's their case. That's the case we have to beat.'

Elly's voice faltered. She hadn't had time to process her husband's betrayal never mind his murder.

'I didn't know Visine drops were poisonous. To me they're just eye drops. I didn't hate James or Harriet. I loved them. I just felt so hurt. I didn't want them to suffer. That's why I deleted that video, the one where I found them together. But by then it was too late. People had taken it and shared it. That's the thing about social media – it's there forever. Jesus, if I could just go back and change what happened . . . I never wanted it to come to this. I didn't want them to be abused online. I didn't want some maniac coming after them . . .'

'Did James have a TikkyTok account?' asked Harry.

Strangely, Elly smiled at Harry. It was only a brief smile. A momentary respite from the pain and stress.

'Yeah, but he took all of his accounts down after my video went viral. He was getting a lot of abuse from my followers. His whole life fell apart. He lost his job. Harriet too. They both deleted their accounts. Why do you ask?'

'Because you put out a lot about your personal life on your social media. That's how this killer was able to know so much about you. Did James post diary videos about his routine?'

'No, he was more private,' said Elly.

'Okay, we've got work to do. We can build a defense. Elly, is there anything else you can tell us that you think might help?' I asked.

She folded her arms, sank into her seat. Her eyes were far away. Thinking. Glistening with fresh tears.

'No,' she said, 'I don't think so.'

Her voice was small and flat, filled with fear and sorrow.

'Thank you, Elly, this has been really—'

I didn't finish my thought.

There was a crash behind us. The sound of a door slamming into a wall.

We all stood and looked toward the door to the office.

Denise was in reception, on her feet, her hands on her cheeks in shock.

Detective Bill Sacks had flung open my office door. He was flanked by two cops in uniform. He had a folder of papers under his arm and a nasty grin on his face.

I came out of the conference room, said, 'Do you know where you are? What the hell is going on, Sacks?'

He took the folder from under his arm and handed me a bundle of pages, stapled together.

'I'm here to do two things, Flynn. First, I'm serving your client with an *ex parte* order.'

'What the hell are you—'

'Next, I'm arresting her for murder.'

'You're what?'

The two cops in uniform strode past me. Elly was still in the conference room with my team. Harry and Bloch got up and stood in the doorway, blocking the cops.

'Stand aside, please,' said one of the cops.

'Son, you'd better back away until we understand what's happening here,' said Harry.

'We said *stand aside*, grampa,' repeated the cop.

'You put one hand on him, and I'll hurt you,' said Bloch.

Both cops took a step back. Bloch didn't mean it as a threat. It was just a statement of fact. One of the officers grabbed the radio on his stab vest and squeezed.

'Four-oh-two to dispatch, we need another unit at Flynn and Brooks to deal with a hostile . . .'

'*Dispatch to four-oh-two, identify the hostile,*' came the reply from the radio.

'It's Bloch,' said the cop.

'*Four-oh-two from dispatch, DO NOT, repeat, DO NOT engage Bloch. Sending three additional units to your location asap.*'

'Only three more units? That's kind of insulting,' said Bloch.

'Wait! Everybody take a second,' I said. 'Sacks, tell me what the hell is happening here. I don't want half a dozen cops bleeding on my floor.'

'Two words, Flynn,' said Sacks. 'NYPD standard detective procedure. Your client poisoned her husband and best friend. When the suspect is charged with multiple homicide due to poisoning, we look at all similar causes of death from those in the suspect's immediate family circle. Standard procedure. We got a hit. Yesterday, we got a court order to exhume the body of Stewart Yorke. He died of a cardiac arrest four years ago. The medical examiner just found traces of tetrahydrozoline in his liver.'

I looked through the glass of the conference room.

Elly had heard every word Sacks had just said.

She buried her face in her hands and collapsed to the floor.

Sacks said, 'Your client is going back to jail. And, unless Bloch steps aside, she's going with her.'

'Who the hell is Stewart Yorke?' I asked.

Sacks smiled grimly, said, 'He was your client's father.'

29

Eddie

'We've got you.'

That's what I said to Elly as Detective Bill Sacks followed her and the two uniformed cops out of my office. She was in handcuffs. White with shock. The two cops were practically holding her upright. I told her not to say a word to the cops, but I didn't think she could formulate speech, even if she had wanted to. She was in shock.

Whatever sliver of fight was left in Elly Parker had been taken from her.

I don't know if she heard me. She hadn't spoken a word since Sacks read her the Miranda warning in my conference room. She had passed out a few minutes before that. I didn't blame her. There are only so many punches anyone can take and for the past few days Elly had been bleeding on the ropes. This one, the arrest for the murder of her father – this was the knockout.

Life sometimes feels like a mountain falling on top of you.

It felt as if Everest was toppling over onto Elly Parker's head.

'*We've got you.*'

Those words felt hollow even as they passed my lips.

We didn't have her. She was slipping away.

Kate, Harry and I took my car and shadowed the cops to the

precinct. Kate and Harry went inside to be with Elly through booking.

I stayed outside and called our opponent, ADA Bernice Mazur.

She took a long time to pick up the phone. The sound of my frustration was made real by my heels pounding the sidewalk as they led me back and forth across the entrance to the police precinct while I waited. I had an image of her walking through the hallways of Center Street Courthouse, one arm lost in that huge handbag, her fingers searching through a haystack of pens, and little boulders of crumpled legal-pad paper and eventually alighting on her cell phone.

She answered and I didn't have time to vent my anger.

'Before you say anything, Eddie, this was all Sacks. He came to me with the standard homicide protocol in poisoning cases and I took it to the judge for an order of exhumation and postmortem. That's it. I did what my client asked me and I'm sorry—'

'You're sorry? Right now, my client is having to deal with the death of her husband, and her best friend, she's been framed for the murder by a psychopath who tried to kill her too, and she just got out of jail right before she got stabbed. On top of that, she's having to process her father's body being exhumed and she's now accused of killing him? You have no idea what she's going through . . .'

'Eddie, has it ever occurred to you that this woman might be guilty?'

'Of course. Then I met her. She wouldn't do this. Elly became famous with a viral video and some psycho saw it and decided she was the perfect mark. This guy with the suitcase likes to kill people and cover it up by framing someone else.'

'So how do you explain the father?'

'I don't know yet. All I know is you and District Attorney Castro are screwing us at every opportunity.'

'That's not how I run my cases. You know that.'

'Then prove it.'

She sighed, said, 'I'll have the autopsy report and video sent to you today. The rest of the discovery in the case will follow in a week. We just got confirmation of the poisoning vessels. Two bottles of water were found in the bedroom. Both of them laced with lethal doses of tetrahydrozoline. Look, I won't oppose bail. We can roll this charge into her current bail package.'

Now we knew. Two bottles of water. They were going to say Elly snuck into her apartment when James was out, poisoned the water bottles. That was their case. We were going to get confirmation of all of this in discovery, and probably we should have had it sooner. I got the impression Bernice was holding this back, waiting for an irate call from me after Elly's arrest. And this was the salve: the cause of death and method of poisoning revealed. In other words, Bernice held back a bone to throw to me when I barked.

'Won't Castro object to bail?'

'This is my case. He's on my back about this one every day, but it's my call.'

I ended the call. Took a breath.

I looked up at the concrete sky high above the buildings of Manhattan. My fingers reached for my chest, poked through my shirt and touched the cold aluminum Saint Christopher's medal I wore on a silver chain round my neck.

It was always tucked under my shirt. Every time I sensed it against my skin I thought of my father. He had worn it every day of his life, since he'd stolen it from a little store in Dublin before he got on a boat to America. Part of him was still in this relic. It gave me strength to fight, not for myself, but for the people who relied on me, for my family, and for the lost souls who wandered into my office as their last great hope.

There is always hope.

Right now, with Elly's situation, I just couldn't find it.

My phone buzzed.

Amy.

'Hi honey, is everything all r—'

'*Dad!* You've got to help! The police just arrested Mom and Kevin for murder!'

30

Eddie

It was almost nine in the evening by the time I climbed the stairs to my office.

Amy trudged up behind me.

All the desk lamps were lit. Denise was brewing coffee. Harry was leaning on a desk, talking with Kate. Bloch was at her computer and Lake must've been out somewhere, probably still trying to chase down Joe Novak.

Amy dumped her backpack on the ground, ran over to Harry and threw her arms round him, burying her head in his chest.

'It's going to be okay, sweetheart,' he said, and his gaze fixed on me. Harry's misty brown eyes were filled with sadness and dread.

As Amy relaxed her arms, and then stared up at him, he softened his look and tried to smile.

'Your old man is about the best lawyer I ever saw. Apart from me, of course. And Kate here, she's the next great one. Your mom and Kevin are in safe hands. We're going to make sure this mess is all cleared up.'

Turning, Amy looked down to find Clarence, panting and nudging at her leg. She bent down and petted and stroked the dog. He licked her face, and she giggled. It was the first time I'd seen her smile in a long time. That little laugh was a strange sound, coming from my daughter. She'd been crying all day, and her throat was raw. It sounded like the laughter hurt.

'Want some pizza?' asked Bloch.

She hesitated, then nodded, and Bloch led her into the kitchen. Amy got another hug from Denise and then Denise fixed her a paper plate with a large slice and a soda, and took her to the conference room. Amy sat at our conference table, eating her pizza, sipping on a Diet Pepsi and flicking through social media on her phone.

Bloch came back to the reception area and sat on a desk.

'How is she doing?' asked Kate.

'Not good. What about Elly?' I said.

'She's back at the hotel. Bernice got the bail pushed through in night court. How's Christine and Kevin?' asked Harry.

'They're just about hanging together. They'll have tonight in booking and then they should get bail in the morning. No record, major assets to put up for collateral and they're both lawyers. Even the craziest judge won't deny bail. Cross was found shot through the head at his front door. Cops recovered the murder weapon hidden in the long grass outside his house. The serial number on the barrel was registered to Kevin. They'd both been arrested and questioned for the attack on Cross, and he had obtained a restraining order. It's not looking good. I haven't told Amy half of this yet. She'll find out soon enough.'

Folding her arms, her head bent low, Kate approached me. She looked like she had something to say that I didn't want to hear. She stopped inches from me, looked up and I saw her lips move and heard her voice falter.

'Harry . . . Harry and I have been talking. I – *we* – think you should step back from this one and let us handle it. You're too close on this case. Your emotions . . .'

'I have an emotional involvement with the clients. I get it.'

Representing someone you love is a bad idea. It can cloud your judgement. It's like running a trial wearing a pair of blinkers – you won't see the roundhouse punch coming from the prosecution.

Harry said, 'I need your word on this, Eddie. Promise me now – you're agreeing to step back and let Kate and I handle the case. You've never gone back on your word to me. Not once in all our long friendship. Promise me.'

I held up my hands, said, 'I give you my word. I think it's for the . . .'

I was exhausted and my daughter had been crying for hours. My ex-wife, who I still loved, was in a prison cell and accused of a crime that could see her put behind bars for the rest of her life. My brain and my heart were fried, but I could still read people.

'Wait, what are you not telling me?' I asked.

'You've promised,' he said.

'What are you not telling me?'

'Here, drink this,' said Denise, as she sidled up to me with a cup of hot coffee.

I took the mug, and brought it to my lips.

'We got an email from the court office. The DA is fast-tracking this case. Grand jury in two days. We think he has a plan,' said Harry.

'Wait . . . you're kidding me?'

Harry shook his head, said, 'I think Castro is going to take this one on himself. He still has beef with you. We don't know for sure, but there's only one reason I can think of to fast-track this trial. On the same day Bernice is making her opening statement to the jury in Elly's case, we think Castro wants to open the prosecution case against Christine and Kevin.'

'He wants to set those trials for the same date to fuck with us?' I asked.

'He hates you and he wants us under pressure, hoping we'll mess up. I don't know for sure that's what he's up to, but it's my best guess,' said Harry.

'Son of a bitch,' I said, loud enough for Amy to drag her eyeballs from her phone to stare at me through the window of the conference room.

'We can stall him, no problem. Christine and Kevin can waive their right to a speedy trial, and we can hold him up with dozens of motions. It doesn't have to be this way. Kate and I will handle Castro, and Christine and Kevin's defense. You take Elly's case. Between us, we've got it covered.'

'Christine will want this over with. She won't want to delay, even if it means our team is split across two trials.'

'That's his tactic,' said Harry, 'divide and conquer.'

Bloch, who had hung back and characteristically said nothing during this exchange, got up from the desk with a wild look in her eyes.

'What did you say just now?' she asked Harry.

'That Kate and I will handle—'

'No, after that.'

'That Castro hates Eddie?' asked Harry.

'After that.'

Harry thought for a moment, said, 'Oh, Castro's tactics. Divide and conquer.'

'That's it,' she said. 'What if it's not just Castro using those tactics?'

'What do you mean?' I said.

'Elly had a ready-made motive to kill her husband and best friend – they were having an affair. The stranger who tried to kill her knew that. Maybe that was why he targeted her. He could use her. If the same man is following Elly's case, he'll know you're representing her. He could have found out about Arthur Cross – those restraining orders are public record. Christine and Kevin were being threatened by Cross, and he alleged they arranged for him to be attacked so he got his own restraining order. For protection.

If something happened to Cross, Christine and Kevin are prime suspects. He could have framed them both. Same MO. It fits.'

My fingers searched for the Saint Christopher's medal at my throat.

Not for hope. For strength. Because, right then, I was afraid.

Thunder rolled over the skyscrapers, and rain began to beat at the office windows.

I said, 'Bloch, did you ever get hold of the landlord for the apartment where Elly was poisoned?'

'Not yet.'

'Ask your forensics contact to meet you there tonight. We can't waste any more time. Kate, can you make sure all the paperwork is ready for Christine and Kevin's bail hearing? Harry, you're with me.'

'Where are we going?'

'My ex-wife's house. Amy has her book bag, but she needs clothes and everything else. And I want to look at that house. If I'm right, it's a crime scene.'

31
Eddie

By the time we got onto the 495 headed east to Riverhead, Amy was asleep. She had curled up in her coat and lain down in the back seat of my Mustang. Harry was in the front passenger seat.

He had started snoring before we cleared the Midtown tunnel.

The rain made it slow going at first. The roads were washed out and the traffic heavy for this time of night. The expressway, headed east, was quieter and as soon as we passed through Queens the rain and the traffic eased.

Harry sat forward with a jolt, the back of his head coming off the head-rest.

'Wha—? Where are we?'

'We've got another forty-five minutes before we get there.'

'Shouldn't Lake or Bloch be here with us?'

'If we find something, we take a photo, then I'll get Bloch out here with Raymond in the morning.'

He looked at me.

I kept my eyes on the road, but I could feel his look.

'What's up?' I asked.

'Everyone has been asking about Amy, Christine and Kevin. How are *you* holding up?'

'I'm worried as all hell, Harry.'

'We'll make sure we deal with whatever comes up. Kate's the best.'

'Christine and Kevin are in great hands. And at least I'm not worried about that creep, Cross, coming after them any more. But this feels a lot worse, you know?'

'Because it's Castro coming after them?'

'That asshole doesn't play it straight. He'll do whatever he can to win, doesn't matter if he's got the right suspect or not.'

'You've got to ignore him. He's Kate's problem. We can take him. All we need is reasonable doubt.'

'That's getting harder and harder to come by, these days.'

In our world, we dealt in doubt and uncertainty. Those were the defense attorney's sacred hills. If a jury has reasonable doubt, they cannot return a guilty verdict. That was the system, but it had cracks that seemed to get wider with every passing year. In today's world, where there was so much division, people carried their beliefs high on their shoulders. The truth was relative. There was your truth, and their truth. Facts and alternative facts. People distrusted the media, especially the news channels. They all had their own point of view, certainly, but only a couple peddled total lies masquerading as the truth. It wasn't news, it was entertainment. The trouble was nobody had told the rest of the country. Not that many of them would care. Most of the country had decided to live in their own world of facts with their own truth, as it suited them.

We dealt in reasonable doubt.

And we lived in a time of unreasonable certainty.

'We know Kevin's gun was found at the crime scene. Somebody stole Kevin's gun, went to Cross's house in Queens, shot him then dumped the weapon at the scene to make sure the police found it. The gun is kept in a lockbox in the kitchen. I asked Kevin when was the last time he, or Christine, had handled the gun. He told me a couple of days ago, when I was at the house. Someone knew about the gun and where it was kept, and somehow they got it out of the house in the last few days without Kevin, Christine or Amy noticing,' I said.

Harry nodded. He said nothing for a few miles. Every now and again he would rub the top of his head. As an old con artist, I couldn't help spotting people's tells, even those who were closest to me. Harry had something he wanted to say, but was trying to figure out if he should say anything and, if he did, how to do it.

'Proving someone broke in and stole the gun without them noticing is a big ask. It's a leap. Castro has a more convincing story to tell right now. Amy was threatened, Cross got beaten up and was fearful of them, the parents decided they had to do what was necessary to protect their family.'

'That's not the truth. That's not what happened,' I said.

'How long have I been trying to teach you this? The truth doesn't matter in a courtroom. This is all about who tells the jury the most convincing story. Right now, Castro's got the edge.'

'I know that. Come on, Harry, spit it out. Just ask the question. I know it's on your mind.'

'Christine would do anything to protect Amy, but she would never take the law into her own hands. I don't know Kevin . . .' said Harry.

'How long have you been waiting to ask me this?'

'Since I heard they got arrested for Cross's murder.'

'The answer is no. And, even if he was the type of guy, Christine wouldn't cover for him. But there's nothing to worry about on that front, Kevin is not built that way. He's the opposite of me. Christine had that life with me, and she didn't want her new man to be anything like the last one. Kevin wears slippers in the house, for God's sake . . .'

'Nothing wrong with a pair of comfortable slippers,' said Harry.

'Now I know what to get you for Christmas. You want a pipe too, Grandpa?'

'Oh yeah, a real *big* pipe – like the one Sherlock Holmes has.

With a huge funnel and a long stem, so I can ram it straight up your assh—'

'Are you two fighting?' asked Amy, cutting Harry off.

'No, no, sweetheart. Your dad and I are just talking. You go back to sleep.'

We drove on in hushed conversation the rest of the way, until I pulled up outside Christine's house as the rain eased off. I didn't park in the driveway, just kept the car on the street. I wanted to check something. We got out, and as soon as I stepped on the flagstone path to the house the security lights kicked in. Two beams from either corner of the house, blinding us.

'We can rule out entry through the front door,' said Harry.

I asked Amy for her set of keys. We went inside, and the alarm system began to beep. Amy ran to the panel on the wall, entered a code and the alarm system beeped loudly once, then fell silent. I checked the corners of the ceiling in the hallway and the kitchen.

Motion sensors.

Amy went upstairs to grab some of her stuff. I'd told her not to bring too much. Just the essentials for a few days, tops, at my place.

I picked up a chair from the kitchen, put it in the corner and stood on it, so I could take a good look at the sensor. There was no wiring behind it, leading into the wall or the doorframe. I noticed sensors on the windows too. I got down off the chair, checked them.

'The sensors must be on batteries. How do they connect to the central security panel?' I asked.

'I've no idea,' said Harry. 'You need Bloch for that.'

'Must be by radio signal or Wi-Fi,' I said.

I checked the shelf in the kitchen and saw the lockbox for the gun. It was still there. Untouched. The police had raided the house this afternoon, and they had impounded both cars, taken the clothes in the closet, the laundry baskets and their contents. Everything would be checked for gunshot residue, and any blood, hair or fibers that could be traced to the victim. But they hadn't taken the lockbox for the gun. They had the weapon already. I guessed there was not much evidential value in taking the lockbox from where it was normally kept.

I checked in the kitchen cupboards and found a box of disposable gloves and plastic freezer bags, put the gloves on, reached down the lockbox and put it in the plastic bag and sealed it.

'If he didn't come in through the front, where is the point of entry?' I asked.

'Here,' said Harry.

He was standing at a window in the hallway that led from the kitchen through to a dining room at the back of the house. There was a window large enough to crawl through, and a sensor beside it. Kneeling down, Harry examined the floor.

'They're not footprints, exactly. But there's some soil and scuff marks. Like someone was wearing swim shoes,' he said, then stood, unlocked and threw open the window. Placing his hands on the sill, he leaned out.

'There,' said Harry.

I took photographs of the floor with my phone, then went out through the front door and walked around the side of the house along the gravel. A strip of lawn, punctuated with some small shrubs and flowers, separated the gravel path from the house itself. I saw Harry leaning out of the window. He was pointing down at the lawn.

There were impressions in the lawn. No tread, not that I could see. But the shape of a pair of feet.

'Barefoot?' I asked.

'No, some kind of moccasin with no tread and no grip. The kind that some special forces use. Because there's no heel and no tread, it's much harder to track.'

I took photos of the lawn and the foot impressions. A man, certainly. About my height maybe, judging by the size of the prints.

No point in taking impressions, they were so flat there was no way to discern the print. Looking toward the rear of the property, I set off that way and found a large, well-tended backyard – lawns and shrubbery. Tall hedges set out the boundary edge of the property along with high fences on each side, to separate them from the neighbors.

The hedges were thick, but there were gaps in certain places low down near the ground. Certainly big enough to squeeze through. I brought out my phone, opened the maps app and tapped to bring up my location. A two-lane highway stretched behind the suburban development, probably why the construction firm planted all of these thick high hedges – to drown out the noise from the traffic. The map didn't show anything on that highway, apart from a gas station.

I crouched down, crawled through a gap in the tree line and when I stood up, my knees were soaked and caked in mud, as were my hands and jacket, which had picked up all the rainwater left on the lower branches.

An area of patchy grass, mud and scrubland separating the trees from the road. The gas station was visible further on up the highway. I looked around, saw some tire tracks about fifty feet away on the grass. Took out my phone, snapped some pictures and sent them to Bloch and Lake, then crawled back through the trees to the yard and made my way back to front of the house.

Harry was waiting on the front porch.

'What the hell happened to you?'

'I was checking round back. I think I found where the killer parked, on the other side of the treeline by the highway. Then he squeezed through the trees and came up on the house from the rear so he could steal the gun. I got some pictures of tire treads, but I don't think it will do much good. Nothing special about the tread pattern, probably widely available. But it might help me explain to a jury what really happened.'

'You mean it might help Kate explain it to the jury.'

I shook my head, said, 'Sorry, I'm just too close to this one. The more I think about it, the more I think I should represent Christine and Kevin.'

'It's exactly because you're too close that you shouldn't represent them. We've got this.'

'But you and Kate do things differently than I do.'

Harry stepped forward, put his hand on my shoulder and said, 'We'll do the right thing. Kate told me about Elly getting hauled off to solitary after she assaulted an inmate. Did you tell Kate to do that?'

I said, 'I didn't tell her to do anything. It was her choice, and she stepped up to protect her client. I know she's been feeling bad about it since. I just can't let Christine go to prison for the rest of her life for a crime she didn't commit. Nor Kevin, for that matter. A couple of years ago, I wouldn't have minded Kevin being out of the picture, but not like this. And not now. I see he's good for Christine, Amy too.'

'You've got to trust Kate and me.'

'I've never doubted your abilities. That's not what I mean.'

'She's not like you, Eddie.'

'I know. She's better. That's the problem. Look, I'm sorry. I can't—'

'I'll do whatever it takes to protect them. I swear to you. Remember, you gave me your word you would step back on this one. Take my word that I will do everything to win.'

He held out his hand.

I took it, and he pulled me into an embrace.

'We won't let you down, kid,' said Harry.

I put my brow on his shoulder. Harry smelled of damp tweed and hard liquor. It was a familiar odor. One I'd grown to love.

'I know,' I said.

We stepped back, Harry punched my shoulder, said, 'Let's get out of here. We have work to do.'

I called out for Amy.

'Just another few minutes,' she said.

Harry said he'd take the lockbox and wait in the car.

I went upstairs, expecting to see Amy lying in her bed. In tears.

She was in her room, her bag packed and on the floor beside her. She sat at her desk, on her laptop.

'What are you doing, sweetheart?' I asked.

'I . . . I was going to watch that show. Your favorite. The "just one more thing" guy, Palumbo?'

'Columbo.'

'Yeah, I started downloading it last night. Thought we could watch it at the weekend. But something happened. Look, the router says the Wi-Fi went out last night. It hasn't downloaded . . .'

32

Bloch

Manhattan at night, in the rain, is a battlefield of color.

The streets ahead of Bloch were painted red by stop lights and the tail lights of cars in front, and every so often an ocean-green traffic light interrupted the deadlock to allow her Jeep to crawl forward. Streetlamps added intermittent cones of pastel yellow on the slicked sidewalks, which somehow only served to make the darkness in between them deeper and richer. The windshield wipers were working fast, sweeping away tides of rain as if washing away a rainbow of digital light. The front driver's-side wheel of Bloch's jeep broke a puddle of neon-pink rainwater, instantly turning it black, and as the ripples diminished the color swirled to life again and settled on its calm surface like a bright veneer.

Bloch pulled up at the apartment building to see Raymond, wearing his waterproof coat and carrying his kit bag, taking shelter in the doorway. Grabbing a fold-up raincoat from her glovebox, Bloch slipped it over her leather jacket, which was already soaked just from the short walk from the office to her car. Her dark blue jeans were black and clinging to her skin. Cold and wet.

She got out of the Jeep, locked it with the fob and joined Raymond in the doorway. A drainpipe on the storefront opposite must've broken loose from its brackets, because a torrent of rain was hitting the sidewalk as fast and hard as a fire hose.

'You picked a lovely night for it,' he said.

Bloch said nothing.

Raymond worked in a lab separate and independent from law enforcement. While he occasionally freelanced for the FBI, it didn't matter to him who paid for his work, because his results would not alter no matter what the fee, no matter what the circumstances of the case may be. He was a scientist, first.

'Is the apartment owner meeting us here?' asked Raymond.

'Not exactly,' mumbled Bloch.

'What was that?' asked Raymond. It was difficult to be heard over the noise from the rain.

Without saying another word, Bloch turned to the panel of buzzers for the apartment complex. About forty in all. Thankfully, the rain was keeping pedestrians off the streets. Nobody wanted to be out in this. Everyone who needed to be anywhere was in a cab, an Uber or their own transport.

She pressed the first ten call buttons on the panel.

As the intercom buzzed, Bloch mumbled, 'Deliveroo . . .'

After a few tries, someone buzzed open the door.

The lobby was tiled and messy, with building supplies stacked in one corner. The elevator was working, and as they got in and traveled up, Bloch took a photo of the lift manufacturer and the maintenance log, which was taped to a panel. The last entry was just a few days ago.

They arrived on the third floor. Bloch and Raymond got out, and checked the apartment number on the door. Raymond dumped his forensic bag, which was silver and thick plastic. It doubled as a cool bag to keep samples at the right temperature. He stripped off his raincoat, took a thick, white latex suit from his bag and stepped into it, then put on his gloves, a breathing mask and then pulled the suit hood over his head and tightened it. He took a flashlight and a UV light, then hooked his bag onto his shoulder.

'Do you have a key? Or is the owner meeting us here?' asked Raymond.

Bloch stood back, then launched forward with tremendous speed, the heel of her boot meeting the door at the lock. The wood buckled and broke, and the frame cracked, but the door didn't open.

There was no apartment directly opposite this one; the closest was a good twenty feet down the hallway. The door to that apartment opened and a young woman came out, wearing pajamas and a bathrobe. She stood just a few feet from her door.

'What the hell is going on? I'll call the pol . . .' she said, but her voice trailed off when she saw Raymond in his suit.

'Sorry, Department of Health,' said Bloch, flashing her PI credentials. She was far enough away for it to look official, but not close enough to read. 'We have a warrant. The owner of this apartment was breeding rats. We have reports some have escaped and we need to neutralize the problem.'

The woman's eyes widened when Raymond, in his hazardous material suit, turned around and gave her the thumbs up.

'Oh shit, sorry. Go ahead. Make sure you get 'em all,' said the woman, hurrying back into her apartment and shutting the door.

'You know anything I find in here can't be used in court,' said Raymond.

'I know,' said Bloch. 'It's not for court. It's for me. We're looking for the man who poisoned our client.'

'Like I said on the phone, this apartment regularly being an Airbnb, there's going to be hundreds of prints and DNA sets. This is going to take a while.'

Raymond moved inside and flicked on the light switch. The apartment was as Elly had described it. Small, sparse. No trash bags, though. The killer had cleaned up.

'Check the bedroom, bathroom and fridge carefully. This man had a cast on his leg. I think he may have cut it off in this apartment. How long will you need?'

'Two, maybe three hours,' said Raymond.

'I'll be back in two hours. I'll be in the car outside when you need me. I'm going to help Lake. He's looking for a witness. With the rain, this guy is going to try and find a dry bed. We need to hit every shelter in the city tonight,' said Bloch.

She rode the elevator to the lobby, used the buzzer to open the door and, pulling up her hood, she went back into the rain, headed for her Jeep.

The sound of fat raindrops pounding her plastic hood, and everything else was way too loud for Bloch's comfort. She didn't like a lot of noise. It made her feel . . . *weird*. The storm drains by the side of the road were covered in foam, the sheer force of the rainwater overwhelming.

Bloch put her hand in her coat, her fingers wrapped round the fob to open the car.

It was then that she heard the noise for the first time.

Footsteps, coming up on her, fast.

Bloch used her other hand to grab for her gun, beneath the raincoat.

It was too late.

33
Lake

Flynn had been right.

Goddamn it, thought Lake.

Flynn was always right.

The lady in the HOME-STAT office who Lake had talked to would not give out any information on the last known whereabouts for Joe Novak. But the HOME-STAT survey-taker Lake found on the corner of East 13th Street and Second Avenue, soaked to the skin in the heavy rain, was just the right kind of guy. His coat sleeve was ripped and his boots were held together with tape. He took the five hundred, made two phone calls and then told Lake to check East 20th Street and Avenue C, in one of the tented villages beneath the FDR.

Within the hour, Lake had made it to the underpass, a concrete patch of shelter from the ribbon of blacktop that was the FDR overhead. There were maybe forty people, some huddled around tents, some crowded around burning oil barrels for warmth. It was a dismal sight. Lake parked his Pontiac Aztek across the street, flipped up the collar of his raincoat and got out of the car. He didn't lock it. No need. Only somebody with a wicked sense of humor would steal this car. It was a bad car when it came out of the factory and twenty years and eighty thousand miles had not added to its charm.

Lake's right foot went ankle deep in a puddle as he crossed the street. Didn't matter. He had been out in this rain for an hour or more and his feet were already soaking with freezing rain.

As he made his way through the village of people, he felt an overwhelming sadness. This wasn't right. In one of the richest countries in the world, it was a disgrace that people didn't have a home, or food, or healthcare as a basic right. He passed a woman sitting outside a tent with a shawl around her head, leaving only her weathered face exposed. The sun in the summer and the cold winter winds ate through people's skin, aging them, and beating down more than just their bodies. Sleeping on a sidewalk will damage your psyche just as much as your spine.

The hard streets of New York break your bones, your heart and your dreams.

'Ma'am, my name is Gabriel Lake. I'm looking for a man named Joe Novak. He's a veteran and he's in trouble. I'm trying to get him some help,' said Lake, holding out a five-dollar bill.

A hand shot out of the shawl, grabbed the cash. She beckoned for him to come closer.

'He's over there, standing around the fire with his pal, Romy,' said the woman, and then a hacking cough cut off all further communication. But the arm did appear again, to point in the direction of the burning barrel.

There were four fire barrels going, but only one in the direction the woman had pointed. Lake thanked her, and made his way to the two guys standing around it, warming their hands with the flames, which licked orange and amber light into their faces.

They both looked suspicious of Lake. Both wore heavy overcoats. Hard to tell in this light what color they were. Both wore thick scarves wrapped round their necks and over their faces, to keep out the cold. One wore an I ♥ NYC ball cap. The other, a beanie pulled tight over his ears. They stood side by side and Lake could see their eyes narrowing and hardening as he approached. It was the only part of their faces he could see.

'Evening, my name is Gabriel Lake. I work for Eddie Flynn, the lawyer. You might have heard of him. He's representing a young woman accused of murder. I think one of you guys might have seen this young lady before. Even helped her. Probably saved her life. Someone tried to kill her and then framed her for murder. The man I'm looking for can save her life again. This is Elly.'

He held up his phone, showing Elly's profile picture from social media.

'Which one of you guys is Joe Novak?'

They looked at each other for a moment. Something unspoken passed between them.

The man in the beanie hat asked, 'Are you a cop?'

'I used to be a fed. I spoke to a couple of your buddies, Pat and Sean. They said there was some other guy looking for you. Someone who was pretending to be a cop. It was Pat and Sean that gave me your name and told me to go look for you around the veteran's center.'

The man in the beanie hat said, 'I'm surprised at Pat. Sean, he was never good at keeping his mouth shut.'

'So you're Joseph Novak?' said Lake.

'I don't want to talk here. I could use some coffee and a place to get warm.'

'Sure,' said Lake.

The man stepped away from the fire barrel, came round and fell into step beside Lake.

'Is there somewhere around here you want to go? Or I could drive us somewhere?' said Lake.

'There's an all-night diner two blocks away. You can drive. Get us out of this rain,' said Joe. 'I don't mind the cold. It's the rain that really beats me all to . . .'

The sound of Joe's voice drifted off for a second as Lake's attention snapped away to something else. He noticed a dark sedan coming through the traffic lights. There was little traffic in this part of the city even at rush hour. Less at this time of night in this weather. The sedan was pointed right at them. It had its full beam headlights on, so it was impossible to see the license plate.

Lake tensed. Already cold and wet, an electric shiver started at the base of his spine and traveled up his back.

As the car turned left, maybe forty feet from them, Lake saw the passenger-side front window roll down.

The rain was unrelenting. The driver wouldn't be buzzing down the window for fresh air.

Lake's instincts took over.

He stepped in close to Joe, shoulder tackling him hard just as the driver popped off his first round. Lake could see the muzzle flash illuminating the interior of the car. It was impossible to make out the driver in the dark.

Five more flashes. Five cracks echoing through the air.

Lake landed on his left side, close to Joe's feet.

The sedan sped away. Engine revving high.

Lake reached for his pistol, but his right arm screamed back at him.

He'd been hit, just below the elbow. He hadn't even felt the round tear his flesh. Now, he gazed at the cuff of his shirt. It turned red as the blood running down his arm seeped through.

Lake turned and crawled over to Joe Novak, who lay on his left side.

Unmoving.

Lake rolled him over. It was too damn dark to see beneath the overpass.

'Joe? Joe? Are you hit?'

Joe's eyes were open. Unblinking.

Lake pulled the scarf away, saw a smear of blood on Joe's lips.

With his left hand, he took out his pocket flashlight and turned it on Joe. Blood was pooling on his chest and throat. Lake wiped it away, looking for the wound, and found two at the top of his chest.

'Joe? Joe?'

Blood was still pumping from the wounds. Lake took the scarf and did his best to staunch the bleed with one hand, while his fingers trembled and his own blood ran over the screen on his phone as he dialed 911.

The other man came running over. Knelt down beside Joe as Lake asked for a paramedic and police.

The other man cupped Joe's face, said, 'He's dead. Oh my God, he's dead.'

Lake took the scarf away, listened for a pulse, checked Joe's breathing.

Nothing.

He started CPR. Told the man to put pressure on the wounds, but not to get in his way.

With every chest compression, Lake felt another jet of blood pumping from his arm. He felt faint and sick. Like he wanted to vomit. But he pushed through, counting off the compressions, then giving Joe mouth to mouth.

Minutes felt like hours. And there was no sign of the paramedics.

Lake's vision blurred. He lost count of the chest compressions.

Gave mouth to mouth. Then pumped Joe's chest again.

'He's dead,' said the other homeless guy.

Lake could hear the sirens getting closer. Sweat and rain stung his eyes. His arm screamed and Lake told himself to stay with it. To keep going. To save this guy. Lake knew he wasn't just trying to save one life – Elly Parker's life was in the balance too.

Suddenly, Lake couldn't hold himself upright. His vision clouded and he collapsed beside Joe. He couldn't breathe. His eyes wouldn't stay open.

Before the darkness took him, he heard the other homeless man in the cap say something weird. At first, he couldn't understand it. It was such a strange thing to say.

'It's the kindness that kills you,' said the homeless man.

34
Bloch

Bloch couldn't tell if the sidewalk was coming up to meet her face, or if she was falling toward it.

She'd heard footsteps behind her on the street, once she'd left Raymond in the apartment, then felt something hit the back of her head, before she could turn round and face whoever was coming up on her so fast. There had been no pain, not yet, but it had been hard enough for her to collapse. Something happens when you get hit just right, enough to rattle the brain inside the skull – your legs just give out.

Bloch wasn't unconscious, but she knew she had been hit hard and managed to bring her arms up, protecting her face as she hit the sidewalk.

Her right forearm took the impact, jolting her shoulder and sending a freezing pain through her elbow that immediately brought gooseflesh to her skin.

She was still awake.

The pain in her arm lit up her nervous system. Cleared her head just as she felt the pain growing at the back of her head and the first trickle of blood on her neck.

She spun round, shoulders to the sidewalk, to face the man standing over her.

He was enormous, and wore a long, black leather coat that bulged from his shoulders and arms, as if he was wearing football pads. But Bloch knew this wasn't padding. She could tell by the large thick hands that reached down toward her. He had a bald head and a beard. Scars crisscrossed his cheeks, and one long slash bisected his right eyebrow.

His name was Bruno Mont. The man who did wet work for Arthur Cross.

Mont knelt down, taking hold of Bloch's coat to keep her on the ground, his left knee digging into her thighs. He let go with his right hand, raised it and sent a massive blow toward Bloch's face. She managed to get her hands up to cover her head and felt her left arm go numb with the impact. Instinctively, she snapped a right hand into his jaw, snapping his head back. But she had no purchase, no power from lying flat on the sidewalk. A second later, she convulsed as his huge fist drove into her side and Bloch heard her ribs snap. She cried out. Reflex kicked in and her arm dropped to protect her side, leaving her face exposed.

A straight right to her mouth hammered the back of her head to the sidewalk. His hand was now in her jacket. He drew out her Magnum and tossed it.

Bloch's vision blurred, stars dancing around Bruno Mont's ugly smiling face.

She was hurt, dazed, but no longer surprised.

Bloch took a second to glance around, getting her bearings. She was beside a line of cars parked along the curb. A black BMW was beside her, just a few feet away, and her Jeep was just beyond it.

Bruno sat up, and reached into his jacket.

Bloch planted her heels on the ground and arched her back, forcing him off, unbalancing him so he fell off her, onto his ass.

She had two choices. Try to get to her feet, and deal with him toe to toe, with whatever weapon he had in his coat.

Or . . .

Bloch rolled onto her left side and swung her right leg as hard as she could into the passenger door of the BMW parked at the curb. A metallic thud from Bloch's boot put a dent in the door, but thankfully something else happened.

The car's alarm kicked in, deafening her. Lights flashing. Horn buzzing.

It was the best thing Bloch could do.

Raise the alarm.

She turned to see Bruno getting onto his feet, a blade in his right hand.

He looked left and right, checking the street. The car alarm would bring any passing eyes directly on him.

Bloch rolled onto her knees, tried to get her feet beneath her. She was panting, her head was fried and her side was in agony. Bruno took one step toward her, sent a boot into her stomach. The force of the kick lifted Bloch's body into the air and slammed her back into the BMW. She landed face down on the sidewalk and heard Bruno's boots again. She flipped over onto her back, and lashed out wildly with her feet, kicking at Bruno, and felt her boot connect with his wrist. She heard the metallic sound of the knife landing some feet away.

He lashed out, sweeping her feet aside, and bent down, taking hold of her by the coat. Bloch made a grab for his wrists, then felt herself being lifted clean into the air, up, over Bruno's head, and then down, fast.

She closed her eyes, locked her fingers behind her head and then screamed as Bruno planted her body through the windshield of the BMW. She heard the sound of glass exploding, felt an unbelievable pain in her lower back, then found herself falling into the passenger seat, her legs draped over the steering wheel.

Over the sound of the alarm, she heard Bruno's boots again, running away before somebody saw him.

Bloch tried to move, heard the glass clinking and rattling around her. She was cut, her right arm bleeding badly.

The effort was too much, and she collapsed as she heard the voices of passers-by running toward her. Male. Maybe two of them. And a female, calling a paramedic.

That's the thing about New York City. No matter what shit goes down, there is always a stranger who will come and help.

35

Logan

His foot still hard down on the accelerator, Logan checked the rearview mirror.

Following the investigator, Lake, had proven useful. Logan had spent his life studying human behavior. He could tell, just by the body language, that Lake had gotten a hot lead from the HOME-STAT surveyor. There was an urgency in Lake's step after that conversation. When Lake spoke to the old woman, who pointed him toward the two men at the fire barrel, Logan knew Lake had hit paydirt. Then his interaction with the men, and the man agreeing to come with him confirmed it. Logan couldn't see much of the homeless men's faces, but he recognized the coat. He'd last seen it being worn by Joe Novak as he was crouched over the convulsing body of Elly Parker.

There was no doubt, Lake had Novak, and now he was bent over the homeless man, giving him CPR.

He couldn't be sure, but Logan thought he had hit Novak at least twice in the chest, high up near the throat. Usually, Logan knew he had landed a fatal shot by watching the victim's expression change. No chance of that with Novak, all wrapped up in that scarf and headgear, but still. The shots were good. He didn't manage to get a clean shot on Lake, though. Just tagged him. Maybe.

It didn't matter.

The witness was dead already, even if Lake didn't realize it.

And so was any hope of a defense for Elly Parker.

Logan put a good mile between him and the scene of the shooting before he pulled over, and got out of the car. He removed the magnetic license plates from front and back, crossed the street to the river, tossed the gun and the plates in the Hudson, then buttoned his coat and made for the nearest subway.

He checked his phone, found a text message from Grace.

> I know what you did. Please come over.

He texted back, said he was on his way. As he stepped down into the subway, he felt his legs dragging. One thing Logan hated was uncertainty. There were only really two ways this could go tonight. Maybe she would be overwhelmed with joy at what he had done. Or she might be really offended and tell him that she didn't ever want to see him again. That would be an unfortunate reaction. For Logan and Grace. Logan didn't want to lose her. Of that, he was certain. If she rejected him, or found what he had done controlling and didn't want to be involved in a relationship, Logan didn't know exactly how he would deal with that.

He rode the trains and thought about how he felt. The mere fact that he was nervous about meeting her wasn't just from the uncertainty – it was also that a big part of him really wanted her. Never having experienced it himself, infatuation was an alien concept to Logan. There are psychological tricks to make up for a lack of empathy, but nothing that came close to being able to fake something like love. Chemicals, hormones, social conditioning, psychology, primal instincts, none of this explained it. Poets came about as close as physiologists.

Logan experienced a weird feeling in his stomach as he climbed the subway steps a block away from Grace's building. His heartbeat quickened when he thought of her. Especially when he thought of those quiet moments, when he was just staring into her eyes. It made him feel more than content. And it was different from the exhilaration of taking a life and hiding the crime so perfectly. The joy and satisfaction of seeing someone else pay for your crime. This feeling when he thought of Grace, it was different to all of them. And more than all of them.

When Grace confessed to Logan about feeling lonely, he'd felt a powerful connection with her. All he had ever known was loneliness. He knew it like he knew the taste of coffee, like he knew the sunrise, even the lines on his own face. And here, for the first time, was someone who felt the same way. It felt, to Logan, that Grace somehow knew his heart, and his deepest sorrows, and hopes, all at once. He felt understood, even accepted.

Fear was part of love, he decided. The fear of losing this person, that connection, was powerful.

Ten minutes later, Grace opened the front door to her apartment wearing her blue pajamas and a bathrobe. A puddle of water had gathered around Logan's feet, his raincoat steadily dripping onto the tiled floor.

Drip, drip, drip.

The sound somehow echoed his heartbeat. The sound of water dripping sent Logan's mind back into a dark, red memory. He fought to clear his head.

Strands of hair stuck to his wet face like cold shards of ice.

Grace said nothing. Her expression was blank.

No joy.

No anger.

Suspicion, maybe?

She left the door open, stepped back and disappeared into the apartment. For a moment, Logan froze. Fear glued his feet to the floor. When he walked through that door, either he would begin the best chance for happiness he'd ever had in his life, or . . .

He didn't want to think of the alternative.

His coat continued its steady *drip, drip, drip*.

A shudder rippled through his body, either from the cold or the fear.

He blinked. Swallowed. Stepped inside the apartment and closed the door behind him.

Grace leaned against the kitchen counter.

There was a brown envelope in her hands. Her beautiful face remained impassive. Neutral. Impossible to read.

Not a good sign.

Logan dug his hands into his coat pockets.

He said nothing.

But his right hand found the switchblade in his pocket.

Shifting her gaze from Logan to the refrigerator, Grace said, 'So you saw my bills on the refrigerator door the other night?'

Logan nodded. He couldn't speak. Didn't want to. It was as if some other part of him was watching this all play out.

'I didn't know I was going to invite you back to my place after our date. As a rule, I *don't* on first dates. But I liked you, Logan,' she said, her tone flat.

That one word replayed in his mind.

Liked.

Not *like*.

Past tense.

His grip on the switchblade tightened.

'I don't have money. You probably realized my student loan came from a private company. Not a bank. I couldn't get shit from a bank so I had to go to a private lender who charges a little less than a loan shark and I'll be paying off interest until I retire. But it's my debt. Lucky for me they don't want the debt paid off early. I called them to transfer the money back into your account. It should be back there by morning.'

'You what? Why? It's a hundred thousand dollars, Grace. That's nothing to me. There's no reason why you should have this debt hanging over you when I could—'

'It's *my* debt, Logan. Not *yours*. I called my landlord and asked him to repay the money you transferred for my back rent. Getting money out of a landlord is impossible. He refused, said he didn't care if it came from Santa Claus or Jesus Christ himself, he was keeping it. It was owed to him. So I went out and borrowed the five grand you paid him. Here, this is for you,' she said, holding out the envelope.

'Grace, you're a great person. And I want to help you. I . . . I like you a lot. And, like I said, it's not a big deal to me—'

'But it is to me. Not the rent or the loan. *You*, Logan. You're a big deal to me. I know we've only had one date, but I really like you. No one has ever talked to me like you did. I felt like we were connecting on a deep level. That this wasn't just a date. It was like you were really talking to me, and I've told you things I've never told other dates. That connection I felt the other night, with you, that was real. I felt it. I know you felt it too. That's what matters to me. I could tell you were wealthy by the watch and the clothes, but I don't care about any of it. And I need you to *know* that. So here – take this back, please. It was so kind, but I don't want it.'

He let go of the switchblade and pulled his hands out of his coat pockets. He stepped closer, and took the envelope, his heart racing. Grace didn't let the envelope go.

'I don't want money, Logan. I want *you*.'

She pulled him in close, and kissed him.

They dropped the envelope to the floor. Logan grabbed Grace, held her, and felt his warm tears trickling across his cold cheek.

Their lips parted, Logan said three words he had never before uttered, nor ever dreamed of speaking in his lifetime.

'I need you,' he said.

36

Eddie

I can't stand those calls.

When your phone rings in the middle of the night, it's never good news.

Those two calls, just hours ago, were bad. They could've been so much worse.

It had been a long, sleepless night.

I got up from my desk and stretched my back. The sun was bleeding the night into morning. Amy was finally asleep in a makeshift bed of blankets and cushions on the floor of my office conference room, Clarence curled up beside her.

Harry had fallen asleep in the chair opposite mine. He was snoring softly.

I left my office and set off for the kitchen. I needed at least two pots of coffee this morning to fire up my brain. Before I got there, I heard footsteps on the stairs: the familiar trudge of Bloch's boots, slower, more halting this morning. And, behind them, the soft shuffle of Lake's shoes.

They came in the main door of the office, spotted me and stopped.

'Jesus, you scared the shit out of me. Both of you,' I said. 'You two should still be in the hospital.'

Lake's left arm was in a sling. He wore a hospital robe under his suit jacket. The robe tucked into his pants. They must've cut his shirt off to deal with the bullet wound.

Bloch was a mess. Her face was swollen on the left side. Her eye, now half shut with the swelling, was turning green and purple. Her arms were a circuit board of Band-Aids and bandages.

'Did you get a CT scan?' I asked, looking at her.

'Mild concussion. Three broken ribs, cuts and bruises,' said Bloch. 'Nothing that would stop me finding Bruno Mont.'

'Leave Mont for now. I know you want him. I would too. But there's a time and a place. You're still breathing, which means he messed up last night. He's gonna lay low for a while. He knows you're going to be on your guard. He'll wait. Some months at least. Enough time for you to become complacent. We'll get him before that.'

'He's going to wish he died fast, like Cross,' said Bloch.

'Did Kate update you all?'

They nodded.

Bloch turned to look at Lake, said, 'You're still wearing a hospital shirt. You went back to your apartment and you didn't put on a fresh shirt?'

'Didn't have a clean one. Don't judge me. I got a lot going on,' said Lake.

'You both sure you're okay to be here?' I asked.

They just stared at me.

'Okay, let me grab some coffee and you both go and take a look at the video on Harry's laptop. I've watched it three times. Something's bugging me. See if you can figure it out.'

They went into my office quietly, so as not to startle Harry. Gently, Bloch put a hand on his shoulder and he opened his eyes. He stood and embraced her. Bloch wasn't comfortable with human contact. Not really. There were few exceptions. Her childhood friend Kate, and Harry.

Bloch tried to smile, not wanting to worry the old guy. It didn't work. Harry watched her grimace as she sat down in one of the chairs arranged around my desk. Lake waved away Harry's concern. I didn't need to be in the room to know what Lake was saying. It was a flesh wound and he'd had much worse. Just before he left the FBI he stumbled into a drug dealers cash house while working a different case. A lot of heavily armed men died that night at Lake's hand. Part of Lake died in that house too. He had walked in an FBI agent, and had been carried out by paramedics as a killer. He'd been set up by someone in the Bureau, and had never found out who exactly was responsible.

It was on my list to find out who some day.

I put four mugs on the counter. Poured black coffee for Bloch and I. Another for Harry, with a little shot from a bottle of Kentucky bourbon I kept in the kitchen. For Lake, I made hot water with lemon. I don't know how he drinks it.

Once I'd carried the drinks into my office, I saw Harry was starting the video.

'In cases of exhumation,' began Harry, 'the key concern for police officers is establishing the chain of evidence for the body. Every second that corpse is out of the ground has to be accounted for. Otherwise, it's Christmas time for the defense.'

'How so?' asked Lake.

'Think about it. They want the body to be examined in the hope of finding evidence of foul play. If a smartass defense lawyer can say that between the time of the body being exhumed and the time the body is examined or tested, there was an opportunity for someone to interfere with the state of the corpse then it renders the test results shaky. They need an unbroken chain of evidence to prove that their examination is accurate, and that no one could have had access to the body to distort their investigation results. Look . . .' said Harry, and hit play on the laptop.

The screen showed a team of police and forensics officers,

together with cemetery workers, breaking ground in a cemetery with a small backhoe. Harry speeded up the video. The gravestone was that of Stewart Yorke, Elly's father. The grave beside it belonged to her mother. Once the hole was big enough, two grave diggers jumped down into the grave carrying long straps. It looked from the video like a peaceful place to be laid to rest for eternity. Beyond the graveyard, the river and the Manhattan skyline were visible.

The canopy of a large tree sat above both graves, providing some shelter for the workers, and for mourners, I guessed.

Once the straps were in place, a telehandler appeared in shot and the straps were attached. It hauled the casket out of the grave and into a black steel case, which sat on a flatbed truck. The case's sole purpose was for transporting exhumed bodies. The lid of the case was closed, locked and for the first time Detective Bill Sacks appeared in shot. He peeled off a police evidence seal sticker from its backing and stuck it over the lid of the steel transport box. Close-ups of the seals were recorded.

The video went blank and started again in a different location with a close-up of the same evidence seals on the steel box, to demonstrate that they had not been broken and were in exactly the same place, but this time the flatbed was at the loading bay of the medical examiner's office in Manhattan. We saw the seals being broken and mortuary workers in white forensics overalls lift the casket from the transport box, onto a trolley and wheel it inside. The camera followed it to an examination room where Dr. Sharpling, the medical examiner, was waiting. He wore a full forensic suit and was only recognizable because of a tuft of white hair sticking out from his hood.

The mortuary assistants opened the casket, and the camera swept over the body of Elly's father, from his shoes to his head.

But the camera stopped at his knees.

'What's this,' said a voice in the video that sounded like Sharpling. He appeared in frame with a pair of long steel tongs. He called for a baggie. Sacks appeared at his side with a transparent plastic evidence bag.

Sharpling reached inside the casket and when his arm came out there was a moth in the teeth of the prongs. The moth was dead, unmoving. As he placed it in the evidence bag, he offered an explanation.

'Probably came from the funeral parlor. Most of them have a room of old, spare clothes to dress the customers who don't have anything formal. This little guy was probably in a suit hanging up in the funeral home and next thing he gets buried with a corpse . . .'

Sacks sealed the bag, then handed it to someone else.

'I've never seen that before,' I said. 'Anything out of the ordinary, it bugs me. The rest of the video shows the autopsy and Sharpling taking samples of tissue.'

'Rewind that back to when the doc holds up the moth,' said Lake.

Harry used the keyboard on the laptop to find the section of video.

'There,' said Lake, 'freeze it.'

Lake and Bloch leaned forward, looked at the screen. The moth was large enough, I guessed, with brown forewings dotted with black spots. The same spots appeared on its scarlet hind wings.

Lake and Bloch looked at each other. They smiled.

'Rewind it further, to the cemetery,' said Bloch.

Harry started the video again from the beginning, showing the backhoe starting to dig up the remains.

'That's it,' said Bloch.

'What?' I asked. 'What did you see?'

Lake smiled and said, 'We just saw heaven.'

'What does that mean?' said Harry.

Bloch stood, said, 'It means we just found a defense.'

PART FIVE

37
Elly

The short months Elly spent in the mid-priced motel in Manhattan felt like years.

She had not posted anything on her social media since her viral video. She had not written anything, or sold her story to any news, TV or publishing outlets despite her agent's protests. As a result, she no longer had any money coming in. Her apartment was up for sale, but buyers were put off by the events that had led to the property appearing on the market. Real estate is at a premium in Manhattan, but no one wanted an apartment that was the scene of a famous double homicide – not even the weirdos.

What little of her savings she'd had left after posting bail, were almost gone. If she didn't sell the apartment, or agree to sell her story soon, she would have nothing.

And Elly didn't care.

She rose from her bed and went to the bathroom, splashed water on her face and stared in the mirror. The energetic, vibrant young woman she had been four months ago was gone. She had swollen red eyes. Her clothes didn't fit properly since she'd lost weight, maybe twenty pounds. The weight loss didn't suit her. It only made her look ill and drawn. Harriet had always gently nudged Elly to lose weight. She would never say anything, but she would give Elly a look if she bought a donut or ordered dessert. Harriet, the model, who had stolen her husband, had always been rail thin.

Memories of conversations she'd had with James took on new meanings. This was a constant source of torture. She remembered asking James, one night at a party, if he thought she should lose weight, and look more like Harriet. He had smiled and told her not to be foolish, but Elly couldn't help but notice the hesitation before he answered, and the way she had caught him looking at Harriet sometimes when he thought he was unobserved.

It all made sense now.

And there was no way to fix any of this.

Betrayal and grief were powerful enemies.

She showered and dressed in a plain black pants suit. White shirt. For court.

No make-up.

Four months ago, the thought of leaving the house without make-up would have been inconceivable. Now, she couldn't recall the last time she had worn any.

No point.

She cried too much.

For her friend. For her husband. For her father, and for herself.

Before Elly left, she turned to the full-length mirror bolted to the wall of the hotel room. A woman she didn't recognize stared back.

Elly had changed. She no longer trusted people. Only Eddie and his team. She had seen the videos about Eddie on TikTok, and like a lot of New Yorkers she had vowed that if she were ever in trouble she would call Eddie Flynn.

She had made the right choice. She knew that.

And yet Eddie wasn't a miracle worker. She knew he had a plan, and that the man would fight for her with his very soul.

But as the strange woman in the mirror stared back at Elly, she couldn't help thinking this was the beginning of another horror.

This trial could send her to prison for the rest of her life.

And there was nothing anyone could do about it.

38
Kate

Kate lay in bed, wide awake, at five thirty in the morning as the wake-up alarm on her phone began to chime.

She had decided to get an early night. Always best to get as much sleep as possible on the eve of the first day of a murder trial. But from ten fifteen last night she had lain in bed, completely and comprehensively awake. This wasn't Kate's first rodeo, but when the clients were her law partner's ex-wife and her husband, the stakes were that much higher. At first, the couple had been arrested on the assumption that they had acted together. Both of them had a reason to want Arthur Cross dead.

The NYPD forensics lab had found two sets of fingerprints on the murder weapon. Kevin's and Christine's. Christine told Kate she had only handled the gun twice. Once at a shooting range, after Kevin got the gun, and once maybe a week before the murder when she had gotten scared by a delivery driver and had taken it in hand.

The prosecution claimed this was a conspiracy to murder Arthur Cross and, with both sets of prints on the murder weapon, they had both been indicted. To make matters worse, Harry had been right – DA Castro had fast-tracked the trial to coincide with the Elly Parker case. That meant the defense of Kevin and Christine fell on Kate's shoulders.

They'd had months of preparation. Bloch had done the legwork, gathered the evidence. Kate had prepared her notes on cross-examination. They were typed up, edited, deleted and rewritten many times. Christine, a good lawyer in her own right, had listened to Kate's theory on defense, and agreed to it. Kevin, also a lawyer, had been impressed.

It had been hundreds of hours of preparation and talks with Eddie and Harry, and now Kate was ready. Organized.

And yet . . .

The defense in this case was weak. The only real point was that the prosecution couldn't prove how Christine and Kevin had got to Cross's house on the night of the murder. It was a hole in their otherwise perfect story. But, in reality, not more than a slim thread for Kate to tug upon. With some luck, it might be just enough. She knew at a murder trial you had to put on a performance. Tell your client's story and rip the prosecution's story to pieces. And do it all with style and panache – for the jury.

The jury had been selected last week. Seven women. Five men. Kate had taken that as a small win. Women, in her experience, had a stronger and deeper sense of justice than men.

The DA, Castro, had worn his famous white suit to court during jury selection, playing the role of incorruptible warrior for victims, for justice and for truth. That was what had been on his last election poster. In reality, it was widely rumored that Castro had bribed several unions to have their members turn out in force for his re-election. Several high-ranking union bosses had had some trouble with the IRS over the administration of some of their pension schemes, and Kate guessed those investigations, with the right kind of pressure from their white knight, would all quietly go away.

Money. Favors. Such things are cities built upon.

And she could count on Castro to fight dirty in this trial.

Apart from the pressure of the case, there was something else that had kept Kate awake last night. What if she had to break the rules to get Christine and Kevin off? Anything can happen in a murder trial, and with the stakes so high for each side the temptation to bend or break the law in order to win was far too tempting for most lawyers.

Eddie didn't think twice about this shit. And she envied him for that. He thought the system was unfair, unjust, and it took a conman to balance those scales of justice. Kate didn't have Eddie's upbringing. Her old man had been a cop for twenty years. She came from the other side of the fence.

She sat up in bed, turned off her alarm and wondered again what she was going to do if she got the chance to hop over that fence, for the right reasons.

Christine and Kevin were innocent. Of that she was convinced.

The only question was whether she could persuade the twelve ordinary citizens of this messed-up city that there was reasonable doubt about their guilt. That was all she needed: a few jurors maybe, even one, to think again.

Doesn't sound like much, but sometimes it's like climbing Mount Everest with a Volkswagen on your back.

Kate showered, dried her hair and dressed. Packed her case for court.

She looked in the hallway mirror of her apartment as she picked up her keys from the table.

A young lawyer stared back at her. Not as green as she'd been a few years ago. Wiser. Smarter. More jaded? Certainly.

She wondered if she was still her father's daughter.

Kate opened the front door to her apartment, stepped out and slammed it shut behind her.

'All rise,' said the court clerk.

Kate rose from the defense table in unison with Harry. Another table had been added to accommodate the defendants. Kevin wore a navy suit, white shirt and dark tie. Christine, navy pant suit, white blouse. They were a unit, these two. It was clear in Kate's interactions with them that they loved each other, and that they provided a great home for Amy. Kevin was the opposite of Eddie, which Kate found curious. They were both smart lawyers, both loved Christine and Amy, but Kevin polished his shoes, loved and respected the law and had never had so much as a parking ticket. Eddie? Well, he was different. Perhaps he had to be. Neither Christine nor Kevin were trial lawyers. They didn't have to stand up and fight in a psychological battle for the life of others.

Surprisingly, Kate had to school them on the courtroom.

Judge Ross came into court, a man in his fifties with a great dye job, soft pink skin, a four handicap and a pleasantly low voice that never rose in anger. He was a box-ticker, like so many judges. He liked to clear his cases as fast as possible – a regular docket rocket. Kate had never appeared in front of him before, but Harry knew him. And knew his weakness too.

Vanity.

Judge Ross had begun dyeing his hair in his mid-forties, in a high-end salon off Fifth Avenue at fifteen hundred dollars a visit. It was a deep brown all over, apart from his sideburns and the tufts of hair over his ears, which were a lighter shade and where he allowed highlights of gray to shine through. It gave the impression that he was graying slowly, and unless you knew he was dyeing his hair you never would have noticed. Dyeing your hair is one thing, but choosing a style to mask the dye job, and paying fifteen hundred dollars for the privilege every month was something else entirely.

'Be seated. Let's bring in the jury,' said Judge Ross.

The jury keeper disappeared through a side door and Kate took the moment to check out the opposition. Castro, white suit and all, was at the prosecution table typing into his phone. Probably checking up on Bernice Mazur, his ADA, who was one floor up, in another courtroom, about to open the prosecution case against Elly Parker. Perhaps sensing Kate's glare, he turned and looked at her.

Smiled and winked.

Kate turned away, checked her desk.

Laptop open. Notes laid out in bullet points in a legal pad. Blue and red pens arranged in a neat row.

Everything in order.

The twelve jurors came in and took their seats. Over the next week, they would have the chaos of the Arthur Cross murder placed in front of them. It was then their job to re-establish order, if they could – if the right defendants were in front of them, and the evidence commanded a guilty verdict.

Kate's job was to keep the chaos in play.

The defendants eyeballed the jury as they settled down for the opening statements, just as Kate had instructed. The guilty don't look at those who would judge them. It's a weird psychological trick, and everyone had an innate understanding of it. Kate told Christine and Kevin to look at the jury whenever they could. Meet their eyes. Hold their gaze. As if their lives depended on building that trust.

In reality, that was exactly the case. These twelve people held Christine's and Kevin's life in their hands.

Running a manicured hand through his rich hair, Judge Ross nodded at Castro.

It was on.

Castro stood, buttoned his jacket and moved to the lectern that separated the defense and prosecution tables.

No man's land in a battle to the death.

'Members of the jury, you all know me. I am prosecuting this case for the People of this city. And I want to tell you about the victim in this case, Arthur Cross. You will hear a lot about this man during the course of this trial, not all of it good. Mr. Cross had a criminal past. He was violent and dishonest, and he paid for his crimes with several stints in our correctional facilities. You will hear that Mr. Cross was stalking the defendants. At first, you might think that you don't like this man. And you are entitled to that opinion. But whether Arthur Cross was a good man or bad man is not the issue you have to decide in this case. You have one job. You must decide if the defendants, Kevin Pollock and Christine White, are guilty of his murder. Because, no matter how bad an individual behaves in our society, no one has the right to execute them at their front door in the middle of the night. Because, have no doubt, that is exactly what happened in this case. The defendant, Kevin Pollock, legally owned a pistol, for self-defense. Last year, in the early hours of the morning, the defendants drove to Mr. Cross's home, and shot him dead. A single bullet went through his skull, killing him instantly. Putting him down like a rabid dog. Then they attempted to hide the murder weapon, and went home, pretending nothing had happened. But they didn't hide the gun well enough. It was found at the crime scene. Both defendants' fingerprints were on that gun. Does it matter which one pulled the trigger when they both conspired in Mr. Cross's murder? Not in the eyes of the law. That is our case. And our forensic evidence will prove it beyond all reasonable doubt.'

He took a moment to enjoy the silence, the attention of the jurors and the gallery of onlookers behind him. Then Castro nodded and took his seat at the prosecution table.

A good opening. Framing the case. Taking away any surprises that the defense might have about Arthur Cross and his criminal past. Short and to the point.

Harry leaned over, said, 'Opening statement B. Take his legs out.'

For weeks, Harry and Kate had been strategizing, not just about the defense case, but also how Castro would handle the prosecution. How he was going to play the ball. He may not mention Cross's past. Or he may lean into it, get it out in the open straight away, thereby taking that element of surprise away from the defense when they tell the jury the victim wasn't nearly holier than thou.

The result was that Kate and Harry had prepared three different opening statements, depending on Castro's strategy, and so they could adapt and use his tactics against him.

Nodding, Kate stood and moved to the lectern. Soon as her low heels took her weight, she felt that familiar churning in her stomach, that strange dry sensation in her throat and mouth. Nerves. Anxiety. Fear. They were all familiar demons. And it was imperative that the jury saw no evidence of their existence. They had to be conquered quickly.

Standing at the lectern, Kate poured a little water into a plastic cup, careful not to grip either item too tightly. She didn't want the jury to see her hands shaking. She took a sip of water, put the cup down and turned toward the jury.

She looked at each of them in turn. Straight. Confident. As if she was claiming each one of them as an ally, even though they didn't know it yet.

'Members of the jury, unlike Mr. Castro, you probably don't know me. My name is Kate Brooks, and together with my colleague Harry Ford we have the honor of representing *Christine* and *Kevin* in this case . . .'

She paused for a moment as the judge looked up from his notes and stared at her. She had the judge in her peripheral vision while she looked at the jury. It's exceptionally rare for any lawyer to be interrupted during their opening speech to a jury. Only if they've said something to deliberately mislead the jury or if they've misstated the law. Kate had done neither, but she had stretched the rules at Eddie's suggestion. He knew how to play Castro.

Kate knew it wasn't custom to refer to the defendants by their first names. The proper way to refer to them was by their surnames or simply *the defendants*. Calling them by their first names humanizes them, turns them into real people for the jury. Makes them more familiar. She wasn't leaping over that tall boundary fence of what was right and wrong – she had just raised her head and peeked over the top of it. And Flynn had been holding the ladder. She could go that far.

But no further.

Judge Ross was weighing whether he should interrupt and correct her court etiquette. Before he made the decision, Kate moved on quickly, making the likelihood of the interruption from the judge diminish. He would have to pull her up on this slip, but he could do that later in the absence of the jury. Easier for everyone and it meant the defense couldn't complain about his behavior if the defendants were convicted and they had to appeal. Judges covered their own asses first. Of course, Castro would have picked up on this too. And Kate knew he was positively bursting to leap to his feet and object.

Something she would exploit later.

'. . . two lawyers with impeccable work records, serving their clients and community for many years in the finest traditions of the legal profession. During this case, you will hear about our clients' past. Their dedication and service to others. Their clean records. Their loving family life. The high regard and respect in which they are held by all who know them. District Attorney Castro won't tell you about any of this. It is true that the victim in this case had a violent criminal past. And that there is *suspicion*, but *only* suspicion, that he may have hurt or killed others and that he was not brought to justice for those crimes. All of this evidence will be presented by the district attorney. We do not care that the victim, Mr. Cross, was an ex-con with a string of convictions, or that he had been suspected of murdering his late wife. That is not our business. That is not the heart of this story, but that is the story that the district attorney will tell. It's *not* the *real* story . . .'

She paused, took another sip of water and let that last hook of a sentence percolate in the minds of the jury. She looked at Harry.

Let the jury see her do it. For a second, the jury followed her gaze to Harry Ford. He turned to Kate, and nodded. Then looked back at the jury. It was a subtle communication.

It said, *Okay, let them have it. Tell them the real story.*

Body language doesn't show up in a court stenographer's transcript of the case, doesn't get discussed in any appeals, doesn't appear in the written judgements of any cases, but it can often be the most powerful weapon in any trial.

Three of the jurors leaned forward.

Kate took another sip of water.

Let the suspense build.

'The *real* story, ladies and gentlemen of the jury, lies in the strange gaps in the prosecution case. It lies in the story the district attorney *will not* tell you. As this case unfolds, you will see holes in the prosecution's story. They are the questions the prosecution can't answer. There are inconsistencies and mysterious events surrounding this case. That is where the truth lies. As those questions and inconsistencies arise, we will point them out to you. We will help you see the real story. Because the truth is that Christine and Kevin are innocent, and the real killer is out there laughing at the district attorney. Because two innocent people are on trial, and the real guilty man is not . . .'

Castro couldn't contain himself any longer. He stood with indignation on his face and spat his objection to the judge. Just as Kate had hoped.

'Objection, Your Honor. Can you advise defense counsel not to refer to the defendants by their—'

'Leave that with me – it's not your place, Mr. Castro. I run this courtroom. Do not interrupt defense counsel's opening statement,' said Judge Ross.

'You see,' said Kate to the jury, 'the district attorney doesn't want you to hear the real story. All we ask you to do is listen, for *the truth*. You will know it when you hear it.'

39
Kate

NYPD Officer Bud Deakins had had his uniform dry-cleaned for this court appearance.

Kate could tell.

Some of the thin, plastic dry-cleaning bag was still visible. A torn piece had been pinned to his shirt beneath the badge on his breast pocket. As if he'd ripped the plastic covering off in a hurry to get into his uniform, maybe late for court, and hadn't noticed some shreds remained behind.

The thumbnail of toilet paper, complete with bloody dot in the center, that clung to his throat confirmed he had gotten ready for his court appearance in some haste and had cut himself shaving.

Good, thought Kate.

Officer Deakins looked to be in his early twenties, a rookie who had a routine encounter with Arthur Cross, never expecting it to lead to an appearance as a key prosecution witness in a murder trial. Deakins would have some limited court experience, but this would no doubt be his most important day on the job so far. Maybe ever.

Hence the shaving cut, the dry-cleaned uniform and the look of fear in his eyes as he took the witness stand. His hand shook as he placed it on the Bible and took the oath to tell the truth, the whole truth and nothing but the truth.

Castro would have spent some time preparing him for today. Peppering him with fast, awkward, even insulting questions – toughening up the kid so that he could better face the evil defense attorneys.

Castro began leading him through the easy questions, his rank, time on the job (only six months out of probation, so still a rookie), his precinct and did he remember attending the home of Arthur Cross in relation to a complaint of assault that Mr. Cross had made.

Officer Bud Deakins answered quickly with a tremorous voice, as if he was standing on a vibrating plate.

'What kind of a name is Bud, anyway?' whispered Harry.

'I have no idea. I thought it was a nickname,' said Kate, then turned her attention back to the witness.

'What happened when you attended Mr. Cross's home?' asked Castro.

'I identified myself as an officer, informed Mr. Cross that I was there to get a report of his complaint and—'

'Just a moment, Officer, can you describe Mr. Cross as you saw him that day?'

'Yes, sir, he was wearing a cast on his arm, and it was held in a sling across his chest. I think he was wearing—'

'That's fine. Just tell us what Mr. Cross told you.'

'He informed me that the previous evening, around ten p.m., he opened the front door and two guys rushed the door, got him onto the ground. They told him to stay away from the lawyer and his family, and then one of them, a very large and powerful man, assaulted him by breaking his arm.'

Kate tutted. Cross couldn't admit that a woman had knocked him to the ground and broken his arm. That would be . . . *unmanly* for a twisted asshole like Cross. And he wasn't reporting Bloch to the cops because he wanted his friend, Bruno Mont, to take his own particular kind of revenge on her and didn't want that attack to be linked back to him.

What he did want was to make things as difficult as possible for Kevin and Christine. His entire reason for existing was to make their lives a misery, and more, until his thirst for revenge had been satisfied. Kate knew that satisfaction would only have come from something dark, bloody and violent.

'I see, Officer Deakins, and did you establish who the lawyer mentioned by Mr. Cross was?'

'Yes, sir. He said it was Kevin Pollock and his wife Christine White. That they must have arranged this assault.'

'What did you do to progress this assault investigation?'

'I visited the home of the alleged organizers of the attack and arrested them, brought them back to the precinct for questioning.'

'And who were those individuals?'

'The defendants, Kevin Pollock and Christine White.'

'What did they tell you during your interrogation?'

'They made me aware that Mr. Cross had been stalking their home, following an outcome from a court case that didn't go in Mr. Cross's favor. They had obtained a restraining order against the victim. But they flat out denied any involvement in the attack on Mr. Cross.'

'What happened next?'

'I provided a statement to the court, in support of Mr. Cross's motion for a restraining order against the defendants, which was successful. It is a much lower evidential bar to obtain a restraining order than it is to get a conviction in a criminal court. I recommended no charges against the defendants considering lack of corroborating evidence of their involvement.'

'Thank you, Officer,' said Castro.

Officer Deakins made to leave the witness stand, but Judge Ross told him to wait there.

Kate and Harry had debated which of them should handle Deakins. Kate decided Harry's approach was more likely to get results.

'Officer Deakins,' began Harry, rising and moving into the well of the court. Harry Ford used to be a senior judge, and he brought his experience and respect with him.

'I have a few questions for you, I know you're nervous and keen to get off the stand, but this won't take very long,' said Harry warmly. He had the indefatigable ability to destroy somebody and make it look like he was very generously doing them a favor. There was nothing to do but admire it.

'Officer Deakins,' he continued, 'you haven't been on the force for very long, have you?'

'I passed my probation a while ago. I have extensive training and mentoring with—'

'That's not necessary, Officer. I'm sure you were very well trained, and that mentorship only served to enhance your natural abilities for the job. Tell me if this is accurate, Officer, from the sounds of it. Mr. Cross wasn't able to give you much of a description of the two men who assaulted him, was he?'

Deakins first looked to Castro. When no help was forthcoming, he looked back at Harry. The thing with inexperienced witnesses, or those holding a large and potentially career-ending secret, is that they do not want to be the one to mess up the case. In the end, the witness stand is the loneliest place on earth for the dishonest man.

'He did give a description. He said one was very large and the other was smaller,' said Deakins.

'Well, that narrows down the list of suspects considerably, doesn't it? I'm surprised you weren't able to make immediate arrests,' said Harry.

The jury smiled.

About five minutes, thought Kate. *That's how long it takes to fall in love with Harry Ford.*

'Your Honor, this is a murder trial,' said Castro. 'I'd appreciate it if Mr. Ford could take this matter more seriously.'

Before Judge Ross could say anything, Harry smacked Castro's fastball into the bleachers as if it was an underarm throw.

'I'm taking it as seriously as this officer took Mr. Cross's assault complaint,' said Harry.

Judge Ross suppressed a smile and said, 'It's your witness, Mr. Ford. Some questions from you might be helpful.'

'Thank you, Your Honor,' said Harry. 'Officer Deakins, given your extensive police training and mentoring, which you alluded to earlier, I take it that you thought it was suspicious that Mr. Cross couldn't give you a more thorough description of his attackers?'

'How do you mean suspicious?' asked Deakins, welcoming the praise, but unsure how to claim it for himself.

'One of them broke his arm. They didn't do that from a distance in a dark alley. They were in Mr. Cross's home. It would have taken some time. They spoke to him. Threatened him. He would have had ample opportunity to view these two men. Indeed, one might say the faces of the men who put the victim through his terrifying ordeal should be emblazoned on his memory forever?'

'I don't know about that. Maybe. I did think he was holding back a little.'

'He wasn't telling you the truth about the attack, was he?'

'Probably not. He did have a broken arm, but maybe he wasn't telling me everything. Maybe he was withholding the truth?' said Officer Deakins, relaxing a little on the stand. Kate thought the officer was enjoying the praise.

'Withholding truth? You mean he was lying?'

'Maybe,' said Deakins, nodding, even smiling a little. Blissfully unaware of the brick wall to which he had been expertly and blindly led.

'You agree he was probably not telling the truth, Officer Deakins, so it's entirely possible that he was lying when he said that the attack had been orchestrated by the defendants?'

Suddenly, that wall appeared in front of Officer Bud Deakins.

'Ehhh . . .'

'Yes? He was lying to you. You've said as much. So, he could have been lying when he said these mysterious, partially invisible men threatened him and told him to stay away from the defendants, *while they were breaking his arm?*'

'Ehhh . . . yeah.'

'Yeah?' asked Harry. 'You mean, *yes*, don't you, Officer? That's how you were trained to answer in court, wasn't it?'

'I mean, my apologies, *yes*, sir. The victim could have been lying about the whole thing.'

Harry strode back to this seat and every pair of eyes in that courtroom followed him there like he was Paul *goddamn* Newman. Except one pair, belonging to District Attorney Castro.

Kevin leaned over and patted Harry on the arm, a small gesture to say good job.

In a low voice, Harry said, 'Don't do that, Kevin. It doesn't look good. Also, we just won an opening skirmish. Castro has the murder weapon at the crime scene, and it's registered to you and has Christine's and your fingerprints all over it. This thing is far from over.'

Castro was on his feet, calling his next witness before Officer Deakins realized he'd been dismissed.

'The People call Detective Alison Withers,' said Castro.

Withers was the investigating officer. The jury was about to hear all about the gun and the forensics.

Kate leaned over to Christine and Kevin, said, 'Buckle up. We're now on a long, hard road. This case is about to become very difficult.'

40

Logan

Logan found walking the streets of Manhattan, with dying winter winds on his cheeks, a good time for reflection.

The months leading up to Elly Parker's trial had been the most joyful of Logan's entire life.

Usually, while he waited for the court case to run its course, and the person he had framed for his crimes to be convicted, Logan felt a little flood of endorphins every time he saw a news article about the case and, when the guilty verdict came in, a wonderful sense of calm.

Order restored.

Then the comedown. His job, his watches, his apartment and possessions looked ever duller with each passing day. And the dullness turned to boredom. And the boredom turned to something like depression. And then anxiety. And longing. A desire to do it all over again.

So sweet.

But not as sweet as Grace.

She had moved into Logan's apartment a month to the day after their first date. They were moving fast, and Grace sometimes worried about it. She said as much as they lay on the couch, listening to music, sipping hot chocolate, talking, being with one another, because, it seemed, that was all that either of them wanted. It was exactly what Logan wanted.

With Grace, there were no troughs, no dips, no sudden flatlining of his mood. He got to lie in bed with her every night, and wake up with her every morning.

Logan slept little, but he enjoyed watching the moonlight on her skin, how blue it appeared, like a volcanic lake, and the morning sun turning that ice blue into warm yellows and browns, and streaking her hair as if it was starlight breaking the blue sky.

After some months, he came to the realization that he loved her. And he loved that he loved her. This was new. This was good.

He wasn't alone.

Logan had grown up in a house. Not a home. There was no love there. His parents tolerated him, but he could not remember ever being held by them, not one single moment of true affection. It was like growing up in a refrigerator. Soon, he'd got used to the cold. And that was all that there was in his world. Thought, rationality, logic, mathematics, the house was covered in books, but not one novel. Not one record, or CD. No radio. No music. Very little TV. No friends came over to the house, not that he made any friends in school anyway.

And then there were the beatings.

From a young age, Logan had been beaten by his father. First, with fists, a punch to the stomach, dropping him to the floor. Never the face. Then, as he grew older, things got worse. His father had a selection of leather belts. Some were thin, and had sharp buckles. As a teenager, he would regularly feel the sting of leather across his back. Just one strike. And, as he aged, the hits grew harder. This could have been for any supposed infraction of the house rules – anything from taking too much milk in his cereal in the morning, to failing to thank his mother for dinner.

She knew, of course. And she did nothing.

In later years, Logan realized that she was afraid of his father and perhaps she too suffered silent beatings.

Grace had asked him once about the scars crisscrossing his back.

Logan had smiled and simply said his father had not been a good man. It was a diplomatic way to close down the conversation. Logan kept his childhood to himself. Better that way.

He had realized during his early forays into psychology that his upbringing was extraordinary. It was strange and brutal. Logan felt as if something had been taken from him by his parents, although he didn't know quite what that might be. He was already formed – his mind and personality forged in a cold, clinical life where fear, knowledge and the power that stemmed from those elements were the most important things.

He sometimes wondered, if his life had been different, would he still be the same person? Something he had asked his father, but not seriously.

It was a rhetorical question.

When he had asked this, his father was lying in a bathtub that was quickly turning red with his own blood. He didn't seem to have an answer. Just a look of total shock on his face. That look had appeared there when Logan put the kitchen knife in his neck, and it had remained there on the face of his corpse. He never got a chance to ask his mother the same question. She had come home from her drinks party to find her husband dead in the bath and called the police straight away. For many hours before she had arrived home, Logan had kept the tub topped up with hot water, to stop his father's body temperature from falling, effectively masking the time of death, and then Logan left the house quietly just before his mother returned. He had waited a long time in that bathroom. Staring at his father's body.

Listening to the leaky faucet.

Drip . . .

Drip . . .

Drip . . .

The medical examiner was able to determine the time of death, judging by the body temperature and the temperature of the water, at around the same time as Logan's mother returned home. He had watched the police take her away, from afar, unobserved, of course.

He never saw her again. At sixteen, Logan was free of the cold house.

After some strange stays in foster homes, Logan came of age and inherited his family's great wealth. And, with it, the knowledge and satisfaction that he could kill someone, and blame that murder on another. And, for a time, that was enough. That was his great pleasure.

Until he found a much greater one, with Grace.

And since that night when he'd shot Joe Novak dead he had not harmed another living soul. More importantly, his dark desire to do so was strangely and welcomely absent. As if a black spider that sat on his brain, like a hemorrhage, had suddenly died and disintegrated, washed away in his blood with all the other waste cells.

He didn't want to think that he was cured, because he did not previously believe that he was sick. Yet he could not deny that he felt better. There was not only love, but relief from the cycle of death that had consumed him, that had had ever-diminishing satisfaction. Logan recognized this pattern of behavior as a cyclical desire to kill. It was a path that had only one outcome. With each kill, the sense of power was not as strong as before, and the sensation lasted less time. This would lead to an increased rate of kills, which would eventually lead Logan into making a mistake. And then he would get caught.

He could not allow this to happen.

Grace had taken away that desire, replaced it with something much more powerful. In many ways, Grace was not only his love, but his savior. His life had been empty before, and he had filled it with horror. Now, he had found someone who filled it with love.

All these thoughts permeated his mind as he walked the streets of the city.

With a destination in mind, he had simply headed south, knowing he would come across it sooner or later. Soon, Logan found himself in Foley Square.

Within minutes, he had arrived at the courthouse.

The district attorney, Castro, had given Logan a welcome and unexpected gift by running the Parker trial at the same time as the trial of Flynn's ex-wife and her new husband. All Logan had wanted was a huge psychological distraction for Flynn, but the timing of the two trials, no doubt designed to put additional pressure on Flynn, was perfect. He would be off his game, not thinking clearly, anxious and worried about the fate of his ex-wife.

Logan could have killed Flynn, but there was no likely suspect for the police to quickly arrest. Killing Flynn didn't fit Logan's pattern. It could just as easily expose him. The murder of Joseph Novak hadn't even made the main news. Page four of the *New York Post*. A homeless man shot in the city – the police didn't care. No one did.

He joined the crowd of Elly Parker supporters and haters gathered outside the courthouse in small opposing groups, holding their banners, their competing chants an incoherent battle. One group shouting for her to be locked up and another protesting her innocence.

Logan joined a group protesting her innocence and watched the front doors of the courthouse. There was a comfort in standing among so many bodies. Usually, Logan took comfort hiding in the crowded streets of Manhattan. Not today.

An uneasy feeling crept up his back. He spun round, one-eighty, checked the street opposite.

Nothing out of the ordinary.

Strange.

Logan had the feeling he was being watched.

He usually didn't ignore his instincts.

But he could see no one who might be watching him.

It had been some months since he had engaged in his dark life. Perhaps he was just out of practice. Perhaps he was just nervous.

He shook it off, joined in the chanting of the small crowd around him, and waited.

He didn't have to wait long.

After a few minutes, Eddie Flynn arrived outside and joined the line to get through security and into the courthouse. Logan backed away from the group, waited until one other person had joined the line behind Flynn, then stood behind them.

All he had on him was his phone, apartment keys and folding cash. No ID. No wallet. He was dressed in black jeans, a black winter coat and a beanie hat. Flynn was just in his suit, braving the cold without an overcoat. He had noticed Flynn's necktie was loose and his top button undone. He had a gym bag filled with case papers on his shoulder. He was nervous. Logan could tell by the way Flynn's right hand, loose by his side, kept a pen in perpetual motion. The silver ballpoint tumbling through his fingers, over and over, in a perfect cycle.

The line moved quickly enough, and Flynn dumped his bag on the security belt, and as he went through the body scanner it beeped, but the officers waved him on. They knew him. He retrieved the bag from the belt after it was scanned, just as Logan put the contents of his pockets in a security tray and stepped, silently, through the scanner. No beeps. No alarms.

Flynn moved toward the bank of elevators. Logan gathered his stuff and followed. By the time Logan turned the corner to the elevators Flynn was just getting into one.

Logan followed.

Flynn pressed a floor button. Logan put his hands in his pockets, and turned to face the doors as he reached the back of the elevator.

There they stood. Side by side. Flynn's head was down. The pen was still moving across and under his fingers. Logan could tell Flynn was in deep thought.

The only sound was the doors rolling shut, then the dull whump of the gears engaging and the counterweight pulling the old elevator slowly upwards.

'Cold today,' said Logan.

Flynn caught the pen in a dead stop, and raised his head toward Logan.

'Sure is,' he said with a sigh, then looked away, facing the doors.

'Are you a lawyer?' asked Logan.

'For my sins,' said Flynn, nodding, but the tone he used brought no humor to those words. It was more like a confession.

'Why? Do you need a lawyer?' asked Flynn.

'No, at least not right now. I'm just spectating. The TikTok murders.'

Flynn didn't reply for a moment. The elevator filled only with the sound of its old gears as they whined and growled.

Then he looked at Logan again, said, 'Have we met before?'

'I don't think so,' said Logan, holding Flynn's gaze, fighting down the electric buzz of fear building in his guts.

'Are you a reporter?' asked Flynn.

'No, I just follow the big trials. I like true-crime cases. I'm thinking of doing a podcast some day.'

'You sure we haven't met? You kinda look familiar. I have a good memory for faces,' said Flynn.

'Nah, I think I would remember,' said Logan.

Flynn nodded.

The elevator began to slow.

Logan's heartbeat accelerated. His face felt flushed, and he realized he was holding his breath.

Flynn stared at him.

Then he looked away as the doors opened.

'After you,' said Flynn.

'No, please,' said Logan, 'after you. I insist.'

Flynn stepped forward, stopped.

But just for half a second – then he left the elevator.

Logan exhaled, shook his hands out to get rid of the tension, then followed Flynn. He turned the corner to the main hallway where the entrances to the courtrooms lined the left-hand side of the hall, flanked by benches for witnesses and those attending court. Flynn disappeared through a set of double doors.

Logan waited a beat before entering.

This had been a mistake. He shouldn't have come. He had never attended the trials of those suspects toward whom he had driven the police's attention. Sometimes they were convicted, sometimes they were never even charged – they just lived their lives under suspicion. It was all about throwing the police's resources and suspicions and attentions toward someone else. Someone other than a complete stranger. The more he did this, the better he got at framing a patsy for his crimes. Sometimes he didn't have to do much. He could be subtle.

And he had always kept an eye from a distance, because, in truth, back then he didn't have much to lose. He was alone. Lost in a spiral of murder.

Now, he had everything to lose. And he wanted to, *had to*, make sure that Elly Parker was convicted. He needed to know that this chapter of his life was done. Case closed. Over.

Finished.

Logan needed to move on, with Grace.

This was all for her, now. This last case.

Logan walked into the courtroom and saw that everyone was already seated. The case had drawn a crowd, and there were no more available spaces on the benches in the public gallery. There were a few chairs arranged behind the last row of benches. Extra chairs brought in for the crowd at the last minute. Two were empty. Logan took one of them, closest to the aisle.

As he sat down, he saw Flynn up front at the defense table, embracing Elly Parker.

Logan dipped his head, rubbed at his brow, just in case she turned round and scanned the gallery. She was the only person who could recognize him, and he had to be careful to hide his face from her. When he looked back, he saw Flynn talking to the investigator, Lake. They were whispering. Lake nodded, then left the defense table and walked down the central aisle of the courtroom. Logan dipped his head, took his phone from his pocket and brought the screen to life, just so that he could have an excuse for looking away from Lake. He heard Lake's feet on the tiled floor, walking past his row, and then the sound of the courtroom doors being flung open, which allowed the low hum of noise from the hallway to invade the courtroom until the doors swung closed again.

Logan put his phone away, and paid attention as the judge came into court, followed by the jury.

The prosecutor, Bernice Mazur, rose and began to speak.

First, she showed the jury the viral video, where Elly had discovered her husband, James, in bed with Harriet, her friend.

'This video has been viewed millions of times, all around the world. Imagine that, ladies and gentlemen,' said the prosecutor, 'the worst betrayal anyone can ever experience, and it's played out for the entire world to see. Imagine the humiliation. Just for a second. What happens then is that two of the victims in this case, James and Harriet, begin to be targeted by the defendant's social-media followers. Both of them lose their jobs, their careers, their friends. And then, two weeks later, the night of the murders, we have phone records to show the defendant called James multiple times that night. It is the prosecution's case that some time earlier that day the defendant managed to poison the victims by placing a toxic substance in their water bottles. The defendant called James that night, for the first time since she'd discovered the affair. James didn't pick up the phone. The reason the defendant called was to make sure that her plan had worked. To make sure the defendants were dead. They had been given a lethal dose of tetrahydrozoline, which induced a fatal cardiac arrest.

'Now, ladies and gentlemen of the jury, in cases like this,cases of sophisticated, premediated poisoning, it is standard police procedure to look into all deaths of those people close to the defendant, to see if any of them were in any way suspicious or had a similar cause of death. You will hear Detective Bill Sacks testify that he found an identical cause of death for a person related to the defendant. It was the defendant's father, Stewart Yorke. Detective Sacks will testify that Mr. Yorke's body was exhumed, and tests were carried out by our forensic pathologist. We intend to prove to you that those results show that the defendant poisoned her father with tetrahydrozoline. Not only that, but we will show you proof that the defendant had large quantities of this poisonous substance. In fact, we can show you a video where she boasts about buying it. The defendant was in financial peril. She had borrowed money from her late father, and after she had murdered him she inherited his home and sold it, solving all of her financial problems.

'By the end of this case, members of the jury, you will have no problem finding the defendant guilty on three counts of premeditated murder. Of that, there is no reasonable doubt.'

41

Eddie

The prosecutor, Bernice Mazur, was just finishing up her opening statement in Elly Parker's trial.

We had a half decent jury. There was nobody there that I thought might be particularly troublesome. One guy, who I knew Bernice wanted, was divorced, in his late forties and came across as slightly misogynistic. Bernice was as straight as they come, but even fair prosecutors don't mind putting someone on the jury who is going to give them an easy ride. I thought the juror could be persuaded. Along with that overly masculine swagger, the guy had something else bubbling away – a distrust of authority. I could use that.

I'd warned Elly already about Bernice's opening, that things would be said in this room that would be incredibly painful for her to hear. That she was not to react. For any normal person, hearing someone say that you had ruthlessly murdered three people who you loved would drive you crazy. You could be forgiven for any number of reactions: standing up and screaming that this was all lies, that you were innocent, or burying your face in your hands and crying at the pain of the accusation. These are all normal reactions.

Juries are smart. When the prosecutor lands a punch, a lot of jurors look to the defendant to gauge how it lands. Sometimes, bad jurors put more weight behind a defendant's body language than the actual evidence they hear in court.

I'd told Elly not to react at all, which is almost impossible. I told her to place her hands on the table. Look straight ahead. And if she needed to cry she had to do it quietly.

I told her that I had to be her voice now. In this place, words matter. How you handle yourself matters. That we were at war. And in war you take some hits.

I also explained that Bernice, and even Detective Sacks, were not framing her for murder. They were following the evidence and motives that had been carefully laid out for them by the stranger who tried to kill her. He was the reason she was in this position.

Bernice finished her opening statement, and I stood up and moved to the well of the court, the very central point in the circle of jurors, judge, lawyers and the witness stand.

'Members of the jury, I am grateful to Ms. Mazur for outlining the main issues in this trial. There are a lot of questions you are going to have to ask yourself before this case is over. I want to help you answer those questions. Some will be difficult. Some will be easy for you to answer. I want you all to keep an open mind, and to remember that the burden is on the prosecution to prove guilt beyond all reasonable doubt. What is the prosecution's case? Their case is my client has murdered three people by administering poison to them, resulting in their death. Ms. Mazur will tell you that these three murders demonstrate a pattern of behavior from a single ruthless killer. Frankly, we agree . . .'

I paused, listened to the audible gasps from the gallery and even a few from the jury.

'All three victims in this case were given lethal doses of poison by a dangerous, psychopathic killer. The only problem is that killer is *not* sitting at the defense table,' I said, pointing to Elly. 'That killer is not on trial here today, but don't worry. During the course of this trial, we are going to tell you all about him. And, yes, it is a man. An extremely dangerous man who is out on the street right now. A dark stranger who is a walking death sentence to anyone he chooses to target. Elly Parker is on trial because this killer wants her to be. He wants her to pay for his crimes. He has set her up. My one word of advice, while you listen to evidence in this trial, is this – ask yourself this question – is there evidence against the defendant in this case because she's guilty, or because someone else wanted it to look that way?'

I turned and looked at the gallery, particularly the front two rows, filled with reporters.

'We're not just going to speculate about some other person who might have committed these murders. We're going to describe this person to you in detail. We're going to show you how he committed these crimes. The defendant is going to tell you how this man almost killed her in the same exact way that he murdered the victims in this case. She's met this man. And she is going to tell you what he looks like. The prosecution will tell you not to take the defendant's word for it. Don't worry – you won't have to. It's not just the defendant that has seen this man. We will call for testimony from an eyewitness who saw this killer. The witness, Joseph Novak, will testify that he helped save the defendant's life after *she* was poisoned by this killer. Joseph Novak will testify that he saw this man. He will describe him to you. He will tell you that this man murdered his friend. Shot him dead in the street, believing him to be Mr. Novak. Once you hear this testimony, at the conclusion of this trial, I have no doubt you will find the defendant not guilty. My only hope is that once this case is over, the NYPD will turn their attention toward finding the real killer.'

I stood there for a few seconds, letting the faint echo of my voice die on the walls of the courtroom, and sink in with the jury. As I took my seat, I checked out the reporters. They were all writing in their notebooks or making notes on their phones. The name of the defense's star witness in the Elly Parker case would soon be on the front page of every newspaper and news site that covered the city and this high-profile case.

Everyone would be looking for Joseph Novak.

I was counting on it.

42

Logan

Logan didn't like surprises.

Hearing Flynn tell the court that Joseph Novak was going to testify for the defense was a surprise, considering Logan had shot him dead months ago. He had felt it in his chest, a sudden collapse, as if all the air was being squeezed from his body. After the initial shock of the revelation, he thought Flynn was bluffing. But it would be very strange to tell the jury about a witness and then not call them to the stand.

Logan's teeth squeaked, and he realized he had been grinding his jaw.

He thought back to that night.

It couldn't be.

He'd seen Joe Novak next to Lake. They were walking side by side. He'd worn the same dirty, ripped coat as he'd worn when he first saw the man. And the shots were on target. Novak had dropped fast.

But he hadn't seen the man's face. It had been covered with a scarf.

Logan closed his eyes, blocked out the sounds of the crowd around him: the low buzzing of breath, shoes shuffling, sniffs, coughs, the ruffling of clothes and coats, and the whispers.

He thought not just about that night. He thought about the days leading up to it. There was no doubt that Novak did not want to be found. That he was frightened.

Could he have given his coat to a friend? Could that person have pretended to be Novak, at least for a short while, with Lake, to allow Joe to make a quiet exit?

It was possible. It was smart. To survive on the streets of New York for a long time takes more than luck. It takes someone to be smart. To be able to read the streets and the people who occupied them to stay one step ahead of the robbers, the thieves, the psychopaths and the cops.

His right fist tightened.

He opened a messaging app on his phone, and sent a secure text to the only contact within that app. A man who sold handguns. The man who had sold him the Beretta he'd used that night.

Now, Logan needed another gun.

There was no doubt now that Flynn and his investigators had Novak hidden somewhere. A place that was safe, secure. And, up until this moment, no one had been looking for him, believing him to be dead.

Now that Flynn had just announced Joe was alive, he would know that Logan would come looking.

This time, when Logan made his move on Novak, there would be no element of surprise. They would be ready.

Lake closed the app.

Opened his messages, sent a text to Grace.

> I'll be home late. Have to meet a client.

The reply came in fast.

> No problem. I'll wait up. I love you.

He typed back.

> I love you too.

Wherever they were keeping Novak, Lake wouldn't be too far away.

As much as Logan wanted to stay and listen to the case, taking out Novak was priority number one. He would need to catch up on the case later through the news reports. One other thing occurred to him – if this case started looking bad for the prosecution, Logan could not risk staying in the city. He would need to get away.

But not yet. He had to make sure Novak didn't testify. Without him, Elly Parker would be convicted. No one would believe her story without a corroborating witness. And, if she was convicted, Logan had nothing to fear. If she was acquitted, the NYPD would come looking for the man with the suitcase who called himself Logan.

He could simply run now, but that would leave his fate to chance. He had to make the last desperate effort to make sure Elly was convicted. He didn't want the police on his tail. Not now. Not ever. Even if he was in a different country, ten years from now, there was always the chance that the police might get lucky, and he could be hauled out of his bed and extradited to New York to face his crimes.

Logan had never failed to accomplish anything he had set his mind to. He did not intend to begin now.

Quietly, he got up from his seat, left the courtroom and went in search of Gabriel Lake.

43
Eddie

While Bernice called her first witness, I texted Harry and asked how things were going one floor up. I didn't want to ask Kate. She was under enough pressure. No way did I want to add to that.

I trusted Kate.

I had to keep reminding myself of that. Had to focus on Elly's case.

There was no denying I was distracted. Half of my head was in the courtroom upstairs, fighting for my ex-wife.

Bernice looked up from a stack of papers on her desk, slid the large-framed glasses from her nose and let them hang round her neck as she stood and called her first witness.

Patrolman John Djawadi was sworn in, and Bernice guided him through his testimony. He responded to a call from one of the victim's parents. James's father couldn't get in contact with him. James wasn't picking up the phone and wouldn't answer the door to his apartment. It wasn't like him. He'd been vilified on social media, lost his job and his friends and his father was worried that James had done something stupid. The patrolman met James's father at the front door of the apartment building together with a locksmith. The locksmith opened the door, and the patrolman entered first, calling out for James.

He entered the bedroom, found James and Harriet dead on

the floor. He got the father out of the apartment and called in the bodies.

'Officer Djawadi, while you and the victim's father were in the apartment, did you disturb anything or touch anything?'

'Just the doorknob of the bedroom. That's all, ma'am.'

'After you had secured the apartment, what did you do then?'

'Like I said, I called in the bodies to dispatch, who said they were sending homicide. I stood outside the apartment and made sure it was secure while I waited for the arrival of the detective.'

'What time did the detective arrive at the apartment?'

'Around ten thirty.'

'Thank you, no more questions.'

I stood up and let Officer Djawadi off the hook. He'd done his job. I could spend a half hour or so picking through his testimony, hitting him with a few jabs and even a body shot or two, but there was no point. This wouldn't win us the case.

No point in wasting energy with this guy.

I was waiting for the right witness.

This case would be won or lost depending on the answer to a single question.

One question.

Wait.

Be patient.

'No questions, Your Honor,' I said, then sat down.

Bernice stood, said, 'The People call James Parker Senior . . .'

'Your Honor,' I interrupted, 'Mr. Parker, the father of the late James Parker, has already been through so much. Neither my client, nor I, wish to add any further pain or injury to Mr. Parker's suffering. We are satisfied that if his statement to the police was simply read to the jury, verbatim, it would also speed up proceedings. We do not intend to cross-examine Mr. Parker. On behalf of my client, we simply ask the court to note our sorrow at his son's passing and offer our sincere condolences.'

A tall, fit man in his sixties with a shock of coiffured white hair, wearing a white shirt and a charcoal suit, came and stood by the prosecution table. Bernice had waved him to a stop. His pale skin had a gray tone, except for the redness around the eyes, as if these were the points through which his soul had been sucked clean out of his skull.

'Your Honor, Mr. Parker Senior is here to testify for his—'

I interrupted Bernice again. 'We all know what he's here for. There's no need to put this man through that kind of ordeal.'

There was no evidential value in calling the father of one of the victims as a witness in this case. He looked strong, but nobody gets on the stand and talks to a hundred strangers in a courtroom about finding their son's body, at the trial of his murderer, and manages to hold it together. Nobody. Mr. Parker Senior would fight through it, but soon his breaking heart would reduce him to tears.

And all of that wasn't for his benefit. There was no catharsis. No closure.

Bernice wanted the jury to see his pain. To feel his pain. And for that pain to turn into anger and for the jury to throw that same anger at the defendant. Juries don't just make decisions with their minds – they make them with their hearts. They would be desperate to give this father justice. And that meant convicting Elly. And I had to stop that at all costs.

'Mrs. Mazur, I'm afraid I am in agreement with Mr. Flynn. It saves court time and spares Mr. Parker Senior from the pressure of testifying in this case,' said the judge. 'The jury can read his statement, and it can be entered into evidence.'

A wave of the hand from Bernice, as if to say, you win some and you lose some and it's no problem for the prosecution. She couldn't really object because she wanted the victim's father to burst into tears and get the jury on her side. She turned to Mr. Parker Senior, who had been following all of this closely.

He shook his head at Bernice, turned toward the defense table and stared at Elly. She stared back, but while Elly's open face was filled with sorrow, for the loss of her husband and for the pain this man was going through, that look was not mirrored by Mr. Parker Senior. His mouth twisted into a snarl, his eyes crawled into a furrow and he leaned forward.

And spat in Elly's face.

She closed her eyes, but otherwise didn't react. I heard a gasp from someone in the crowd behind me. Bernice skipped out from behind the prosecution table, and lightly took his arm to guide him away, but he wrenched free from her grip, and with a final look of disgust at Elly he strode back to his seat in the gallery.

I looked at the judge. He shook his head.

So did Bernice. I gave Elly my handkerchief. She was crying softly now.

The judge could've admonished Mr. Parker Senior. Even held him in contempt. It was technically an assault on the defendant, and contempt of court. But Judge Quaid didn't do anything. There was no point because there was no punishment fitting for this man. Very little in this world could have added to his suffering.

'Your Honor, the People call Detective William Sacks.'

The first witness of any real consequence.

This was Detective Sacks's big day and he had dressed for it. As he raised his hand to take the oath, his beige sport coat rode up. It may have been made to measure, probably five years ago. Made to measure a detective who was twenty pounds lighter, perhaps. Sacks wore a dark checkered shirt and a red tie beneath the tight jacket. Charcoal pants.

The formality of a court appearance in the biggest murder case of his career didn't extend far enough for Sacks to wear formal shoes. When he had passed me by on the way to the stand, I clocked his red socks beneath his black Crocs.

As Bernice asked her first question, I noticed a sheen of sweat on the detective's top lip, and his cheeks were flushed. He was feeling the pressure of this case. Bernice, always looking to move the case on as quickly as possible, ran through the circumstances of Sacks getting to Elly's apartment after the patrolman and the late James Parker's father had found the bodies. Sacks had given fast, direct answers. The speed of his delivery and the fact that he was looking squarely at Bernice as he answered confirmed his anxiety.

Cops are trained to take their time and to look at the jury as they give their answers, not at the counsel.

'Would you please describe, for the jury, what you saw in that bedroom?' asked Bernice cleverly. She had included a reference to the jury in her question in the hope it would remind Sacks of his training – that he should be addressing them, not the lawyers.

Before he answered, he cleared his throat, then took Bernice's subtle clue and turned to look at the jury as he delivered his response.

'I saw two people in the bedroom. One, the female, whom I later identified as Harriet Rothschild, was lying face down on the floor on the right side of the bed. The other individual was male, and later identified as James Parker. The upper half of his body was on the bed. He was lying on his back, but his feet were hanging off the bed, one of them on the floor. There was a distinct odor in the room. I stepped inside and—'

'Detective, let me stop you there for just a moment. You had mentioned to the jury that you smelled something. Could you elaborate on the odor you detected?'

Sacks took a breath, closed his eyes and nodded, then exhaled. It was only natural to be nervous in a case like this, with the world watching.

'My apologies, yes,' he said, then looked at the jury. 'There was a strong smell of vomit in the room.'

'Were you able to determine the source of that odor?'

'Yes, I saw a large pool of what appeared to be vomit beside the female victim's head. There was another smaller pool on the bed beside the male victim.'

'I see, thank you. What did you do next, Detective?'

'I gave the bodies of the victims a visual inspection, of course careful not to touch them or move the bodies before forensics or the medical examiner arrived. I could see no signs of blood on the floor or in the room at all. No pooling of blood and no blood spatter anywhere. I could see no signs of violence anywhere on the bodies of the victims. No cuts, no bruising. In addition, there were no signs of asphyxiation.'

'And what were you thinking at that moment?'

'I hadn't completed a full inspection of the victim's bodies, so I could not rule out physical violence pending the medical examiner's autopsy conclusions, but at this moment I thought that either they had overdosed on drugs or, alternatively, death may have been due to poisoning.'

'Is poisoning an unusual cause of death?'

'It's quite rare, but not unheard of. I thought about it in this case because there was no evidence of drug use in the apartment. No drug paraphernalia, no burnt spoons, no needles, no burnt foil, no drugs, nothing that I would expect to find in the apartment if this was a case of death by drug overdose.'

'So what did you do next?'

'While I was waiting for the forensic team, I made notes and took pictures of the water bottles in the bedroom. There were two of them. I guessed they each belonged to the victims. And I made a note and took pictures of all the items in the refrigerator and the cupboards, the cleaning products, the bathroom products, everything in the garbage bag in the kitchen – basically, anything that may have carried or contained a potential source of poison. I wanted the forensics team to examine and test all of it.'

There's always a lot of information to take in during a murder trial. Some testimony is more important than others. Juries usually don't miss the key stuff. You underestimate the intelligence and understanding of a jury at your peril. Even so, they'd had a lot to take in, so far. And Bernice was about to get into important details.

'Your Honor,' said Bernice, 'might we take a short comfort break?'

'Twenty minutes,' said Judge Quaid.

The break was for the jury, so that when they came back with their bellies filled with coffee and stale donuts, they'd have a better chance of remembering the key testimony that was about to come out.

I checked my phone to see if Harry had replied. I wanted to know if things were okay in Christine's case.

I had one message.

From Harry.

He could have lied to me. Told me everything was going just fine.

But that's not Harry Ford.

Amy had to grow up with me as a father. She needed her mom. And, in truth, she needed Kevin.

The text read –

> We're losing. We need a miracle.

44

Kate

As Detective Alison Withers testified, Kate took notes.

She studied the witness.

Detective Withers wore black pants, a pale blue blouse and a dark jacket. She was in her forties but looked older. The lines around her eyes were deeper than most women her age. Kate wondered if working homicide did that to people, whether the daily horrors of the job took their toll on the body, and the skin, and the eyes, just as much as they stained and weathered the soul.

While she took notes, Kate occasionally glanced at the jury. They were paying attention. This was important.

The testimony was detailed, accurate and indisputable. Detective Withers was telling the simple truth, and her words were hitting her clients hard. Kevin had slid down into his seat, his head bowed. Christine, the more experienced trial lawyer in the marriage, was watching the jury. She was smart enough to see the extent of the damage being done.

'Detective Withers, let's just recap for the jury,' said DA Castro. 'You testified that once on scene you formed the theory that Mr. Cross was shot once through the forehead with a low caliber weapon, and you asked the other officers on the scene to conduct house to house enquiries with neighbors. What happened next?'

'The lawn on either side of the path leading to the victim's home was overgrown. The grass was maybe a foot and a half tall. I was scanning it with my flashlight to see if there was any other potential evidence at the scene—'

'What kind of evidence were you looking for?'

'I was looking for the shell casing, initially, from the fatal shot fired at Mr. Cross. But I was keeping my eye open for other important pieces of evidence such as shoe or boot impressions, or any trace of the assailant that they may have left behind.'

'And did you find anything?'

'Yes, we found a Smith and Wesson revolver.'

Castro took the exhibit in his hand, the revolver inside a plastic evidence bag. He had it logged into evidence and handed the weapon to Detective Withers.

'Is this the revolver you found?'

'Yes, I discovered it approximately ten feet from the porch. It was all but invisible in the tall grass. I opened the chamber of the weapon and found that one of the five rounds had been fired and the empty shell casing was still in the chamber.'

Holding aloft another evidence bag, this time containing the spent shell, Castro had it logged with the court as prosecution evidence.

'Is this the spent shell casing you found in the revolver?'

'Correct.'

'The defense has reserved their right to call their own firearms expert, but I wanted to ask if you had an expert conduct an examination of the weapon and the shell casing.'

'Yes, an NYPD forensic technician was able to match the caliber of the round which killed Mr. Cross to this weapon. Forensic firearms testimony shall be given by my colleague, but we believe that this is the murder weapon.'

'Was anything else revealed by an examination of this weapon.'

'Yes, the revolver has a serial number to allow us to trace the registered owner. The defendant, Kevin Pollock, is the registered owner.'

'Were any other forensic tests carried out on the murder weapon?'

'Objection,' said Kate, 'draws a conclusion. It has not been established as fact that this is the murder weapon.'

Swiping his fingers through his dyed hair, Judge Ross gave Castro an admonishing look and said, 'Sustained.'

'Apologies, Your Honor, I'll rephrase. Detective, were any other forensic tests carried out on the weapon, registered to the defendant Kevin Pollock, which was found at the crime scene?'

'Yes, fingerprint analysis was conducted and both defendants' fingerprints were found on the weapon.'

'Thank you. Are you aware of any potential motive for this cold-blooded murder?'

'The defendants and the victim were known to each other, and each of them had taken out mutual restraining orders. Specifically, in the last few days of his life, Mr. Cross claimed he was assaulted by men acting for the defendants and had obtained a restraining order against the defendants, fearing for his life and personal safety.'

'What happened after you made these enquiries?'

'Given the evidence found at the scene, the gun, specifically, and the apparent motive, I formed the strong belief that the defendants were responsible for Mr. Cross's homicide. They were arrested and charged with first-degree murder.'

'Thank you, Detective. I think that's all the jury needs to hear.'

Kate quietly shook her head in disgust – Castro couldn't resist getting in his little jabs whenever he could – anything to help sway a jury toward a guilty verdict.

Kate stood.

Took a breath. Let that air flow through her lungs, filling her chest. She held it, then let it out slow and laid the groundwork for the defense with her opening question.

'Detective Withers, you've painted a detailed picture of the crime scene with your testimony. However, there are some important details missing, isn't that right?'

'I don't know what you mean?' said the witness.

'You found blood on the victim's porch consistent with this location being the scene of the murder, correct?'

'Correct.'

'You are asking this jury to believe that on the night of the murder, the defendants were at the victim's property, and they shot him in the head on his front porch, dropped the murder weapon and then went home, correct?'

Withers swallowed, took a sip of water. She'd been prepped well by Castro. She knew this line of questioning was coming.

'We have not been able to establish the mode of transport used by the defendants to get to the crime scene, no. But that kind of detail is not significant considering the evidence found at the scene.'

'Your forensic technicians impounded and examined both of the defendants' family vehicles, correct?'

'Correct, the GPS units in both vehicles did not show any movement on the night of the murder.'

'So how did they get from their home to the victim's property?'

'As I said, we have not yet established their mode of transport—'

Kate cut off the detective, said, 'Don't you really mean to say that, even on your case, you can't prove that the defendants even left their home on the night of the murder?'

Withers opened her mouth, drew breath, hesitated and stared hard at Kate. She wanted to fight back, but understood, being an experienced witness, this was not a battle she could win.

'We do not yet have the evidence to prove that, no.'

Kate glanced down at Harry. He nodded. There was a lot in that small nod. Reassurance and confidence. *You've made that point. Won it. Move on.*

'Let's turn to the security technician's report obtained by the defense,' said Kate, taking a document from the defense table. The report was entered into evidence without objection from Castro. He was busying himself with reading over his notes, nonchalantly. She had prepared a legal argument for this moment, but since there was no objection there was no need to argue the law.

Castro was not the type of man to let anything slide, particularly when it helped the defense. Suddenly, the general nervous anxiety Kate felt when she was on her feet cross-examining kicked itself up a notch. She could feel heat at her throat. Her cheeks were beginning to burn, but she had no choice but to go forward.

Perhaps more cautiously.

'You've had the opportunity to read this report, Detective?' asked Kate.

'I have,' said Withers.

'This report details an examination of all video recordings and data logged on the defendants' home-security system for the night of the murder, correct?'

'Yes.'

'The report prepared by the defense's engineer confirms that the video doorbell recorded footage of the defendants and their daughter entering the property at approximately six thirty in the evening, correct?'

'That's what that footage records, yes.'

'And the next time the motion sensor video recording kicks in is at eight in the morning, the following day. Isn't that right?'

'Yes.'

Kate heard Harry's chair creaking. She was aware of him leaning forward and placing his elbows on the defense table. They had not been expecting to get such an easy ride from this witness. Something was up. She had no choice but to keep going now.

'So the footage corroborates the defendants' version of events, that they were at home on the night of the murder, doesn't it?'

Detective Withers paused again. She was considering her answer. If something was going to pop up and bite the defense on the ass, now was the time.

'On the surface, yes,' said the detective.

Kate could have doubled down. She was wary now. And moved on.

'The report also details an outage in the security system in the early hours of the morning. A period of eleven minutes, where the Wi-Fi and radio signals that the system uses were offline, correct?'

'I read that in the report.'

Kate took a second and looked over her notes. All her questions had led to this point. She knew what she had to ask next. But she was anxious. There was something she wasn't seeing.

She bent down and lifted their first physical piece of evidence, the gun lockbox, and had it logged as a defense exhibit.

'Detective, this is the lockbox used by the defendants to store the gun which was found on the victim's property. This has been examined by defense experts: a fingerprint analyst and a DNA expert. Those reports have been agreed and submitted to the court in evidence. Those reports show that there are no fingerprints, nor any trace DNA found on this box, not even on the keypad. Do you dispute that?'

'I can't dispute that.'

'It is the defendants' case that, on the night of the murder, someone jammed the transmitter signals to their home-security system, snuck into their home and stole the Smith and Wesson revolver belonging to the defendant Kevin . . . wiped any trace of their theft from the lockbox and used this weapon to shoot and kill the victim, Mr. Cross. Wishing to shift the blame for the victim's murder onto the defendants, this person left that weapon at the crime scene in the full knowledge that it could be traced back to the defendants.'

'No,' said Detective Withers, 'I do not agree. It is my belief that the defendants deliberately killed the security system so they could leave their home undetected, perpetuate a false alibi, murder the victim and return home where they gained access through the rear of the property without triggering the camera system with their arrival.'

Kate felt those words like a knife.

They cut deep.

A glance at the jury. Some of them were covering their mouths. Some just let their jaws fall wide open. It was the same look that people wore when they'd just seen a car crash.

She was bleeding out. She needed to staunch the wound. Right now.

'So let me get this straight,' said Kate. 'The prosecution's case is that the defendants took great care to wipe their own fingerprints and DNA from their gun lockbox, temporarily disable their own home-security system, get to the victim's home somehow, but not using their own vehicles, shoot the defendant, leave their own gun with their fingerprints on it at the crime scene and get back to their house and get inside again, without the home-security system logging their re-entry?'

'Every murderer makes mistakes. They panic, adrenalin is high and their plans go astray,' said the detective.

'This seems to have been a mix of meticulous planning and absolute stupidity. They seem to have taken great pains to hide their participation in this crime apart from leaving their own gun at the crime scene. On your case, they may as well have left their driver's licenses behind?'

'It's more plausible than a mystery man breaking into their home undetected and stealing their gun,' said Withers.

Kate reserved the right to recall this witness for further questioning, and sat down.

Harry had his phone tucked underneath the desk. She guessed he was keeping Eddie informed. She wondered if he'd told him that they just got their ass handed to them. Harry leaned over, whispered, 'The security system was a double-edged sword. It did us just as much bad as it did good. Don't sweat it. This happens. We pick up and move on.'

Kate silently cursed. She should have seen this coming.

She didn't. Probably because she was too worried about what she might have to do to win this case. Flynn had a plan.

A plan that would compromise everything Kate stood for.

A plan that she wasn't sure she could be a part of.

45
Eddie

After the short recess, Detective Bill Sacks resumed his place on the witness stand and Bernice reminded the jury where they had left off – that Sacks had suspected that James and Harriet had been poisoned, and had ordered the water bottles and potential sources of poisoning to be seized for examination and treated as potentially hazardous material.

'Did the forensics lab carry out tests on the items taken from the apartment immediately?' asked Bernice.

'No,' said Sacks, 'I wanted to get toxicology results and a full medical examiner's report first. That would hopefully tell us what type of poisonous substance we were looking for and then we could test for it. When they did eventually test the items, they found traces of tetrahydrozoline in both water bottles found in the bedroom.'

'Are these the water bottles?'

Bernice put a picture on screen, a close-up of two plastic bottles with some water remaining in both. The caps were screwed tight. The label on them was the same – Ethos Water.

This was the one part of the case that I couldn't figure out.

With no traces of breaking and entering, how the hell did the man who called himself Logan get into Elly's apartment and poison those bottles without anyone seeing him?

'Your Honor,' said Bernice, 'I have already spoken to Mr. Flynn, and it has been agreed, subject to Your Honor's view, that we take the detective's testimony in stages. We are dealing with three murders in this trial. The first stage is his initial investigation into the deaths of James Parker and Harriet . . . I would propose to pause there and let Mr. Flynn cross-examine on the testimony so far. Then I would propose to call our expert toxicologist and the medical examiner who will testify and be cross-examined on their testimony regarding all victims. Then we can resume Detective Sacks's testimony.'

Judge Quaid nodded in agreement.

I stood up, said, 'I have no questions for the detective so far.'

Bernice whipped off her glasses, put her pen down and looked at me as if I'd had a stroke. Asking police officers questions in a multiple murder trial is not only expected, it's the job.

This case came down to one question. It wasn't yet time to ask it.

Sacks was replaced on the stand by the toxicologist Dr. Curry, an acknowledged expert. A bookish type who wore tweed and highly polished shoes.

'You examined bloods from the victims James Parker and Harriet Rothschild. What were your conclusions?'

'Both victims had a high concentration of tetrahydrozoline in their bloodstream.'

'And you examined and tested part of the liver from the first victim, the defendant's father Stewart Yorke.'

'I did, and again found traces of tetrahydrozoline.'

'What is tetrahydrozoline?'

'It's found in eyedrops, mainly. But if it is ingested, even in relatively small quantities, it can prove fatal. It acts as a vasoconstrictor, restricting blood flow, which can result in fatal cardiac arrest.'

'Thank you, Dr. Curry. Mr. Flynn will have some questions.'

I stood, said, 'No questions for this witness,' and sat down.

Bernice froze.

Then stood up and approached me, whispered, 'Are you trying to throw this case? If you're trying to build grounds for appeal for your client because of ineffective representation from counsel, it won't work.'

'I'm not up to anything shady. I'm choosing my moment, Bernice.'

'You're breathing – that means you're up to something shady,' she said.

'Not this time. I'm playing this one straight. Shame your DA isn't doing the same in the case against my wife.'

She turned, thanked Dr. Curry and called the medical examiner Dr. Sharpling, otherwise known as Dr. Death.

He was the only reason this case got on so quickly. There was not a single pathologist on the eastern seaboard who had anywhere close to the level of experience of poisonings as Dr. Sharpling. He was the leading expert, and he was retiring and moving to Costa Rica in two weeks, with the understanding that he would not be called upon to testify in any cases once he hung up his license and retired from his post.

As he took the Bible in his hand and swore his oath to tell the truth, I took a second to appraise him. A tall, gray-skinned individual with silver hair and pale eyes. I don't know what it is about medical examiners, but the idea of working with the dead every day, cutting them open, and seeing what stories their bodies would tell, just made me uncomfortable. I always got the impression medical examiners were cold people. They had to work in morgues, which by their very nature were cold, but I thought Sharpling had ice in his veins anyway. By all accounts, he was a decent man. Thorough and respectful. Called the corpses he dealt with his 'customers' and would sometimes spend time with the bereaved families of those customers to reassure them or simply to tell them exactly how their loved ones had died – so they didn't have to wait for a week on his report.

He was dressed in a steel-gray suit. The only strong color was in his dark navy tie.

'Dr. Sharpling, you examined the bodies of all three victims in this case, did you not?' asked Bernice.

'I did, and without the benefit of having viewed Dr. Curry's toxicology reports, which were prepared afterwards.'

Dr. Death was an old hand. He'd been cross-examined more times than most. He knew all the lawyers' tricks. He was cutting off potential lines of attack already. If, for example, he'd had a toxicology screening before he'd conducted the autopsy, there was the potential for his findings to be biased because he had the benefit of knowing there was a lethal poison in the bodies. Then, he would look for signs of that poisoning and the damage it had done to organs and arteries, which may have meant he missed some other vital clue showing an alternative cause of death for his customer. Defense lawyers call it confirmation bias. And he was avoiding it.

Smart.

'What were your findings in relation to James Parker?'

'The same as those of Harriet Rothschild. Death was caused by fatal cardiac arrest. There was no evidence of chronic heart disease in either of these individuals. They were much too young. I concluded, given the relative findings in the heart and unobstructed arteries, that the heart attack was chemically induced.'

'Is an overdose of tetrahydrozoline one such possible cause of chemically induced heart failure?'

'It most certainly is. It narrows the arteries, temporarily, and cuts off blood flow. With little to no blood flowing to the heart, the consequences are inevitably fatal.'

'As a consequence of your findings, did you have cause to examine a third body?'

'Yes, the defendant's father. I have dealt with a large number of poisoning cases. More than many of my colleagues. In my extensive expert experience, a poisoner will nearly always have multiple victims spread out over time. Once the type of poison used has been identified, and in particular the cause of death related to that poisoning, then it is common to find multiple victims within the suspect's personal circle. It didn't take long for me to search death records and find an identical cause of death in the case of the defendant's father. I informed Detective Sacks that, given my findings, the death of Stewart Yorke should now be considered a possible homicide.'

'What happened after you informed Detective Sacks about your suspicions?'

'A court order for exhumation and examination was obtained. I instructed the detective to make a video recording of the exhumation to establish chain of evidence and custody of the body as it was delivered to my mortuary table. This was to ensure that there had been no disturbance or potential for contamination of the body from any outside source prior to my examination.'

'What were your findings in relation to the body of the defendant's father?'

'The body had been through the usual embalming procedures, which meant there was no blood to test. However, if tetrahydrozoline had been administered in sufficient quantities before death, I would expect to find some trace to remain in the liver. I took a sample of the liver for testing. The tests returned with confirmation of the presence of tetrahydrozoline. This confirmed, in my mind, that there was a strong probability this victim had had a cardiac arrest due to tetrahydrozoline poisoning.'

'Thank you, Doctor,' said Bernice, and sat down.

Elly hung her head. She began to cry softly.

I whispered to her, 'Your father loved you. And I know you loved him, and you didn't do him any harm. We're going to show that.'

I stood, with Elly still crying in the seat beside me.

Trials are brutal.

I had one important question, but not yet. I needed to do some prep work first.

In a trial, it's not just about asking the right questions. It's not even about asking the right questions in the right order. It's really about making sure you get the right answer.

It's a little like playing three-card monte. A hustler bends three cards in the middle so that they stand up on their sides, like little roofs. With two of the cards, it doesn't matter what suit they are, or what number. But there always has to be a queen. He places the three cards, face down on a little table, turns over the queen to show the mark where it is in the line-up, then returns it face down. He then shuffles them around. The hustler will shuffle slowly enough to allow the mark to follow the queen.

Find the lady.

The mark points to the center card. He's right. He wins five dollars.

Now he's hooked.

Now he can be conned. Double or nothing. And the mark will play, and play, and play, and this time the dealer moves too fast for the mark to see. He will never find that queen again.

Now I had to start the game with Dr. Death.

First job, show him the queen.

'Dr. Sharpling,' I began, careful not to accidentally call him by his nickname, although it wouldn't have been the first time an attorney had called him Dr. Death during his testimony. 'Why did you ask Detective Sacks to make a video recording of the exhumation of Stewart Yorke?'

'I thought I had made it plain. It was to ensure that there was no opportunity for anyone to tamper with the body. If, for example, the body was left alone in a morgue or funeral home overnight, then a smart defense attorney like yourself could argue that the poison found in his liver could have been placed there after his corpse had been exhumed. I wanted to rule out any interference.'

'I see. So, hypothetically, it's possible that someone could inject a poison into the liver of a deceased person to make it look as though they had been poisoned?'

'It is not hypothetically possible in this case. We have the video evidence to prove that the casket seal was not opened from the moment it left the burial site to the time when I opened that lid in my facility and conducted my examination.'

'But, just to be clear, if the body was not observed for any length of time, it would just be a matter of someone injecting tetrahydrozoline into the liver to give the appearance of poisoning?'

'Correct, but impossible in this case.'

'Impossible because you can prove that no one had a chance to interfere with the body from the moment it was exhumed to the moment it got to your lab?'

'Correct.'

I looked at the clock. It was almost four.

I needed to ask my question now.

The court would soon be finishing, and I didn't want to get into something complicated now and then break overnight. I needed the jury to be able to follow this point from start to finish. Also, I didn't want to tip off Bernice.

'Your Honor, I have one question for Dr. Sharpling, then I would like to get into a long and complex area. I think it would be better for the jury to begin hearing that portion of testimony tomorrow, to ensure that they follow it.'

'It's been a long day already,' said the judge. 'Ask one more question, then we'll move into that more difficult area tomorrow.'

I thanked the judge, turned to Dr. Death, and casually asked the only question in this whole trial that mattered.

'Dr. Sharpling, are you certain that all three victims were murdered by the same person?'

I phrased it as dryly as I could. Made it sound flat. Like a question that I had to ask because I was doing my job. It wasn't sloppily phrased, but I didn't give it any bite on purpose. I wasn't throwing a softball here, but I wasn't exactly unleashing my fastball either.

'Mr. Flynn, given my extensive experience, and the fact that the same poison was used, I am one hundred per cent convinced that all three victims were poisoned by the same person. And that person is *your* client.'

Two jury members blinked when they heard that response. Whatever kind of ball I'd thrown with that question, Dr. Death had gotten all of it with his baseball bat of an answer, and it was now sailing clean out of the stadium.

Home run.

Or so he thought.

46
Eddie

I had my back against the wall, in every way possible.

Court adjourned for the day. Legs crossed, head down, I felt cold marble at my shoulder blades as I sat on a bench in the hallway of the courthouse, considering a decision. I glanced up, saw Denise with her arm around Elly, telling her it would be okay. She was going to take Elly back to her hotel. Denise would be telling her not to worry. That things would work out. That Elly should trust me.

Elly nodded, said she trusted me. But her eyes said something else.

Life can beat you down as surely as a pro boxer.

At this point, Elly was on the canvas, the referee was up to an eight count and the timekeeper had his hand on the bell, ready to ring it when he got to ten.

Not many people get up from this position. Even if I could save Elly, which was a long shot, there was every chance she would never recover. Not really. All I could do was fight for her in that courtroom. All I could do was my best, or my worst, depending on how you looked at it.

Right now, I carried that burden. Her life was in my shaking hands.

The stranger called Logan had really done a number on her. On us all. While preparing for the trial, Raymond had examined the apartment where Elly had been poisoned, and had found only DNA from the last occupants, an elderly couple from Nantucket who had come up for the week to see some Broadway shows.

There wasn't even any trace of him on security cameras. Bloch had managed to get a hold of someone in Secure One, who confirmed that one of their employees had wiped the entries for the day of Elly's attack. He had somehow run over a kid in a parking lot, sent a suicide note to his boss and then shot himself in the head.

I felt the hand of the stranger in these deaths too.

But I couldn't introduce it in court. I had no evidence to link him.

Elly's case stood on a knife edge.

I glanced to my left, watched as Harry talked to Christine and Kevin, who had come to my floor to check in. Christine wore that look. The one I'd both dreaded and grown accustomed to in our marriage. It was fear. This time it wasn't fear for our relationship, but for her life, for Kevin and for our daughter. Kevin was trying to smile through it. He was sticking his chest out as far as it would go, rubbing Christine's lower back, nodding along with Harry as he was trying to reassure them both.

It had been agreed that I wouldn't get involved in the case. I had to concentrate on Elly. And my love for my ex-wife and daughter clouded my judgement. I was no good as their lawyer.

But I didn't want to be their lawyer. I just wanted to make sure they got acquitted.

Kate approached me as Elly got into the elevator with Denise. I'd heard Kate's slow walk. Kicking her heels with every step. Those footsteps sounded heavy with resignation. She swiveled round and leaned against the wall beside me, her shoulder touching mine.

'You get your ass kicked today?' she asked.

'Yep. You?'

'Yep.'

I didn't say anything for a time. Let the low mood pervade for a while, then said, 'I think I can turn it around tomorrow. Can you?'

She nodded, said, 'At the moment we have some seeds of doubt planted. Harry did well with the cop. They know Cross probably lied to police about who exactly broke his arm. That gives us some credibility issues to work on.'

'It's not enough for reasonable doubt,' I said.

'I know. It's just a seed. Hopefully tomorrow we can make it a sapling.'

'It's my ex-wife's life on the line here, Kate. Why not bring your own fully grown tree and plant it in the middle of the goddamn courtroom?'

She sighed, said, 'Because your idea is highly illegal.'

'I think it will work.'

'I think it could get us thrown in jail, or worse.'

Harry joined us. He'd been listening to the conversation as he idled across the hallway.

'You're correct,' said Harry. 'It's risky and it's sure as hell illegal, but you know there's a difference between morality and the law. My mother grew up under Jim Crow laws in the South. She couldn't vote, couldn't sit on certain seats on a bus and couldn't drink in the same bar as a white person. By law. Sometimes, you find justice by breaking the law.'

Kate looked at Harry, then stared at me.

'You two think I don't know this? It's not that easy for me. It's not the way I was raised.'

'You bent the rules before,' I said. 'You told Elly to assault someone in Rosie's. That's illegal, and it saved her life.'

'You don't need to remind me. Somehow, I knew stepping across that line wouldn't be the end. It would be the beginning.'

'You saved her. You did the right thing.'

'No, I incited an assault. I did the wrong thing. What kind of a lawyer breaks the law to help their client?'

I raised an eyebrow.

'I wasn't talking about you. This isn't about you. It's me. This is different from telling your client to smack somebody in jail. This is . . . This is a lot more dangerous.'

Kate Brooks was better than me in every conceivable way. She was a better lawyer, smarter, braver and she had an absolute belief in what is right and what is wrong. No one tells you that when you become a lawyer you have to make moral compromises. You have to put aside your beliefs and trust the system. That's where Kate found herself at this point in her life. That system of professional ethics is a set of guard rails for lawyers, to allow them to sleep at night. I had already gone past this, a long time ago. I now knew the system didn't work, and I had to stick to my belief in what was right and wrong and that had nothing to do with the law. If I had to break the entire justice system to do the right thing, then that's what was going to happen.

If this was any other case, I would let Kate do whatever she wanted. I wouldn't interfere. But this was my family.

She wanted an excuse. She didn't want to go down this road, but there was no other way to save her conscience. She wanted me to order her.

'You don't get it. If you're a lawyer that gives a damn, then it's never about you. It's only about the client. I don't want to tell you how to run your case,' I said, 'but I don't think there's another way to win this one. I can't let anyone risk Christine and Kevin's life. It's not their decision either. Christine would rather spend the rest of her life in jail than let us do this, so don't tell them. This is all on me. I'll take the blame.'

Kate swallowed. I could see this was tearing her apart.

I said, 'This is my family, or what's left of it. You can play it straight and gamble their lives on a long shot you can't make, or you can do it my way and save them.'

She stared at me for what felt like a long time. I watched as part of her broke. This case was going to take a piece of Kate. And that piece would be forever lost.

Without another word, Kate walked away toward the elevators, leaving Harry and I in the empty courthouse hallways.

'Do you think she'll do it?' asked Harry.

I nodded.

'Will it work?'

'It has to. It's the only shot we have for winning Christine and Kevin's case.'

'How are things going with Elly's case?' he asked.

'I've got cards to play. We'll see how they fall. I've had so much on my mind that I haven't been able to figure out the last piece of the puzzle. How did Elly's stranger get into her apartment and poison those water bottles? I just can't work it out.'

'There was no sign of a break-in, right?'

'Right.'

'Elly had her keys the whole time. What about James's keys?'

'Two sets were listed in the inventory in the apartment. I'm guessing one was James's, maybe the other was Harriet's or it was just a spare set.'

'So there's no way he could have gotten into the apartment without us knowing about it?'

'Correct,' I said, and stood. Stretched my neck and back.

'We're idiots,' said Harry, smiling.

'Tell me something I don't know.'

'No, no, you're not hearing me. There's no way the killer could've gotten into the apartment without us knowing about it. With all the shit going on, you've been thinking about that as a question, instead of thinking about it as the answer,' he said.

My eyes flared with an idea. Same idea lingering behind Harry's smile.

'If he couldn't get into the apartment, that means he didn't get into the apartment,' I said.

'Now you've got it,' said Harry.

I thanked him, took out my cell phone, dialed a number and ran down the hallway, heading for the elevators.

47

Logan

Ten after five in Manhattan. Rush hour. Logan stood at a crowded bus stop on First Avenue, sipping a coffee and staring diagonally across the street, at the five-story redbrick apartment building on the corner of First and East Fifth Street. Only two sides of the building had windows, the east and the south sides, and from his position at the bus stop he had a view of both. The other sides of the building buttressed the rest of the block. The east face had a pizza shop on the ground floor and an old dressmaker's store – Logan saw the mannequins and dressmaker's dolls in the window. On the south side of the building was the entrance to the apartments on the upper floors and a wrought-iron fire escape that went down as far as the second floor.

Logan watched the windows in the building. Only a few lights were on. Two on the third floor on the east side. One on the fourth floor on the south side. The rest of the building was in darkness.

Two minutes ago, Gabriel Lake had left the pizza place on the ground floor, carrying two large pie boxes and two one-gallon bottles of water. He'd turned the corner, used his key and entered the building on the south side.

Logan was waiting to see if any of the other windows became illuminated.

He guessed that they would not.

He guessed, from the two large pizzas and the two bottles of water, that Lake was visiting someone who was home already.

Someone who already had a light on.

He watched the lit windows carefully, mindful to allow his peripheral vision to pick up any other lights suddenly being turned on in the building.

But no other lights came on.

Instead, he saw what he had been looking for.

The blinds parted on the third window along, on the third floor on the south side.

And Gabriel Lake checked the street below.

This was a safe house.

To keep Joe Novak hidden.

As if to wash away any nagging doubts Logan may have had, the woman investigator, Bloch, pulled up outside the building, parking next to Lake's old Pontiac. She got out, retrieved a man's gray suit from the back seat, still in the plastic from the dry-cleaners, and entered the building.

Joe Novak would need a suit for his court appearance.

Logan dropped his coffee in the trash and felt that strange sensation again.

He scanned the street. The prickles of tension crept up the small of his back.

That feeling again that he was being watched.

He told himself he was paranoid. It was the first time he had played the game having so much to lose. It was just fear. He told himself he should welcome this feeling. It would help keep him sharp.

Logan walked a few blocks before disappearing into the subway, heading home.

He ate dinner with Grace that night, although he only managed a few mouthfuls out of politeness. Logan was too tense to eat. He smiled and told her the pasta was delicious, but somehow he knew she wasn't buying the false praise.

While they cleared the plates away together, she finally relented. 'What's wrong?'

She asked it flat out in that way which neutralized any thought of a lie in response.

'Things are very difficult at work. I need to clear up some problems tonight, or I won't sleep.'

'Are you sure that's all it is?' she asked, grabbing him round the waist. 'Are you sure you're not getting tired of me?'

He cupped her face in his hands, kissed her, felt her cool lips against his, then said, 'I am doing everything for you, now. For us. So we can be together more.'

'I love you,' she said, and her hands slipped inside his sweater, her fingers clasping his back.

If she had done this when they'd first met, Logan would have recoiled. Now, he didn't mind. Not even when he felt her fingers tracing the scars on his back when she held him in the night.

'I love you more than I have ever loved anyone,' said Logan, from the heart.

'I'll be here when you get back,' said Grace.

For a second, he thought of Bloch and Lake. Both were formidable.

'If things don't go as well as I'd planned tonight, I might want to go away for a while. I need a break. I need to leave the city. Would you come with me?'

'For how long?'

'I don't know. A few months? A year?'

'A year? I can't, I have college and work . . .'

'But you can defer college for a year. And I'll take care of you. We could go anywhere in the world. Anywhere you want.'

'Anywhere?'

'I have a lot of money. We could go to Europe, Asia, the Caribbean . . .'

'The Caribbean? Wait, wait, this is not real. This is not real life . . .'

'It is real. We could get a boat, spend a year cruising the islands. I don't want to leave New York, but some of the people I've had to deal with lately . . . I didn't know it at the time, but they might be dangerous. I may have to leave, and I want you to come with me.'

She took a step back to study him. To read his expression. Her eyes searched his face. Looking for some hint of insincerity.

'I love you and all, it's . . . It's just a lot to take in. Things have been great between us, but we haven't known each other that long and this is all so sudden . . .'

'You're scared, aren't you? You're frightened that this is not real. I promise you, what we have is . . . You're the best thing to ever happen to me. I want you with me. And I want to make sure you're taken care of. If something happens to me tonight, these are my account numbers, and the passwords.'

He took a slip of paper from the notepad in the kitchen, and wrote down the details for his three accounts.

'There's twelve million dollars there. I have more, but if something happens to me I want you to have it. I want you to know that this is real. Hold out your hand.'

She held out her palm. Logan folded the note and placed it in her hand.

'What kind of trouble are you in?'

'I'm not in any trouble at the moment. The people I've worked for have gotten in bed with some criminal types. Bad people. I can't tell you anything about it. All I can say is I want out. And I want out clean.'

'Don't go tonight,' said Grace.

'I have to. I'll be back before morning. But, just in case, maybe pack a bag.'

She took hold of him, and they kissed long and passionately.

As Logan left his apartment building and stepped back into the cold, dark streets of Manhattan, he thought about the task ahead.

One target.

One location.

Two armed hostiles. Lake and Bloch.

His odds of taking out Joe Novak were not good. He had no choice. He couldn't risk Elly being acquitted. That would mean the police would start looking for the man with the suitcase. Part of what he told Grace was the truth – whatever happened tonight, he needed a clean break. Something had to happen to make sure no one came looking for him.

He thought of lying on a beach beside Grace. The warm ocean lapping at their feet. A blazing Caribbean sun overhead. Their boat anchored in the jetty nearby. Total freedom, from the cops, from Flynn, from his crimes and, most importantly, freedom from his dark nature.

He knew going into that building was fraught with danger.

If things went wrong, he needed a back-up plan.

Logan took out his cell phone and made a call.

While he waited for the call to be answered, he had an idea. An insurance policy. Something that would protect Grace.

If he failed to kill Novak tonight, it would be better for Grace if he died trying.

48
Bruno

Bruno Mont sat on a busted leather chair in a portable cabin that he used as his site office, flicking through the channels on his TV remote. The cabin was surrounded by seven hundred tons of scrap metal, mostly cars and refrigerators, and a single magnetic crane and a car crusher, which while technically were not scrap could certainly qualify under anyone else's definition of the word.

As junkyards go, Mont's Scrap Metal was one of the worst.

They didn't need a junkyard dog to guard the place at night.

Bruno provided all the security that was required, largely through reputation. He'd taken over the family business from his father five years ago after his dad passed on. The first weeks on site, Bruno experienced the same problem that had plagued his father – thieves climbing the fence at night to steal the stockpile of catalytic converters. The cat converters are rich in rare metals, and sell for between five hundred and a thousand dollars each. After ten of them went missing one night, Bruno bought a TV and a cot bed and stayed in the junkyard overnight.

He caught a thief red-handed. A kid, maybe eighteen years old, part of a gang who stole cat converters from parked cars and junkyards. The rest of his crew knew he'd been caught, and they waited round the corner for the sirens.

But the cops never came.

All they heard was the grinding of the crusher, and the screams beneath it. And they never saw the kid again.

Now, all that Bruno needed to do was put on the light in the site cabin, and nobody would ever dare climb his fence again.

He sat in his chair, found the local news. First, he watched the coverage from the Parker case, and then the Cross murder. There wasn't much reported about his friend. Bruno didn't really have friends. Not in the real sense. But he'd found a companion of sorts in Cross, a single individual who he could be around without having to hide his true nature. And that was important. Cross appreciated Bruno's skills and his desires. Even fed off them.

His cell phone rang.

Too late to be a customer.

He answered, 'Mont's.'

'I have a disposal job for you,' said the voice. Male, unfamiliar.

'We're closed,' said Bruno.

'I'm interested in a particular kind of disposal.'

Bruno leaned forward, opened his desk drawer, took out one of half a dozen burner phones. He called out the number written on the back of the phone with a silver sharpie, then hung up and turned the burner on.

The call came through right away.

'Who is this?' asked Bruno.

'Best if we don't use names. I got a referral, couple of years ago, from an old friend of yours, Arthur Cross. I was sorry to hear he passed.'

'Arthur was murdered.'

'Shit, sorry. I didn't know.'

'I guess you could say Arthur had it coming.'

'Are you still working?'

'I'm working. What do you need?'

'Two targets. Both are ex-law enforcement. I don't need them to disappear – I just want them dead.'

'That'll cost you.'

'What's the damage?'

'Depends. Somewhere between fifteen and twenty is the normal price, but for ex-cops I gotta charge more. You're looking at twenty-five apiece.'

'I can do that. Two things you need to know. One of them is a woman. You got a problem with that?'

'Not in the slightest.'

'You sure? 'Cause I had this problem before with contractors. They're all gung-ho when they get their deposit, but they pussy out when it comes time to pull the trigger on a bitch. You're not going to pussy out on me, are you?'

'This wouldn't be the first time I done a woman.'

'I don't know. I need to be sure you're going to go through with this. This is a time-sensitive thing.'

'I took out a little old lady in her own house. Broke her neck then dumped her over her balcony. Then I drove to an all-night diner and ate steak and eggs and then some pie. That make you feel better?'

'I'll take your word for it.'

'What's the second thing I need to know?'

'I need them taken out tonight.'

'Tonight? It's like seven already? That's not possible.'

'I know exactly where they will be. And they damn sure won't be expecting you. I can add another ten to the deal. That's sixty grand for a night's work. Half now, half on fulfilment.'

Bruno stood up from the desk, looked out of the window at the mountain of rotting scrap. He'd had to stare at that pile of metal garbage all day. Every day. Just like his old man had. He didn't know this guy, but if he knew Arthur well enough for him to give a recommendation for his friend, then he must be on the level.

And he sounded desperate.

'Why tonight?' asked Bruno.

'I don't think you need to worry about that. It's got to be now or never. That's all you need to know.'

A huge rat, the size of a small terrier, scuttled over the rusted hood of a Ford Pinto that sat atop the mound of junked cars.

'Seventy-five,' said Bruno. 'Half now. Half when the job's done. Or find somebody else.'

A pause.

For a moment, Bruno worried that he had priced himself out of the market. He had some cash squirreled away, but not enough to live on. The money from the Betty Le Saux job had never come through. That lawyer had done Cross out of his inheritance. Cross had been a smart guy, and Bruno knew that if he was ever going to get a big payday, it would likely come through Cross. The Le Saux job had been a washout, but now one of Cross's old pals might just come through for him. With that kind of money, Bruno could sell up and ship out. His days of doing five-grand hits for gangbangers and dirty cops were over.

One more job.

Tonight.

He could be in Baltimore by morning, then catch a plane and by this time tomorrow night he'd be sipping a cocktail in a bar in Boca Raton.

If he hadn't blown it already.

'Deal,' said the man.

Bruno smiled, but it quickly faded. There was nothing really holding him back. He could get out of the city anytime, but a strange sense of loyalty as well as a lack of funds had kept him in his father's junkyard. He had promised Arthur that he would take out Bloch. She had managed to get away when he'd tried to kill her quietly. He hated leaving loose ends. And he would feel bad leaving without fulfilling that promise to his late friend. But seventy-five large was enough to at least make him feel better.

'Give me your information and I'll do the transfer,' said the voice on the phone.

'Just one word of warning,' said Bruno. 'When the job is done, you transfer the rest immediately. If you don't pay, you become the next target. You understand?'

'I got it. Your targets are Gabriel Lake and Melissa Bloch. You can find them in . . .'

As Bruno wrote down the information on a notepad, his heart filled with the promise of destiny fulfilled.

He was meant to have this job.

This was a gift from Arthur, from beyond the grave.

Everything felt right.

Or it soon would, soon as he shot Lake and Bloch dead.

49

Logan

Logan hung up the call, completed the transfer of funds on his phone, then disappeared into the subway.

When he exited again, he walked five blocks and saw a man in the doorway to a dance club. The doorman was smaller than most, but his neck and shoulders were thick with muscle, filling out his black bomber jacket.

Logan nodded at the doorman as he went inside the club. He paid the girl at the coat check ten bucks, but refused the stamp on his wrist. The club had five floors. The first floor was a chill-out zone. Muted lamps, couches and a long bar. Only a handful of patrons. It was still early in clubland. A man in a long black coat sat at the corner of the bar, four cell phones in front of him.

Logan approached the man, said, 'I'm just picking up my order.'

'You got the chit?' said the man.

Logan brought out his phone, showed the man a QR code. He scanned it on his phone, nodded, said, 'Did you want the German, Austrian or American?'

'Austrian,' said Logan. 'I ordered a potato too.'

The man checked his phone.

'You sure did,' he said, and nodded at a waitress standing at the bar. She gestured for Logan to follow her. They moved through the room toward a hallway with a bathroom sign on the wall. She led him into the lady's bathroom. Logan followed. She shut the door behind her.

She went into a cubicle, removed a panel from behind the toilet bowl and reached inside. She came back out with a Glock and a suppressor, both wrapped in plastic. Logan removed the plastic, slid out the magazine from the Glock, checked the load in the clip and clicked it back home. He screwed the silencer into the barrel, made sure it was tight and a good fit. He chambered a round and tucked the weapon into the inside pocket of his jacket.

'Happy?' asked the woman.

Logan nodded, left the bathroom and the club and picked up his rental car.

He drove to the building he had been watching that afternoon, on the corner of First and East Fifth.

The street was quiet.

Coming up on nine thirty in the evening.

Dark.

But not yet dark enough.

Streetlights seemed to shun the south side of the building, at the entrance. As if the city wanted to keep that doorway discreet. There were still people on the sidewalks. It wasn't yet late enough for people to seek the comfort and security of their homes. Crime was up. The city that never sleeps was increasingly somnolent late at night. People stayed off the streets. Bad things happened in the dark.

Logan parked down the street from the bus stop he'd occupied earlier, so he could observe the building.

The same light was burning in the apartment window. Lake's Pontiac Aztek was still in the space outside the building, next to Bloch's Jeep.

Logan became very still.

And waited.

50

Bruno

Bruno had seen enough.

It was three in the morning.

He'd been round the block a few times in his van. Walked the street twice. Up and down.

There were three ways in.

The front door that led to the small lobby for the apartments.

The pizza place.

And the dressmaker's.

Both of those businesses would have back doors leading to the alley at the side of the building. Had to, by law. The apartments would have the same access to the alley. That meant there was a hallway that connected the whole building. There was no alarm system on the dressmaker's. They probably didn't carry that much cash; they wouldn't keep it in the building overnight and their stock was largely worthless. No point in paying for an expensive security system.

Bruno checked the street.

It was empty.

He slipped a crowbar from under his long coat, stepped up to the dressmaker's door and jammed the head deep between the door and the frame, right above the lock. He was a large man, and very strong. Anyone else would struggle, but Bruno leaned back, yanked the bar toward his chest. He could easily lift a full stack, maybe four hundred pounds, on a lat pull-down machine.

One pull tore the locking mechanism from the frame in a cloud of dust and splinters. And he was inside. Smooth. Easy as opening the door with a key.

Bruno stood in the dark store. No motion sensors. No alarms.

He pushed the door closed behind him, knowing it wouldn't fully shut. Looking around, he saw a small table by the register. He lifted it and jammed it against the door to keep it shut and then moved through the store. There was something eerie about the place, cluttered with dressmaker's mannequins, headless torsos on sticks that appeared animate in the dark. Moving through to the back of the store, he found the hallway that dog-legged left to the alleyway. He turned right, went through another door and found the small lobby for the apartments upstairs, a staircase and a single elevator.

He strode up the stairs to the second floor. Took a moment to readjust his geography.

The information he'd gotten said the middle apartment on the south side.

The hallway was lit tastefully with four lamps, evenly spread out on the walls.

There was an apartment door behind him, one at the end of the hallway, before it turned left, and a single door in the middle. This was where Bloch and Lake were hiding out, protecting a witness.

He stopped and listened. Heard nothing. Either the apartments were unusually well soundproofed, the tenants were all asleep at this time of night or the apartments were unoccupied.

He had expected at least someone to be up watching TV. It was likely at least one of the PIs was awake. If they were smart, they would take watch in shifts. So he could expect either Lake or Bloch to be awake when he went through the door.

Bruno reached under the glass shade of the first light in the hallway and unscrewed the bulb. It was hot and he found the glass sticking to his leather gloves. There was thick padding beneath the leather, so it didn't burn him, but he had to shake the bulb loose to get it out of his grip. It fell to the floor but hit the carpet from just a few feet of a drop and didn't break.

He did the same with the next bulb.

And the next.

As he moved along the hallway, he heard nothing.

The entire floor was now in darkness.

Bruno drew his pistol, a Sig Sauer, and put his back to the wall beside the door to the apartment where Bloch and Lake were supposed to be. He listened.

There was no sound.

He could knock on the door, lure one of them into the dark hallway. Take them out, then get inside and deal with the next target.

This had its own difficulties.

He would need to breach the apartment when there was at least one live target inside who would be alert and expecting him.

Better option was to go in hard and fast right now. Keep the element of surprise.

The hallway was in darkness to disguise his escape. Anyone else on this floor stupid enough to open their door to see what was going on would hopefully only see a large shadowy figure disappear down the stairs.

He checked the load in the Sig.

Thought about how to get through the door.

There might be security chains or deadbolts on the door, operated only from the inside. No real way to tell.

If he shot out the lock, or shot out the hinges, that would require multiple shots and he may as well call the police himself.

Better he used the crowbar. If he jammed it in between the door and the frame just right, it didn't matter what kind of security they had on the other side. The door itself was not very sturdy. It would give or break with enough pressure.

Bruno tucked the pistol into the front of his pants, and took the crowbar from the sleeve inside his long coat. He stepped out from the wall, levelled the head of the bar and faced the door now. Unless someone had their eye right at the peephole, that didn't matter. He placed his right hand near the bend just before the head, his left round the crook. His eyes fixed on the exact place to stab the bar into the tiny space between the door and the frame.

He didn't know if he heard something or felt it.

But he froze.

Then he definitely heard something.

'Don't move,' said the voice to his left. A woman's voice.

A voice he'd heard before.

Bloch.

51
Bloch

The camera Bloch had fixed inside the air vent in the hallway ceiling was motion activated.

She had taken the first apartment on this floor through Airbnb. The front door looked down the entire length of the hallway, as did the camera.

The first thing she heard was the beeping from the remote camera app on her phone, picking up motion. She checked the feed and saw Bruno unscrewing the lightbulbs along the hallway. Lake would have gotten the same alert on his phone. But, just to be sure, she sent him a text message. She drew Maggie, her beloved Magnum 500, turned off the small lamp in the living room and approached the door.

It was just a question of when to open it.

Ideally, when Bruno was focused on breaching the apartment door just down the hall.

She waited until he'd put his gun away and taken out a crowbar.

Bloch had already greased the locks and hinges of the door to this apartment so that it opened with no more of a sound than silk brushing skin.

She pointed Maggie at him. He was side on, facing the door to Lake's apartment.

'Don't move,' said Bloch.

It was dark. No light spilled from the apartment behind her. She could just about make out his silhouette.

At this point, Bloch regretted not bringing a flashlight. She couldn't have any light on in her apartment, because Bruno would have seen it when she opened the door. Now, she just wanted to be able to flick on a powerful flashlight and bathe her target in bright light.

'Drop the bar. Put your hands in the air,' said Bloch.

Bruno froze.

She heard rattling.

The security chain coming off the door to Lake's apartment.

The door opened fast and the arc of light from inside the apartment swept across Bruno, but as soon as the door began to open, he sprang forward, into the apartment, the crowbar held out in front of him across his chest.

Bloch let a round go, but it just took a chunk out of the wall where Bruno's head had been just milliseconds before.

Bloch swore and ran for the open door to Lake's apartment.

It was only twenty-five, maybe thirty feet of hallway. No more.

Her boots pounded on the carpet.

She heard a shot from inside the apartment.

Just before she reached the open door, she slowed, stopped, jammed her back against the wall and performed a fast peek, ducking her head forward and back to get a look at what the hell was happening inside.

Bruno had his back to her. He was straddling Lake, the crowbar raised above his head.

Bloch spun through the door. There was no time to grab the bar.

A bloody hole in Bruno's coat, at the shoulder, already told her the story of who had fired and where the bullet had gone. But Lake's gun was on the floor, just out of reach. Bruno's arms curled behind his head, ready to whip forward and cave in Lake's skull.

Bloch fell into a crouch, fired once.

Bruno's coat rippled.

The crowbar fell harmlessly over his back, and he fell forward.

Lake reached up, shouldered the falling Bruno out of the way, pushing him to the right to make sure he didn't land on top of him. Then Lake scrambled backward, lifted his gun from the apartment floor and stood, aiming it at Bruno, who was now face down on the floor.

Bloch had to do a double-take. Lake's face and shirt were covered in blood.

She looked along the path of her firing line, saw a dinner-plate-sized chunk taken out of the cement wall.

'Round came through,' said Lake. 'If you'd fired from a standing position the round would have taken me out too, and maybe the neighbors on the floor below.'

'Are you hit?' asked Bloch.

He shook his head, trained his weapon on Bruno as he stepped forward. Bloch joined him, and carefully, guns trained on him, they turned his body over onto his back.

A pistol was tucked into his pants. Lake grabbed the butt of the gun, between finger and thumb, drew it and threw it into the corner of the room. The gun had sat below a large exit wound in Bruno's abdomen.

He coughed, put his hands on his stomach to stop the bleeding. There was little chance of that happening.

Bloch stood over him, said, 'Do you want a paramedic?'

He stared up at Bloch, eyes bulging, and nodded.

'They're not going to make it. I can call the coroner?' she said.

Bruno coughed blood onto his face.

'Tell me. How does it feel, bitch?' said Bloch.

Bruno's eyes shifted toward the door.

Bloch ducked and spun round just as the first bullet zinged past her head.

52

Bloch

As she spun round, Bloch levelled her weapon at the door.

She hadn't heard a shot. Whoever fired must've been using a suppressor.

She caught a glimpse of a man in the doorway, wearing black. A gun in his hand.

A scar on his chin.

Bloch fired.

Lake fired.

The doorframe exploded in clouds of dust and wood splinters as the man ducked back into the hallway. Bloch moved to the right, keeping low, narrowing the angle. Lake dived onto the ground, lay flat, gun trained on the doorway.

'It's him,' said Bloch.

A voice came from the hallway.

'I don't have much time. Send out the witness and I'll let you both live.'

'Come and get him,' said Lake.

Keeping her gun trained on the doorway with one hand, Bloch reached into her jacket, took out her phone and brought the screen to life. It still had the feed from the camera in the hallway.

They saw the man, back to the wall, inching forward toward the door. She put the phone on the ground.

She took Maggie two-handed, looked at the phone.

Looked at the wall just to the right of the doorway.

Adjusted her aim.

Squeezed the trigger.

Maggie bucked in her hands.

She looked at the phone, saw a blow-out of plaster on the other side of the wall, right at the man's left shoulder. For a second, he disappeared in a cloud, but she saw him duck down, clutching his left arm.

Bloch adjusted her aim.

The man set off running for the stairs, just as Bloch let off another round. She followed his trajectory, firing through the wall as he vaulted the railing, dropping down a flight of stairs.

'Go,' said Bloch, but Lake was already moving.

Before she followed him out of the apartment, she put in her AirPods and hit dial on Eddie's cell phone. She glanced at Bruno.

He was already dead.

Eddie picked up as Bloch started running.

'What's happening?' said Eddie.

'Bruno is down. The stranger appeared. I tagged him in the arm but he's on the run. We're in pursuit. Get down here right now.'

53
Eddie

'You're calling on the river?' I asked.

Amy looked at me with that same disappointed expression. She was a teenager, and that meant she knew infinitely more about the world, and everything in it, than I did.

'I'm calling. He's bluffing,' she said, glancing across the table at Joe Novak.

'I ain't saying a word,' said Joe.

'You should listen to your father,' said Christine. 'This is his wheelhouse.'

Christine and Kevin were on the couch in the corner of my apartment. I was sitting at the small dining table, playing poker with Amy and Joe, who was staying with me while Bloch and Lake did everything possible to give the impression that Joe was stashed away in Lake's apartment on East Fifth Street and First Avenue. Elly had come over too. At the moment, Flynn and Brooks was at war, and I just wanted everyone around me. We'd had pizza and sodas, and now I was teaching Amy poker.

Thanks to Harry, I had something new to show the court tomorrow in Elly's case. Something that would change things dramatically.

Elly came out of the bathroom and sat on a chair facing the

couch. She was quiet. I'd invited Kate over too, but she had declined. Said she was working.

Kate was struggling.

'Dad, I know what I'm doing,' said Amy.

'Okay, I'm just offering some friendly advice,' I said, then reached for my phone in my pants pocket. It was buzzing.

Bloch was calling.

'What's happening?'

'Bruno is down. The stranger appeared. I tagged him in the arm but he's on the run. We're in pursuit. Get down here right now.'

'I've got to go. Bloch and Lake are chasing the stranger,' I said. I grabbed my coat and keys and ran out. I heard Elly calling after me, but I ignored her. I had to move.

Within thirty seconds, I was behind the wheel of my Mustang, racking up speeding fines as I blitzed downtown, blowing two red lights.

Bloch was now on speaker in my car. I could hear her breathing heavily, her voice punctuated by the pounding of her boots on the sidewalk. She was running fast.

'He just got into a black Toyota Camry. I'm headed back to my car.'

'Where's Lake?' I said.

'He's ahead of me, waiting at my Jeep. Where are you?'

'I'm five minutes away. Second Avenue, headed south. Just passing Twenty-fifth Street. Where's Lake's car?'

'Beside mine. He's a terrible driver and his car is a piece of shit. He'll ride shotgun with me.'

I could hear her breathing slowing, her pace decreasing. The sound of her Jeep unlocking and then, seconds later, the roar of the engine.

'He's turned east on Sixth. Black Camry, New York plate but I can't get close enough to read it yet.'

I slammed on the brakes for a red light, let five cars pass in front of me. Waited until it was clear then blew through the red before it could change.

'I'm passing Seventeenth Street,' I said.

Bloch had put me on speaker. I could hear Lake swearing in the background.

'Watch it!' he cried.

'You okay?' I asked.

'Fine, he's turning onto Avenue A.'

'How far ahead is he?'

'Two blocks, but not for much longer,' she said, the engine revving high, the gear changing, then more revs.

If he was headed south with a car on his tail, there was little to no way to shake it unless he was a highly skilled driver. My guess was he was nowhere near as good as Bloch. In that case, he had one chance – get off the island to give himself more options, including the interstate.

'Don't get killed,' I said. 'Just stay on him. He's going for the Williamsburg Bridge. I'm going to stay on Second and cut onto Delancey Street, see if I can head him off.'

For once, even at this hour, I had a clear road ahead. Green lights all the way.

I crushed the accelerator into the floor, hit seven thousand revs, then heeled and toed the gear change into fourth and watched the needle on the speedo climb past eighty miles an hour.

At this speed, it didn't matter what happened to the lights. If they turned red, there was nothing I could do. I pulled round a yellow cab, heard the horn blasting after me and prayed I didn't run into the NYPD or a truck driver coming out of a side street.

I gripped the wheel, eased off the gas as I shot through the intersection onto Chrystie Street, blew past Sara D. Roosevelt Park and held my breath.

Foot off the gas. Clutch. I dropped into second, slammed the wheel left and pulled the handbrake. The tires smoked and screamed in the turn as I laid rubber across three lanes and arced onto Delancey Street where I let the brakes go and hit the gas, fighting with the wheel to correct the slide and wrestle the Mustang into a straight line.

'I'm on Delancey. Where is he?'

'He's on Essex, turning into Delancey now. Lake called it in. Police are on the way. They're going to close the bridge on the Brooklyn side.'

Up ahead, maybe a block and a half away, I saw a black Toyota Camry fire straight across the intersection, its tail flicking out, catching another vehicle. The horns blared, but the bump helped the Camry bounce back on course.

I chanced a glance down Essex Street, saw Bloch's Jeep easing out of the intersection. She fell in behind me.

Now there were two of us bearing down on the Camry.

And gaining.

The Camry's brake lights flashed red, then it pulled out and overtook a camper van.

Sparks flew from the exhaust as it hit the slipway for the bridge and began to climb.

'At this speed, he'll be across the bridge in under a minute,' I said. 'Those cops better close it.'

'They're almost there,' said Lake.

We climbed, and I followed the Camry, weaving through the light traffic as we rose above the city. Soon we would be over the East River.

This guy was incredibly smart. That's what made him predictable. One way or another, this would all be over once we made the other side of the bri—

Jesus!

He was stopping.

I stood on the brakes.

The Mustang fishtailed, angled toward the concrete barrier separating me from a hundred-foot drop into the river. I fought the slide with the wheel, then pulled the handbrake.

The Camry, instead of speeding to get over the bridge before it could be closed, had pulled up in a cloud of tire smoke and angled his car to block both lanes of the bridge. The Mustang came to a stop just a few feet from the Camry. Then the driver's door opened and a man, dressed in black, dived out onto the ground.

I unhooked my seatbelt, threw myself on the passenger seat just as the man's head came up again over the hood of the Camry, a pistol in his hand. I heard three shots, two through the windshield and the third blew it out, showering me in broken glass.

More firing. This time I heard the rounds hitting metal, but not my car.

I took a quick peek in my side mirror, saw Lake and Bloch getting out of the Jeep, guns in their hands, using the heavy doors for cover as they fired back.

This was my chance.

I kicked open the passenger door, crawled out as fast as I could onto the asphalt and, keeping low, I made it to the trunk of my car.

Over the sound of gunfire, I heard sirens.

I never thought I'd be glad to see the cops, but tonight was an exception.

'Drop the gun and step out!' I cried. 'The cops are blocking the other side of the bridge. You're not going to make it to the interstate. You got nowhere to go.'

The firing stopped.

I heard a voice.

'I was never going for the freeway. I know when it's over.'

A volley of shots from the stranger saw Lake and Bloch duck behind the Jeep doors, holes appearing in the hood and side panels of the car.

As the firing stopped, I peeked out.

The man stood in the middle of the highway, staring at an empty gun. He spun and vaulted over the concrete barrier onto the balcony beneath one of the support towers.

Bloch and Lake started running toward me. I turned and ran for the stranger.

I jumped the barrier, and my feet slid on the iron-grille walkway as I landed. It was an area not much bigger than a barbershop floor, but bags of cement, stacks of traffic cones and a Porta-Potty took up most of the space. This was an area for the highway and construction workers who were always carrying out repairs to the bridge. A railing wrapped round the semicircular balcony. At the apex of that half circle was an iron streetlight, with three globe bulbs, each of them about three times the size of a soccer ball – the old-fashioned, ornamental type of lights that gave the bridge so much of its charm.

I heard Bloch and Lake coming over the barrier, their feet stomping on the iron walkway.

At first, I couldn't see the man we'd been chasing.

Then, from behind a stack of orange water barrels, he grabbed hold of the iron streetlight pole and levered himself up to stand on the railing.

'Stop!' I cried.

Bloch said, 'Don't move.'

He looked back over his shoulder at the three of us. Then looked down.

Through the grille, I could see the East River, maybe a hundred and twenty feet below, dark and swirling. The wind was strong and as sharp as ice up here.

I took out my phone, held it low, angled the camera lens toward the lights and hit video record. It was then that I noticed he held his left arm stiffly. Blood was dripping from a wound there.

'Cops are almost here. Don't do it. Step down. Tell them what you've done. You can still do some good. You can tell them how you poisoned James and Harriet.'

He said nothing, just stared down into the river below.

The sirens grew louder. Getting closer now.

'Come down. Don't do it.'

I held up the phone, capturing the man in full frame.

Even when I looked back at the footage from that night, I couldn't tell what happened first.

Did he jump first, or did I move first?

Impossible to tell.

The man raised his right leg, held it over the edge for a second, and then hopped into the air and disappeared.

I ran to the edge, grabbing the balcony railing. Lake and Bloch joined me on either side and stared into the darkness below. We saw the man falling, hitting the water with a terrible *schtoooom* sound, like a missile breaking a wave. The splash was ten feet high, white water flowing through the air and crashing back down.

Rolling red and blue lights painted the green iron bridge as the sirens roared to a stop.

For five minutes, none of us moved. We stared at the water, looking for signs of life.

There were none.

54
Eddie

You have to choose your moment carefully.

Trial law can be like chess.

You know the final move, the winning move, will be made with your queen. But before that move is made you have to cut off the other means of escape for your opponent's king. That winning move comes from the dozens of little moves before it. The strategic placements of rooks, knights and even pawns. Some of your pieces will be lost, and that's fine. As long as you meant to sacrifice them.

And then, when it's the perfect time, your queen slides across the board and it's game over.

Checkmate.

Dr. Death had changed his suit from yesterday. This one was a navy pinstripe, with a pale blue shirt and black bowtie. His expression hadn't changed, though. He still wore that demeanor of professional boredom.

I played the video from yesterday, just a minute or so, and paused it right at the moment when Dr. Death reached into the casket with tweezers, just after the lid had been removed.

'Just to remind the jury of what you'd said yesterday, Doctor. You said that you were completely satisfied that between the casket being exhumed and it being opened in your lab, there was no possible way for anyone to interfere with its contents, correct?'

'Correct,' he said.

'So this casket was sealed and showed no signs of any interference?'

'Yes.'

'And, furthermore, you are one hundred per cent sure that the same person murdered all three victims?'

'Correct.'

I played the video for twenty seconds, then paused it.

'Doctor, you found something at the foot of the casket. This video shows you removing it with tweezers. What did you find?'

'A dead moth.'

'A moth? Is that unusual to find in caskets?'

'I think I may have even mentioned it at the time. Most funeral parlors keep some spare clothes around. Suits and dresses, that kind of thing, in case they have to perform a burial where the deceased person, or their family, don't have appropriate clothing for the body. It wouldn't be unusual to find moths where you store old clothes.'

'I take it you retained this moth for evidence?'

'Yes, that's standard protocol. And we took photographs.'

I asked for a blown-up photograph to be shown on the screen.

'Is this the photograph of what you found in the casket?'

'Yes.'

I asked for a different photograph to be displayed and entered as a defense exhibit.

'Would you agree that this is the same type of creature that you found in the casket?' I asked.

The doc took a long look, said, 'Yes, I think so. Same markings.'

'For the record, you're referring to the forewings, which are brown with black spots. The hind wings are red, black and white, again with black spots. And these markings are identical to the ones you found on the moth in the casket?'

'Yes.'

'There is only one problem with your testimony, Doctor. That is not a moth.'

'It's not?'

'It's a bug.'

I asked for a third picture to be displayed. This was an information-and-warning memo issued by New York City's Department of Parks and Recreation.

'As you can see from this memo, which includes the picture you just saw, this creature is what's commonly known as a spotted lantern fly. It's considered a pest.'

'Objection, Your Honor,' said Bernice. 'While this is all very interesting, Dr. Sharpling is here to testify about his findings as an expert pathologist, not as a moth expert.'

'Your Honor,' I countered, 'this goes to the heart of the defense.'

'What is the relevance?' asked the judge.

There was no way around it. I needed to blow this up in testimony from the stand. If I explained to the judge the meaning of all of this, it would give Dr. Death the heads up. Effectively, I'd be telling my opponent exactly what moves I was about to play on the chess board, and that couldn't happen.

'Your Honor, it was the witness who said that he found a moth. He offered that opinion freely. That opinion has direct bearing on his findings on the examination of the body of Stewart Yorke. If you refuse to allow this line of questioning, then I'm going to have to ask for an appeal on your ruling.'

The judge looked at me, then Bernice.

'I'll allow a few more questions, but get to the point.'

'Thank you, Your Honor. Dr. Sharpling, what is the date of death of Stewart Yorke?'

'Seventh of January 2017.'

'And you testified that there was no possible way this casket was opened, from the exhumation until it got into your lab.'

'Correct.'

'As this memo from the Parks and Recreation Department records, the first recorded sighting of the spotted lantern fly in New York was in 2020. Three years after Mr. Yorke was buried.'

Bernice's pen moved angrily across the page. Dr. Sharpling had finally seen the punch headed his way.

'I cannot explain that.'

'You have already confirmed, twice now, that the casket showed no signs of interference. What is the casket made from?'

'I believe it is constructed from brushed steel.'

'Doctor, this is a photograph of the tree beside Mr. Yorke's grave. Its name is *Ailanthus altissima*, but it's also known as the tree of heaven. It is the preferred food source of the spotted lantern fly. You can see from this photo there is a large colony of spotted lantern flies on the bark of this tree.'

The photo I brought up on screen, and entered into evidence, spoke for itself.

'Are you suggesting this fly burrowed underground and into the casket? Because the casket was sealed with no damage, Mr. Flynn. I don't think that's possible,' said Dr. Death, trying to head me off.

He called it wrong.

'No, Doctor, I'm not suggesting that. Like you said, it's impossible. What I am suggesting is that on the seventh of November, while my client was in police custody, someone dug up Stewart Yorke's body, and injected his liver with traces of tetrahydrozoline to make it appear as if he had been poisoned. While the casket was open, this fly got inside.'

Silence.

Dr. Death looked at Bernice, and I could see his desire to push back. This was the last time he would appear in a courtroom, and he was desperate not to let this one be a loser.

'I find it hard to imagine that someone could dig up a body in a cemetery without anyone noticing,' said the doctor.

'I agree,' I said, and watched Doc Sharpling's eyes widen.

'On the seventh of November last year, a nightwatchman in the cemetery was brutally murdered. Some empty beer cans were found scattered around his body and the NYPD took fingerprints and DNA from those cans. They arrested the three minors who were known to police through their DNA and fingerprints, but all three had solid alibis and did not face charges. It is more likely that the individual who murdered the nightwatchman attempted to frame some innocent kids for this murder, just as he was attempting to frame my client for murder. Do you have any opinion on that, Dr. Sharpling?'

He said nothing. The last time he'd shot out a defense answer, it had come back to bite him. He was taking his time.

'I'm just here to offer my opinion on the cause of death.'

'Dr. Sharpling, the casket is plate steel. The bug you found in the casket was not present in this part of the country for many years after Mr. Yorke's death. The only possible way that bug got into the casket is if someone dug it up and opened it. Isn't that right?'

Dr. Death sighed, bit his lip, then nodded and said, 'Yes.'

'You already testified that tetrahydrozoline could be present in the body of Stewart Yorke if someone simply injected his liver with this substance, correct?'

'Correct.'

'Is it possible, Dr. Sharpling, that if you hadn't found tetrahydrozoline in Stewart Yorke's liver, that his death was accurately recorded the first time around as a natural cause of cardiac arrest?'

Dr. Death's skin grew paler as he said, 'Yes, that's possible and, now I am satisfied that the body could have been interfered with by a person unknown, I don't believe I can continue to stand by my initial findings.'

The crowd in the gallery grew noisy. They could tell the DA's case was falling apart spectacularly.

'One final question: what date do you estimate to be the date of death for James Parker and Harriet Rothschild?'

'That's in my report. November second.'

'Your Honor,' I said, 'I would like to call Detective Sacks to the stand.'

Bill Sacks's Crocs squeaked across the floor of the courtroom as he made his way to the witness stand, the lanyards round his neck jangling softly. The clerk reminded him he was still under oath.

He smiled at me. I looked at Elly.

She sat up straighter today, staring right at Sacks. She wore a little make-up, and had had her hair styled in a salon round the corner before she came to court, while I was at the Starbucks headquarters with a subpoena. Being around my friends and family last night had helped Elly, I thought. She didn't feel alone. She felt the weight of the whole team behind her. I'd told her about my phone call with the head of human resources in Starbucks while she was at my place, and for the first time since I'd met her I saw hope in her eyes.

And something else.

Anger.

'Your Honor, at this time I would like to introduce evidence which came into the possession of the defense this morning. A security footage recording from a Starbucks from November second last year . . .'

As I spoke, I watched Detective Sacks's expression change.

The smile faded. The color drained from his rosy cheeks and his hands gripped the chair handles. His knuckles were pale with the effort.

'Objection, Your Honor,' said Bernice. 'Security footage is routinely only kept for around sixty days by Starbucks. I've had direct experience of this. The defense has been holding on to this footage for some time and now wants to ambush the prosecution. I haven't seen whatever is on this video, but the defense has an obligation to comply with discovery. I object to its introduction.'

The judge looked at me.

'Your Honor, this footage was retained by Starbucks human resources because it formed part of an internal investigation. This store is located in the same block as the defendant's apartment, right outside the front door of her apartment building. It seems there were ongoing cash discrepancies with the register. As a result, management retained all security footage and even stopped taking cash payments for a while in order to find the member of staff suspected of stealing from the register. I obtained this footage this morning, having contacted the human resources department last night. If need be, I can have a Starbucks head of HR testify to—'

'What is on this footage exactly?' asked the judge.

'It shows how James Parker and Harriet Rothschild were poisoned, Your Honor.'

Elly sat back and folded her arms, staring at Bill Sacks.

He chanced a quick glance at her, swallowed and quickly averted his gaze.

'I would like to have a short adjournment to show this footage to Mrs. Mazur first, Your Honor. Perhaps we can agree to it being introduced into evidence . . .'

'Take a half hour,' said the judge.

Ten minutes later, in a DA's office on the ground floor, Bernice reached across the desk and closed the lid of my laptop.

'Is that what I think it is?' she asked.

We had just watched a man in a ball cap sitting at a table in the Starbucks, nursing a coffee. As James Parker and Harriet Rothschild walked through the front door of the Starbucks, the man got up and walked quickly into the line for the cash register. He had a messenger bag on this shoulder. *Without* James or Harriet seeing him, he took two bottles of Ethos still water from his bag, and placed them on the refrigerator shelf in front of the other bottles there. James picked up those two bottles, totally unaware that they had just been placed there a few seconds ago by the man in front of him in the line. The man stayed in line, got a coffee, watched while James paid for the two bottles of water, and then both James and Harriet left, headed for the apartment upstairs.

The man in the cap left shortly after. His face was largely covered, but the scar on his chin was plain from a number of angles.

'I have Elly Parker and Joe Novak who will testify that this is the same man who tricked Elly into that apartment the next day and poisoned her. My investigators will testify that this is the same man who tried to kill Joe Novak last night before he leapt to his death off the Williamsburg Bridge.'

'Jesus,' said Bernice. 'And you really just found this last night?'

I got up from the desk, stood a little distance away from Bernice and studied her closely. Her reactions to the footage were real, and honest.

'I got it last night, but Detective Bill Sacks took a copy of this footage two days after he arrested Elly Parker.'

'He what?'

'Didn't you see his face when I mentioned it? He was like me. He couldn't figure out how the water bottles were poisoned. Ethos Water is only sold in Starbucks, and he must've put two and two together a lot faster than me and checked the footage. It's luck, pure dumb luck, that they still had this footage. They fired somebody a month later and they were afraid they might get sued, so they kept all the security footage for October and November. But Sacks had exculpatory evidence that he never showed you. And, more importantly, he never disclosed it to us. I'm going to level with you – I didn't think Sacks had it in him. I thought he was playing this straight. Turns out, he thought he'd made the case that would crown his whole career, get him another promotion, so he could sit behind a desk in his Crocs. He had his murderer in the shape of Elly Parker, and no way was he going to miss out on closing the biggest murder case in the city just so he could go chasing a mystery man that he would probably never find.'

Bernice took off her glasses, stood, said, 'Eddie, I swear I didn't know anything about this . . .'

'I believe you. I know you're a straight shooter, Bernice. Sacks had me convinced too.'

Here's the thing about cops. Corruption is easy. Playing it straight is hard. When you've got a solid case, it's too easy to look the other way when you find evidence that doesn't fit. Sacks did what a lot of cops would do in the exact same situation. It's their job to make cases, make arrests and get convictions. The truth is somebody else's problem.

'Now you know about Sacks. The question is, Bernice, what are you going to do about it?' I asked.

I sat at the defense table, and I did something I'd never done before.

I took my client's hand in mine. Elly held on to me, and I could feel her heart racing as Bernice stood to address the judge.

'Your Honor, the People have a motion before the court. We wish to dismiss all charges against Elly Parker with prejudice . . .'

Her voice was drowned out by the cheering crowd.

'I would also like to say something, Your Honor, as I know members of the press are here and I won't be taking questions at this time. I simply wish to apologize to Mrs. Parker, who should never have been on trial for these crimes. The DA's office is opening an investigation into a person unknown who we believe is responsible for multiple homicides. We are also recommending an internal affairs investigation into Detective William Sacks. If it pleases the court, that is all.'

I liked Bernice. And I wouldn't want to be Bill Sacks. She was going to crucify him. And I was going to be there, that day, to watch.

I stood with Elly, her hand in mine, and we turned to face the crowd.

I raised her hand in the air and listened while the cheers and applause filled the courtroom.

I let go of her hand, told her Denise would look after her, and I ran for the exit, fought my way through the crowd and found the stairs.

Christine's case was still running . . .

55
Kate

This was it.

There was no more time.

Christine and Kevin sat at the defense table, unaware of what would happen next. Eddie had deliberately kept them in the dark. They knew he had something up his sleeve, as he almost always did, but they didn't know what.

Kate stood, took a moment to look at her clients.

Good people. They hadn't harmed anyone. Kevin had done the right thing for his old client and had drawn the ire of a deranged killer. She couldn't blame him for what he had done. He could not have known the risks that came with his actions. No one could. In fact, Kate surmised that if she had been in Kevin's shoes, she would have done the same thing.

She had a decision to make.

Save these good people.

Or obey the law.

Harry stared straight ahead. He would say no more to her. He had made his mind up. He knew what had to be done. Perhaps, she thought, Harry always had a mild disrespect for the law. And it was only when a young con artist appeared in his courtroom, and he and Eddie had become friends, that this innate underlying rebellious streak had come forward.

Kate's father had been an NYPD cop for most of his life. He had taught her right from wrong. If her father knew the decision that faced her, she guessed he would tell her to stick to the law. Don't take a personal risk for a client, no matter who they are. Don't compromise your professional ethics.

She hung her head.

Listened to Castro whispering to his assistants.

Detective Withers cleared her throat.

They were all waiting for Kate.

Some people on the jury coughed or shuffled their feet.

In the midst of the hum of the courtroom, Kate closed her eyes, thinking of Amy living with her father, while Kevin and Christine spent the rest of their lives in a hellhole prison.

She opened her eyes, and looked at Detective Withers with a determination she had never felt before.

Kate said a silent apology to her father and asked her first question.

'Detective, you are aware that the deceased, Arthur Cross, was suspected of murdering his wife very recently. I think we established this?'

'He was suspected, but no charges were brought.'

'To be specific, it was suspected that Mr. Cross had paid an associate of his, Bruno Mont, twenty thousand dollars to kill his then elderly wife, Betty Le Saux?'

'That was the suspicion. That was all it amounted to. Suspicion.'

'Do you know the amount Mr. Cross stood to inherit?'

'I'm not sure, but I believe it was many millions of dollars.'

'How about twenty million dollars?'

'I will take your word for that.'

'The defendant, Kevin Pollock, managed to get the will overturned, and a previous will through probate so that Mr. Cross inherited nothing. Correct?'

'Correct.'

Kate tapped her laptop. A financial statement appeared onscreen.

'This is Mr. Cross's bank statement. We can see here a payment, before Betty Le Saux's murder, to Mont Salvage of twenty thousand dollars. And another payment, just recently, of fifteen thousand dollars. Do you see that?'

'I do.'

'Mr. Cross made that second payment, the day after he was allegedly assaulted by the defendants, even though he was unable to give an accurate description of his attackers that day?'

'Yes, that timeline appears to be correct.'

'So right after he had his arm broken, Mr. Cross pays Mr. Mont another fifteen thousand dollars, agreed?'

'Yes.'

'Your Honor, I would now like to play a recording which came into our possession yesterday. The first voice you will hear is Mr. Bruno Mont.'

'Who is this?'

'Best if we don't use names. I got a referral, couple of years ago, from an old friend of yours, Arthur Cross. I was sorry to hear he passed.'

'Arthur was murdered.'

'Shit, sorry. I didn't know.'

'I guess you could say Arthur had it coming.'

'Are you still working?'

'I'm working. What do you need?'

'Two targets. Both are ex-law enforcement. I don't need them to disappear. I just want them dead.'

'That'll cost you.'

'What's the damage?'

'Depends. Somewhere between fifteen and twenty is the normal price, but for ex-cops I gotta charge more. You're looking at twenty-five apiece.'

'I can do that. Two things you need to know. One of them is a woman. You got a problem with that?'

'Not in the slightest.'

'You sure? 'Cause I had this problem before with contractors. They're all gung-ho when they get their deposit, but they pussy out when it comes time to pull the trigger on a bitch. You're not going to pussy out on me, are you?'

'This wouldn't be the first time I done a woman.'

'I don't know. I need to be sure you're going to go through with this. This is a time-sensitive thing.'

'I took out a little old lady in her own house. Broke her neck then dumped her over her balcony. Then I drove to an all-night diner and ate steak and eggs and then some pie. That make you feel better?'

'I'll take your word for it.'

'What's the second thing I need to know?'

'I need them taken out tonight.'

'Tonight? It's like seven already? That's not possible.'

'I know exactly where they will be. And they damn sure won't be expecting you. I can add another ten to the deal. That's sixty grand for a night's work. Half now, half on fulfilment.'

'Why tonight?'

'I don't think you need to worry about that. It's got to be now or never. That's all you need to know.'

'Seventy-five. Half now. Half when the job's done. Or find somebody else.'

'Deal.'

'Give me your information and I'll do the transfer.'

'Just one word of warning. When the job is done, you transfer the rest immediately. If you don't pay, you become the next target. You understand?'

'I got it. Your targets are Gabriel Lake and Melissa Bloch. You can find them in . . .'

Castro launched to his feet and began complaining, but the judge waved him away, and then asked Kate, 'Miss Brooks, the first voice on the recording you say is this Mr. Mont. Who is the other person speaking?'

Kate said, 'My law partner, Eddie Flynn.'

The rear doors of the courtroom burst open, and Eddie came through them.

He held up a hand to apologize for the interruption and took a seat at the back of the court.

Speak of the devil . . . thought Kate.

'Detective Withers,' said Kate, 'Mr. Mont tried to kill our investigators last night and was fatally injured in the attempt. NYPD are aware of the circumstances. During this call, you hear what Mr. Mont normally charges to kill somebody, he admits murdering Betty Le Saux, and he threatens the caller that if they fail to meet their obligations to him they in turn will be murdered. Is that a fair summation?'

The detective nodded. Kate pressed her for a verbal reply and she said, 'That's fair,' for the record.

'Detective, Mr. Cross was set to inherit millions of dollars from his wife. He didn't. He paid the down payment for the hit to Mr. Mont, so that he would kill his wife. I put it to you that when Mr. Mont didn't get the rest of his fee he broke Mr. Cross's arm, and threatened to kill him. That's why another fifteen thousand was paid by Mr. Cross to Mr. Mont the day after the assault. That's why he was unwilling to describe his attacker to police. When Mr. Cross didn't come up with the rest of the money, Mr. Mont disabled the alarm system on my client's property for eleven minutes, snuck into their home, knowing they had reasons to want Mr. Cross dead. He took their firearm and shot and killed Mr. Cross.'

Detective Withers' mouth opened, but no words came out. She stared at the jury. Castro stared at them too.

It didn't matter that Kate had just established reasonable doubt, corroborated by bank statements and a timeline – now the jury knew Cross was a killer, they didn't give a shit about him.

'Detective? That's a reasonable theory as to who may have killed Mr. Cross?'

Castro started to object, but he was too late.

.'This information was not in the prior possession of police. This is the first time I am seeing this evidence. It is reasonable—'

Kate turned to the judge, said, 'Your Honor, I move for a dismissal of this case.'

While she waited for the judge to respond, Kate thought of all the professional ethics and laws she had just broken.

Someone had framed Christine and Kevin for Cross's murder.

Now, she had done the exact same thing.

She had framed Bruno Mont for Cross's murder.

Eddie had used the stranger's own tactics against him.

Never try to con a conman.

Kate waited for the judge to speak, and Harry took her arm.

Christine had covered her mouth with her hand, and Kevin was wide-eyed, staring at Kate.

'In light of this new evidence . . .' began the judge.

56
Eddie

I stood with my back to the cold marble in the hallway outside court.

Kate and Elly were in an embrace. Tears streaming down both of their faces. It was the first time I had seen Elly smile in real life. That smile seemed to come from a deep place within her that had lain dormant and subdued for months. It was good to see.

She was free. The case against her had been withdrawn, with prejudice, by Bernice, who now stood beside me.

'One of these days, things are not going to go your way,' said Castro. 'Be careful, Eddie. You made a lot of powerful enemies today. And you could've gotten yourself and your own people killed in the process.'

'Bloch and Lake knew Mont was coming for them. And they guessed that the stranger would come too. NYPD still have no idea who he is. They've done a facial recognition scan, but they don't hold out much hope of finding his identity. All I know is he's dead. Elly knows that too. Kevin and Christine, and Elly, are free. My people are safe. And that's all that matters. Apart from one thing.'

'What's that?' asked Castro.

'If you ever come for me or my family again, I'm going to take you out.'

'Take care of yourself,' said Castro. 'I don't want to be prosecuting somebody for your murder one of these days.'

I turned and watched Amy throw her arms round Kevin. He was crying. So was Christine. They embraced one another in the hallways of this old courthouse, ignoring the people milling around them.

They looked like a family.

I put my hands in my pockets and headed for the elevator.

A hand on my shoulder stopped me.

'Thank you,' said Christine. 'I know what you did. What you all did. Lake and Bloch risked their lives for us.'

'It was Kate. She won the case . . .'

'I know, and I already thanked her. But I know you. She wouldn't have gotten that Mont guy on tape if it wasn't for you. That was your play. Thank you.'

We hugged, and I left Christine, Amy and Kevin to themselves and headed back to the office.

It was dark by the time Harry, Kate, Lake and Bloch got back. Denise had been busy all afternoon, handing out small checks to the former customers of Richard Reynolds Bail Bonds. He'd sold his car collection, and we were making good on our promises. Denise said he was booked on a flight to Toronto in the morning.

I watched through the glass partition in my office, as first Lake, then Bloch, Denise, and then Harry hugged Kate.

I stood up as she came into my office.

'Eddie, I don't know how to say this—'

'Then don't.'

She swept her hair away from her face, blew out her cheeks and stared at the floor.

Then she looked at me.

'It's not you—'

'I know what you're going say. You're leaving. And it is because of me.'

'No, it's the job. You're the best. You know that? Three people are walking around free today because of you. And I wouldn't and couldn't have done that. I need to take a break and figure out what I want to do with my life.'

'You're a lawyer, one of the best.'

'I need time. I know I can't do this job. Maybe I'll come back to the law in a while. I just don't want things to be awkward between us. It's really not your fault. It's the job. Sometimes you need to do whatever it takes to save somebody. And I don't know if I can do that.'

She skipped forward, wrapped her arms round me.

'Thank you for everything you've done for me. I've learned so much.'

I put my arms round her, said, 'You have a family here. Whether you own half of the business or not. These people will always be here for you. Me too. Whenever you need me.'

She stepped back, wiped away a tear.

I said, 'I'll split the business with you any way you want. You can take half of what's in the business account and I'll buy out—'

She waved her hand at me. 'Don't worry. We'll work it out. I don't care about money. I just want to clear my head. See my dad.'

She turned, opened my office door and stepped out.

'Kate,' I called after her. She swung round. 'Take Harry and Bloch to lunch. When you feel up to it. They'll be broken-hearted. When you've decided what you want to do, let me know and if I can do anything to help you I will. But you owe me coffee, once a week at least.'

'Deal,' she said.

I grabbed my coat. I couldn't watch Kate clearing out her desk. Harry picked up Clarence's lead, forced a smile, said, 'Let's take a walk.'

We stepped out into the dying winter chill of Manhattan. I threw my collar up and started walking.

We hadn't got to the end of the block when I stopped. Something wasn't right.

Clarence and Harry halted too. It was then that I realized what was bothering me.

'You forgot your cane.'

Clarence stared at me. Then Harry.

'I'm okay now. The physio said I could leave it behind for a while. Clarence agrees.'

Sure enough, he hadn't barked when we'd left the office without Harry's walking stick.

Just then, he reached into his jacket pocket. Checked his phone.

'Look, Elly posted a new video.'

He angled the screen so we could both watch. Elly was in her hotel room. This was the first video she'd posted since she'd been arrested.

'Hi,' said Elly. 'Thank you for all of your messages of support. It's meant so much to me. Now the truth is finally out there, I am so relieved. I'm going to be posting more from today, but it's not going to be about me. I just heard from my agent that she's sold the book rights to my story, so you can read all about what happened over the last few months. I'm going to be okay, thanks to my legal team. So I'm only going to post here about my random acts of kindness. Most of you don't know what happened to me on the subway when I tried to help a stranger. It almost cost me everything. But that doesn't mean people are all bad. That's just one sick person. It doesn't undo all the good that comes from helping people in need. So I want you all to share with me your random acts of kindness. I'll be doing the same. It's how my parents raised me. To help others. We could all do with more kindness in the world. Help me spread a little of it . . .'

The video ended. Harry put the phone away.

We walked on in silence, crossed the street and Clarence came to a stop outside a bar.

He sat at the entrance and stared up at Harry.

'This dog has more sense than I do,' he said. 'I'm going to go and get good and drunk, then probably get into some trouble. Would you care to join us?'

'I'm going to walk for a little while longer. Get my head straight. Ask the bar tender to put on a pot of coffee. I'll be there soon.'

'Kate is going to be okay, you know?'

'I know,' I said.

Harry followed Clarence into the bar.

I didn't know where I was going. I let my feet carry me through the streets.

All I knew was that from now on things would be different around here.

Kate had made a choice to turn away. To do what was right for her.

I'd had that choice once.

I chose different.

Not a day goes by when I didn't wonder what would have happened if I'd chosen an easier life, saved my marriage, and been there for my kid.

My cell phone rang. A number I didn't recognize.

'Hi, is this Eddie Flynn?' said the male voice.

'Yeah, it's me. Who is this?'

'Chuck Buchanan, of Buchanan and Duff, attorneys. I've got a referral for you. Homicide case. Fair warning, this one is difficult.'

'Is the client innocent?'

'She's pleading not guilty, if that's what you mean.'

'No, it's not what I mean. Is she innocent?'

Silence on the phone.

'She's innocent.'

I stopped walking. Looked up at the dark skies covering the city.

'Sounds like I'm your guy,' I said.

57
Logan

Logan raised his right foot off the rail, crossed his arms in front of his chest . . .

And jumped.

In mid-air, as he fell, he locked his feet together.

Felt the wind rushing over his body.

Right before he hit the water, he raised his knees toward his belly, then, both feet together, he kicked down, punching through the waves as he disappeared into the water.

Daily cold plunges meant he didn't feel the shock of cold water any more.

But this water wasn't cold.

It was the warm, azure blue of the Indian ocean.

Logan swam to the surface, the blazing sunlight hitting his eyes as he gazed back at the yacht he'd just leapt from. There, standing on the deck, was Grace.

She wore a silk sundress over her bikini, and she smiled down at Logan.

He swam back to the boat, grabbed the ladder and climbed back on board. He grabbed his swim shorts and squeezed most of the water from them, then found a chair on the deck and sat down to dry in the hot sun.

They were a mile out from the coast of South Africa.

Far away from New York City.

That final day in Manhattan, Logan had known his odds of taking out Joe Novak were very slim. That night, once he'd left the apartment he'd shared with Grace, Logan had made a phone call.

To a company that chartered private jets.

Logan knew that if things went south, he had to end it. Only way to be sure that Flynn and his crew wouldn't come looking for him, was to make them believe he was already dead. That leap from the bridge was never going to be fatal, not for someone who knew how to dive, not for someone who had conditioned his body, for years, to survive in cold water without going into shock.

He'd come home to the apartment in the early hours of that morning, told Grace he had cut his arm in a fall, and that things had gone badly in his meeting with that difficult and dangerous client. They had to get out of the city.

Grace had already packed a bag, like he'd told her to.

They flew first to Barbados and spent a few weeks there. Now, in their second week in South Africa, Logan had hired this small yacht so they could be alone.

He enjoyed the solitude of the ocean.

He heard Grace padding toward him. He turned round and looked up from his seat, shielding his eyes from the sun.

'Here you go,' she said, and handed him a glass of whiskey with ice.

'Nikka Yoichi,' she said, 'your favorite.'

'Where did you get this?' he asked, taking a drink.

'I ordered it from the hotel. I paid a little more than you normally would. They had to order it from Cape Town. I figured you'd enjoy it out here. It might help you relax.'

'Thank you,' said Logan, and took another sip.

He relaxed his shoulders, closed his eyes and breathed in and out, feeling the gentle rocking of the ocean against the boat.

He was the luckiest man alive, he thought.

He had the woman he loved. He had money. And no one was ever going to find him. He had faked his own death. No one comes looking for a dead man.

This would be the start of a new life. A peaceful one.

A life where he would never feel alone.

He thought back to that day when they'd met on the subway. She had looked so beautiful wearing that floral print dress, and her bright green cardigan. The soles worn thin on her Converse. He wondered what would have happened if he had not spoken to her that day, if she had not tried to save that passenger's noodles from falling onto the subway car floor. How different his life would have been.

'What are you smiling about, handsome?' asked Grace.

'I was just thinking about the day I first laid eyes on you in the subway car. You looked so cute in that dress, and that cardigan.'

He drained the last of the Nikka Yoichi. The salt in the air had altered the taste, somehow enriching the flavors.

'Oh, I wasn't wearing that, was I?'

He opened his eyes and saw her walking past him. As she did, her fingers traced the scar on his arm from the shrapnel kicked up by Bloch's magnum. He saw her touching the scar, but he couldn't feel it. He guessed there was some nerve damage there.

Grace sat down in the seat opposite him. Damn, she was beautiful.

'Oh, you definitely were. I'll never forget it.'

'I think you're not remembering correctly, darling. When we first saw each other, I was wearing blue jeans and a tight little white tee. It was summer and it was hot.'

Logan's smile faded.

'What are you talking about? I saw you on the train in November. You saved that woman's noodles, remember?'

'That was much later, darling. You'd been following me for months by then.'

'What?'

'Oh, don't worry. I didn't mind. I saw you that first day. You were so good-looking. And that watch, the Patek Philippe. And the hand-made Italian shoes. I knew you were a catch.'

'You saw me?'

'Oh yeah. I knew then you were someone special. I knew you would make a move on me sooner or later. Like I said, I knew you were a good catch. And you confirmed that right after our first date. You saw the bills pinned on my fridge, in my apartment, and you paid them the very next day. All of them. Over a hundred thousand dollars. Normally, it's like half a dozen dates before my gentlemen do the gentlemanly thing and pay off some of my debts. Then I move apartments and find another wealthy gentleman.'

Logan's head swam. He felt dizzy. What the hell was she talking about?

'I own all the companies that issued those debts. Never had a guy pay them *all*, and never on the first date. That's why I gave you the money back. It was a *convincer*, as we call it in the trade. Something to make you trust me. I knew then you were a big fish, Logan. But I didn't know you were a killer . . .'

The whiskey glass slipped from his hand, shattered on the deck. His heart was thumping so hard it was deafening.

'You had something to do with those TikTok murders. I saw you outside of the court. I followed you.'

Logan remembered standing in the crowd of Elly's supporters, and the sensation of being watched.

'That gunshot wound on your arm confirmed it. I read the news. I know you tried to kill a witness in that case and the police chased you to the bridge. You're a dangerous man, Logan.'

'Grace, wait, you have this all . . .'

He tried to finish his sentence, but his throat dried up. He tried to lean forward, to get to his feet, but . . .

He couldn't move.

Fear took him.

'The nerve toxin in the whiskey is fast-acting,' said Grace. 'You're not going to suffer for long. I've got your account numbers and passwords. I thought about taking your money in New York. But I knew you'd come after me. And you'd probably find me and kill me. I needed it to be clean. If I'm going to have my biggest take ever, your *millions*, I had to make sure I did it right.'

Logan's mouth opened, but no words came.

And no air came in either.

His eyes bulged. He couldn't move his arms, his legs.

It was as if he was encased in cement.

'It took me a while to figure out you were a killer. I sensed you were dangerous before we'd even met. What you didn't know is that I'm dangerous too. You remember that story I told you about the melon farmer who went missing, and the whole town went out looking for him? I told you we searched for him and then found out he'd moved to Atlanta and met a stripper. Well, he didn't move. I buried him deep in his land, Logan. So deep, no one was ever gonna find him. I was blackmailing him, and he decided he didn't want to pay. So he had to die. Now it's your turn. You'll die in the next minute, and then you'll go for another swim. A long one this time. Right to the bottom of the ocean,' said Grace.

She stood and, as she walked away, she said, 'Never trust a stranger, Logan. Didn't your mother ever tell you that?'

Logan wanted to scream. To fight. To kill.

He could do nothing. His chest would not move. His lungs would not expand.

There was no air. His eyes felt heavy. And there was no longer sight.

Only sound.

The sound of the seawater, dripping from his swim shorts onto the deck.

Drip . . .
Drip . . .
Drip . . .

Acknowledgements

At the time of writing this, I have just realized that it is ten years since I published my first novel. A lot has changed in that time. My life has certainly changed, and I am reminded how grateful I am to everyone who has helped me along this road. As always, the greatest thanks and praise to my amazing wife, Tracy, who makes these books so much better, and for her love and support and for making me laugh every day.

Thanks to Jon Wood, Safae, Sam, Tristan, Katharina, Stephen, and everyone at RCW Literary Agency. Thanks to Toby, Joe, Ruth, and everyone at Headline publishing in the UK. Thanks to Sean Delone, Ali, Maudee, and everyone at Atria Books in the USA. I am sincerely lucky to be working with such talented editors, publicists, agents, and everyone else who works tirelessly behind the scenes to get these books into bookstores all over the world, and into your hands.

A special thanks to David Torrans of No Alibis Bookstore in Belfast, for always supporting me.

Thanks to all my family and friends, for all their warmth and support.

And of course, thanks to you, dear reader.

Did you think I'd forgotten about you?

That list of very talented people you read about in the earlier paragraphs, well, they all work for you, not me. Everything we do together is aimed at delivering a book to you that we all hope you enjoy. So on behalf of all of those people, thank you.

And from me, I really hope you enjoyed your time reading. There are plenty more books in this series to come, God willing. Until next time, thanks again for picking up one of my books, and I hope you are well, and happy, and safe.

My very best wishes to you and your family.

Steve Cavanagh.

RAISING READERS
Books Build Bright Futures

Dear Reader,

We'd love your attention for one more page to tell you about the crisis in children's reading, and what we can all do.

Studies have shown that reading for fun is the **single biggest predictor of a child's future success** – more than family circumstance, parents' educational background or income. It improves academic results, mental health, wealth, communication skills and ambition.

The number of children reading for fun is in rapid decline. Young people have a lot of competition for their time, and a worryingly high number do not have a single book at home.

Our business works extensively with schools, libraries and literacy charities, but here are some ways we can all raise more readers:

- Reading to children for just 10 minutes a day makes a difference
- Don't give up if your children aren't regular readers – there will be books for them!
- Visit bookshops and libraries to get recommendations
- Encourage them to listen to audiobooks
- Support school libraries
- Give books as gifts

Thank you for reading.
www.JoinRaisingReaders.com